Ta

A Novel

MW01136259

ISBN-13:978-1482662467
Amazon : ASIN B008G3PEAE

Cover photographs: JoMarie Cook &

Stephen Tritto

Cover layout & design: Zhiping (Z) Yu

Thanks & best wishes.

Steve, 4/27/2013

i

Stephen Tritto

To Peggy:
With Love and Thanks for a Great
First Forty

Taking Flight

Acknowledgements

My heartfelt thanks to Dan McInnis who read every line multiple times always telling me what I wanted and didn't want to hear; a dear friend and a great reviewer.

Special thanks to Lulu Santana who helped me understand the soul and the people of El Salvador.

Special thanks to Suzanne Helfman

Endless thanks to my fellow writer's who dedicated three years to helping me get it right: Amber Marince and Raquel Gonzales who were there from the beginning, and Audrey, Ben, Charles, Suzie and Swann who contributed so much along the way.

Many thanks to my friends for their support and kindness: Patty and Willy Falk, Roseann Rasul, and Mario Zelaya, my Salvadoran friend.

My thanks and my love to my family who never thought it absurd that I would try to write a novel, and whose love and support have sustained my belief that I could: Peggy, Christopher, Matthew, April and Lori.

Stephen Tritto

Source and Inspiration for the Title

Excerpt from Sombrero Azul (Blue Hat)
By Alí Rafael Primera, The People's Singer.
Alí Rafael Primera Rosell was a musician,
composer, poet, and Venezuelan political
activist. He was born in Coro, Falcón,
Venezuela on October 31st 1942 and died
in Caracas on February 16, 1985.

The Salvadoran people have the
sky for a hat
So high is their dignity in the
search for the time
When the earth will flower for
those who have fallen
When happiness will come to
replace this suffering
When happiness will come to
replace this suffering
Dále* Salvadoran, Dále
There's not a single bird, Dále
Which, after **taking flight**, Dále
Stops in midair.

*Come on, go for it, Do it!

Taking Flight

Chapter 1

Anthony spent the afternoon preparing for war. That's how he saw tonight's get together hosted by he and Bernadette. The arrangement of a round robin supper schedule was organized by Bernadette and her best friend Sarah. While familiar with the couples invited, Anthony still categorized them as his wife's friends and their spouses. He was doing this for Bernadette. Having them in her home was important to her, just as being the King of the Castle was important to him.

As host, he would impress their guests by subtly presenting subjects to discuss about which he was well informed, have a few self-deprecating remarks at the ready to display his humble side, and a few politically correct funny stories to demonstrate his wit. The background music he selected for the guests' arrival included *Pachelbel, Rodrigo's Concerto* and *Musetta's Waltz*, any of which he could quickly identify if queried. His selection of wine included an expensive Syrah, some trendy reds and whites and a modest, but respected Champagne for a welcoming toast. A non-alcoholic sparkling cider was there for Nancy who did not consume alcohol. Cordial glasses were set aside in the kitchen for an after dinner drink. He planned to substitute the milder amaretto for brandy. For this occasion, Anthony and Bernadette had made an investment in overpriced snack tables topped with an inlaid tile that were sold in sets of four. They agonized over buying twelve instead of eight. Anthony suggested they bite the bullet to be sure no one would have to balance a plate on their lap.

Anthony had arranged his hardback copy of *Acts of Faith*, a fictionalized account of the chaos and brutality taking place in Sudan to be visible on the end table in the living room. A worn, paperback version of Norman Mailer's *Harlot's Ghost* noticeably protruded from the bookcase in his study. Also visible was a current copy of *Sea Kayaker* to at once display his athletic and adventurous interests and his love for the water.

He dressed in freshly pressed grey flannel trousers, a grey and black, small check button down shirt and black loafers without tassels. He had a haircut three days before and was very satisfied with the way it looked tonight. For a final touch, he selected a black V-neck sweater which was a favorite and always looked good on him. Some clothes seemed to have the perfect fit, the perfect look and this sweater had never failed him. He knew it would be uncomfortably warm as the evening progressed, but thought *that's the price you have to pay.*

War requires a well thought out strategy, proven tactics and adequate materials and supplies. So did hosting Bernadette's friends whom he would entertain for the evening by dazzling them with himself. His final preparatory step was to assume a meditative stance, close his eyes and recite his mantra for the evening: "Fuck 'em all."

Bernadette had just finished laying everything out on the dining room table. His jobs of preparing the bar and the music were done. She stepped back and turned to him.

"Does everything look all right? I want it to be perfect."

"Everything *is* perfect" he replied. "In fact it's too good to waste on these guys. Let's invite some people we really want to impress."

"Please don't talk politics or philosophy tonight. You know how you can be."

"I promise to say only mundane things that will offend no one," he said.

"You know what I mean," she countered. "I just want everyone to have a nice time."

"I'll be good" he said with a smile. "Bring on the bastards."

"And no profanities," she pleaded, "Regina has issues."

He reassured her, "Don't worry. I'll save them for after they leave."

He marveled at how good she looked dressed and undressed. She could throw rags on and be the belle of the ball. He loved her breasts. He was always surprised at how much larger they looked when she was naked. He concluded that it was the size of her rib cage and her tiny waist that made her breasts appear larger as well as perfectly formed. As much as he was fascinated with them, it was her eyes that knocked him out. They were large with dark pupils rimmed with a hazel ring that sparkled and cut right through him. It was her eyes that got him to drop all his bullshit and just be himself. She dressed to emphasize her small waist. "Might as well before it all turns to shit," she would say in a rare use of vulgarity. He knew other men found her attractive, *but that's the price you have to pay*, he thought.

The door chimes signaled the first arrivals of the evening. After a quick 360 degree check, Anthony headed for the door and Bernadette darted to the bathroom. He checked his fly, took a deep breath, exhaled, put a presentation smile on his face and opened the door. He was surprised to see all eight guests, uncertain if they coincidentally arrived at the same time or met somewhere else before coming. He welcomed them into the foyer and offered to take coats, scarves and handbags which he collected and promptly delivered to the guest bedroom. Bernadette charged out of the bathroom with a high pitched cross between a cheer and a cry.

"Oh, I'm so happy you're all here."

With that began a series of hugs befitting a reunion of survivors of a traumatic wilderness adventure. Anthony let Bernadette have her moment and shook hands with the men. He invited them to sit in the living room in the long leg of the L shaped layout connecting it to the dining room. Bernadette was already conducting a tour that would be sure to avoid the guest bedroom and laundry room where so much was piled up to make the other rooms more presentable.

Three of the women were Bernadette's college friends. The fourth, Regina, was a Human Resources Representative at Mayfield's Department Store where Bernadette worked as a Buyer of women's formal wear. The upscale department store was the first and only employer of both women since they left their respective hallowed halls of academia six years ago.

Carla was a part owner of a travel agency that catered to sophisticated and well-heeled business travelers and those seeking exotic cruises, safaris, cultural and religious expeditions. By doing well in this niche, her company avoided the onslaught from Expedia, Travelocity and Orbitz, or as Carla put it: "travel for the ordinary." Carla looked, acted and spoke like she came from money, except when she presented a comedic, slutty side. She was married to David, who was on the partner track at a prestigious law firm. He was a graduate of Columbia Law which no one would ever mention without immediately adding "he must be very smart." His condescending manner and sarcastic wit motivated Anthony to test Carla's fidelity, but the code of his youth created a barrier. That you don't mess with your friend's spouse was extended to include Bernadette's friends. Besides, he had never cheated on Bernadette.

Sarah was Bernadette's closest friend since their college years. She was a third grade school teacher in a local public school. Her father's connections had enabled her to get assigned to a school in an affluent area rather than the hell of the inner city. At the time she started, she didn't realize that prosperous parents created their own version of a teacher's nightmare when their progeny were not nurtured according to their specifications. Sarah had a uniquely woman's sorrow that comes from working with children after suffering two early stage miscarriages. Anthony thought she was pretty and had a nice figure, but sadness was etched in her eyes. She was married to Martin, who Anthony had sized up as an O.K. guy, and had grown to like.

Martin, an oral surgeon, was fascinated by teeth, jawbones and his work. At their last gathering, he showed the group a series of digital pictures of a young boy whose mouth was severely damaged in an automobile accident. Martin had restored his upper and lower teeth, saving some, and capping and replacing others. The results made an impressive "before and after" pictorial essay of which he was undoubtedly very proud. At first, Anthony thought this was a display of an enormous ego, but ultimately concluded that Martin was sincerely humbled by how he had been able to help the boy.

Nancy was a social worker who was out to save the world. In addition to eradicating world poverty, eliminating illiteracy and re-distributing the nation's wealth, she wanted to save the environment. When the time came, she would consider adopting children rather than give birth to more users of the earth's limited resources. Left unchecked, she would start a passionate, long winded dissertation of how little it would take to straighten out the world if everyone just got off their asses. Anthony actually enjoyed engaging her in serious discussion. He thought this was how a Jane Goodall or Amelia Earhart must have been driven when they were young, but poor Nancy was unable to break the bonds that held her back. Her church, her parents and all the bastards who influence the choices made by idealistic young people conspired against her.

Aaron was a Podiatrist and an accommodating husband who supported Nancy's causes. Sometimes he invoked supplemental information no one really needed in an attempt to give one of Nancy's passionate rants more credibility. Aaron always looked like he was recovering from an illness. His complexion had an almost jaundiced coloring. The whites of his eyes were a sickly blend of yellow and red. Even his hair and lips didn't seem healthy. Anthony could not understand why Nancy or any other woman would be attracted to him unless they were sickly or needy themselves.

Les was the only male in the group who was part of Bernadette's past. Regina's husband came from a strong traditionalist, if not religious, Jewish family. He married a girl whose background was so Catholic her parents had a Mass for her soul when she and Les were married in a civil ceremony. Les' family shared the spirit by considering their offspring to be dead. Les had a very good sense of humor and usually found a way of getting everyone to laugh with a witty remark or a funny story from a vast mental library.

6

Taking Flight

Anthony suspected this was Les's way of gaining acceptance and scotch guarding his inner self. Les worked as a Floor Manager in a Garment Center showroom. He entertained department store buyers from all over the country. Les worked under the tutelage of his uncle, his mother's brother, who at her behest hired him even though he had married a shiksa.

It occurred to Anthony that the occupation of each guest was so easy to understand. Most people, and no one in this room, knew what a Product Manager did, or what potential the position had. They assumed that since Anthony worked for a high tech company, he was probably well paid and his job had some substance to it. Anthony had no pictures of a wounded mouth, courtroom adventures, the latest in orthopedic shoes, or naughty tales from Seventh Avenue to share. And so his party persona would be based on good books, wine, food and music. After that, it was "Fuck em all."

Bernadette had created an attractive buffet of hot and cold treats including seasoned artichokes, Swedish meatballs, spinach and cheese crepes, cold shrimp, triangular sliced ham, dry salami, a variety of sliced and block cheeses, pate and spreads along with soft rolls, sliced rye bread, hard crackers, cherry peppers, olives and celery sticks all presented in a flow of colors starting with the reds and ending with the greens. Napkins surrounding silverware were bound by a different colored ribbon for each guest. Plates were stacked neatly at both ends of the table. A separate table that normally supported a lamp now hidden away displayed a feast of Italian pastries that would be served for dessert. Anthony was in charge of the wine. He had opened a Chardonnay and Pinot Grigio he selected for the whites, and a Syrah and Cabernet for the reds. He

7

had a Merlot and Fumé Blanc standing by if needed. He began his duties by skillfully removing the volatile cork from the champagne bottle. He poured for everyone except Nancy to whom he served the sparkling cider in a fluted glass. The hosts decided not to show any hard liquor, but kept some in the cabinet below the wet bar in case it was requested.

When they returned to the dining room the women were chatting about the current scandal involving an attractive female high school teacher who reportedly seduced a seventeen year old student. Carla gave David's legal perspective of the case, to which David shouted some corrections.

Sarah offered Martin's perspective with a smile. "Martin said she must have had beautiful teeth."

Regina rolled her eyes toward Les.

"Les wanted to know where these teachers were when he went to high school."

Aaron offered, "I'll second that," to which Nancy responded with a wince and shook her head.

David was admiring, or at least evaluating the flat panel TV that hung on the living room wall. He suggested to Anthony that he consider adding a home theater system to get the full benefits of the viewing and listening experience. Anthony told him that they had been uncertain about locating the TV in the living room, but once they did, they did not want any wires traveling across the room.

David suggested, "You know Tony, wires can be concealed in the walls and ceiling."

"It's Anthony not Tony," he replied. "Yes, that's true, but we weren't ready to take that project on right now."

David went on, "You can even get a TV that doesn't look like a TV when it's not being used. They have some disguised as mirrors or framed pictures."

"Yes, that's right," said Anthony, who shifted into sommelier mode and offered everyone a glass of wine, "White, red, or we have chocolate, vanilla and strawberry, whatever you like."

"Do you have Chablis?" asked David, to which Anthony smiled and offered the Pinot Grigio instead.

David replied, "Whatever you have is fine."

You bastard, Anthony thought, continuing to smile as he filled the glass.

Bernadette invited everyone to help themselves "to our simple buffet" to which several of their guests exclaimed almost in unison "it looks to pretty to spoil."

Les volunteered to be first and began helping himself. The others immediately followed. After everyone took seats in the living room, Anthony made sure that each glass was full and everyone had a snack table. The sofa faced the loveseat and at each end were chairs from the dining set forming a rough oval. Bernadette took a chair at the edge of the dining room so she could have easy access to the table and the kitchen. Anthony sat opposite her between the two couches. A conversation led by Sarah had to do with the announcement of a divorce by one of her former classmates that some of the women knew.

Nancy responded first, "Oh, I always feel so bad about that kind of news. It's such heartbreak."

"Well, divorce isn't all bad," said David. "It keeps the less talented lawyers busy. Besides, statistically speaking, half of the couples in this room will split up sooner or later. And if you didn't have divorce, where would we get our waitresses?"

"Wow, that's cold," said Martin.

"No, that's disgusting," added Regina.

"Just kidding," said David, "Give me a break here."

"It is true about the rate of breakups though," said Carla. "You wonder sometimes if our whole society is breaking down."

"My father always says that divorce has been made too easy. It removes the incentive for people to work out their problems," said Martin.

"My father always said that no matter what you do, you should wear comfortable shoes, preferably Italian," said Les to a chorus of giggles.

"My father determines good days or bad days by the quality of his bowel movements," said Aaron. "Forget war, peace, tragic times, happy times, booming market, bust market. A good bowel movement and everything is good or can be worked out. A bad one and nothing is good; period, end of story. That's my old man's philosophical contribution to the world."

"Enough with the toilet talk. Your father's a nice man," said Nancy.

"My father wasn't much of a philosopher, but he used to say that everything has a ten percent shit factor," said Anthony. "He believed that everything you plan to do: take a vacation, buy a flat panel TV, even the more important things like getting married, having children, buying a house, that no matter how well you plan it or how much advice you get, ten percent will always go wrong. If you believe that, your expectations won't fall short. And if you consider this as an immutable law of physics, you consider the ten percent shit factor in a context of ninety percent success. You can therefore conclude that each of these things came out well instead of dwelling on the ten percent that didn't."

"Your father sounds like he's right up there with

Aristotle and Thomas Aquinas," replied David.

"He may not have been an educated man, but he had a strong moral compass and clearly defined values," said Anthony. "I wish I could say the same for myself."

"Anthony's dad was a sweetheart," said Bernadette. "A big teddy bear with a warm heart. He passed away a little over a year ago. Young by what you would expect these days."

"Here's to ten percent shit factors," said Sarah raising her glass. "I like that."

"Me too," said, Carla.

Everyone raised their glass, "Hear, hear," they said in unison.

"What fascinates me," said Anthony, "is that as a society, we seem to have all the knowledge and recorded wisdom that we need to live a good life, and yet we screw it up all the time; over and over again."

"Define what you mean by a good life," said David.

"One that is fulfilling," replied Anthony. "Where people are personally fulfilled, give to others, have shared values about families and the well being of the community, live a healthy lifestyle, appreciate all that we have, especially here where we live better than most of the world's population."

Bernadette sat upright in her chair with an interruption at the ready in case Anthony was going to go off on one of his sermons.

"What's fulfilling to us may not be fulfilling to everyone else," said Martin. "I'm sure there are tribes living in some remote jungles without electricity or running water who are quite happy."

Anthony was getting wound up. "I'm sure different cultures and societies have varying definitions of fulfillment, but just think about it. You can go to any book store and find dozens of books that have taken universal truths and turned them into clichés. I'm not talking about Whitman, Thoreau, Buddha or Thomas Aquinas, but Jesus…"

"You're not going to talk about Jesus are you?" asked David, "Les is Jewish."

"Not at all, smartass," said Anthony, "but just in terms of our little society, forget the whole of western culture, forget the USA, just put New York City in the center of a circle that has a diameter of fifty miles and…"

"That's pretty much the whole of Western Culture," piped in Les.

Anthony went on, "…think of the society and culture we grew up in and live in now. We can all recite how money doesn't bring happiness; how no one ever said on their deathbed that they wished they had spent more time at the office; or gosh, by the time the kids grew up, I realized that I didn't even know them; then there's doing for others brings more fulfillment than doing for yourself, and on and on and on. You have the Poppa's Book of Wisdom, the Momma's Book of Common Sense and fifty Hallmark varieties of the same. You have all these guys pontificating in PBS seminars, writing books, and selling DVDs. You can probably get a podcast that will provide an instant fix to any life problem. People buy this stuff up and two weeks after they've read, watched and listened, they get depressed and moan about how empty their lives are! How screwed up is that?"

Bernadette jumped in "Hey guys, we have plenty of more food out there and regular and decaf are brewing in the kitchen."

David asked, "Anthony, do know what your problem

is?"

"I didn't know I had a problem," he replied brusquely.

"What you don't realize is that most of the people you're talking about are assholes. Face it, they're lemmings. They don't think. They just follow. They eat up the bullshit that everyone feeds them without making any intelligent choices, and then when they're about to die, they realize they've wasted their lives."

"That's very dark," said Martin. "I think a lot of people get up in the morning, go out to their jobs and work their asses off in the hope of being secure and that their progeny will be safe and better off, and that at the end of the day, they're tired and just want some peace or maybe a little fun. I think that's true for the professor and the factory worker."

"Sounds like a great title for a book," said David.

Anthony shifted getting ready to speak when Bernadette stood and asked, "Who would like seconds?"

Les immediately raised his hand.

Bernadette continued, "The coffee is ready in the kitchen and please help yourselves to our dessert tray. I'm sorry, but we only have sugar, no Sweet and Low. I hope that's all right."

"Sure it is," said Sarah as she stood. "I'll help get these dishes inside in case an armed conflict breaks out."

"Thanks" said Bernadette, as she looked over at Anthony making sure that the dialogue was over.

"Take it easy," Sarah said. "Boys will be boys. At least they didn't pee on the furniture."

As the guests got up from their seats, some moved back to the dining table to help themselves to seconds, while others migrated to the tray of pastries. Anthony made his way into the kitchen to prepare after dinner drinks. He decided to pour the amaretto without asking. When he turned carrying the tray of cordials, he found himself looking through the doorway that led to the dining room. David had his arms wrapped around Bernadette with his hands clasped at the base of her spine, just high enough to not be resting on her ass. Bernadette was listening to whatever he was saying with a smile on her face and didn't seem at all disturbed by the closeness of his body to hers.

"Is one of those for me?"

Anthony turned and looked at Sarah who was smiling at him.

"Sure," he said, "take your pick."

"I liked the story about your father's ten percent shit factor," she said as she helped herself to a glass of amaretto.

"My father died being afraid," he said, looking over her head toward the dining room.

"Of dying?" Sarah asked.

"Of living," Anthony said with a very serious tone, this time looking right into her eyes.

"So what are you afraid of?" She asked.

"Nothing and no one," he answered, again distracted by the couple in the dining room. Bernadette was still locked in David's arms; his hands were lower than before.

"Everybody is afraid of something," said Sarah.

"Maybe I'm afraid of myself," he said.

"Do you mean not meeting your own expectations?"

"Or that I will," he said as she looked at him curiously.

"Then don't be afraid of David and Bernadette," she said following his gaze.

That got his full attention. This time when he looked at Sarah, he noticed how fine featured she was. There was a regal look to her forehead, cheekbones, nose, mouth and jaw that he hadn't noticed before. While she had a nice

14

smile, a more serious expression emphasized the nobility of her features.

"The fact that he's one step short of dry humping my wife shouldn't bother me?" he asked.

"Relax," said Sarah. "That's just David's thing. Bernadette can handle him. Everyone in this room, with the possible exception of you, knows that if he ever stepped over the line, Carla would castrate him. No one knows that better than David. So this is how he gets his jollies, and she lets him have his fun."

"And everybody buys that?" he asked, shaking his head in disbelief.

"That's it," she replied.

"So you think I should ignore ten minutes and counting of David's slow dancing without music because everyone thinks it's okay?" he asked.

"He's just your ten percent shit factor tonight," she said. "Besides, most of the men in this room are harmless, trust me," she said.

"Most of the men? Okay," he asked, "who's not harmless?"

"You could possibly not be harmless," she said.

"Hey Anthony," Martin interrupted, "Great party, the food was delicious, and the pastries are from heaven."

"Thanks," said Anthony. "Bernadette did all of the work. I just poured the drinks."

Later, when everyone was gone, Anthony and Bernadette spent forty silent minutes putting away the perishables and stacking the dishes, silverware and glasses in the dishwasher. He put the dispersed chairs back in the dining room lining their legs up with the indentations left in

15

the carpet. Bernadette announced that she would finish cleaning up in the morning. These were the first spoken words since her last "goodbye." She went into the bath off the master bedroom to begin her nightly routine. Anthony stayed back to listen to the soft music and sip an amaretto. It was close to 1:00 A.M., but he felt wide awake. The events of the evening took another stroll through his head. He reminded himself of his goal to make this a good evening for Bernadette. His thoughts slowed to a crawl, as he pictured David's arms locked around her waist.

He went into the bedroom and saw that Bernadette was standing by the bed. He looked for the silent signals they had developed to suggest she was ready for lovemaking, or to see if she was looking for signals from him. There was no thanking him for his help tonight while standing on his toes. No asking for a lotion rub on her shoulders. No kneeling on the bed with her arms holding her up in a way that let her nightgown reveal more than her neck. Instead, she pulled the covers back and got into bed commenting only on the amount of leftover food. She turned on her side away from the center of the bed.

He knew it was the wrong time to bring up David.

"David seemed to enjoy your company tonight," he said.

"Yes, he spent a great deal of time telling me what a great guy you were," she replied.

"I guess he needed to be sure you heard every word," he shot back.

She pulled the covers up to her chin, reached up and turned off her bed lamp. Anthony knew the discussion was over for the night. He thought to himself, *So much for good food, wine and music. Tonight sure turned to shit in a hurry.*

16

Taking Flight

Chapter 2

On Sunday morning, Bernadette was distant, spending most of the day running errands and doing some personal shopping. Upon returning home she used the leftovers from their party for supper. The couple ate while watching the late football game on their new TV. Anthony drifted into the study to review the work papers he was to turn in the next day. When he was finished shortly after nine, Bernadette was asleep in bed with a book resting in her lap. Her head was propped up by two pillows. Her brushed hair fell over the temples of her reading glasses. A few freckles on her nose were making their nightly appearance to coincide with the stars. He gently lifted the book careful not to close it before placing her flowered bookmark on the open page. Anthony lifted her glasses from the bridge of her nose, then raised the ear pieces and placed them and the book on the night table. She stirred slightly and turned to her side. As he was getting ready for bed, he wondered how what had started yesterday as an upbeat social evening could have turned so bad so fast and leave them hardly speaking.

On Monday morning, Bernadette left the house while Anthony was in the bathroom so she could shout her daily farewell, and not have to fake a more pleasant departure. Anthony tried to put the weekend behind him and switched his mind to the affairs of work. Driving east on the Southern State Parkway, he took in the beauty of the orange and red leaves dressing the trees that lined the road. The leaves would soon be gone and the bare trees would allow visibility of the ugly single story strip malls on the street above and parallel to the roadway. As a child, he had always been impressed with the trees in full bloom during the summer trips his parents took from Brooklyn into "the country" as they referred to Long Island.

He appreciated driving against the commuter flow to the Misty Harbor Industrial Park that housed SkyTel, the technology company where he had been a rising star since joining them four years earlier. After starting as Product Specialist responsible for marketing programs and managing product life cycles, he took on more responsibilities and was promoted to Product Manager. His current and most important assignment was presenting the company as an acquisition prospect to NordSTAR, the German communications giant that lusted after SkyTel's technology. NordSTAR preferred an acquisition rather than risking two or more years to develop a competing technology. The German company was evaluating three companies with the intention of buying the one most suited to fill its needs. Anthony's job was to make sure SkyTel was selected.

Anthony had researched NordSTAR's corporate culture, management style and customer base in order to present SkyTel as a potentially good corporate partner as well as a source of advanced technology. He took it upon himself to learn conversational German so that he could demonstrate respect for the prospective parent company and work through introductions and social events in their native tongue. To the engineers at SkyTel, this was unnecessary showboating because all the "suits" and "techies" at NordSTAR spoke English very well. Anthony knew, however, that it was important to honor their position in the negotiations and to distinguish his company (and himself) from the alternatives NordSTAR was considering. Over a four month period, Anthony had played a larger and larger role in the company strategy sessions and negotiations.

Three weeks earlier, the primary content of the meetings shifted from technology issues to business terms; a very positive signal. One of the German executives personally congratulated Anthony on the quality of the information he provided. His praise was spoken in German. Anthony knew that bode well for him. He was savvy enough not to bring this to the attention of the SkyTel team.

SkyTel was headed by its founder and Chief Scientist, Dr. Edwin Albright and his second in command, Henry Trenholme. Albright was a believer in the superiority of all scientists, and considered himself in the top tier of this special species. Trenholme had a financial background, but served primarily as Albright's lackey and hatchet man. Trenholme publicly revered Albright. He did all of his dirty work, and to his credit had created a mythology about the unique and outstanding achievements of Albright that served the company well. Anthony realized that Trenholme had created alternative professional histories of Albright's accomplishments to suit various purposes. No one ever challenged their veracity. Anthony recognized the contradictions in accomplishments attributed to Albright, but this was a boat he was not going to rock. With a potentially lucrative stock option package, Anthony knew that an acquisition by NordSTAR would bring him a substantial reward as well as a bigger arena to play in. Albright and Trenholme would become millionaires if the deal went through. Their holdings were many times greater than his, but Anthony's opportunities would be more than satisfactory. He knew that the technology was Albright's baby, but Anthony was the principal architect of the deal that was now on a fast track. By impressing the executives at NordSTAR, he could eventually have a job free of the ego, pill popping and paranoia of Albright and the ass kissing of Trenholme.

Last week, Trenholme had asked him to prepare a Phase-Out Program for two product families that had served SkyTel as cash cows, but were now less and less competitive. Relying on programs that he had developed for other products, Anthony had drawn up maintenance contracts for the customer base, estimated the replacement parts requirements and defined customer incentives for upgrades to newer SkyTel products. He was to leave the completed package in the form of a CD with Trenholme's Administrative Assistant, Jeanne Marsh. His other assignment was to provide a printed, up to date status report of the contract negotiations and all related engineering and business activities with NordSTAR directly to Trenholme at 11:00 A.M.

When he pulled into the parking lot at 9:00 A.M., he had plenty of time to transfer the content of the SkyTel CD to his office computer and have it printed and bound in the usual manner. Upon entering the SkyTel building, the difficulties of the weekend faded away. He went to his office, checked for phone messages and emails and started the report completion process. He was surprised to find that his voice mail and email accounts were empty, unusual even for a Monday morning.

He looked over the Wall Street Journal just to be sure there was no mention of what NordSTAR was doing these days. At 10:55 A.M., he dropped the CD containing the Phase Out programs at Jeanne's desk with an ignored smile. He knocked on Trenholme's door before entering.

Trenholme invited him to sit, extending his hand to receive the status report. He browsed through it carefully, asking only about the demonstration program that was being modified by the Engineering department. Anthony reported that the Engineers had run a finalized version over the weekend, and with the exception of updating its accompanying Power Point presentation, it was ready to go.

Anthony added, "The new demo will knock their socks off."

Trenholme sniffed and curled his nose in a manner that demonstrated his lack of appreciation for the effort and importance of a custom made demonstration using actual NordSTAR data.

"Anthony," he said, "I have a rather difficult assignment this morning."

"Is it something, I can help with?" asked Anthony.

"Anthony, although everyone here appreciates the value of your services and the contributions you have made to the company, I am afraid that we are letting you go."

Anthony was stunned. "What?" was all he could say.

"I've convinced Edwin that we should offer you what I think is a very generous separation package; full salary and benefits for three months, providing of course that you agree to resign, to speak to no one about this, and turn over your files and clear out your office today. Your stock options will be surrendered since you are not fully vested yet, and of course, we will not say anything negative about you to prospective employers contacting SkyTel for job references. Jeanne has a paycheck that brings you current. Severance paychecks will be mailed to your home at the regularly scheduled pay periods."

The blood drained from Anthony's face. He could feel his body stiffen as Henry went on as though he were reciting a corporate policy or biblical passage.

"In the event that you have not found gainful employment at the end of the three month severance period, you will be eligible to enroll in COBRA, although I doubt that someone with your drive and talent…"

Anthony interrupted, "Is Edwin okay with this?"

"Anthony, decisions like this are always made final by Edwin. In fact, it has caused him severe anxiety, and he had to see his doctor today because of the manner in which this subject has taxed his nerves."

"*His* nerves?" said Anthony.

Henry did not appreciate the irony.

"Can I talk to Edwin?" asked Anthony.

"Anthony, you must consider that Edwin has been under considerable strain working endless hours in the Lab so that NordSTAR would have a full appreciation of his technology."

"What endless hours?" asked Anthony. "The technology has been stable for eighteen months. The engineers have been customizing files and demos to meet the specific requirements of NordSTAR. Edwin hasn't had to do anything but pop meds for the new disorders he discovers and retain the mystical air that convinces everyone he's a genius."

"Ah, you see Anthony, there is your problem. You neither appreciate the mind of Edwin nor the team approach we like to have here at SkyTel. We all agree that you are a bright, industrious worker, but you just don't fit in." Henry seemed to be enjoying his role now.

Suddenly the Buddhist concepts Anthony had been studying on the *Noble Truths of Suffering* came into his mind. *Slow down*, he told himself. *Go easy*.

"This is bullshit," said Anthony. "I have busted my ass

for this company. The prospects for the NordSTAR deal would have faded months ago if not for my efforts."

"Indeed, we do appreciate your contribution in presenting the value of Edwin's work to the NordSTAR people, Anthony. However, you should not overestimate your role," said Trenholme rather dismissively. The sniff and curling of his nose reappeared.

"So this is a done deal," said Anthony.

Trenholme took some papers from a manila folder.

"There are papers for you to sign. Of course, you are entitled to review them with an attorney, but I can assure you this is a very generous package that required my considerable persuasion of Edwin. If you sign them now, Jeanne will immediately give you the paycheck that goes through the end of the current pay period. If you wish to wait, your check will be mailed when she receives the signed separation agreement. In either case, I would like you to turn over all your files to Jeanne and vacate your office today. If you prefer to do that after 5:00 P.M., feel free to take the afternoon off and come back then. Jeanne and I will be here."

"Do the Germans know about this?" asked Anthony.

"The NordSTAR people have been informed."

"How long has this been planned?" asked Anthony.

"Would you prefer to complete this now, or come back after Five?" asked Henry.

"Give me the fucking papers," said Anthony as he reached for a pen.

Chapter 3

Anthony was a few miles from his former office before he realized his hands were very tightly wrapped around the steering wheel and his jaw was clenched. He had been in a daze when Jeanne Marsh and Trenholme accompanied him to his office. He turned over all his computer files, manuals, company papers and keys and sorted out his personal things. Jeanne brought in a set of Office Depot fold-away cartons without so much as a pretense that they were not purchased just for this occasion. He packed his belongings: pictures, reference books and a framed poster of the 1955 Brooklyn Dodgers World Champions, his father's team. Before his heart started pumping normally again, the car was packed, and he was out the door facing a brave new world.

He decided to exit the Southern State and head for a small marina that he and Bernadette visited upon occasion. Anthony liked being around the water and near fishing boats in fair weather or foul. He parked where he had a clear view of the shoreline and could see the moored boats bobbing in the shallow water.

"Anthony Bartolo, you've just been fired, cooked and had for lunch" he said out loud. "The bastards got you and you didn't even see it coming. Well, fuck 'em all."

He left his car and walked to Marina Coffee Shop and got a cup to go. He strolled along the small pier studying the sea gulls while sipping his coffee before returning to the car. He replayed the morning experience over in his head. He knew he should have taken the papers with him before signing. Hell, he didn't even read them carefully. He knew though, that the die had been cast, and anything he objected to would have to be dealt with later. In truth, the facts were simple. They were done with him. Right then, he didn't care to negotiate for more severance pay, letters of recommendation or anything else. He had just wanted to get out of there. He felt calm now, but also as tired as after a day of kayaking, something he had not done for months. Realizing that he had some time to develop a recovery plan, there was no need to panic. For the first time in a very long time, his thoughts drifted to Rita.

He and Rita Suarez had been together for almost a year and apart for another year before he and Bernadette became an item. Anthony and Rita worked for the same company way back when. They both reported to Jack Mullen the Division Marketing Manager. Anthony had been a first year Marketing Support Rep in his first job out of college. Rita was the one person Regional Marketing Communications Department responsible for marketing presentations that described the company and its products to the outside world. She was two years his senior. The first time he saw her, he thought she was the most beautiful girl he had ever seen. She was tiny at barely five feet tall and proportionately slim. No big boobs, no grapefruits in her ass, but her whole being exuded femininity, confidence, and sex without a trace of slut. Her clothes, hair style, and makeup were all conservative. She did have a slight accent that just emphasized her allure. After gradually getting to know her, he asked her out.

"Why does a nice Dago Boy want to go out with a

Rican?"

Anthony figured that she was going to make him work for it. He decided he would.

"I have good taste," he said. "I know something special when I see it."

"Have you ever been to Puerto Rico?" She asked.

"No."

"I was born there," she said. "Have you ever been to Spanish Harlem?"

"Sure, to Manny's restaurant and a club or two, but I can't say I hang out there," he said honestly.

"Yeah, same for me," she said with a little smile. "I live in the Village."

"So will you go out with me?" he said.

"You're going to be very disappointed and horny if you expect to get me in bed."

"I won't be disappointed in you, and I'm always horny anyway," he said.

"My Bachelor's is in English Lit, but my minor is in High Standards."

"In that case we sound perfect for each other."

"Okay, Dago Boy, we can go to an early dinner Friday night after work. Does that work for you?"

"How long are you going to call me that?"

"How about if I call you DB instead? I'll stop when it's the right time. You'll know when that is," she said.

"Friday night after work, Rita."

"High Standards, DB." she said.

They saw each other regularly for three months after that first dinner, each successive month with increased frequency. They did dinner, shows, parks, the beach and a couple of concerts. Anthony still shared an apartment with a college buddy so they seldom went there. Sometimes, they would just stay in at her place. In all that time, he waited for her. He came to love her dark hair, dark eyes and light, bronze skin. He loved the feel of her arm linked through his. He loved to hear her speak with her soft accent that was so different from the harsh New York sound he was so used to. He knew that the time would come when she would be ready. He knew he loved her.

One Sunday night as they were finishing dinner at her apartment, she asked him a question.

"Anthony, what do you know about Cape Cod?"

"Well", he said, "It's nice. I've only been there twice, once for a ... " he was halfway through his answer when he realized that for the first time outside of the office she called him Anthony instead of DB.

"Would you like to go there?" he asked.

She had a smile on her face. He stood facing her and put his hands on the back of her chair, bending slightly, just taking her in. She undid the clasp in her hair letting it fall to the sides of her face. She remained silent while he gently clasped her hands and lifted her from the chair. He scooped her up and brought her over to the studio bed.

"Undress me," she said. "And leave the light on."

Chapter 4

Anthony was startled as an SUV pulled up next to him. Two women got out, collected their children from the back seat and headed toward the marina shops. He realized that he had become aroused thinking about Rita. He took a long sip of the cooling coffee. A feeling of self consciousness came over him. He wondered if he looked like a pervert hiding out in his car as he and Bernadette had so often suspected when seeing lone men in parked cars. His thoughts of Rita faded and the events of the morning popped back into his head.

Trenholme was right about him not fitting in. Anthony enjoyed stirring the pot and pushing people's buttons. His comments at meetings would take colleagues right to the edge. If a deadline was missed by Engineering, Anthony would highlight it. If a product feature was dropped, he would not let it pass. If a competitor developed products faster, he would wonder aloud about how they were able to do it. It was not beyond Anthony to make remarks that poked fun at Edwin's hypochondria and self adoration even though Edwin's sense of humor was not his strength. Anthony pushed people with critical honesty and very little diplomacy. It pissed them off and today they kicked his ass. He should not have been surprised.

He finished the coffee and started up the car knowing it was time to bring home the news and face the music. Bernadette would be caught off guard, but he would reassure her that he would find work quickly and that their lifestyle wouldn't change. *She'll be able to handle it*, he thought. *She'll be in his corner. She always was.*

It was earlier than usual when Anthony approached their house. He left his car in the driveway so Bernadette wouldn't be startled seeing him when she came in. He decided not to change from his business clothes into something more comfortable as he usually did. He browsed through the papers he had signed earlier and made some notes in the margins before putting them away. To kill some time, he brought in the mail, paid some bills and renewed a magazine subscription. Finally, he put everything away and started watching the clock.

He thought about how he would tell Bernadette the news of the day and anticipated her possible responses. It was approaching four o'clock when he poured himself a snifter of Amaretto and waited in the living room where they had entertained her friends two nights before. Bernadette didn't arrive home until after 6:00 P.M. with three bags of groceries. At that hour, she was not at all surprised that he was home. Anthony helped her carry in and store the groceries.

Expecting they would watch the Monday night football game, she suggested a simple dinner of soup and salad. He agreed and added that he had something to talk about before dinner and poured her an Amaretto. Bernadette sensed that this was going to be a continuation of their argument of Saturday night. She was reluctant to get into that again, but agreed to listen.

"So," he said, "I've got some not so good news."

"What's the news?" she asked cautiously.

"Well, it looks like I don't work for SkyTel anymore."

"What do you mean?" she asked.

"I've been canned," he said.

"Oh my God! What happened? Why?"

"To be honest, I didn't see it coming. I was told this morning, but apparently it had been in the works for a while," Anthony said.

"How could this happen?" Bernadette asked, "I thought things with the German company were going so well."

"They are. Better than ever. The acquisition will be concluded soon. Edwin and Trenholme will get very rich."

"But I thought you were the key person putting it together. I don't understand," she said.

"I was the key person. The deal is at the stage now where it can go through without me. No one was more surprised than me. I'm sure I ruffled some feathers along the way, and this was an opportunity for them to unload me before my stock options vested. Edwin and Trenholme were never really big on sharing the spoils," said Anthony.

"Can they do that?"

"They just did," said Anthony as he slumped a bit in his chair giving up his air of confidence.

"This is terrible," she said.

"It's not so bad," he said unconvincingly, "I'll get paid for three more months. I can find a new job by then."

"But you've worked so hard for them. You said this could go a long way once the Germans took over the company; that there might even be a promotion coming."

"Yeah, well, I'll put it in the lessons learned column," he said.

"Anthony, is there anything you're not telling me?"

"What do you mean?"

"You know. Did you tell Edwin or Trenholme to fuck off or something?"

The question startled him. She didn't like that word and never used it.

"Whoa, slow down. I can be abrasive, but I'm not stupid," he said.

"Anthony, how long have we been together? I know how you can be."

"Jesus Christ," he said, knowing it would upset her sensibilities. "I can't believe this. I go in this morning after completing some reports over the weekend including a glowing update on the situation with NordSTAR, which I have handled beautifully by the way, while working my ass off. Everything looked so good that I was calculating the rising value of my stock options and how they're going to help us, and you' re asking me if I fucked up! Wow. Thanks a lot for the vote of confidence. I deal with that paranoid hypochondriac and his ass kissing sycophant every day while managing the merger deal to the point where the Germans are ready to sign, and you want to know if I told somebody to fuck off?"

"I'm sorry Anthony, but they did fire you."

"Yes, they did. And I'm not the most likable, easygoing person on the planet, but that doesn't make what they did right, or this my fault. I did my job and I did it well. The job I started for them will come to a successful conclusion because of how well I did it. And for that I am supposed to be rewarded. But they want to keep the prize for themselves. And sometimes, that's just the way it goes!" he said.

"Please don't shout," said Bernadette.

"Jesus, give me a break here."

"And please stop saying Jesus."

Anthony looked at Bernadette with a mix of anger, contempt and self pity.

"I'm going for a walk," he said.

"Fine," she said. "Go."

He grabbed a jacket from the hall closet. "I'll be back soon. I need to cool off."

She turned and walked toward the kitchen.

"Yeah, great," he said as he turned and walked out the door.

He walked for three blocks and had made two right turns before he realized where he was. It was cold and dark except for the yellow phosphorous glow the street lights poured through the bare branches of the maples lining the street. He turned right again continuing east instead of making the last right turn in the direction of his house. He started thinking out loud.

"What the fuck is wrong with me? How do these things happen? Is it me? Am I asking for this shit? Am I too fucking smart, or too fucking stupid? Is the world fucked up, or am I?"

At that moment he felt a wrenching in his stomach. He put an arm against a maple and bent over as far as he could to avoid puking on his good shoes. His stomach heaved, but it was empty except for coffee and Amaretto. He gagged violently again and again with nothing coming up except acidic bile that seared his throat. The heaving in his empty stomach would not stop. He struggled to catch his breath between spasms. Finally, it subsided. His whole body was soaked with perspiration. Braced against the tree, he straightened up and took several deep breaths. He looked to see if anyone had seen him, and was relieved to see the street was empty. Anthony wiped tears from his eyes with a handkerchief before drying the rest of his face and neck.

"Fuck 'em all, fuck 'em all," he said, saying it louder the second time. He started walking again gradually picking up his normal pace. When he reached the house, he checked his shoes under the porch light before going in.

Taking Flight

Bernadette was in the kitchen. He shouted that he was back and went straight to the bathroom to wash his hands and face and brush his teeth. He changed from his work clothes into a pair of sweats before joining Bernadette in the kitchen.

"You look kind of pale," said Bernadette.

"I'm a little tired. It's been a helluva day," he said.

"I'm sorry we fought about this," she said.

"Yeah, me too," he said.

"I made some salad, and I'm heating up the soup. Maybe you'll feel better once you've had something to eat," she said.

"You know what? I think I'll just have some tea with a few crackers for now. I'm sorry if you've already fixed something."

"No big deal," she said, "I'll get the tea."

"Thanks," Anthony said as he slumped into the chair at the kitchen table where they often ate when it was just the two of them.

"Do you think that maybe, you should talk to someone?" she asked when she returned with the tea.

"Like who?" he said.

"Well, what about a lawyer?"

"Quite frankly, Bernadette, I know as much about this stuff as lawyers do. Remember, I have fired a few people myself. I learned all the rules of the road about how to avoid lawsuits. I assure you that Trenholme followed the same roadmap. Besides, to the outside world it will appear like a voluntary resignation. That's why my salary will continue for three months. And I don't have to tell a future employer that I was sacked. No muss, no fuss. That's how it's done."

"But you lost your stock options," she said.

"They were useless until I became vested eighteen months from now, or immediately after somebody acquired us, whichever would come first. As long as neither has happened, I have to kiss them goodbye."

"That seems so unfair," she said.

"The term "fairness" is never included in stock option agreements. Besides, we don't have a personal attorney."

Bernadette fell silent looking down at the table.

"Oh no," he said. "Don't even go there. If you're thinking about that pompous ass, who by the way, had his hands all over your ass the other night, forget it," he said.

"He did not. Besides, David is supposed to be very smart, and he works for a top law firm. Maybe he could just recommend somebody from the firm who handles these things," she said.

"What things? I got fired. It happens every day. Besides if you sue or something, it gets around and for sure the next job will never come."

"It wouldn't hurt to just talk, to get some professional advice."

"Bernadette, look, this is my world. I know how things work. I understand what happened, and what I have to do about it. I admit that I got blindsided. I should've seen it coming. I should've been better prepared or somehow protected myself, but I didn't. That's my mistake, but we'll get through this. I know enough people in this business. I'll decompress for a couple of days. Then, I'll put a recovery plan together. I'll be working someplace better and with more opportunity in a few weeks."

"This is scary," she said.

"I know. I know. But we'll be okay. Trust me."

They went to bed that night without making love, but not with the anger of the weekend. They were lying in the dark wide awake.

"Bernadette?"

"Yes?"

"Why did you let David hold you close and grab your ass in front of me and all your friends?"

Chapter 5

Anthony spent the next two weeks at home getting used to the idea that he no longer had a job. It was strange watching Bernadette go off to work the first day in his new position as a soldier in the army of the unemployed. That's overstating it he thought, since the paychecks would be coming in for a while. This could be a good thing, he told himself. He had time to think about his career, assess the opportunities in the job market and make a wise move. He decided that he would continue to wake up at his regular time and go through his usual morning routine except that jeans or khakis would become the uniform of the day. He would pick up the NY Times or Newsday at the local newsstand and read the news to start his "business" day. To free his mind of the recent events, he made a list of house projects that he or Bernadette wanted to get done. In the coming weeks, he would install overhead cabinets in the garage, prune the rosebushes, have a minor recall notice for his car taken care of and mount two candleholders that Bernadette had picked up for the living room wall. Post-season baseball relieved some of the quiet boredom, but he was aware of his mind drifting as he watched the games with little more than a passing interest since the Yankees were eliminated in the first round.

He finished reading Stephen Hawking's *A Brief History of Time* after several false starts. He had the tenth anniversary paperback edition which had been gathering dust. Anthony believed that it was an important book to read, or be able to say he read, even though the chapters detailing quarks, particles and anti-particles were mind boggling. When he read the section on wormholes and time travel he remembered how grateful he was to receive a C minus in a required Physics course in college.

Nevertheless, Anthony struggled through the Hawking book. He took a particular interest in the author's reference to God. Anthony concluded that Hawking invoked God only to make the point that there are things about the formation of the universe and the laws that govern it that we don't understand yet, but when we do there will no longer be a need for God. This interpretation had a profound effect on Anthony. He and Bernadette had been having issues about religion and church. They had settled on "growing spiritually" which to her had meant getting back to practicing her faith. To him it had meant having a license to explore philosophical concepts of good and evil and alternatives to the religious beliefs he had been taught and practiced since childhood. He also vowed to reward himself with some pulp fiction for his next read.

On Thursday of the second week, he announced to Bernadette that he was so caught up on house projects that he found himself waiting for suspect light bulbs to burn out.

"It's time for me to get back out in the world!" he said.

She reacted tentatively as she had been doing since he was fired from SkyTel, not sure whether to laugh about the light bulbs, offer encouragement, reassurance or exercise caution.

"What's your next step?" she asked.

"Well," he replied, "I'm going to have lunch with Jack Mullen of CommData tomorrow. I called and proposed getting together next week, but he's going out of town so he agreed to see me tomorrow.

"That was nice of him," said Bernadette.

"He always respected my work. There were times when I was his "go to" guy. I always felt good when I delivered for him. Jack is a stand-up guy. He'll be good to talk with."

"Are you going to ask him to hire you back?"

"No, no, no. I'm just going to bring him up to date on my situation, see what he has to say, and just go from there."

"But…" Bernadette started then stopped. "Well, I hope it goes well. You always spoke highly of him. I used to think that you were sorry about leaving that company."

"I'm looking forward to seeing him," said Anthony.

Anthony started the following day like he would any other workday. He selected a soft textured, gray plaid suit and a solid tie knowing that Jack favored plaid suits and sport coats. *When you visit a customer, dress like the customer*, he had been told in an early CommData Training program. *Dress like the people you're calling on. That way, they won't be intimidated or alarmed by you. Your dress will announce your membership in the same club.*

At ten o'clock he walked to the coffee shop halfway between the house and the train station. On the way, he picked up a copy of the New York Times and Wall Street Journal and put them in his otherwise empty briefcase. After ordering coffee and a plain bagel, he read the hallowed words of the Journal. He came across a small article about a new CommData subsidiary that he could bring up during his conversation with Jack. After making sure that the Times had control of world affairs, he gathered his belongings and headed for the train station to catch the 11:05 A.M. to New York City.

The train was a milk run at this time of the day, stopping at every station along the way. By the time they pulled into Penn Station, he had finished the Wall Street Journal but brought it with him for its appearance value. *No different than wearing the right tie*, he thought. He decided to walk to the office even though it was a chilly day. It felt good to be in the city. The hustle and bustle was invigorating. He felt like he was getting back in the game; taking control. He looked forward to seeing Jack. Today was going to be a good day.

By the time Anthony arrived at CommData, it was just after Noon. He entered the building lobby and found the elevator as he had hundreds of times before. He *was* back in the game. Arriving at the third floor where Jack had his office, he was startled by seeing a new face behind the reception desk.

The comely young woman asked, "May I help you?"

"I have an appointment with Jack Mullen," said Anthony.

"What is your name, please?"

"Anthony Bartolo," he said, realizing it would mean nothing to her.

"Please sign in," she said, handing him a clipboard. "Print your name and company name followed by your signature."

While he was printing his name, the woman picked up the phone and said, "Mr. Barolo is here to see you."

Anthony started to correct her, but thought better of it. In less than a minute, Jack was approaching the reception area. He already had on his coat suggesting that they were going straight out.

"I booked us at The Customs House. They still have

the best steaks," said Jack with a smile, while extending his hand.

"Great," said Anthony. "It's been a long time since I've been there."

They walked two blocks before descending three steps to the entrance of the restaurant. They walked past the long bar already three quarters occupied before reaching the Maitre D's station. He greeted Jack by name.

"Good afternoon, Mr. Mullen, your table is ready."

Anthony was glad to see that their table was in the back where the restaurant was less noisy. They would be able to talk without having to shout. Both men ordered the Petite Sirloin with a House Salad. Jack had iced tea. Anthony asked for mineral water.

Jack had been invited to Bernadette and Anthony's wedding. Not able to attend, he sent a crystal vase as a gift. The thank you note Bernadette sent was probably the last exchange of correspondence between them. They went through the required catching up. Jack asked about Bernadette. Anthony asked about Jack's wife, four sons and daughter. They concluded that everyone was terrific and got down to business.

"So what's up, Anthony? To what do I owe this honor?"

Anthony smiled and said, "Hey boss, I'm in the job market and just starting to get back into that part of the universe." Afraid that Jack might misconstrue what he said as asking for a job, he quickly added, "I was hoping to run my game plan by you to get some feedback."

"Sure," said Jack. "What happened at SkyTel?"

Anthony paused for a moment. "I got canned," he said. "In thinking about it, I worked my butt off, and I think I did good work, but I was probably abrasive especially to the top guys who were very sensitive to criticism."

"I appreciate your candor, Anthony. It looks like not much has changed."

Anthony was surprised by Jack's comment and became defensive. "I didn't think I was abrasive when I worked for you," he said.

"Not to me you weren't," Jack said. "But I remember a number of encounters you had with people in Headquarters and some with the field organization. You did not discriminate when it came to being, let's say, a little pushy."

"I just called things as I saw them. I don't think I was mean spirited. I thought it was okay to do that," said Anthony. "I never knowingly criticized anybody unjustly. I just did my job."

'Well, let me put it this way, Anthony. When you left, at least a half dozen people called to say they were glad you were gone."

Anthony sat stunned hearing this from the man he respected so much.

"Wow," Anthony said. "And here I thought I did a good job for you."

"You did do a good job. Every project you handled was done correctly, on time and presented flawlessly. I'm just saying that you did not make a lot of friends along the way."

"I didn't like to kiss ass, or play the political games," said Anthony.

"There is a difference between that and showing respect for your colleagues, especially if they disagree with you."

Anthony slowly shook his head in disbelief. "I guess this is not the time to ask for a job reference."

"Anthony, I'll be happy to give you a letter of reference. I can address it to 'To whom it may concern.' That probably will be better than having someone call me."

"Why?"

"First of all, I would have to refer them to the Human Resources department at Division, and no one there will remember you. Besides they will only give whoever calls your name, rank and serial number. They're more concerned with avoiding litigation than helping former employees."

"So you couldn't just say a few positive things about me?" said Anthony

"Of course I could, Anthony. But if I did that, any caller worth his salt would see the obvious which is that you worked for me four years ago. In terms of responsibilities and accomplishments that I can speak about, they're ancient history."

"Yeah, but still, having…"

"And then, even if I speak well about what you did here, they would ask the code question that would circumvent the need for me to not say anything negative as corporate policy dictates."

"Which is?" asked Anthony.

"Would you re-hire this person? Unless I gave an immediate and positive response without qualification to this question, he or she would interpret it as 'No.'"

"And you don't feel you can do that?"

Jack paused, "No Anthony, I don't."

Anthony could not believe what he was hearing.

"Which is why," Jack went on, "a letter would be better. It will describe your attributes, which are several. It will avoid the coded question and it can omit any shortcomings you may have. I'll make it a very good letter.

You'll have it by Monday."

The steaks arrived while Anthony was trying to absorb this without showing his shock and disappointment.

"Suppose someone calls you anyway?" said Anthony.

"I will recite the corporate policy and refer him to Division."

"Thanks," said Anthony. "I appreciate the letter." Knowing that this part of the conversation was over, Anthony switched subjects and mentioned the Journal article he read about CommData. He also asked about certain product lines while struggling to swallow his steak. When the conversation moved into the mundane, Anthony surprised himself.

"Does Rita still work for you?"

"She left CommData about eighteen months ago.

"Do you ever hear from her?" asked Anthony.

Jack paused and gave Anthony a long look before answering.

"From time to time."

It was clear this was a subject Jack was not going to discuss. Anthony could not finish the small steak and declined the waiter's offer to wrap it. Upon leaving the restaurant, Anthony mentioned that he had some errands to run for Bernadette which would take him in the opposite direction of Jack's office. They exchanged pleasant goodbyes, promised to stay in touch and offered their regards to each other's families. Jack wished Anthony good luck and Anthony thanked him for the letter once more. Anthony turned away and began walking uptown in the cooling afternoon air knowing that he would never see or speak to Jack again.

Chapter 6

Anthony and Rita had spent a great deal of time together during their year of courtship. Although he had kept his share of an apartment, Anthony had camped at Rita's almost every weekend. The frequency of Anthony's visits to his parents' home had been reduced by half to one per month. He and Rita had been apart for three months when he called to invite himself to dinner and an afternoon at the firing range with his father.

As had become their custom, he and his father met at the Prospect Park Firing Range for about an hour before heading to the house in Brooklyn. Anthony didn't particularly enjoy the firing range, but appreciated sharing the hobby and having time with his father. He thought it was ironic that a man who didn't have a violent bone in his body would revel in firing guns.

"I appreciate the precision with which they are made, the feel of them, and the concentration and control it takes to fire them accurately" his father had told him. He didn't like shooting at living things so he substituted targets at the range for animals and birds.

After their first few times together, Anthony declared that he had a "sissy shoulder" that couldn't handle the kick of a rifle, and had switched to hand guns. One experience with a Magnum 47 drove to him a Glock 9mm before he settled on a Smith and Wesson 38mm. When he found a gun he felt comfortable with, his expertise improved to marginally acceptable marksmanship.

Taking Flight

Anthony brought flowers for his mother and a bottle of his father's favorite Chianti to dinner that night. The house still looked comfortable to him. His folks kept the place up by replacing kitchen cabinets, installing new appliances, upgrading the bathrooms and adding new flooring and window coverings. They even took down the wood paneling his father had loved and his mother had hated. His parents knew that he had broken up with "that Puerto Rican girl" as Anthony's mother still referred to her.

After a wonderful dinner, his mother served espresso coffee. Anthony declined dessert, but placated his mother by agreeing to take some home. Waving off any help, she began to clear the table. His father suggested he and Anthony go to the garden to enjoy their coffee while there was still some daylight. He and Anthony had had many "special talks" there when he was growing up. Anthony suspected he was in for another one today.

"So, are you okay?" his father asked.

"Yeah, Pop, I'm okay. I miss Rita more than I can say, and I hurt inside, but I'm still walking and talking. I guess Mom's happy now."

"Oh, you know your mother. She was concerned about the girl being of mixed race. It's a carryover from the old days. After all, you are her Prince and like most mothers, she worries about the decisions you make," he said. "What about Rita, how is she?"

"I hurt her to the point where she can't forgive me. She's tough though. One of us will probably leave the company. It's too hard seeing each other every day. I'm looking around for a new job. I've had enough of

CommData, anyway," said Anthony.

"New job. Eventually a new girl. It's a new beginning. You'll survive," said his father. "Everybody goes through something like this. It's too bad though. I really liked her."

"Not at first, you didn't. You were standing in Mom's camp."

"That was to keep the peace. When I met Rita and got to know her a little, I said to myself, 'My boy knows how to pick a good woman.' She was beautiful, smart, and had a spirit that I liked."

"Pop, we broke up, she's not dead," said Anthony shaking his head. Then he hunched over and buried his face in his hands. They were sitting on wooden chairs under the grapevine covered arbor his father had built. The long narrow yard had a sense of privacy despite neighbors' yards running parallel on both sides. The fencing was hidden by trees and shrubs that absorbed sound and blocked sight. The yard was broken into three sections; the arbor area where they were sitting, a flower garden with a fountain at its center and his father's treasured vegetable garden in the rear. This was his father's place, Anthony thought, his sanctuary. It was this yard that defined his father.

"Look, I don't want to meddle, but are you sure you can't get back together?" his father said, as he put a hand on Anthony's shoulder.

"No, Pop. I screwed up big time."

"I don't need to know the details," his father replied.

Anthony couldn't stop.

"Everything was going great. Every day was better than the next. I loved being with her. When I traveled on *business, I couldn't wait to get back. We kept our private lives out of the office, although my boss, and probably everybody else knew we were together. The company frowns on office romances, so we played it down. After work, we would meet outside most nights, rather than leave together. Nobody really cared, but it was a way of saying this was private, not for conversation, our own business. In the office we behaved as professionals and kept our private lives outside.*

"Then about three months ago, this guy, Garrity, my boss's boss, comes down from Division HQ in Framingham. He was here to spend the day reviewing our operations. Although our company is established, our division is new and still in the growing stage. We showed him how we had divided Manhattan into four sectors and how each would become a separate sales branch as the territory developed. We showed him an impressive list of companies who were committed to our product lines. We described our strategic plan in detail, and he loved it.

"After lunch, Rita came in and using her laptop, gave a slide presentation we have used for prospects on Wall Street. It was great stuff. When she leaves, Garrity turns to my boss and me and says, 'Jesus, Joseph and Mary, that is one sexy piece of ass. I bet if she fucked a gorilla, the gorilla would quit before she did.' I must've looked like I was in shock because Jack, my boss, jumps in and says, 'Mac, Rita is one of our best people.' So Garrity says, 'What is she, Cuban, Latino, Spic, what?' My throat is dry and I hear myself saying 'She's Puerto Rican' hardly able to get the words out. He says, 'I hear they put chili peppers in their pussy to keep it hot all the time.' He's laughing and

I'm fuming at this Neanderthal, but I didn't say a word so Jack takes over and closes out the discussion.

"Garrity says he has a few hours before his flight and suggests that he and Jack have a couple of pops before he takes a cab to the airport. He invited me along, but I told him I had some work to do for a customer meeting the next day. He left his briefcase and overnight bag in the office and went with Jack to a bar around the corner. I finished up around 5:00 P.M. and was making some notes for the next day when Rita passed by to let me know she was leaving and she'll wait for me outside. A few minutes later, Garrity came back without Jack to get his stuff. The smell of liquor is pretty strong. When he saw me, he says, 'Hey kid, good job today.' I'm aware that his opinion is important, and I was glad to get the strokes. He rules the Division and has a lot of weight with Corporate. I say 'Thanks' and start to pack my briefcase. He says, 'You know that girl is downstairs at the corner. Must be waiting to pick up a gorilla,' and then he starts to laugh like he's just heard the funniest joke in the world. And I say back, 'Yeah, you know how those Spics are.'

"Pop, I couldn't believe I said that. Then he says, 'Look, I have still have some time before I head out. Let's get a drink. I want to talk to you about your future. I talked to your boss and he's okay with this. In fact he's your biggest fan. I know there's opportunity here in the city, but there's going to be a key spot opening up at Division. You could be a good fit. It would be a nice promotion with bucks and benefits.' I knew this was important, but there was no way I wanted to go to Framingham, Massachusetts.

Taking Flight

"I told him, 'That's very flattering, but I don't know. I'm a Yankee fan and you're talking about Red Sox country' trying to put a light touch on it. He ignores me and invites me out for a drink again. I knew Rita was waiting downstairs, but I agreed to go. I figured if I had just turned down his offer, I should at least have a drink with him. We grabbed his stuff and headed downstairs. When we came out of the lobby, we see Rita standing near the corner. Garrity said, 'Hey, maybe we should invite her along.'

"'No, I say back. She might bring her gorilla.' He laughs heartily, and we go around the corner to the bar. We spent another hour together before he left for the airport. I told him I appreciated the offer, but I was really happy living in New York. He told me to think about it some more, and we left it at that. I got in a cab and went over to Rita's.

"When she opened the door she said, 'I got the picture when you came out together, you don't have to explain.' I tell her 'I feel like I need to take a shower.' 'Want some company?' she asks. 'No thanks,' I tell her. 'I have to get rid of the stench.' Later after we ate, I told her everything that was said. I thought that by being honest, she would understand that I felt trapped and was sorry, and was temporarily out of my head.

"She just sat there, stone faced and said nothing for a long while. Finally, she said, 'You denied me, Anthony.' 'What? I said.' 'You denied me. As a person, as a Puerto Rican, as your lover.' 'But..., I tried to explain again.' 'There are no buts. This isn't a misunderstanding. We didn't have a quarrel. You didn't flirt with somebody. You

didn't forget an important date. You denied my existence. You denied my role in your life. You denied who I am.'
'Rita, I got caught up in...' 'Anthony, I know we all make mistakes, but you threw me out of your life to suck up to a drunken boss in a disgusting and unforgivable way. ' 'Rita!'
'Go, Anthony,' she says. 'High standards, remember. Take your things and just go.'

"And that was it, Pop," Anthony said facing the ground, his face still in his hands. "No more discussion. It was over."

"No more discussion was necessary," his father said, looking very sad.

They sat in silence for a while longer.

"I screwed up the best thing that ever happened to me."

"Yes, you did," replied his father. "You screwed up and you'll never forget it. If she were to call tomorrow and say she forgives you, your future would always be marred by that moment. To be honest, my heart goes out to Rita. She lost something too. I think if the circumstances were reversed, she would have handled them much differently."

"Yeah, Pop, yeah."

Taking Flight

Chapter 7

Anthony and Bernadette were getting ready to leave for another Saturday night with her friends. He was not comfortable meeting with them after losing his job. Yesterday's experience with Jack Mullen was unsettling. He had given a toned down version to Bernadette, emphasizing the value of Jack's letter of recommendation and didn't mention Jack's other comments. He knew Bernadette had told her friends about his leaving SkyTel, but wasn't sure of how much detail she provided. Anthony and Bernadette had not spoken about it or much of anything else since it happened. To Anthony, she seemed to remain in a neutral zone, leery of bringing up anything that would cause him to become upset. Anthony remained uncommunicative except to provide the minimum facts coated with a layer of reassurance. When the subject did come up, he repeated his mantra that he had a plan and that everything would work out.

They stopped at the door so Anthony could key in the exit code of the house security system he had installed two years earlier. He had called it a "modern necessity of the privileged."

"You look very nice," she said as they were about to leave.

"Thanks. You look great," he said, admiring the fitted pale green knit sweater over her dark green slacks visible under the open leather jacket that matched her black pumps.

Bernadette smiled as she stepped out. Their car was in

the driveway ready to take them to Martin and Sarah's house. Anthony locked the front door, peeked through its small window to be sure that the "security system activated" light was on. By the time he reached the car, Bernadette was already fastening her seat belt.

"You know, we've been out with them a lot, but I've never been to their house. If you give me their address, I'll put it in the GPS system," he said.

"Why don't I just give you the directions as we go? It's pretty easy and they don't live that far."

"We bought this thing so we could use it," he said.

"*You* bought it because you like gadgets. I don't want to hear her step by step instructions tonight. Just head toward the Sunrise Highway. Please."

Anthony decided not to argue the point.

"So, does everybody know I got fired?"

"Everybody knows that you no longer work at SkyTel, and that you're looking for something else," said Bernadette.

"How much detail do they have?" he asked. "I'd like to know what I'm in for."

Bernadette said, "Look, they know you lost your job. They know that you didn't quit. I never said whether you were fired, laid off, cut back or anything else, but they know it wasn't your idea. They know it came as a surprise to you, especially after all you had accomplished there. Anthony, these are my friends. They are not going to be judgmental or assume you did anything to deserve this. Probably, no one will even bring it up. If someone does, it will be because they care about us. They will be supportive."

"I don't need to be cared for," he said.

"Well maybe I do. Can't we just have a nice evening?

I've known most of these girls and Les for years. They're important to me. And the guys are all nice."

"And every one of them is working," he said.

"Anthony," she said, "You're feeling sorry for yourself. Please relax and try to have a good time."

"You're right," he said. "I'm sorry."

"Turn right on the next corner where the coffee shop is. Drive three blocks and turn right again," she said.

Anthony realized they had just turned by the coffee shop where he had stopped before going into the city to meet Jack.

"Did I tell you that Jack said he wouldn't hire me again," said Anthony.

Bernadette looked puzzled. "I thought you weren't going to ask him for a job."

"I didn't. But if someone calls him and asks if he would hire me again, he said he would have to say no. So he's going to write a good reference letter instead. If someone does call, he'll just give them the corporate drill and refer them to Division."

"That doesn't sound so bad," said Bernadette.

"Jesus Christ, Bernadette, the man said that he wouldn't hire me again!"

She let his use of the Lord's name pass. "This is where you turn right. The house is just two streets down on the left; Number 2240. I'll point it out."

When they reached the house, the driveway was full of cars, and there was no place to park within sight.

"Do you want me to let you out?" he asked.

"No, of course not. I'll go with you until we find a parking space."

They found one about a half block away. On the walk back toward Martin and Sarah's house, Bernadette said,

"Anthony, I'm very sorry about what Jack said, but I wish you had told me when you came home last night, not now as we're about to walk into a dinner party."

After a few more steps, he stopped and took her arm.

"Look, you're right again," he said. "I'm whining and I can't stand it. I hate the idea of feeling sorry for myself. I just haven't got my arms around this yet. I promise that I'm going to drop it right now and not think about it until the light of day. When I do, I'll figure out what to do next. But before dropping it, something to remember is that I have an interview with Stewart Ogilvie on Monday. There are positive things to look forward to. Now, I'll shut up about it and we can join the party."

"Everything will be fine," she said as she linked her arm with his.

As they approached the house, Anthony realized that all the houses around him were huge. They were at least twice the size of the house he and Bernadette owned. Everything was oversized. The frontage was much deeper and the side to side space could have held another house. He estimated this house to be at least five thousand square feet. Although the grass was already browning with the season, you could see that the grounds were professionally maintained. The flagstone walk was laid out beautifully with mixed colors, shapes and sizes just waiting to appear in a magazine spread. They reached the solid oak double front doors with stained glass insets and a large brass handle.

"This thing looks like it could pump gasoline," he said. "I'll bet he didn't get this house by fixing the teeth of indigenous peoples for Doctors without Borders."

"Martin has a very good practice," said Bernadette. "He has two offices on the Island and one in Manhattan.

And as a matter of fact, last year he did spend two months in El Salvador working free in an impoverished village. I think he is supposed to go again in the Spring."

"I had no idea," said Anthony.

"Ring the bell and let's just go in," said Bernadette.

He did so and as they entered, Sarah greeted them with a big smile and gave each of them a warm hug. Bernadette removed her coat. After a second or two of staring around, Anthony did the same.

"Just give me these and head straight back." Sarah said. "They're all in the playroom shooting pool."

Anthony learned later that the playroom housed an eight foot tournament pool table, a card table that could seat six, and a standalone bar with four stools opposite a stone fireplace. This room was not be confused with the family room that had a home theater system with complete surround sound and speakers strategically placed around the room without a wire in sight, or the downstairs recreation room which was outfitted primarily for children to accommodate Martin and Sarah's nieces and nephews when they visited. *Jesus*, thought Anthony, *and I thought I could impress them with a fucking canolli.*

Anthony and Bernadette joined the others, interrupting a game of Eight Ball as everyone greeted them. The women hugged them and the men shook Anthony's hand, hugged Bernadette and exchanged pleasantries. Martin brought them each a glass of wine. When the game resumed, it became clear that Martin and Sarah were teamed up against David and Carla. Regina was substituting for Sarah who had left to greet Anthony and Bernadette, and then went on to retrieve appetizers from the oven. Regina wasn't very good, but when Les volunteered Carla said that broke the boy/girl substitution rule so Regina struggled hoping that

Sarah would return quickly. Nancy didn't play so she and Aaron had wandered off toward the family room. Sarah came back holding a tray of hot appetizers.

"They smell so good," said Regina. "You can take your turn now. I'll take care of these."

"Wait, I have one more tray to get," said Sarah.

"Let me do it," said Regina. "I can handle an oven much better than a pool cue."

"Regina, that sounds so hot," said David.

"Carla, you need to take care of this boy," said Regina, as everyone laughed.

Sarah took the cue stick. Martin reminded her that they were solids as she started to line up the striped fifteen ball. She shifted her position lining up the four ball for a corner shot. As she looked up, she caught Anthony staring at her. She lowered her gaze and made the shot. Everyone around the table cheered. Anthony turned and joined Bernadette at the bar. When the game was over, Martin and Sarah begged off the winner's right to play again.

"Bernadette, why don't you and Anthony play? Martin has to get the barbecue going, and I have a few things to prepare," said Sarah.

"Can I help?" replied Bernadette.

"No thanks, I have it all under control. Please take our turn."

"Isn't it kind of cold out for a barbecue?" asked Anthony.

"Martin loves to barbecue twelve months a year. It's his specialty. Tonight he is making kabobs with marinated beef instead of lamb. They are to die for," said Sarah.

Anthony was ready to play, but waited until Bernadette agreed. When she did, Martin and Sarah went about their hosting duties.

"Help yourselves to the wine. There's more behind the bar," called out Martin as he approached the French doors leading to the patio.

Anthony offered David the opening break. David declined at first since he and Carla lost the last game, but Anthony insisted.

"Fine," said David. He placed the cue ball on the table as Anthony racked the numbered balls. Before the first stroke, the game had the air of being a contest. Anthony proved to be more than a match for David, and it wasn't long before the table was clear of all but striped balls and the eight ball. Carla could not make her shot leaving Bernadette with a clear path to pocket the eight. With one to go to win the game, she got ready and lined up the shot. Nancy and Aaron joined Les and Regina as spectators. Bernadette completed her stroke; the cue ball struck the eight which spun off to the side hitting the ten ball that in turn dropped into the side pocket as the spectators gasped.

"I believe that is a scratch and we have just won the game," said David with a smile. "Sorry Bernadette."

Anthony smiled back. He placed his cue stick on the table as a gesture of defeat, but he did so knowing that he had shown David how to play the game. He went over to comfort Bernadette who was holding both her hands to her cheeks.

"I can't believe that happened," she said.

"It was close to being a very good shot," said Anthony. "It had just a little too much side spin. Besides, winning at pool is a sign of a misspent childhood."

David invited Les and Regina to play. Les wanted to, but Regina felt she wasn't good enough.

"Bernadette, why don't you play in my place so Les can have a chance," said Regina.

"I'm not sure I'm good enough after that last shot," said Bernadette.

"Oh, go ahead," said Anthony. "You did fine except for one shot."

"Madame," said Les with an exaggerated bow, "I would be honored if you would join me in a game against these imposter pool sharks."

"Go ahead," said Regina. "I enjoy watching more than playing."

"Looks like you're up," said Carla.

Bernadette consented and David agreed to take the winner's break shot as Les racked the balls. Anthony walked over to the bar and filled two wine glasses. He brought one over to Bernadette.

"You go ahead and play," he said. "I'm going to check out the palace and visit with Martin for a while."

"Okay," said Bernadette. "Thanks for the wine." She was relieved to see that Anthony looked at ease.

Anthony strolled through the beautifully decorated rooms. The family room was a knockout. One would never miss going to the movies, he mused. The elegant dining room housed a table that could comfortably seat ten. A breakfront with beveled glass panels displayed china and crystal that were undoubtedly high end. A wine cabinet and service table were in the corner negating the need to travel to another room for an additional bottle of wine. The walls were lined with Central American art, mostly farm or village scenes peopled by peasants who were working, dancing or eating. Anthony sensed an earthy quality in them that he instinctively envied.

As he worked his way back to the playroom from the other side, he reached a second set of French doors that led to the patio. On the adjacent wall was a sophisticated security system control panel. It had scrolling displays describing the position of every door and window in the house. It had a speaker and an array of buttons and lights that left Anthony dazzled. He opened one of the doors and walked out to the patio. The non-slip ceramic tiles of differing shades, shapes and sizes were masterfully connected by a dark grout that provided an accent to the earth tones of the tiles.

Thirty feet from the door there was a spa connected to a winding pool not quite kidney shaped, but with enough curves to complement its beautifully landscaped setting. Martin was at the built-in stone grill that had a large cooking surface and work space. An exhaust fan insured that any smoke would be carried away from guests during an outdoor party. Industriously preparing the evening meal, Martin looked up with a welcoming smile.

"Beautiful place you have here," said Anthony.

"Thanks," said Martin. "I'm glad you were able to make it. We use the outdoor area a lot. Cooking here is kind of a hobby of mine. Here, let me know what you think of the marinade I used for this beef," he said, handing Anthony a fork holding a bite size piece of meat.

Anthony took the fork and tasted the beef. He could not believe how sweet and tender it was.

"This is great," he said." I won't even ask how you prepared it."

"It's a recipe I picked up in El Salvador. The people in the villages there are so poor and the quality of the meat is so bad that they use local herbs and spices to improve the flavor."

"I remember reading," said Anthony, "that the French developed their great sauces and gravies during World War II when the condition of their cattle, game and farm animals was so bad. Sort of a "Necessity is the Mother of Invention" thing."

"Yes," said Martin, "except the French were able to reverse their wartime circumstances and return to their earlier prosperity. The Salvadorans had been oppressed by one outside group after another until a native born ruling class evolved to exploit the poor. The peasants have not known anything else for generations. Now they have relative peace and can survive from one generation to the next, but there is not much hope for things getting better."

Anthony was moved by how sincerely Martin spoke. He was searching for a reply when he heard a voice from an intercom speaker.

"Martin, honey, I have to bring some soda cans upstairs and the cases are sealed and heavy. Will you be able to give me a hand soon?"

"Sweetie, I can either do that or destroy dinner. Your timing is bad. However, Anthony is standing right next to me, and I'm sure he's willing to help."

"You bet," said Anthony.

"Okay. Thank you. I'm down in the recreation room. Martin, please tell him how to find the stairs. Oh, and I also want to bring up a few extra bridge chairs," said Sarah.

"You'll find the stairs off the kitchen. A set of café doors lead to them. Be careful, they are steeper than they should be. One of the only design flaws in the house," said Martin.

"I'm on my way," said Anthony, then he stopped and turned back. "Martin?"

"Yes?"

"I enjoyed talking with you," said Anthony. "You have a beautiful home."

"Thanks, Anthony. You're welcome here anytime."

Taking Flight

Anthony turned and walked toward the French doors. He worked his way through the kitchen admiring the oak and glass cabinets. The antique white traditional French farm table and chairs had a pitcher of fresh flowers resting in the center. The oak work island with copper pots and pans hanging above it completed the potential photo layout for *Architectural Digest*. He found the café doors and pushed while stepping through. There was a small landing, but thereafter the steps were steep. He descended cautiously calling out Sarah's name.

"Hey Anthony, over here," said Sarah as she stood by a stack of soda cases in a corner of the room. She wore an apron that somehow looked flattering over her silver top and black slacks. Anthony walked over taking in the hobby horse, life size inflated Muppet characters, a toy chest and two cushioned sofas. Next to the boxes in front of Sarah were a washer and dryer, utility sink and a refrigerator.

"This is quite a home you have," said Anthony.

"It's a lot for two people," she said. "We haven't had any luck adding more occupants."

Not catching her meaning, Anthony said. "I didn't realize you were a princess."

"Don't call me that!" she said sharply.

"I didn't mean…"

"Martin has worked hard to build a successful practice. He devotes one, sometimes two months a year to helping the poor in El Salvador. He also does pro bono work in the Bedford Stuyvesant section of Brooklyn one day a month. I work as a teacher and give half my income to charity and the other half to help my parents deal with medical expenses. So don't call me a princess."

"Sarah, I apologize. I was born with this incredible ability to put my foot in my mouth. More importantly, you

61

and Martin are the nicest people in this group, and I wouldn't want to offend either one of you, or lose your friendship. That is, if we can be considered friends. I mean I know that you and Bernadette are friends, and I've always considered this group as her friends, but with you and Martin, I feel like I would like to earn that friendship as well. As for my big mouth, I just meant that I was overwhelmed by your house. It seems like a palace. And a palace is for a princess. So before I screw it up again, I'm sorry and you're beautiful. You and Martin, I mean are beautiful people. The things you do and…"

"Okay, I get it," Sarah said. "Anyway, I overreacted. Martin and I are very sensitive to all that we have while so aware of the poverty around the world and close to home. I just didn't expect to hear that from you."

Anthony let that sink in without responding right away.

"So, how can I help?" he asked.

"Well, I want to get one case of club soda and one case of ginger ale upstairs. Of course, they are on the bottom of this pile. Then I want to bring the bridge chairs upstairs. They are right inside that closet door."

Anthony flexed his arms. "Strong like bull" he said with a fake Russian accent, smiling as he lifted the top soda case from the pile and put it off to the side. He noticed that they were dusty and stepped back to brush off his sweater.

"You better wear the apron," Sarah said, "even though it might spoil your manly image."

She walked over to Anthony and untied the apron straps behind her back. She lifted the neck strap over her head and placed it over his and brought it down to his neck. She flattened the apron against his chest, then handed him the straps so he could tie them behind his back. She took a step back.

"That'll keep your clothes from becoming a mess," she said.

"Yeah, thanks," he said almost in a whisper.

He continued to remove the soda cases until he reached the bottom two. He moved them aside, and then put the others back where they came from. He picked up the cases of club soda and ginger ale and asked, "Where do you want these?"

"In the playroom, please. There is a mini fridge under the bar," she said.

"I'll be back for the chairs," said Anthony.

He realized on the third step that it had been a mistake to take two cases at a time, but he continued. Arriving at the landing with a twinge in his back, he rested for a minute before bringing the cases into the kitchen. He set them carefully on the table. From there, he took them one at a time into the playroom. As he arrived with the first one, he saw that David had his arm draped over Bernadette's shoulder. Bernadette turned toward him and David let his arm fall as she did.

"Where have you been?" asked Bernadette, noticing the apron.

"I've been hired as Martin's food taster and Sarah's heavy hauler," Anthony said with a bright smile as he placed the case on the bar. "I would like to stay and chat, but duty calls. No rest for the weary and all that."

He returned to kitchen and retrieved the second case and brought it into the playroom. He noticed that Carla was standing in front of David with her pool cue pressing into the bottom of David's chin. Anthony suppressed a smile. *A pool cue now, castration later?* He opened each case and put the cans in the mini-fridge. Those that didn't fit, he took back to the kitchen and put in the refrigerator. He navigated his way back down the steep stairs to the recreation room. He found Sarah sitting on one of the sofas. He was about to tell her about his putting the extra cans in the refrigerator when he realized that she was just staring off into space with a sad look in her eyes.

"You okay?" he asked.

"Sure," said Sarah. "Just a little tired. It's been a long week."

He caught himself and suppressed a wisecrack about how tiring it was to carry the soda.

"Can I get you anything?" he asked.

"No thanks, but if you can bring up those chairs, I'd appreciate it."

He walked over and kneeled in front of her.

"I meant what I said about being sorry for being a jerk," he said.

"I know."

"And if …"

She looked at him as he rose, turned and picked up four chairs and carried them to the stairway feeling the twinge return to his back.

When he arrived at the playroom with the chairs, Martin was inside announcing that "Kabobs a la Martin" were ready to be served. He invited everyone to freshen their drinks. Martin and Les had already set up two six foot tables behind a sofa. Each was dressed with a red and white check table cloth. One table held the plates, silverware, napkins and a huge platter of Kabobs a la Martin and smaller platters of vegetable sides. The other was adorned by two lit candles.

Although Martin and Sarah had chosen a picnic style dinner, each guest had a place card. Anthony could not help notice that David was assigned to sit as far from Bernadette as possible. *This must have been the work of Sarah or Carla*, he thought, deciding finally that it must have been Carla. Sarah joined them after everyone had begun helping themselves to the food, the sad look in her eyes contrasted by a pleasant smile.

After the group settled into their seats, Martin softly asked for their attention. Everyone paused and he said, "Thank you all for being here and joining us in breaking the bread of friendship. We recognize how fortunate we are to have such riches as good food, good wine and good friendship. To the less fortunate, we wish better times. For our guests we wish continued camaraderie."

"Hear, hear," said Les.

"Hear, hear," said everyone raising their glasses.

Before anyone could finish a sip of their drink, Anthony excused himself and headed for a bathroom that he had passed on his self-guided tour. Once inside, he flushed the toilet and turned on a faucet to cover up the sound of a deep sob that seemed to come from the bottom of his soul. He looked in the mirror and saw that his eyes were red. He could feel his nose running. "What the fuck is wrong with me?" he asked softly out loud. His body shook soundlessly as he tried to suppress sobs that were determined to escape. When they subsided, he washed his face. He found a wash cloth that he soaked and placed over his eyes. He drank some water and rinsed his mouth. He patted his face with a towel, and then tried exercising his face muscles so they would eradicate any trace of this experience. He took some deep breaths before opening the door. When he did, Bernadette was standing there.

"Are you all right?" she asked.

"I'm fine," he said, forcing a smile.

"If you want to leave early, it's okay," she said.

"No, no," he protested, "I'm fine, really. Let's go and enjoy the party."

When they rejoined the group, Martin came over and asked if he could get anything for them, and if everything was okay.

Anthony rebounded quickly saying. "Martin, I have to tell you that I was so overcome by jealousy of your kabobs that I had a momentary physical reaction. I did sample them, after all, and knew they were better than anything I could prepare. Now that I'm over that, I'm ready to dig in."

"That's too bad," said Les. "I had my eye on your kabob and was kind of rooting for an upset stomach." Everyone laughed.

"Eat your heart out Les, but stay away from my kabob," said Anthony.

"Hey," said David. "If you guys keep talking about your kabobs, some of us may get the wrong idea."

"Shut up and eat your dinner," said Carla.

"Hear, hear" said Nancy, who had been quiet all evening.

"Here's to Kabobs a la Martin," said Aaron.

Bernadette reached down and took and Anthony's hand and intertwined her fingers in his. She smiled as he looked at her. Sarah noticed them and smiled through her sad eyes.

When Anthony and Bernadette arrived home that evening, Anthony skipped his routine of checking for phone messages and making notes of thoughts that uncontrollably popped into his head. Instead, he washed up and brushed his teeth while waiting for Bernadette who was in the other bathroom. He stripped down to his shorts, sat on the bed and waited for her to come out. When she did, she was wearing a nightgown. He got up and went right to her, pulled her to him and kissed her as passionately as he ever had.

"Anthony," she started to say.

"Please. Let's not say anything. Let's not talk. Please."

With that he bunched her nightgown in his hands and raised it over her head. He kissed her again and this time she responded as passionately as he. They staggered toward the bed tripping over each other until they found it. She lay back and he quickly looked at the body he adored. He bent to kiss her breasts, but she pulled him up.

"Come inside me right now," she said huskily. As he did, she wrapped her legs around him and the two moved harmoniously until her body shuddered, followed quickly by him. They lay breathing heavily, he still on top of her, still inside her.

"Anthony," she said, "This is the first time since we had that argument. That's a long time for us."

"I know," he said. "It's my fault, being so self absorbed."

"Anthony?"

"Yes?"

"My diaphragm. I didn't use it. I didn't expect…"

Chapter 8

Anthony was glad now that his meetings with Jack Mullen and Stewart Ogilvie were separated by the weekend. He had originally planned to have them in the same week to formally launch his job search, but Jack's travel schedule did not permit that. *Appreciate small blessings*, Anthony thought. The meeting with Jack was an unexpected blow. It took a couple of days for the effect to wear off. This was a new day and a new week. Anthony was looking forward to seeing Ogilvie.

Anthony had used the services of Ogilvie's recruiting company to find some key players at CommData and SkyTel and had recommended Ogilvie's services to others. Ogilvie was able to expand his business to include high tech companies and reach into new geographic territories at least in part due to Anthony's effort. Anthony knew his assistance to Ogilvie would be reciprocated.

Preparing for his meeting today as he had for Jack Mullen, Anthony adjusted his schedule to arrive at Penn Station at a later time since he and Ogilvie would not be having lunch. Upon exiting the busy terminal, he took a cab to the financial district. Rather than run up the fare navigating narrow and congested streets, Anthony left the cab on Broadway. He walked three blocks to the building that housed Ogilvie Management Services and several investment banking and brokerage firms. The lobby of the old building was designed at a time when the height and décor of its ceiling was more important than energy efficiency. It had the scent of ruthless tycoons and legalized larceny. Tall, sculpted columns resting upon worn marble floors reached three stories high to ceiling paintings depicting the "iron horse" moving west. The brass trim on the ornate windows matched the trash receptacles adjacent to the small coffee and sundry shop.

The lobby had a post 9/11 security gate at the entrance to the elevator bank. It was complete with metal detector, armed guards and tables to support briefcases, assorted carrying bags and outer garments that could be searched or scanned. Each new arrival not holding an employee badge had to sign a visitor's log. The name entered was compared to a pre- approved list. If there was no match, the person had to step aside and bear the uncomfortable scrutiny of the approved. Further checking by the guards would result in either belated approval or the person being asked for identification to be recorded before being turned away.

Anthony survived the entrance process, found his way to the wood paneled elevator and leaned against the brass hand rail at the rear. The rising box quietly carried its silent occupants to their destinations. When the doors opened on the forty-seventh floor, Anthony stepped onto the carpeted foyer leaving behind his fellow passengers. His armpits were damp despite the cool weather. He smoothed his jacket, checked the positioning of the knot in his tie and patted the hair on the back of his head. He considered a quick visit to the restroom, but gave priority to being five minutes early for his scheduled appointment.

He opened one of two walnut doors on which mounted brass plates identified the inner occupants. He found a receptionist who served the several offices inside. After introducing himself, Anthony was asked to be seated in one of the chairs forming a semi-circle with easy access to a coffee table covered with current newspapers and business magazines. He politely declined an offer of coffee, tea or water. After fifteen minutes, he wished he had stopped in the rest room. He was considering going just as the receptionist announced that Mr. Ogilvie was ready to see him. Ogilvie didn't come out to greet him as a professional courtesy. Anthony followed the path suggested by the receptionist's pointed finger until he found the correct office. Once at the doorway, Ogilvie stood and invited him to take a seat.

The office was small with two flat screen monitors mounted on the paneled walls. One displayed scrolling stock market results. The other offered a barely audible summary of the day's financial events by a woman who could have been a candidate for the Sports Illustrated calendar. Bookcases lined the other walls containing reference books, books touting the trendiest business and management techniques and pictures and trophies that presented Ogilvie's accomplishments for all to see. On his desk was a gold pen and pencil set mounted in a marble holder and a uniquely shaped keyboard that controlled the wall mounted monitors and the computer screen on his desk.

"Stewart, it's good to see you again," said Anthony extending his hand.

Ogilvie shook his hand and repeated the offer of something to drink. Anthony declined and was about to start the conversation with a few prepared remarks when the phone rang. Ogilvie raised his hand, took the call and turned the swivel chair and his back to Anthony. After a conversation that lasted a minute or two, he apologized to Anthony and added that they only had about fifteen minutes before he had to leave for an unexpected, but very important meeting. Anthony felt the control of this meeting slipping away and went right into a full court press.

"Stewart, I'm here because I resigned from SkyTel due to differing views with management. There is no question that I made valuable contributions to the company especially in optimizing the life of their product lines, and more importantly, structuring an acquisition that I really cannot discuss in detail, but which will be of great significance to the company. The bottom line is that I am putting myself in the job market, and I could certainly use your expertise in finding the next career opportunity."

"Do you have a current resume?"

"Yes" said Anthony, as he opened his briefcase and handed him two copies that Ogilvie placed on his desk without a glance.

"What are you looking for, Anthony?"

"A position that takes me to the next level. I'm very good at Product Management and Product Marketing, but I think my experiences over the past year or so prove that I have the business acumen to develop and execute major deals between companies. I'm talking about structuring strategic alliances and that includes working in the international arena."

"Anthony," said Ogilvie, "that may be a bit overstated. Your work in this arena as you call it, has not delivered any results yet. And when it does, you will not be able to claim them as yours. I happened to be speaking to Henry Trenholme on Friday. While he did not say anything directly, I got the impression that he is not your biggest fan and would hardly give you credit for the accomplishments you claim."

"You spoke to Henry?"

"Yes. It seems that he is seeking a replacement for you and called me to see if I could help. Since he is my client, that's all I can say about that conversation."

"Stewart," said Anthony, "we've worked together in the past. You know my track record. You know I have excelled at my job. I brought you into SkyTel because of my respect for your work which I always thought was mutual."

"Of course, Anthony, which is why I'm trying to help you. I am simply advising you that prospective employers may not see your merits in the same light as you do."

Anthony remained silent as Ogilvie continued, "Why don't you write a piece, an essay if you will, describing your accomplishments, career ambitions and why you feel qualified to achieve them. Then I can look it over, polish it a bit and append it to your resume. When we have a client who is looking for someone whose needs you match, we can pursue the opportunity. You must also remember that in our business, the client comes to us as Trenholme just did. We do not go out seeking prospective employers. Besides, doing this exercise might help you focus on a position for which you are specifically qualified. Sorry to say that I really must be going. I have to be uptown in thirty minutes."

Anthony mentally jumped on the word "exercise." He recalled a past conversation with Ogilvie about how you get rid of someone hounding you for a job, or help in general. Ogilvie's advice was to keep giving the person "exercises" to do. 'Sooner or later,' he had said, 'they give up and go on to nag someone else.'

Anthony stood up. "I appreciate your time," he said, looking Ogilvie straight in the eye.

"Yes, yes, and give my best to your wife and children," Ogilvie said, forgetting Anthony had no children.

"Thanks, I will," said Anthony as he left the office. He

walked past the reception area and into the foyer hoping that the elevator would arrive quickly.

When he was outside, a homeless man in a worn tweed coat that reminded Anthony of one he had once owned came up to him with a cup.

"Can you help me out? I'm having a hard time," said the man.

The anger that had been brewing inside of Anthony suddenly erupted in laughter.

"I know the feeling my friend," Anthony said, still laughing while he reached into his pocket, found a ten dollar bill and put it in the man's cup.

"God bless you," said the man, wide eyed at the discovery of his newly found treasure.

"Whatever works," said Anthony as he started the long walk toward Penn Station.

Chapter 9

It was almost 3:00 P.M. by the time Anthony returned home. He entered the house, turned off the alarm system, and removed his jacket and tie. He wished he had taken the car to the train station because he felt like being near the water. It would help him absorb today's meeting and think about what he had to do. After Mullen and Ogilvie, it occurred to him that his next stop should be the unemployment office. The words rolling around in his head sounded foreign. *Unemployment office? Me? Government handouts? This is crazy.*

It occurred to Anthony that if he wanted to be near the ocean, he could go to the ocean. There was no place he had to be! Bernadette would not be home for three more hours. He could beat the commute traffic going east, and there would be little coming back. He walked in a circle three or four times in the middle of the living room, stopped in the bathroom to wash his face and headed to garage. Once in his car, he felt a sense of excitement. Without thinking, he drove to the Southern State Parkway, turned on the eastbound ramp and headed toward the marina. As he thought about the conversation with Ogilvie, he caught himself and realized he wasn't reacting the same way he did after the meeting with Jack Mullen. He wasn't devastated or depressed by it. It was as though the players in this drama were lining up on a football field. He could see Albright, Trenholme and Ogilvie on one side with Mullen behind them choosing not to commit either way. On the opposite sideline were Bernadette, Martin and Sarah looking on to see what he would do.

Albright and Trenholme decided to box him out before he could receive credit for facilitating the merger and before his stock options would have any value. He wasn't sure if they did not want *him* in the picture or *anyone* in the picture. It didn't matter because the result for him was the same. They secured Ogilvie in their camp by contracting with him to find a replacement. That made it seem personal, but the truth is his successor would not have as generous a stock option package because he would be joining the team so late in the game. None of this mattered, he concluded. This was *war*. The first objective would be to survive the recent events. The second was to re-start his career in a positive direction. The third was to make the bastards pay.

Anthony was still considering his objectives when he reached the exit that would take him to the marina. At this time of year, especially on a weekday, he would practically have the place to himself. Entering the parking lot, he picked a spot right in its middle, got out of the car and took a deep breath. He loved the smell of ocean air, and the taste of salt that came with it.

Only the coffee and bait shops of the six stores on its east side were open. He walked to the edge closest to the water and looked out. *I am going to handle this*, he told himself. *I am not going to let those bastards beat me*. He sucked in another deep breath and walked to the coffee shop and ordered a cup to go. Outside again, he paced up and down the wharf, sipping the coffee while playing the tape of the morning's conversation over and over in his head. What a set-up. Ogilvie knew why he was coming in. He had already cooked a deal with Trenholme, and proceeded to treat him like shit. The leverage Anthony thought he had was just vapor. Ogilvie didn't give him a dime's worth of respect. He just sold himself to the highest bidder.

As Anthony continued to pace and ponder, he came upon two women walking with their arms around each other's waist. He shrugged and decided to give them some room by walking more slowly and angling away from them. They stopped and faced each other, embraced and kissed passionately. They hugged again before one made a move to leave. She got into a nearby car while the second woman stood with her hands in her coat pockets looking after her. She gave a small wave as the car pulled away. Anthony had moved back in the direction of the water to give the car a clear path. He was looking out at the waves when the second woman turned and began walking toward him in the direction of her own car. She was about five feet away when he looked at her and blurted out, "Nancy?"

Nancy looked up, then turned and looked toward the parting car, and back to Anthony.

"Anthony! What a surprise seeing you here. I just came down to do a little shopping at the nautical shop, but it's closed. Aaron has admired one of those model ships in a bottle, and he has a birthday coming up."

Anthony just looked at her not saying anything.

"You saw, didn't you?" said Nancy as she covered her face with her hands.

"Saw what?" Anthony tried to say convincingly. "I just got here."

Nancy began to tremble visibly. "Oh my God," she said.

"Nancy, it's okay, it's all right. Please don't be upset."

"Oh my God, I can't believe this is happening," said Nancy, whirling around still clasping her hands to her face.

"Nancy, this is none of my business. I'm just here to collect my thoughts and look at the ocean," said Anthony.

"Well, I sure gave you some thoughts to collect, didn't I?"

"Nancy, please, this is your business, not mine. As far as I am concerned, I didn't see anything."

Nancy looked up through parted fingers. "Do you really mean that? You're not going to judge me? You won't tell the others?"

"Tell them what?" replied Anthony. "Look, the rest of my coffee is cold. How about we go and get a cup and just calm down a little?"

"Coffee?" she asked.

"Yeah, I could use a cup. Actually, I could use something stronger. This is the least exciting thing that has happened to me today, but the bar here doesn't open until five."

"It must have been some day," she said, "to beat seeing your wife's friend making out with another woman."

"The only making out I saw was by those seagulls over there. Shameless, those two. Come on, I could really use another coffee," he said.

They entered the small coffee shop. Only one table was occupied by an old guy reading a newspaper. After checking with her, he ordered one cappuccino and one regular coffee. Nancy sat at the only table not near a window as Anthony brought the two cups from the counter.

"Do you know," he said, "that in Italy, it's very bad form to order a cappuccino after lunch?" he said.

"Really? Where did you hear that?"

"From a cousin who went there on a vacation and became an expert on Italian customs and now pontificates on such things. He even went so far as to give up cappuccino in the afternoon or after an evening meal despite having always enjoyed one. Kind of dumb, huh?"

"Anthony, if anyone were to find out…"

"Find out what? I don't know anything. Besides, like I said, your business is your business."

"Everyone thinks the world has changed and everyone is more accepting saying 'not that there's anything wrong with that.' But when you live it, it's different. Your job, your friends, your family… to them there is something wrong with that. It's only for someone else that it's okay."

"Nancy, I'm not an expert on how people think. I appreciate your sensitivity to your situation. I'm not the guy who sees these issues with infinite wisdom, but I know that people are good or bad, usually a combination of both, but that's not determined by whether or not they're…"

"Gay," she said finishing the sentence for him

"Gay," he said.

"Did you know that I once had a serious crush on Bernadette?"

"Jesus," he said smiling, "I'm trying to be cool here and you're positioning yourself as a competitor!"

"It's true," she said. "A long time ago. She never knew, at least I don't think she did. I got over her, but she's always been special to me."

"Yeah, me too," he said.

"Well you better be good to her, or I might move in on you," she said with a laugh.

"It's good to hear you laugh."

"You're sweet, Anthony. I didn't know what to expect when I saw you."

"Don't go around saying I'm sweet. You'll spoil my rep as a tough guy. Maybe make me ineligible for a job as a wise guy."

Nancy paused for a moment. "Aaron knows," she said. "Well, kind of. We don't talk about it directly, but he knows. He has issues of his own. Not like mine, but he has some things…"

"Not my business," Anthony said in a sing-song voice.

"We give to one another in all ways. We support each other. We take care of each other. It works for us."

"You're beginning to sound like a very put-together person. More so than a lot of people I know."

"There are people who believe that people like me are evil," she said.

"And then there is Buddhism that does not embrace the concept of good or evil," he said.

"What do you know about Buddhism?" she asked.

"Not very much," he said. "I looked into it once because I have a problem with Christianity generally and Catholicism specifically, which is the religion of my family. Eastern religions and philosophies looked very attractive and wise from a distance. But as I learned more, I had just as many problems with them as with how I was raised. In fact, my problem with Buddhism is the absence of accepting the concepts of good and evil. How can anyone not believe they exist?"

"You are turning out to be much different than I thought," said Nancy.

"Yeah well," he said, "you should see me when I've had a few. I can wax eloquently for hours on things I know nothing about or don't understand at all."

Nancy smiled. He could see that she had calmed down and was comfortable with him.

"Well, I'd better be going. I came out here to clear my head about some things that happened today before I discussed them with Bernadette," he said.

"Did I interfere with that?"

"Not at all. As a matter of fact, I feel a lot better about things just from talking to someone about something other than what's on my mind."

"I feel a lot better too," she said.

"Come on," he said, "I'll walk you to your car. I can slay any dragons that may get in your way, or maybe whack somebody, or put out a contract if they're bigger than me."

As they reached her car, she turned to him and stood on her toes to give him a kiss on the cheek.

"Thank you, Anthony," she said, "You were very cool."

Taking Flight

Chapter 10

On the drive home from the marina, Anthony felt a lot better. He was calm with a renewed sense of well being, and the temporary relief that comes from learning someone else has a problem greater than your own. Anthony liked having secret information about someone in the group, and that he and Nancy shared the secret of his knowing. He decided not to mention any of this to Bernadette. Rather than having to lie or betray a confidence, he just wouldn't bring it up. Satisfied with his decision his mind drifted back to his job situation.

In his revised assessment, Anthony realized his strongest cards, Jack Mullen and Stewart Ogilvie had been played and he was trumped. He had to start fresh by establishing new contacts and cold calling on companies that could arguably use his skill sets. The place to start would be with competitors of SkyTel. The idea of using on-line job sites or classified ads with the possible exception of those in the Wall Street Journal would be a waste of time. He had learned from being on both sides of the recruiting process that both were ineffective. The closer you got to a personal contact or a referral, the better. He would start identifying recruiting firms to contact and potential employers to cold call this week. He would get the Wall Street Journal on Wednesday, traditionally the heaviest employment ad day. He would use the Sunday Times to check out recruiting firms. He would do some due diligence on the internet before making any calls. He would market himself as he would a product; define the market, objectives, resources and strategy. Then, *watch out world, Anthony would be on his way!*

As a practical matter, he knew he should sign up for unemployment insurance the next day. As repugnant as the idea was, he knew he had to get in there and sign up. He could jump start the one week eligibility waiting period in case it took a while to find a job. The notion that it might take a while was one he quickly suppressed. Anthony was still thinking about his job hunting strategy when he pulled into the driveway at home. It was later than he thought. After bringing the car in the garage, he retrieved the mail. He was standing in the driveway looking through it when Bernadette pulled up beside him.

"I'm surprised to see you just getting home," she said.

"Actually, I came home earlier and went out again," said Anthony.

"Let me bring the car in, and you can tell me all about your meeting."

Rather than say anymore now, Anthony went into the house and poured two glasses of white wine. He offered her a glass when she came in.

"Why don't we sit and talk for a few minutes and then decide if we're going to eat in or grab something quick in town."

She took the wine and put it down. "I don't know about going out, but okay. Just give me a minute to freshen up."

When she returned, she retrieved the wine and stood opposite him.

"So, how did it go today?"

Anthony looked at her admiringly. She had removed the blazer of her business outfit. Her peach colored blouse provided a warm setting for her skin and hair. It was also fitted to show off her figure in a subtle and classy way. The pleated skirt ending just at the knee displayed her curved calves which he had always found attractive. "I've always been a leg man," he used to tell her.

"Cheers," he said, raising his glass to hers. The glasses clinked and they both sipped the wine then sat facing each other.

"Does this mean we have something to celebrate?" she asked.

"If you mean about the day's events, no, not exactly. Things didn't go well with Ogilvie. But if you would like to toast to new beginnings based on my current mindset, it would be appropriate."

"Okay then, to new beginnings," she said raising her glass again.

He responded in kind, taking a longer sip.

"So, are you going to tell me about your meeting?"

"Well, the short version is that Ogilvie didn't give me the time of day. SkyTel had already contracted with him to find my replacement and he treated me like yesterday's news."

"Wow, what's the long version?"

"The long version includes the fact that the self-important, pompous bastard didn't even consider the opportunities and the money he received as a direct result of working with me. Didn't even give me a sign of respect as a professional. I got the bum's rush and a 'say hello to the wife and kids, and don't let the door hit you in the ass on your way out.' It really went well."

"Sounds like it," she said. "So to mark the occasion we're going out to eat?"

"I thought maybe we would run out for a burger and fries. Comfort food with not having to worry about pots and pans and dishes to clean."

"Tell you what. Why don't we both change. I'll throw some chicken pot pies in the oven. I have your favorite from Amendola's Market. We can have them with this wine and maybe watch a movie afterwards."

"You sure?"

"Sure," she said. "We can even use paper plates. The cleaning up will be easy."

They both changed into sweatshirts and jeans while Mendola's pot pies baked in the oven sending out a pleasant aroma and the promise of comfort food providing you didn't examine the Nutrition Facts on the package; comfort came with lots of salt, preservatives and saturated fat. They ate in the kitchen while Anthony retold of his meeting with Stewart Ogilvie.

"He didn't pretend to be sympathetic to my situation. It was clear to me that he didn't want me coming back for more help, or that he would even keep me in mind if something came up," he said.

"Sure he will," said Bernadette. "He sounds like somebody who is loyal to himself and his business. If something came up where he could make money by recruiting you, he would do it in a heartbeat."

Anthony was surprised by her assessment of Ogilvie, but knew she was right.

"Hey," he said, "you're getting to know how these characters operate."

"I may know better than you. You expect them to have loyalties, a sense of fair play and ideals that don't exist in business. I see it all the time. If a vendor wants to sell us something at the store, he will do anything to make the sale. He will trash his competitor, offer little bribes like theater tickets, and so on. It goes on all the time. That's why they have such strict rules. Even so, people turn their heads as long as the favors are small ones. Then you have Sally Bingham who used to be our Buyer for furniture. She must have had her whole house furnished on the cuff. When they found out, they just quietly let her go. Making a big fuss about it might have harmed the store as much as her. They just secretly let the other Buyers know that she got sacked in order to send a message."

"But," Anthony countered, "That's the retail business. The high tech business is different."

"Anthony, people are people, and business is business. High tech, retail, it's all the same."

Anthony smiled. "That's naïve to say," he said. "This industry was formed by giants like IBM and Hewlett Packard whose founders set very high standards. Ethics and business practices were very clearly defined at the birth of the high tech industry and remain in place today."

"Now who is being naïve? Anthony, what you just said is contradicted by everything that has happened to you over the past two weeks. Or is it just the people you work for who violate the code everyone else subscribes to? That would suggest you have very poor judgment in selecting who you work with, or that you are living in a dream world."

Anthony looked at her in disbelief.

She went on. "Anthony, you have this moral code, which I admire. It is one of the reasons I was attracted to you and fell in love with you. You love to talk about your father and how he could see things so clearly, about the value he placed on honor and duty and loyalty. Anthony, he was a wonderful man, but he wasn't a boy scout and neither are you. You have unrealistic expectations about how people should behave, about how you should behave.

"You're expecting everyone to practice lofty principles while they're just looking out for themselves, trying to survive and get ahead. And when push comes to shove, you'll do the same thing. When you realize that no one out there wakes up each day to the thought of 'How can I help Anthony Bartolo today? How can I fix his career? How can I get him a job? How can I make sure he can afford GPS systems and flat panel TVs?' you'll understand that nobody cares. And when you're in a position of trashing somebody who's after the same job, or reminding someone of the favors you did for them, you'll do that because that's the way the world works. Morality doesn't work in business, including the job market so you can't go around complaining about how these people didn't meet your standards of behavior. It's not personal."

"When did you become an expert on business ethics and behavior? Do I detect a cynical edge to my sweet, 'the world has a lot of good in it' wife?'" he said, with a joking tone that bordered on mocking.

"Even David says you have to treat this impersonally. Business is like the law. The only way it can work is to be entirely objective, to evaluate facts and circumstances fairly and apply the law coldly without regard to where your sympathies may lie."

"What do you mean, David says?" Anthony asked, there no mistaking the challenge in his tone.

"I talked to David about the hard time the company was giving you the night we had dinner at Martin and Sarah's place. He understood the anxiety that you must be going through. Today he called me to ask if everything was going okay, and if there was anything he could do for us, as a lawyer or as a friend. We talked a little about how you're handling it, and that's when he said what he did about the impersonal nature of business and law."

"You're discussing my handling of my job situation with David? He's calling you at work to ask how things are going? What the hell is going on here? It's not enough that he grabs your ass in front of everybody in our house, now he's calling you at work to check on your feelings? To offer comfort and support?"

"Anthony, will you stop. He's just trying to be helpful. Maybe he feels badly that you and he haven't hit it off. Maybe it was even Carla's idea that he call."

"Yeah, right." Anthony said. "Listen, you may have some valid points about business dealings, but let me tell you something. When a guy calls a woman, an attractive woman, to offer comfort and support, he is thinking of providing it on a mattress. He's had a hard-on for you at least since the time I've known him."

"Oh, come on! David is harmless. Sure he flirts a little, but that's just the way he is. I think he was being sincere when he called."

"Bullshit."

"Anthony, don't be crude. It doesn't become you."

"Oh, great! I'm going to end up being the bad guy here."

Bernadette got up and cleared the paper plates, forks and wine glasses. After that, she went to the bedroom closet and started moving clothes in and out. Anthony drifted into the den and made himself busy at the computer. A couple of hours passed, each doing their own thing. Finally, Bernadette went to bed. Anthony found her there reading while he undressed and put on a pair of short cotton lounge pants he used as pajamas. Without saying goodnight, he got into bed and lay on his side with his back to Bernadette. A short while later, she turned out the light and moved toward him. With her breasts against his back, she put her hand on his hip then slipped her fingers under his waistband. Anthony did not move or say anything. He could feel her hair on his waist and back as her hand moved further down.

"I don't think this is such a good idea right now," was the most resistance he could utter.

Bernadette borrowed an old line of his that he had borrowed from a movie they had seen together, "But, I want to pleasure you, my dear," she murmured, pushing down on the waistband. Without saying anything, he rolled over on his back.

Chapter 11

Bernadette was gone when Anthony woke up. Before leaving for work, she had left a note on her pillow. 'Love you. See you tonight. It was my pleasure! B.' He didn't know what to make of last night. He had wanted to tell Bernadette about his new mindset that would help him pursue a new job with a positive attitude. Instead, he ended up giving her a detailed description of what went on with Ogilvie and probably sounded like he was feeling sorry for himself. Then she spelled out how the world works in a way he couldn't deny. All of sudden David was in the picture calling to offer comfort and get closer to nailing her. The evening was shot. He felt miserable, and then ended up on his back while Bernadette took over and nailed him. They had always had a pretty adventurous sex life, but last night the mixture of emotions leading up to it left him off balance. He suddenly realized that he never mentioned his encounter with Nancy. Well, at least he didn't lie or withhold. It just hadn't entered his mind.

Today was the day he would sign up for unemployment insurance. He decided to approach it as a practical step, an obligatory part of the process and not let it bother him. At the same time, he couldn't escape the feeling of dread that someone he knew might see him there. Not sure of where it was, he skipped the internet and pulled out the phone book and looked under state government agencies. Unemployment compensation services were listed under the Employment Development Resources Department noting the further evolution of political correctness in the naming of government agencies. General information numbers were offered for English, Spanish, Vietnamese and Mandarin languages. He wondered why the Koreans and Arabs were not represented. It couldn't be based on numbers. He caught himself going on a racist riff before he stuffed the idea. *Crappy times bring out crappy ideas*, he thought. He found the office location listed on Sunrise Highway, one town over from Hempstead and jotted down the address.

Anthony was uncertain about what to wear. Do you wear a suit and tie, the purpose of which is to announce that you no longer have a job and would like to apply for assistance from the great state of New York? Or do you dress casually to symbolize your current participation in a life of leisure unencumbered by the travails of heavy commute traffic, crowded trains, or the need to impress clients or customers? Perhaps dressing poor is more appropriate to indicate need. Clothes stained or torn might elicit compassion from the bureaucrats who had the power to dispense or withhold funds. The same bureaucrats who would probably never have to apply for help because the State of New York did not think like the Edwin Albrights and Henry Trenholmes of the real world. However, such clerks might see tattered clothes as a sign of disrespect. Don't the poor dress as well as they can when going to see a priest or minister? Anthony caught himself again and heard Bernadette's words ringing in his ears. He sat down on the bed looking in the closet full of nice clothes, organized by type; business wear, dressy casual, casual, knock-arounds for the house and stuff to wear while working on a yard, attic or garage project. *Just get dressed and get out of the house,* he told himself.

After settling on a pair of gray slacks with a blue

button down oxford shirt, open collar and black loafers, Anthony fixed himself a cup of coffee and a slice of toast before leaving the house. As a crutch, he brought along his small brief case that contained a copy of his employment termination agreement, a new resume in case he needed to describe his work experience, and a lined pad, pen and pencil.

The morning commute had already escaped the small town. Traffic on the Sunrise Highway was such that he was able to cruise at the posted speed and make the metered traffic lights with only two stops between home and his destination. The Employment Development Services Department building was set back from the Sunrise providing an expansive parking lot that anticipated bad times. It was a half mile east of the Green Hills shopping mall and was surrounded by unattractive office buildings whose occupants served those needing to post bail, get a divorce quickly and a private school that offered classes in automotive mechanics, air conditioning repair and court stenography. *At least*, Anthony thought, *none of his acquaintances were likely to be nearby.*

He parked and headed toward the gray, almost windowless building that welcomed those invited by the Statue of Liberty "to bring your asses here for a handout." Whatever his impressions were of the sad, colorless, drab exterior of the building, he was not prepared for its interior. Everything was gray; battleship gray. The floor was gray. Gray pillars held up a gray ceiling from which hanging fluorescent lights seemed to add a gray cast to the applicants at tall gray work tables and clerks sitting at gray desks separated by gray partitions. The plebeians were on one side of a gray barrier waiting to plead their case to the patricians on the other side.

He approached the Information Window where he received an application form and a brochure explaining how the unemployment compensation system works. After completing the form at one of the work tables, he became aware of several hanging and posted signs. They advised those who entered to pick a number from the gray ticket dispenser and compare it to the number that appeared in a bright red LED display that stood out as a beacon of light and hope. Once your number appeared, the applicant was to present him or herself with their ticket to the next available service representative. Several other signs instructed the ticket holders to stand behind the yellow line approximately fifteen feet from the service representative's window to insure privacy to the applicant being served. Anthony picked number 183 and stood near the yellow line trying to size up the geography and activity of the place. Number 162 appeared in the lighted display. To get an idea of the amount to time he would have to wait, he counted the number of open windows and estimated the time each applicant spent there.

A tall Hispanic man standing behind him offered that the officer two windows to the right of center was a stand up guy who always tried to help, but the four eyed bitch on the left end acted like you were asking for money from her own bank account.

"If she's the next available when your number comes up," he suggested, "find a reason for getting out of line and starting over again."

Anthony looked at the man who was dressed as though he worked in construction and thanked him.

"I haven't been down here before," he said.

"Yeah, it shows. Remember what I said about the four eyed bitch and you'll be all right."

"Thanks again. I'm Anthony." Anthony offered his hand for him to shake.

The man looked at him quizzically, and then put out his hand. "Ramon," he said. Ramon pulled out a newspaper out of his pants pocket folded to the classified ads and began to read.

"Good luck," said Anthony, genuinely grateful for a touch of kindness.

"You too," said Ramon.

Forty minutes went by when the red display flashed 181. He felt hopeful that his journey into this gray bureaucratic hell would soon be over. He was looking over the active windows trying to estimate if the four eyed bitch would be available soon when he was approached by a security guard. He wore an olive drab shirt and dark green trousers held up by a black belt containing two leather cases, one rectangular, one oblong. The guard's stomach reached way out over his belt and looked liked it needed a leather case of its own.

"Sir, I'm afraid I have to ask you to give me your ticket and that you get another from the dispenser. After doing so, please make sure you stand behind the yellow line in order to afford the person at the window his or her maximum privacy."

"What are you talking about?" said Anthony.

"Sir, there are six posted signs facing every direction instructing applicants to stand behind the yellow line. You sir, have your feet inside the yellow line which is against policy. As a result, you have to give up your ticket, get another one and wait your turn behind the yellow line."

"But, I'm not intruding on anyone. I can't hear what anyone up there is saying," said Anthony trying to keep his rising anger under control.

"Sir, you clearly crossed the yellow line. That·violates the Department's policy."

Anthony saw 182 flashed in red. The four eyed bitch took the next applicant.

"Hey, I'm sorry," he said. "I'm new here. This is my first time. I made a mistake. Look, I'm up next."

The guard looked over his shoulder and waved to someone.

"Sir," he said firmly, "You were not standing behind the yellow line."

"Well, if you want me behind the yellow line, you better paint another one in front of me," said Anthony, his voice rising.

Just then, two other guards appeared along side of Anthony. The red light flashed 183. Anthony stepped forward. One guard removed a remote control device from his belt case, pointed it at the red light and 184 appeared.

"Sir, we are asking you to leave now and return tomorrow or anytime after that. If you refuse to do so, we shall have to fill out a report that will require that you meet with a service representative who will determine whether a penalty should be applied that will affect your eligibility."

"Are you fucking insane?" said Anthony.

When the guard turned to call someone else over, Anthony turned and headed for the door.

"Keep your eligibility and handouts," he said as he neared the door. The three guards watched as he left through the exit door. Once outside, Anthony stopped as his eyes adjusted to the sunlight. He saw Ramón standing by his truck looking his way. Ramon shrugged his shoulders, turned to get in the truck and drove away.

"I wonder what Bernadette and David will have to say about this," Anthony said out loud as he got into his car.

Taking Flight

Chapter 12

Anthony was furious as he left the unemployment office. He was furious at the notion of having had to go there and apply for benefits. He was furious at the security guard and his damn yellow line. He was furious at his inability to just get through the humiliating application process without incident. He could hear Bernadette's admonitions ringing in his ears: *You know how you can be*!

He reached his exit on the Sunrise Highway before his mind came back to the present. His body was still tense. He didn't want to go home, and he wasn't ready for another trip to the marina. He settled on going to the coffee shop as he had before his trips to Manhattan.

When he arrived, he looked over the bagels, rolls, muffins and treats on display. The thought occurred to him that the baked goods must have been displayed according to a designer plan that maximized the appeal of their shapes, textures and colors. They couldn't look that good by accident. He decided to pass on food and just ordered a cappuccino. He smiled to himself thinking it was still early enough to not upset the Italians or his cousin. He carried his coffee to a quiet table in the corner. As he sat down, his foot caught on one of the table legs and he flopped awkwardly into the chair. The coffee spilled and soiled the sharply pressed gray slacks that he had chosen to wear to the unemployment office. It seemed appropriate after the way the morning started. No amount of napkins would dry the slacks quickly. He would just have to endure the stained dampness and the pants would have to go right back to the dry cleaners.

Early on in their marriage, he and Bernadette had divided up household chores. One of his jobs was to bring their clothes to and from the cleaners. He and Max, the owner South Shore Dry Cleaning and Laundry, were on a first name basis. Max knew that Anthony preferred no starch in his shirts and the overall preferences of the couple. They would chat about the Yankees, Mets, Knicks or Rangers in the appropriate season. Their verbal exchanges defined the boundaries of their relationship. Now, Anthony wondered if he should push the boundaries and mention that he was out of work. Might Max think differently of him if he knew? Unless Anthony continued to go at the end of the work day or on Saturdays, Max might catch on. Anthony's cappuccino had cooled in the time he devoted to worrying about Max's response to his job loss. He decided to just go at the usual times and not bring it up.

Anthony got a fresh coffee, opened his briefcase and took out his SkyTel resignation agreement. He was skimming through it when his mind drifted back to the experience of the morning. He should have handled the security guard in an entirely different manner. If for no other reason, it was in his best interests to do so. He knew better and he blew it.

As he turned the pages, he came to the heading titled New Employment. The essence of this article was to say that if he found new employment during the ninety day period in which he was being paid by SkyTel that such payments would cease. Anthony was familiar with the concept since the continued salary was designed to protect income. If he was employed by another firm that protection would no longer be needed. He went on to read that upon acceptance of this agreement which included the ninety day extended salary, he would agree to not work for a SkyTel competitor for a period of one year in order to protect the confidentiality of SkyTel's technology.

Anthony carefully re-read the article realizing that he should have negotiated a reduction in the one year non-compete clause or have lengthened the severance pay period. His temper led him to sign the agreement without reading the fine print. Once again, he should have known better. He put the papers back in his briefcase and took out the brochure he had picked up at the unemployment office.

After skimming through the eligibility requirements, he came across a paragraph stating that a one week waiting period would begin with the date of the applicant's last paycheck. The whole morning had been a waste of time! He would not be eligible to apply for another two and a half months. *Maybe they'll forget who I am by then*, he thought. As he reached for his briefcase to return the brochure, he sensed that someone was standing at his table. He looked up and saw Sarah.

"You look very engrossed in your reading," she said. "If I'm interrupting, I'll say hello and goodbye and be on my way."

Surprised, Anthony stood up and said "No, no, no. I was just putting this away."

He realized that she was looking at the large coffee stain on the front of his gray slacks.

"Oh," he said, "this is a kind of a ritual I practice whenever I have coffee by myself. Please sit down so I can and not display my wet pants to any more people."

"Well then, please sit while I get some coffee. I'll join you if you're sure it's okay," she said.

"Yes, and try not to spill any on you. I would hate to see you copying my ritual because it's the in thing to do."

Sarah went to the counter while Anthony put away the brochure unable to escape the sinking feeling that came from knowing that he couldn't work for a SkyTel competitor for a year. When Sarah returned, he started to get up again, but she extended her arm with her palm facing him.

"Once is enough," she said smiling. "So what are you doing here?"

Anthony paused for a moment to take her in. She had a burgundy sweater with a darker shade burgundy skirt. She wore a simple gold chain around her neck with a matching set of ear rings. Her hair was brushed in a different style and framed her face perfectly. For the first time since they met, the look of sadness in her eyes was gone. She was unconditionally beautiful.

"I stop by every once in a while," he said, "usually on my way to the train station."

"Are you taking the train today?" she said.

"No. I just came from a visit to the unemployment office and stopped by on my way home. How about you?"

"Well," she said, "I live only a few blocks from here as you know. I was out walking and decided to treat myself to a cup of coffee which I don't do very often, and here you were."

"Great," he said. "It is really nice to see you, especially since I've had a really bad morning."

"Oh. Were the people there less than kind?"

Anthony wasn't sure if she was sincere or making fun of him.

"You know what, I'd rather just chalk it up to a bad morning and forget it. By the way, that was a great dinner party you guys put on Saturday night."

"Thank you again for coming."

"Say," he said, "Aren't you normally working at this time of day."

"Yes," she said. "But I arranged this day off to help Martin. He has been asked to go to El Salvador next week in place of a colleague who was in an accident. I've been helping by working with the relief agency. His office is jumping through hoops to re-arrange his schedule and get coverage for his patients. It's not easy on such short notice."

"Couldn't he have just said no?" Anthony asked.

"Yes, he could," she said looking right at him.

"I'm sorry. I know Martin is very dedicated to that work. Saying no was probably not an option."

"It was the last option, but it's all working out. He'll be able to make the trip and his patients here will be taken care of."

"What about you?" he asked.

"What about me?"

"How do you handle the abruptness of all this? Isn't it unsettling?"

"Of course," she said. "But you do what you have to do. You realize that these things happen, and if you are serious about what you're doing, you respond the best way you can."

"You guys amaze me," he said.

"It's not that amazing" Sarah said. "We have great resources and have been very blessed. We want to give back. Martin came across this program quite accidentally and just took to it. I love him for it and support what he does in every way I can. It's simple really."

"Maybe it is," Anthony said, "but it's not common. A lot of people in your position wouldn't do this. Don't underestimate its importance and value. You're both special people."

"Wouldn't you do something like this if the opportunity and resources were there?" she asked.

He paused for a moment. "I don't know," he answered honestly. "I don't know if I would ever reach a point where I would say I can now devote a portion of my life to others, or to a cause. I'm not sure I know where that point is, or when I would say I have enough or have gone far enough professionally."

"I hope you'll know someday," she said. "In the meantime, how is the job search going, or should I be polite and not ask?"

"Well, it certainly isn't a dull process," he said grinning. "It'll be all right. I just have to figure out a few things."

Sarah looked at him earnestly and after a short pause she asked, "What did you mean that night at your house when you said your father was afraid of life more than death, or something like that?"

"Well, my Dad reached a point where I think he just felt very tired of struggling with life. It was a whole combination of things. A lot had to do with my mother. You know after he retired, he really got into things like picking a burial site. He was so excited about this plot he found at a cemetery. It was on a knoll and had a beautiful view of rolling grass hills that stretched for a mile with plenty of trees in the landscape. He made it sound like he would be going there on a picnic. Like every evening, he was going to rise out of the grave and have some wine and cheese and look at the sunset instead of being under the ground in darkness."

"You sound angry," Sarah said.

"Maybe. I just think he gave up on life too soon. That

he thought death would bring peace."

"Did he believe in an afterlife?"

"I don't know how anybody can. When do we outgrow all that superstition about Hades, the River Styx, Paradise, Hell, Purgatory and Heaven? The church finally got over Limbo. Do you know how many believers went to their graves in agony because their innocent un-baptized children were condemned to never seeing the face of God because some old guys sitting around a table in Rome said so? And then they changed their minds!"

"Anthony, tell me something nice about your father," she said.

He thought for a minute. "I never saw my father cry except when I graduated from college."

Sarah was quiet for a moment. "That's sweet," she said.

Anthony took a deep breath and exhaled slowly. "Well, Dr. Sarah, I see our time is up now. Perhaps in our next session we can discuss my fascination with blueberry pie. I expect that can be very revealing."

They both laughed.

"This will teach you to treat yourself to a cup of coffee," he said, a little embarrassed about how he had been talking about himself.

"Nancy told me that you saw her at the marina," she said.

Anthony wasn't sure what she meant by "saw her."

"She said you were sweet about her situation, not at all what she expected."

"So you…?"

"Of course, I know. Nancy and I have been friends for a long time," she said.

"I said you were special. Special and trustworthy."

"Anthony, you may not have a cause or a project yet, but you're special too. You're just too preoccupied with what's wrong in the world. When you figure out what you want to do to make one thing right, you'll be fine. Now, I'm afraid I have to go."

Sarah rose to leave.

"I think I would have liked your father," she said before turning toward the door.

A minute or two later, Anthony picked up his briefcase and headed toward the door totally unaware that two young girls were giggling at the stain on his gray slacks.

Chapter 13

On the way home, Anthony could see the bicycle shop on Sunrise Highway where he and Bernadette had purchased their mountain bikes. At the last minute he pulled into the driveway entrance of the upscale mini-mall that housed South Shore Bicycles and a dozen or so independent stores offering men and women's clothing, home furnishings, attire for dogs and cats, one Chinese and one Mexican restaurant and a fitness center offering personal training. He parked in the rear and made his way to the double sliding glass doors surrounded on both sides by a row of chained bicycles starting with children's models on the left with models for adults and those with advanced skills and bank accounts on the right.

Upon entering the automatic doors, he was struck by the protected display of a 1949 Schwinn Black Phantom 26" boys bicycle. It was the introductory year's model; black frame with red trim and chrome fenders. It was as much a symbol of America's post war prosperity as well as the new standard of recreational bikes that would offset the growing popularity of "English Racers" with skinny tires and three-speed gear mechanisms. Anthony studied its details; the key locking front fork, chrome plated coiled shock absorber, tan leather seat, black carrier mounted over the rear fender, chain guard with the Schwinn logo and the aerodynamic headlight mounted seamlessly on the chrome front fender. It was heavy, with a single speed sprocket and balloon whitewall tires, but it had style. It was not unlike the Cadillac of that era distinguished by its pronounced tail light fins. The bike was a classic, thirty years older than Anthony.

He saw Tom, the shop owner, and was disappointed not to be recognized even though almost three years had passed since he and Bernadette purchased their bikes.

"Can I help you?" said Tom.

"I'm just here to check on how well you're taking care of my Black Phantom," said Anthony.

"Well, we're doing the best we can." Tom said with a smile.

"I'm just looking around," said Anthony. "You helped my wife and I pick out a couple of mountain bikes a while back."

"Sure," said Tom. "Are they going okay for you?"

"Oh, yeah. We haven't been out much during the summer, but now that the cooler weather is here, we'll get to it. I prefer biking this time of year as long as it's dry."

"Well, we're having a tune- up special on all bikes before we get into the holiday season. If you haven't used them for a while, you may want to bring them in. We can check the gears, chains, brakes, tires and so on. Right now, we can turn them around in less than a week. Once the holiday rush starts it would take a month."

"I'll think about that," said Anthony. "I guess the holidays are an important time for you. I hear that most retailers do 75-90 percent of their business during the Christmas season."

"For us it's about fifty percent, and then we get a big spike in the Spring," said Tom who seemed to be enjoying having someone to talk to.

"Right now is probably the slowest time of year for us, sort of the calm before the storm. That's why we have the tune-up and maintenance specials."

"Is that a significant part of the business?" asked Anthony.

"Well, more dollars from it stay in the store because it's labor intensive. We get more revenue from the bicycle sales, but then we have to pay for the merchandise."

Anthony looked at the bikes mounted in stands on both sides of the floor and hanging from racks attached to the ceiling. There was every size, shape and type of bicycle. Toward the rear of the store was a section devoted to clothing, helmets, carrying cases and all kinds of biking gear. A glass case separated the customer area from the maintenance section. It displayed bicycle instruments and specialized GPS systems. Behind the case, two bicycles, one upright and one upside down were mounted in maintenance stands. Above the work area, at least a hundred tires hung from the ceiling. Power tools, hanging lights and part bins were all neatly arranged on the rear wall. Cans of spray lubricant and hand tools were laid out on a bench below the bicycles. The smell of rubber and grease defined what was done here.

"Well, take good care of my Phantom. I'll probably be back for the tune-up," said Anthony as he headed toward the exit.

"Sure, come back anytime," said Tom as Anthony departed through the sliding glass doors, got into his car and drove home.

The smell of the shop was still in his nostrils when he reached the empty house. He went through the ritual of changing into sweats and sneakers then walked into the garage through the door off the family room. Their bikes were hanging side by side from hooks he had anchored on an exposed beam. They were high enough for him to walk under without bending, but low enough to reach with extended arms. He squeezed the tires and found that they were soft. He knew keeping the bikes suspended would preserve the tires, but over time the tires would lose air. He spun the wheel and watched the spokes as it turned. He liked the appearance of his dark green bike, but it was no Black Phantom.

In the family room he found himself walking in circles. He knew he had to figure out a new game plan now that working for a competitor was not in the cards, but he just wasn't up for it. *Maybe I should give it a rest for a day or so*, he thought. He considered putting on some music or reading a magazine or starting one of several new books he picked up when he and Bernadette had last went to Barnes & Noble, but he just kept circling the room. Finally, he went over to the wet bar and opened the lower cabinet. He bent and peered toward the back and spotted a bottle of Jack Daniels. He had bought it specifically for a small dinner party he and Bernadette had hosted for Stewart Ogilvie and his wife two years ago. It was shortly after he had introduced Ogilvie to SkyTel. Stewart was a bourbon man. Although Anthony had never quite acquired a taste for it, he reached for the bottle. *Early in the day and no lunch*, he thought. *Perfect*.

Anthony got some ice and poured himself a Jack on the rocks.

"Bartender," he said with a drawl to the mirror over the wet bar, "just leave the bottle." He took the bottle, glass and a coaster to the sofa, placed them and his feet on the coffee table and took a long sip. The bourbon smelled like bicycle tires. His mind replayed the fiasco at the unemployment office, the papers he read at the coffee shop, the unexpected encounter with Sarah and his visit to the bicycle store. He twirled the melting ice cubes in his glass

with his index finger. He sipped more bourbon. The smell
of rubber hadn't gone away.

When Bernadette arrived home a few hours later, he
was still on the sofa. The bourbon was on the coffee table.
Alongside it was a glass about one quarter filled with
melted ice. The room was not quite dark, but at a point
when Bernadette had expected a light to be on if anyone
was in the room. At first she thought Anthony was asleep,
but she realized that his eyes were open, and he was just
looking straight ahead. She turned on a table lamp.

"What's up Anthony?"

"Not much," he said, "just waiting for you to come
home."

"I don't think I've ever seen you drink bourbon," she
said.

"Maybe it's a time for new things," he said.

"Anthony, are you drunk?"

"No Ma'am. I am not drunk. However, I may have
been slightly over served."

"That's not funny. You know how I feel about getting
drunk. I had enough of that with my father."

"I'm not really drunk. I borrowed that line from an old
comedian named George Gobel. My father used to love the
Johnny Carson show so I got him a set of DVDs of
Carson's classic shows a few years ago. One night we
watched one together, and this guy Gobel was on with
Dean Martin and Bob Hope. They were big time stars and
Gobel had an okay TV show, but was a minor leaguer by
comparison. So anyway, this Gobel guy had two great lines
that stole the show that night. The first, in the context of
being surrounded by these big names, he says to Carson 'I
feel like the world is a tuxedo, and I am a pair of brown
shoes.' Dean Martin laughed so hysterically, it looked like

he was going to pee his pants. A little while later, Carson asked Gobel if he had ever been drunk to which Gobel replied, 'Never. I have never been drunk, but I have, on occasion, been over served.' Carson, Martin, Hope and the whole audience went nuts over that line which Gobel delivered in his dry, hokey style. It was unforgettable."

Bernadette just looked at Anthony not saying anything.

"Well, I guess you had to be there," he said. "But the point is, I had a couple of drinks, but I'm not drunk." He noticed a slight slurring of his speech. "Well, maybe a little."

"This is not like you. I'm going to make some coffee," she said.

"Can we just sit and talk a minute?"

"We can sit and talk after I make you some coffee," she said as she walked to the wet bar with the bourbon bottle.

She returned in about fifteen minutes also dressed in sweats and sneakers carrying a pot of coffee and one cup. While she was gone, Anthony had washed his face and combed his hair. She sat on the other end of the sofa after pouring him a cup of coffee.

"Okay, let's talk," she said.

He decided to skip the long story of the employment office and the coffee shop experience except to tell her that he wouldn't be eligible for unemployment compensation until after the paychecks from SkyTel stopped in a couple of months. Then he shifted gears.

"You know that bicycle shop on Sunrise, where we bought our bikes?"

"Sure. Right next to Pedro's Restaurant."

"That's the one," he said. "Well I stopped there today."

"Why?"

"I don't know," he said. "It was an impulse. So I start talking to the owner, Tom, the one who sold us our bikes. We're talking about his business, and I'm looking around his shop admiring the bikes and his whole set up, and I'm thinking, 'this is really cool.' The guy lives near his work so he doesn't have a bad commute. His work varies from being a salesman, to a small business manager, to working with his hands on the bikes. He knows people in the community. Kids probably see him as a savior when he fixes their bikes, parents are glad they don't have to assemble the damn things which have become so complicated, and I bet at the end of the day he makes a pretty good buck what with the sales and service of bicycles, accessories, clothing, and all. Did you know they even have GPS systems made especially for cyclists?"

"No, I didn't," she said.

"So anyway, I get home and I'm thinking maybe I ought to consider something like this for myself. Maybe I should have a shop like his. Maybe even buy in as a partner. I can sell. I'm good mechanically. I like biking. I could give up working with guys like Albright and Trenholme in a heartbeat. By now, I'm starting to feel pretty good about the idea. So then I have a glass of my friend Jack D, and I think some more about it. I start thinking about how I could do it. Buy in as a partner there or someplace else like it and learn the business. You know there are dealers, trade shows, and the whole retailing thing. Then I can maybe buy the whole thing or sell my share and set up my own place. Now I'm thinking five years down the road on my way to becoming the Big Bicycle Banana from Brooklyn, when it hits me."

"What hits you?" Bernadette asks.

"The tires," he said.

"What tires? What do you mean?"

"This place, and don't get me wrong, it's a beautiful shop. But it's got these tires hanging from the ceiling. You know. That's part of the business. Replacing and fixing tires."

"Yes, so?" Bernadette asked, completely confused.

"Bernadette, if I walked into the same store every day of my life and I had those tires hanging over my head with that smell of rubber in my nostrils day in and day out, I would go absolutely nuts. I don't know if anybody could hang themselves with a bicycle tire, but I might be the first one to try. I could see that place getting smaller and smaller every day. I could see the kids coming in whining about their chain slipping off the gears and me pulling out a shot gun and running the little bastards off. End of story. I decided that having a bicycle shop is not for me."

"Please don't drink bourbon anymore," said Bernadette.

"Hey, wait a minute, there is a serious side to this message."

"Let me guess. You want a GPS system for our bikes," she said.

"No. No more about bikes, shops, or working in the community."

"What then?" Bernadette asked not sure if he was drunk or not.

"I was thinking about change. Since I don't have a job right now and the prospects for staying in the same field are not too terrific, maybe I should look at something else."

"Like bicycle shops," she said impatiently.

"No," he said, "but something new and different that has value and different kinds of people."

Bernadette saw that if he had been drunk, it was

wearing off. He was speaking clearly and passionately now, the way he did when he really cared about something. It was a quality she admired about him.

"Do you have any idea of what that would be?" she asked cautiously.

"No. But there has to be something important I can do that can make a difference. Look at the work Martin does. He goes off to places that aren't very far from third world. Not to the metropolitan centers that have the all the amenities and comforts of home, but to native villages of indigenous peoples, and he brings them help that for them can be life changing. That's the kind of thing I mean."

"Anthony," she said, "that's very noble and idealistic, but think about it. Martin is a health professional. There is an organization in place that is designed to bring his services to these people. Besides, he has accumulated a lot of wealth. Sarah has told me that if he wanted to, he could retire right now, but he loves his work, and he is really into this program in El Salvador. You can't forget that he can afford it. He didn't start doing this when he was out of work."

"Ouch."

"I didn't mean that like it sounded, just that there are practical issues to consider."

"The thing is," he said, "if another job comes along like the one I had at SkyTel, I would probably take it, and life would go on as always, and the opportunity to change and do something noble and idealistic and personally enriching would go away. Who knows if that kind of opportunity will ever come our way again?"

"Anthony, you have an idea, not an opportunity. There is no organization calling that will utilize your skills for the betterment of mankind, and certainly not one that will also pay for our home, cars, vacations and so on, to say nothing of the fact that we have talked about having children and the meter is running on that one, by the way."

"I know, I know. It's just that as long as I have to think about changing jobs, I want to broaden the playing field. I want to think in terms of how we live and why we live. I'm not going to do anything crazy. I just don't want to be stuck in a box when there's a whole world out there."

"Stuck?" asked Bernadette, "That's how you feel? Stuck?"

Bernadette felt her marriage being threatened for the very first time.

"I don't mean anything bad by that. I just want to consider this situation as an opportunity."

"I'm going to put on dinner," she said. "How about pasta and a salad?"

"Sounds good," said Anthony.

As she left for the kitchen, Anthony went to the wet bar, opened the cabinet and reached for the bourbon.

Taking Flight

Chapter 14

Anthony woke up on the sofa the next morning feeling very uncomfortable having slept in the same clothes of the day before. The headache brought on by the bourbon and the foul taste in his mouth provided an unfortunate reminder of the evening. He made his way to the bathroom as the stiffness in his neck and back added to his discomfort. Bernadette had already left for work. No note was to be found. He wasn't quite sure how their conversation had ended after dinner, but his presence on the sofa explained all he needed to know. He wasn't much of a drinker, but she had a very low tolerance for anyone who over imbibed. He concluded that the pain far outweighed the benefits of bourbon.

He took an antacid and began a head and body overhaul that started with a long shower followed by a shave and a series of stretches that he remembered from a Yoga class he and Bernadette had taken. After putting on some fresh clothes, he made himself scrambled eggs like those he occasionally made for the two of them on Sundays. His "culinary secret" was adding a little milk to the bowl of whipped eggs before pouring them into a preheated frying pan that was coated with sizzling butter. While the eggs were cooking, he dropped some wheat bread into the toaster and ground coffee into the coffee maker. He carefully transferred the eggs to a plate, retrieved the toasted bread to which he applied lightly salted butter and poured his first cup of coffee into the awaiting mug. He was proud of the simultaneous completion of each breakfast element. The eggs were perfect and the coffee hit the spot. He was sorry now they only had delivery of the Times on Sunday. A newspaper would have provided good company.

Halfway through his breakfast, Anthony stopped eating. Everything that had gone on since he lost his job was racing through his mind again. He got up from the kitchen table leaving the remaining eggs and one slice of toast. He refilled his coffee mug and took it with him to the adjacent family room. He opened the sliding glass door and stepped onto the backyard patio. The air was clear, but had an autumn chill. He dismissed the idea of going back in for a jacket and walked the brick perimeter of the concrete patio. The maples that provided a seasonal protective screen from the neighbors to the rear were mostly bare. Some leaves still clung desperately to the branches resisting the fate of those that had already succumbed to the changing season. The lawn that began at the bricks was turning a yellowish brown. He inspected the deflowered shrubs and dwindling flower beds that lined the two side fences. He sipped the coffee and looked up at the sky taking in the clouds that filtered the sunlight. Before he headed back to the house, he made a mental note that it was time to remove and store the cushions from the patio furniture and put the winter cover over the table umbrella.

Anthony turned and took two steps toward the house, stopped and pivoted on the soles of his feet to face the maples. He took another sip of coffee and extended his arm, palm up, and with a very bad Russian accent said aloud to no one, "This land is mine as far as the eye can see. And someday, it shall all be yours." As an overhead cloud blocked the sun and shaded the patio, the smile on his face disappeared and his eyes narrowed. He inhaled deeply hearing the sound of air rushing into his nostrils. He took a step forward and brought his right arm back, fully extended. Bringing his arm forward nearly full circle, he released his anger and the coffee mug smashed into countless pieces. Coffee stained his clothes, the concrete and brick edging and followed the mortar lines into the fading grass.

A short while later Anthony found himself at the desk in his study holding the sides of his head in his hands. He was trying to think, but was unable to connect two thoughts that made any sense. He tried closing his eyes and taking deep breaths in order to collect himself. An attempt to clear his mind and listen only to his breathing failed as a barrage of random thoughts penetrated a porous shield of tranquility. He left the study for the open space of the family room where he dropped into his favorite chair.

He sat with his head back and eyes closed. *I wish I was connected*, he thought. *I would have Albright and Trenholme whacked in a heartbeat. I would have it done slowly and painfully with each of them fully aware of the inevitable outcome. Of course, a sincere apology would be extracted. Making them beg for mercy would be a nice touch. For Albright, he imagined having him dangled by his feet for about five minutes before being dropped onto a mountainous terrain, his body bouncing on unyielding and penetrating rocks each taking its toll. His wounds would leave his consciousness intact and aware of a broken body that would take hours to expire. For Trenholme, he would prefer his being dropped into a huge clear glass vat of human excrement. Inside the vat would be the steps and railings of a ladder that would reach to within two feet of the rim. His feet and hands would be unable to sustain the grip necessary to haul him up. Outside the vat would be a gathering of all the employees that had ever worked for him. As he would shout to them for help, his mouth and lungs would fill with the vile ingredients of his habitat until he could no longer breathe, no longer see, no longer hold onto the ladder.*

The images in Anthony's mind finally turned to blackness. At last, he could hear only his breathing. It took on the tone of synthesized sound with an artificial richness that one might hear in a sound chamber. For thirty minutes he remained in a trance before he stirred and pushed himself out of the chair. He undressed on his way to the bathroom and went straight to the shower where he ran the water as hot as he could stand it. The water began to cool when the hot water heater could no longer keep up with his demand. He turned it off, stepped out and walked dripping wet to retrieve a fresh towel. After he dried himself, he picked out fresh underwear, a pair of jeans, blue cotton polo and a gray hooded fleece jacket, socks and sneakers. He dressed, left the house and went for a long walk through the bare tree lined streets of Hempstead.

When Anthony returned an hour later, he went immediately to the backyard and cleaned up the patio. He collected as many pieces of the broken coffee mug as he possibly could. He hosed and brushed the coffee stained cement and bricks. He deposited the debris in a garbage can kept on the side of the house. Anthony went back into the house and picked up the clothes he wore after his first shower and added them to the refuse in the can. He then retrieved the patio cushions, bundled them in plastic tarps as he had each winter and brought them to their storage place atop the false ceiling in the garage. While there, Anthony retrieved the umbrella cover and an old towel he had used as a rag whenever he worked on the cars. Outside again, he secured the cover over the closed umbrella. Next, he took some flower pots that were hanging from Sheppard hooks strategically positioned on the rim of the grass and brought them to a safe harbor against the back of the house. Finally, he took the greasy towel to the garbage can and placed it over the remnants of the coffee mug and his discarded clothing.

Chapter 15

During the two weeks following his visit to the unemployment office, Anthony and Bernadette developed a routine based on the new circumstance of his being home during the day. He took care of the winterization of the house: removing screens, installing storm windows, checking insulation, collecting and disposing of fallen leaves, and the cars – changing the oil, strengthening the antifreeze and installing dedicated snow tires and wheels. He also did more household shopping and prepared meals more often. His days started with a two mile run, a practice that he had abandoned some time ago, but always intended to revive. Each day after lunch, he would read the newspaper which was now being delivered daily. He checked employment ads and looked for articles concerning businesses similar to SkyTel. He examined business opportunities for those interested in buying a franchise or starting a home based business. He dismissed the idea of retail shops, selling vitamins or anything to do with real estate sales or multi-level marketing. He came to understand the coded subtleties of the advertisements; "looking for highly motivated people" meant sales jobs with commission only income. It became much easier for him to disqualify a business opportunity than become interested in one. As his analysis skills became more proficient, the more he understood that his career was in trouble.

Anthony gradually thought less and less about finding noble work that would make a difference to mankind and more about not drowning in a sea of jobs for which he had no interest, experience or qualifications. After studying or browsing through books that addressed job hunting strategies, common traits of successful people, and making money in the new economy, his reading drifted toward pulp fiction and sports biographies. His social interactions were confined to getting together with Bernadette's friends. The most recent event had been a week ago when Sarah gave a bon voyage cocktail party for Martin who was going to El Salvador for four weeks. The usual crowd attended with the exception of David and Carla who begged off but sent a magnum of champagne in their absence. Anthony still admired Martin's pro bono work, but now saw the context as a service that Martin "could afford to provide." Anthony also admitted to himself that Martin seemed naturally predisposed to the concept of helping others whereas he never gave it much thought. Anthony's own network of friends had diminished in recent years. Contact with old friends and college buddies fell off as each built their own lives, relocated, got married, had children and developed social circles that centered around their evolving lives. His own life had centered on Bernadette, their home and his career. Although he occasionally missed some former friends, he didn't take any steps to re-establish contact. The idea of doing so now made him uncomfortable given the amount of time that had passed and his current job situation. His growing sense of isolation became a physical ache that resided in his upper stomach, varying in degree at times, but always present.

On Wednesday morning, at about 9:30, the phone rang. He was about to shower after his morning run and decided to let the call be picked up by the answering machine. He screened it in case it was Bernadette only to be surprised by the sound of Henry Trenholme's voice.

"Good morning, Anthony, this is Henry at SkyTel calling. It's about 9:30 on Wednesday morning. I have some information that may be of interest to you. So, when you are available, please call me during regular business hours at your convenience. If Jeanne Marsh should answer, tell her you are returning my call and she will put you right through. If I happen to be away she will find me and I will return your call shortly thereafter. I shall look forward to speaking with you."

Anthony had lunged toward the phone upon recognizing the caller stopping seemingly in midair as Trenholme completed his message. With his arm extended and hand wide open over the handset, Anthony froze making an instant decision not to answer so that he could prepare himself for a response to whatever Henry was calling about. Postponing his shower, Anthony replayed the message over and over listening for clues he might decipher from Henry's words and tone. In the end, he concluded that Henry was typically Henry, leaving no clue and revealing no emotion or meaning. *But he called,* thought Anthony. *The reason might not be clear, but it was not to wish me Happy Birthday, or to see how I was doing in my job search. He wants something.*

Anthony decided to wait before returning the call. He completed his morning routine, all the while replaying Henry's message in his head and mentally preparing for his response. After being screwed so badly, he realized that it could not be bad news. The severance agreement locked up all the conditions the company wanted. When Anthony considered the possibility that this could be something breaking in his favor, he dared not explore what that might be. He considered calling Bernadette, but decided against.

She would be either overly cautious or too positively excited. Better to know more before discussing it.

Deciding to put the return call off until about 3:30 P.M., Anthony prepared by placing a note pad and a separate sheet of paper with a list of key words next to the phone. The list addressed all possible scenarios likely to be presented by Trenholme. A minus column with the word 'Attorney' would be used if there were further negative developments. Anthony would respond by "needing to discuss this with his attorney before commenting further," and then worry about what to do next.

A plus column had the words stay "calm, be cool, need time" to help him be unemotional, professional, seem interested, but needing a little time to think it over. He added the phrase "considering several things right now." Anthony also set up a portable tape recorder so he wouldn't have to depend on notes to recall the conversation. He also prepared a cup of coffee and had a cold glass of water on hand. At precisely 3:30 P.M. he made the call.

"SkyTel Corporate Offices, may I help you?" Jeanne Marsh answered in her practiced unfriendly style that she mistook for professionalism.

"Hi Jeanne, this is Anthony Barto…"

Before he finished the sentence, Jeanne interrupted with "Hold on while I transfer your call."

Anthony was already upset by her manner and the concepts of calm and cool were slipping away. The phone was ringing again as he tightened his grip on the receiver.

"Hello, Anthony, this is Henry," the new voice said. No welcoming tone, but no sneer built into it either.

"Yes, Henry. I'm returning your call."

"Thank you for doing so, Anthony. The reason for my call earlier today was to invite to you a meeting with me at our office in the next day or so at a time we can work out."

"What's the subject of the meeting?" Anthony asked.

"Well, I would rather not go into any details over the phone, but I'm sure that the subject would be of significant interest to you, and that your visit here would serve your interests well."

"That sounds inviting, Henry, but I would like to know more."

"Well, for now, let's just say that it concerns NordSTAR and the pending acquisition of SkyTel. It would really be inappropriate for me to say more at this time. Further, this meeting shall require that you sign a Non-Disclosure Agreement before we can get into any details."

"Henry, you already have my confidentiality agreement on file, why would I have to sign an NDA?"

"Anthony, your confidentiality agreement covers all the information you had been privy to up until your resignation. What I would like to discuss with you concerns new information. Now, I really cannot go any further than that. If you are available, this meeting, which will be in your best interests, should take place this week. If you are not available, just say so, and we can move on."

Anthony had made a note to put any meeting off until next week as a measure of his coolness. He caved.

"Well, tomorrow is not good. I could come in Friday, but it would have to be in the morning, and I would have to leave no later than Noon," he said, trying to sound as though his available time was limited.

"Fine. Be here at 10:00 A.M. We shall look forward to seeing you," said Henry.

The phone went dead before Anthony realized he said "we." Did he mean "we" as in more than one, or the royal, editorial or corporate we? Anthony had second thoughts about having put the meeting off until Friday. *This has to be good for me* he thought, but the ache in his upper abdomen intensified.

Anthony spent the rest of the day thinking about his Friday meeting. He shelved those thoughts temporarily during dinner out of fear that he might say something to Bernadette. She had some work-related reading to do so the evening was a quiet one they spent separately; she retiring before him.

When he got to bed, his mind was racing. He was negotiating all kinds of imagined scenarios, storing conditions in prioritized columns. He knew that the most important principle in negotiating was to know in advance what your "must have" requirements were, and what you would be willing to concede.

There was no need for a minus list. His simple answer for any negative scenarios would be the same, "I will have to speak with my attorney." Besides, bad news is not given in person. They needed something from him. All he had to do was to defer any response to proposals or requests until he had time to think them through. He made another mental list:

Write things down as they speak. Keep a poker face. Ask questions with a flat tone. Avoid sarcasm or any kind of commentary. Would Albright be there? Is that why Henry said "we"? What was NordSTAR's interest in this? Would this get him back in the game?

It was 4:00 A.M. when he last saw the red numerals on the clock radio. When he awoke, his mind went immediately back to the phone call with Henry. He thought to himself, *I have to get out of the house today, do something physically challenging. I need space and exercise or my mind will explode.*

Chapter 16

Anthony started the new day with his usual routine. After his morning run, he cleaned up, put on his "at home uniform" of jeans, sneakers and polo, grabbed his fleece jacket and headed for the garage. In a hurry to get on the water, he skipped checking the tide tables and drove to Blue Waters Kayak Sales & Rentals at the shore. He rented a sit on top model after his request for a sea kayak was turned down by a substitute clerk who didn't know him. Since he hadn't completed a qualifying course at this facility, the clerk would only rent an open hull boat. Being on the water was important enough to Anthony to make the concession.

After donning the wetsuit, a life jacket or "personal flotation device" as they are now called, he selected a paddle, went to the beach and picked a Perception Swing. The boat was more stable than fast, and the offshore breeze suggested it was a good choice. He dragged the kayak from the sandy beach into the water until there was enough depth to float the boat with his added weight. He stood on the left side of the boat, swung his right leg over the hull and from a straddling position, bent, put a hand on each side of the boat and lowered himself into the molded seat. He lifted the tethered paddle and pushed off with very little side to side rocking. The incoming surf lifted the boat and Anthony used the paddle skillfully to keep the bow pointed seaward. Once out of shallow water, he relaxed a bit, got his bearings and headed eastward toward the jetty about one mile away. He took note of the wind which could make his return to the launch site difficult. Wind is not the kayaker's friend, he learned when taking a kayaker's survival course some years ago at Cape Cod. A course too dated and distant to qualify him for a sea kayak rental today.

Anthony maintained good form until he approached within twenty yards of the jetty which was home to mussels, crawfish and ocean debris. Forty minutes of continuous paddling earned him a rest. He stretched out his stiffening legs and dropped them over the sides of the hull. His lower back was tightening up so he stretched upward as much as he could from a sitting position. His bare feet felt cold in the water, but his legs and upper body were warm in the wetsuit.

A higher than usual wave came toward him. Anthony turned the bow directly into it and the boat was gently lifted and lowered as the water's surface changed height. It might have been a rogue wave, but the wind was picking up and blowing in a more easterly direction. It would require more energy on the return route. He decided to head back by paddling directly west into the wind to minimize the rocking of the boat and then cut a sharp shore bound turn when he was even with his original launch point.

He took a few deep breaths and regretted not bringing a water bottle with him. His mouth and throat were hot and dry as he sat in this vast area of forbidding cold and wet. He straightened his back, positioned his legs, extended his arms and began paddling aware of the distant shore line to his right. The paddle westward had the feel of much greater speed because of the water rushing toward him as it was propelled by the wind. After twenty minutes he had gained only about half the distance covered in the same time on the way out. He dared not stop knowing that the kayak would be pushed back and he would lose ground.

After continuing steadily for an hour and a half he could see the shack of the rental place on shore to his right. He waited for a wave to pass before he turned by paddling on the left leaning his body slightly starboard. When the turn was completed, the bow was facing directly toward shore. Happy that the hardest part of the return was over, he made a mistake.

Taking a deep breath, he lifted the paddle with his arms and stretched upward in hope of getting some relief to the growing tightness and ache in his back. With the paddle out of the water and his body not ready to lean as a counterweight, an oncoming wave caught him broadside lifting and capsizing the boat. Anthony instinctively held his breath before he was in the water. Life jacket or not, his head was under for a few seconds. He remembered to look for the paddle which was tethered to the boat, but couldn't see it or the kayak. *Stay cool*, he told himself, *stay cool*.

Anthony turned himself around first observing the direction of the shore, then seeing the boat already ten yards further east and drifting seaward.

"Oh shit," he said out loud. He looked toward the shoreline about a half mile away and knew that with the life jacket, he could make it to shore safely, but further east than his starting point. He indulged himself by imagining that he would walk back to the rental clerk, look him in the eye and say "You should have given me the sea kayak." He laughed to himself and felt a slight chill.

Anthony checked the movement of the boat. It was moving slightly faster than he, drifting away from him. He looked to the shore once more. "No!" he said defiantly and began swimming toward the boat. He tired as he reached within ten feet. With every stroke after that, the boat moved further away from him, becoming impossible to reach. He realized that his motion was causing the boat's movement to accelerate. He stopped to take some deep breaths then paddled gently with his hands below the water line so that he could keep even with the boat. His breathing became less labored, and he made his decision.

Trying to move with as little effect on the water as possible, he unzipped his lifejacket and gently slipped it off. He tried, but was unable to tie the lifejacket strap to his foot. Committed to his plan, he let it go and watched it drift away.

He inhaled as deeply as he could before diving to three feet below the surface where he swam as hard as he could toward the boat. With eyes open, he could see the shadow of the hull above him. He moved toward the surface when his back went from being tight into a full spasm. His extended arms couldn't reach the boat. When his left hand broke the surface of the water, he felt a coiled object in his palm and was about to pull his hand away when he recognized it as the tether connecting the paddle to the boat. He wrapped his fingers around the coiled plastic, pulling it to bring the capsized kayak directly over his head. His right hand reached up and grabbed the side of the boat. His left hand followed still clinging to the tether. With a little effort his body elevated so that his head came out of the water. He sucked in air and rested his head against the side of the overturned boat.

Anthony was not sure how long he stayed in this position. It could have been five or twenty minutes. He tried to relax his back but the increasing cold through the wetsuit made it difficult. He knew the rest of what he had to do. Each side of the kayak had a rubber handle at the midway point of the hull. He centered himself alongside the hull gripping the handle in front of his face with his left hand. Holding it, he lowered himself in the water and moved under the boat until he could reach the opposite handle with his right hand. As his breath was released through his nose, he pushed up with his left hand, pulled down with his right and pushed himself upward suffering the agonizing pain in his back. The kayak righted itself and Anthony lay across it, perpendicular to the hull, face down, with his head and feet above the water. All he had to do now was shift his body so that it would lie in the same direction as the kayak, then move to a sitting position. He rested for a minute staring at the water inches from his face as the kayak bobbed up and down with the movement of the waves.

Very gently, Anthony shifted and turned his body being careful to keep his weight evenly distributed. His feet came even with bow and his head was face down at the stern. His whole body was now supported by the boat. In slow, jerky movements, he rolled his body over until he was looking at the beautiful sight of a cloudless, dull gray sky. As tempting as it was to just lie there and rest, he pushed himself up and onto the seat and reeled in the paddle by pulling on the tether. Wasting no time, he began the paddle shoreward. He decided on a route of going to shallow water closer to the shore even though it would be rougher going west from there.

Anthony was exhausted by the time he was in swimming range of the shore close to where he started. A Coast Guard running boat pulled up alongside him. A seaman stood starboard facing Anthony.

"It gets pretty rough this time of day. Not such a good idea to be out here by yourself," he said.

"Got it," said Anthony. "I'm heading in right now."

"Where's your PFD?"

"I lost it back there," said Anthony.

"I should write you up."

Anthony just shrugged.

"Do you need to be towed in?"

"No thanks, I'm good."

With that, the officer driving the boat turned away and sped off. Anthony continued toward shore.

Anthony pulled in the paddle as the kayak approached the beach and coasted in until the bottom of the hull scraped the sandy shore. He tried to straddle and exit the boat, but he couldn't raise his legs high enough. He tried again to no avail. Finally, he leaned to the left and the kayak tilted on its side. Putting both hands under his thigh, he lifted his leg over the side of the kayak and let it fall in the water. Then he went back and grabbed his right leg and pulled it over to the same side. He ended up on his hands and knees in three inches of water. Feeling self conscious, he remembered kidding Bernadette about her girly-girl exit from a kayak while he always executed a manly-man exit.

He pushed himself upright and stood next to the beached kayak. He reached down slowly and lifted the paddle holding it as though he were about to paddle away. Anthony extended his arms overhead and looked up to the sky. The coiled tether was strained. At the top of his voice, he shouted,

"I am Kayak Man! I shall not go down!"

When he was sure the Kayak Gods had heard him, he brought his arms down and was about to drag the boat out of the water and onto the beach. Just then the clerk who had rented him the boat came down and said, "I'll get that. You can change back into your street clothes up at the shack."

"I want to buy the tether," said Anthony.

"Fine, I have different lengths at the shack. They come

in yellow or black. Pick the one you want, and I'll meet you at the counter."

"No," replied Anthony. "What I mean is I want this one."

"But it's used. The ones at the shack are brand new."

"How much are the ones at the shack?" asked Anthony.

"The black are $12, the yellow are $13.50, but I can't discount this one if that's what you're thinking."

Anthony looked straight at him and said, "I'll give you $20 for this one to cover the tax and your trouble for swapping them out."

The clerk looked at Anthony and shrugged. "Go ahead and take it," he said.

Anthony reached down and undid the Velcro wrap around the paddle shank and the hook connecting it to the eyelet on the kayak.

"Thanks," he said, wrapping the tether around his neck. As he started making his way toward the shack, he turned and said, "I also owe you for a life jacket."

He took an outside shower rinse with his wetsuit half off. He dried himself off, changed into his street clothes, dropped the wetsuit in a cleansing tank and moved to the office area of the shack. He put his credit card on the desk, settled up, thanked the clerk again and walked out to his car. When he got in, he removed the tether that was still around his neck, put it in the glove box and drove home.

Taking Flight

Chapter 17

By the time Anthony arrived home, he decided to add his misadventure at kayaking to the list of subjects he was not sharing with Bernadette. The encounters with Nancy and Sarah, and the call from Trenholme were all neatly tucked away in a mental Non Disclosure Box. He was exhausted from the experience and had to be in top form for Trenholme the next day. The evening went quietly with only a few words exchanged during dinner. He and Bernadette watched TV until retiring for the night. As he was getting into bed, he told her that he would be meeting with a recruiting firm the next day, and that it was just a "getting to know you" type of meeting without any agenda. He knew lying was a step beyond withholding information, but he felt he needed a cover story for being out in case she became aware of it. The explanation immediately struck him as stupid and unnecessary, but the words could not be taken back.

Anthony slept well during the night, as a benefit of unintentionally almost drowning. When he awoke he felt very calm about what he expected from the day. The anxiety and constant mental rehashing of possible scenarios were gone. He felt confident that there was no need for further preparation. After Bernadette left for work, he dressed for his meeting with Henry Trenholme. He selected a dark blue business suit, but left off the tie keeping an open collar on his starched pale blue shirt. He packed his briefcase with a notebook and two pens and off he went.

Anthony arrived at SkyTel at 9:45 A.M. He parked

further from the building than was his custom and sucked in the crisp autumn air as he walked toward the entrance. Once inside, he noticed a sign on the receiving desk to call Extension 722 for a receptionist. He walked passed it until he came to Jeanne Marsh's desk. She looked up, pointed to a chair and picked up her phone. After another minute or two, Henry Trenholme came out to greet him, offered coffee which Anthony declined, and led Anthony to his office. When they were seated, Henry made an abortive attempt at small talk before getting down to business.

"Anthony, we have run into a snag with NordSTAR and we would like your help in resolving it and to get our negotiations back on track. To entice you to do that, we are prepared to make you a very generous offer that we believe you will find more than satisfactory."

"Tell me more."

"We will keep you on your regular salary for the duration prescribed in your termination agreement. In addition we will provide…"

"Sorry for interrupting Henry, but I meant tell me more about the snag."

"Well, the details don't matter, suffice to say…"

"The details do matter, Henry. I'm willing to listen to whatever you have to say, but I need to know what's going on and why you need me."

Trenholme blinked for the first time. He shifted in his chair and after pausing a moment, went on.

"It seems that Edwin became agitated as NordSTAR increased its demands of project management and access to work under development as it relates to the acquisition. When he reminded them of his stature in the industry and uniqueness of his abilities, he did so in a way that insulted the executives and engineering staff of NordSTAR. Had they been Japanese executives, they would have walked away from the entire deal. NordSTAR however, is less interested in saving face than getting the job done on their terms."

"Which are?" asked Anthony.

"In recent discussions, NordSTAR proposed that one of their engineers join the development team that was adapting and adding performance features to the SkyTel software that is at the heart of the acquisition. He would remain their employee, be compensated by them, but have full access to the project details and status. This was unacceptable to us because of our vulnerability if the deal were to fall through."

"I take it that's where I come in somehow?" said Anthony.

"When we could not agree to their proposal and Edwin raised the issue of potential software piracy, we took a break for a day so that cooler heads could prevail. Edwin remained steadfast about not allowing "outsiders" to have access to the software until the deal was done. It was then proposed that you be brought back in to be a Project Manager dedicated to this program, and that you would furnish each company with a bi-weekly status report of the project."

"And this was proposed by…?"

Trenholme continued, "NordSTAR made the proposal. To insure objectivity on your part, they will pay one half of your compensation for your efforts until the project is completed or abandoned. Under the circumstances of your departure, we would continue your salary as defined by the terms of your Termination Agreement. They will enhance your compensation by paying SkyTel an equal amount which in turn will be transferred to you. All of your compensation will therefore come from SkyTel although NordSTAR would be underwriting half of it. At the successful completion of the project, which includes a signed acquisition agreement, NordSTAR will underwrite fifty percent of a bonus to be paid to you equal to six months' salary. Summarily, you will work at twice the salary rate as before until the project is completed. Upon successful completion, you will receive a handsome bonus."

"That sounds very attractive," said Anthony.

"Good," said Trenholme. "I can have the papers drawn up by Monday. You can start immediately thereafter."

"You're forgetting something," said Anthony.

"What is that?" asked Trenholme. He shifted in his chair as he finished the question thinking Anthony was going to ask for an apology.

"My stock options," said Anthony. "Technically, under the terms of this arrangement I would continue as an employee until the deal is done. When that happens, my stock options automatically become fully vested. That my stock options remain intact until that happens has to be part of the agreement. If the acquisition does not go through, I'll give them up."

"Anthony," said Trenholme, "don't let greed get in the way of this very generous offer. I doubt I could convince Edwin to agree. He is very protective about stock ownership."

"If I lose mine, his and yours will be worthless. Another suitor like NordSTAR won't come along for a long while, if ever."

"Anthony," said Trenholme with a very steady voice, "you are proposing a potential deal breaker that will be harmful for all concerned."

"Henry," he said as he stood up and extended his hand. "I will give your proposal very serious consideration. But I must tell you that my position on the stock options is non-negotiable. If you and Edwin can work your way through it, I think we can do business. If you reach a favorable position I can have my attorney review the papers you draw up, and I can give you a reply within a day or two. Thanks very much for inviting me in."

Henry looked at him with a hint of a smile on his face.

"I'll do what I can," he said. "If we work together, I will expect you to negotiate as well with NordSTAR on our behalf."

Anthony smiled at the compliment and turned to leave. As he passed by Jeanne Marsh, he leaned over and put his lips close to her ear.

"Jeanne," he said. "I just have to tell you that you look really hot today."

She gave him her "drop dead" look, but was blushing at the same time.

Once outside, he got into his car trying to contain his exuberance. He reached into the glove compartment and took out the coiled kayak tether and draped it over his neck. He did not dare make a sound until he was back on the Southern State Parkway after which he shouted, "Yes. Kayak Man lives!"

Before reaching home, he stopped at the bicycle shop. He paused briefly upon entering to admire the Schwinn Black Phantom when he was greeted by the owner. Anthony was pleased that he was remembered.

"Hi Tom," said Anthony.

"Hi young fella. Checking up on your old Schwinn again?"

"I always enjoy that, but I'm here for something else as

well," said Anthony.

"What can I do for you today?"

"I'd like to pick up one of those GPS systems designed for bikers and hikers."

"Sure," said Tom. "Come back to the case and I'll show you what we have."

Tom gave Anthony a short course on portable GPS systems after which Anthony decided to go for a top of the line model that could be used for biking, hiking and even kayaking. Trails, pathways, shipping channels and city streets were all there. Altitude, latitude and longitude, time of day and mileage appeared on the display.

Admiral Perry, eat your heart out, Anthony thought as Tom put the unit in its carrying case, ready to use.

"Tom," Anthony said, "My wife has a mountain bike that has a really hard seat. Is there a cushier model that can replace it?"

"Sure," said Tom. "I've got one that's padded and has a double coil spring for extra support."

After looking it over, Anthony asked Tom to wrap it as a gift which took a little effort, but Tom was happy to do it. Making one more stop, Anthony bought a bottle of champagne to bring home.

At the house, Anthony put the champagne in the refrigerator, put Bernadette's packaged bicycle seat on the coffee table in the family room and changed from his business suit to jeans, polo and a pair of sneakers. He put away his briefcase, checked the answering machine and sat on the family room couch with his new toy and the GPS owner's manual. The sky was getting dark when he finally heard Bernadette's car coming into the garage. He put the GPS system back in its case. Anthony was about to get the champagne when she walked in. She had a serious look on her face and she sat down before removing her coat.

"Can I have a glass of wine, please?" she said.

"Sure," said Anthony. Clearly something was wrong, so he put his plan on hold. After getting each of them a glass of white wine, he handed her one and sat opposite her.

"What's up?" he said. "You don't look so good."

"I'm not," she said looking down at the floor.

"Tell me."

She looked at him and said, "David and Carla split up."

"Wow! That is news. How is she taking it?"

"I don't know," she said. "I haven't talked to her."

"So how ...?"

"David called me at work. He was devastated."

"You mean Carla left David, not the other way around."

"Apparently she has been seeing this guy, some big shot client, for almost a year. She sat David down and told him that she wants out of the marriage. She told him he can have all their major assets except her business. The big shot will cover her losses."

"Jesus." said Anthony. "Right away I figured she caught him fooling around, and he either walked out or she threw him out."

"I've been telling you that he's really not like that. He was really devoted to Carla, and is actually a very sensitive guy."

"So, what do the others think about this?"

"No one knows yet. He asked me not to tell anyone. He wants to do it himself, but he needs a little time."

"So the only one he told was you?"

"Well, I'm sure he told his mother. She lives in

Florida."

"But of the group, you're the only one he told?"

"I guess."

"Why do you think that is?" he asked.

"He must have needed to tell someone, and he knew that I, that we, were having problems about your job. You know, I told you…"

"So you and he are sort of confidants lending support to one another?"

Her back straightened. Bernadette stared at Anthony.

"I can't believe this. I come home with terrible news about two of my friends and you're making this about him and me? What is wrong with you?"

"Hey, I'm just saying that you two seem to have become close lately to the point where he confides in you before any of his other friends. He calls you at work, makes suggestions about my job situation, and offers a friendly ear and now this."

"Anthony, you need to find a job. You have too much time on your hands, or something. Jealousy doesn't suit you."

"Well, it turns out that I do have a job, or will very soon," his voice growing louder."

"What are you talking about?"

"I met with Henry Trenholme today and they offered me my job back. We have details to work out, but we left that until next week. It turns out that they need me, not forever, but for now, and they're willing to make it worth my while."

"That's wonderful news," she said

"Yeah, except that your snotty girl friend has been banging one of her clients and her horny husband has been hovering over you. Fuck Carla! Fuck David! Fuck the job!

And Fuck …"

"Don't you dare say that to me. Not now. Not ever!"

"Look. I was right about my job. I'm right about this. I'm sorry that Carla dumped him, but this guy has been coming onto you, and you either don't see it, or you like it, or I don't know what."

Bernadette turned away from him. They each stood silent for several minutes. She pointed toward the coffee table.

"What's that box?" she asked softly

"It's a present. A bicycle seat. A padded one for your tush."

"Maybe you haven't noticed lately, but my tush has more padding of its own."

"It's still a great tush. It should be protected. Besides, how I could I buy a GPS system for my bike without buying something for you?"

"So that's it," she said smiling, "The old guilt gift to cover the one you got for yourself," she said as she unwrapped the box.

"You got me," he said.

"Anthony, I don't know what's happening, but I love you, and I want things to be right between us."

"Yeah, me too. I know I've been hard to live with since the job thing, but I know I'm right about this guy."

"Maybe after dinner, we should have some make-up sex," she said.

"I have champagne. Who needs dinner?"

Chapter 18

Anthony woke up before Bernadette on Saturday morning. He tried not to disturb her as he eased his way out of bed. He picked up his clothes from the night before and brought them into the bathroom to dress as quietly as he could. He threw some water on his face and headed for the kitchen. After making some coffee, he picked up a bath towel and brought it with him to the patio. He placed it over a chair to take the chill out of the metal frame. The morning was overcast and the air was cold, but he wanted to be outside to think things through. His mind kept bouncing between his meeting with Trenholme, the news about David and Carla and his suspicions about David's interest in Bernadette. Last night was extraordinary. He and Bernadette were almost savage in their love making. He decided that if things were that good in bed, she was not interested in another man. Still, he did not trust David or any other man's intentions for that matter.

Today, he would tell Bernadette the details of his meeting with Trenholme. It went so well, he wouldn't have to embellish it. He thought that later, they could go for a bike ride and try out their new toys. He hoped that tonight they could have a nice dinner out and celebrate, just the two of them. Perhaps tomorrow, they would drive out to a fruit and vegetable farm on the Island, pick some apples, and check out the progress of the pumpkins making their way to a Halloween harvest. The traffic would be reasonable now that the season at the Hamptons was over. The weekend would allow them to recover from the stress they were enduring since he was let go from SkyTel. Things were back on track. Still he was uneasy, and his upper abdomen was not handling the coffee very well.

As he ran the meeting with Trenholme through his mind, he thought about the two of them sitting face to face having a discussion as though there were allies. The previous animosity between them had dissipated as Bernadette had suggested it would. The men worked through the issues as though Edwin was a problem they had to solve. They were now colleagues with a common cause, he and the self righteous hatchet man who only weeks ago seemed to take a special pleasure out of firing him. Trenholme had acted as though Anthony was a misfit, an overrated malcontent for whom SkyTel no longer had any use. Now, they were buddies, joined at the hip in pursuit of a common goal defined by greed and stock options.

Anthony got up and went over to shrubs planted at the perimeter of the patio. He stooped to pull out some new weeds making their presence known at the base of the shrubs. He thought of his father as he patted down the earth that came up with the weeds. What would he think of this situation? When practical matters and principles clash, what do you do about it? Anthony had had an epiphany while seeking the help of business colleagues and learned the difficulties of finding a new job. Still, joining forces with Trenholme and Albright seemed…?

Anthony went inside for more coffee and to get a sweatshirt, when Bernadette strolled into the kitchen wearing her robe. She walked up to him and gave him a hug and clung to him with her arms wrapped around his back.

"You must have been up early," she said. "I had a great night's sleep." She removed her arms from his back, pushed up his shirt, opened her robe and hugged him again pressing her flesh against his.

"Thank you for last night," she said.

"You're welcome and thank you back," he said, putting his arms around her shoulders. "We have some things we need to talk about. I was hoping we could have a quiet weekend to just chill."

"Okay," she said, "but how about letting me have some coffee and a shower before we talk about anything serious?"

"Sure, I'll even make breakfast," he said.

After they had eggs, toast and coffee and were showered and dressed, they sat in the family room to talk about the saga of Anthony and SkyTel. Anthony fudged a bit by telling her that the phone call from Trenholme came in yesterday morning and he decided to give SkyTel a priority over his meeting with the recruiter he had invented. Other than that, he gave Bernadette an accurate description of the meeting. He related all the details in a flat, unemotional tone like she might hear from a broadcast journalist.

"That is really good news," she said. "Do you think you'll get the stock options back?"

"Yes. They're a mere pittance compared to those owned by Trenholme and Albright. If they were to tell the folks at NordSTAR that they were a deal breaker, the Germans wouldn't tolerate it. It's more a matter of principle than money, although, for us the monetary value of the options is more than chump change. Besides, I'm enjoying breaking Albright's balls over this."

"When would you return to work?" she asked.

"If the deal goes through as I expect it to, I'll probably be asked to go back before the week is over."

"So you have a few days to relax and prepare, that's nice," said Bernadette.

"If I accept," he said.

"What do you mean? I thought you said they offered you a great deal."

"Yes they did, they did, but I'm not sure if this is what I want to do."

"Anthony, how can you say that? You seemed genuinely pleased that they gave you this offer, and they had to eat crow besides. You were so upset by Jack Mullen not doing more than he did. You went nuts over the way that Ogilvie guy treated you. You said the job market and the terms of your severance agreement did not bode well for you. What is there to think about?"

"It's hard to explain," he said. "These guys are dirt bags. They took their best shot at screwing me with no consideration for what I did for them. Now they need me because the head dirt bag has an ego so big it couldn't fit in a Mack truck and they want to make nice. If NordSTAR pulled out tomorrow, they would say to me 'Sayonara baby. It's been a lot of fun, but Edwin gets upset at the sight of you, so it's time to leave.' That's who I'll be working with, talking to everyday, and shaking hands with when the deal is done."

"That's why you're getting everything in writing," said Bernadette, "to protect yourself. You said it could be done so that you would be completely protected. The only question is about the stock options which you said are based on success. You said that was fair. In the meantime, you would be making twice as much as before. You couldn't have asked for a better outcome for the situation you were in."

"There's something else to think about."

"What?" she asked.

"Look," he said, "I know that I'm not going to eradicate hunger and poverty in the third world. I know I'm not going to open a bicycle shop and befriend the snotty little bastards of Nassau County. But I also know that there has to be a way I can do something useful with my life; something that has some value; something that has some meaning; something that has some integrity. There has to something other than working with these sickos.

"And I'm afraid of becoming just like them. I was pleased when Trenholme grinned at my demand for the stock options. Do you know what I did as soon as I knew the job crisis was over? I went out and bought toys. All was well again. I could afford more stuff. We could drink champagne. If I take this offer, things will never change. I'll always be the same. We will always be the same. We would be driven by our income and security. We'll not make choices based on how we want to live, but on what we want to buy! This is like a last chance to do something different, to do something better.

"That night," he went on, "when your friends came over, we talked about how the world knows that there is more to life than acquiring stuff. That meaning and happiness is never realized by going to the department store, or buying a bigger house or living in a vacuum. And yet we all do it. Your friend David was the only one honest enough to admit he likes it that way, and that he doesn't give a rat's ass about anybody who struggles just to survive because he thinks they must want it that way. I go on about the great thinkers and philosophers, but I'm no different. If I accept this offer, I'm nailing that door shut. You can write my epitaph right now. 'He lived. He worked. He bought stuff. He died.' That's what there is to think about."

He sat looking at his hands, not knowing where all the words came from, not even sure if they were his. Now he wouldn't be able to hide from them, or pretend they were never spoken.

Bernadette got up. "I think we need a break," she said, as she walked toward the bathroom. When she came back she poured a glass of orange juice for both of them. She sat quietly just gathering her thoughts when the phone rang.

"Let's let it go on the machine," she said.

"I'll screen it," he said, as he got up and went to the kitchen.

Bernadette could hear a voice on the answering machine, but couldn't make it out before Anthony picked up the phone. She heard him speak with a strained voice, but was unable to hear the words. Even though it was the weekend, she suspected the call came from SkyTel and something was wrong.

When he returned Anthony looked shaken to his core "What's up?" she asked.

"This is really bad," said Anthony.

Bernadette became frightened, "Anthony?"

His voice trembled as he spoke, "That was Sarah. Martin is dead. He was killed in El Salvador."

Chapter 19

Anthony and Bernadette were at Sarah's house within minutes of receiving the call. They met Aaron and Nancy on the walkway. The men shook hands; the women hugged and whispered about how terrible this was. The front door had been left unlocked; they entered after knocking gently. Les and Regina were already there. Regina was preparing coffee and tea while Les was standing uncomfortably beside Sarah who was listening to a stranger dressed in a dark blue suit. Sarah interrupted him and greeted the new arrivals with a hug. Her eyes were swollen, and she was a bit unsteady. Genuine sadness and sincerity accompanied each expression of shock, sympathy and offer of support.

Sarah introduced her friends to the blue suit.

"This is Michael Reisner from MATES, Medical Aid To El Salvador. That's the agency that administers the health services provided by Martin and his colleagues. He came here to give me the news in person and has offered the assistance of the agency to repatriate Martin's remains." She went on as her voice started to tremble. "Apparently, it's a little complicated because of him dying in a foreign country." Sarah's voice drifted off leaving an awkward silence in its wake.

Michael Reisner turned to the others. "We work with the State Department to arrange the services provided by our health professionals. Many agreements are made in the process of obtaining permission from the host countries in order for us to provide our services to their citizens. Unfortunately, the death of one of our participants creates an unusual amount of red tape that complicates matters. As a result, Martin's remains are not available for repatriation until an investigation is completed and the surviving family agrees not to hold the government or any entity operating in El Salvador responsible for the loss."

Nancy asked, "Can you tell us what happened and what we have to do?"

Michael looked at Sarah, who after hesitating briefly realized he was waiting for her permission to answer the question. She nodded and he went on.

"There was an explosion at the facility where Martin worked. The early reports indicate that oxygen bottles and various chemicals had not been stored properly and somehow the oxygen was ignited. The explosion was followed by a fire and the entire facility was consumed. Martin and the others died very quickly."

"There were others?" asked Les.

"Three. A medical assistant by the name of Ynez Órnelas who also served as an interpreter, Juanita Herrera, a clerk who kept whatever records they had, and Jesus Moreira an orderly and handyman. They were locals all of whom had been doing this work for at least two years."

"What about patients?" asked Les.

Reisner shifted uncomfortably. This wasn't what he came here to do.

"As far as we know, the clinic had just opened for the day, and there were no patients being treated at the time."

Nancy looked at Sarah, then back to Reisner.

"Was there any possibility of foul play?" she asked.

"To the degree that we have been able to ascertain, all the information indicates that this was an accident," said Reisner.

Nancy cleared her throat and the others shifted

uncomfortably.

"Look," he continued, "we all immediately think about terrorism when we hear about an explosion, especially with the death of an American on foreign soil. But this was an unfortunate and tragic accident. A full report will be available in a few days."

"Who prepares the report?" asked Aaron, who had been quiet until now.

"The Salvadorian government will issue the report and turn it over to State. They in turn will send their own report to MATES."

"So by the time we get to see it, if we get to see it, it will have been handled by three agencies including a foreign government, the State Department and the agency that arranged for him to be there," said Aaron. "That's not very reassuring."

"I assure you that as tragic as the news is, if there was anything out of order, Sarah would be so advised."

Nancy looked at him and said, "Perhaps this is not the time."

The others nodded in agreement. Nancy went to sit next to Sarah.

Just then David walked in and introductions were made. David gave each of the women a hug and a word of consolation starting with Sarah and ending with Bernadette. Anthony thought the hug he gave Bernadette had a little extra squeeze to it, but quickly chastised himself for being suspicious. Les brought David up to date after which David announced that he would be representing Sarah in any related legal matters and that his firm had several lawyers specializing in international commerce and their expertise would be available to expedite the repatriation of Martin's body.

"There is no body" said Reisner.

He looked to Sarah who did not seem to grasp the words.

"Because of the explosion and the fire, the remains, after being identified, were cremated. This caused a stir in the village where the facility was located because the Catholic Church, although it permits cremation under certain conditions, has not approved the practice in El Salvador. The people there have cultural restrictions against it. That's why the government worked with the church before taking any action."

"So now we have two governments, a service agency and the Church to deal with," said Les.

David looked at Les, then back to Reisner.

"Let's try and stay on point," said David. "Can we correctly assume that Martin's remains from the cremation are intact and safely stored under the custodianship of a responsible government agency?"

"Yes."

"Do you or your agency have the required documents Sarah needs to complete in order to claim Martin's remains?"

"I have them with me."

Sarah let out a soft moan. Nancy took her into another room.

"I'd like to have them," said David. "They'll be completed on Monday. My firm will address any special requirements of the U.S. and Salvadoran governments in order to repatriate the remains. Can we rely on your agency to provide its full assistance and complete cooperation?" said David.

"Of course," said Reisner.

"Good. Why don't we go into the dining room and

look over the papers."

Reisner picked up his briefcase and followed David's lead. The group sat around the living room, not saying very much. Regina asked who wanted coffee or tea and had a few takers. When she returned with a tray, Carla had arrived and was talking with Sarah. Regina placed the tray of cups and servers for coffee, tea, milk, sugar and lemon slices on the coffee table. Les gave Carla an update.

Aaron said, "David did an excellent job with that fellow."

"The schmuck is a good lawyer." Carla snapped back. "He'll be able to help Sarah through any legal issues."

Shortly after, David returned with Reisner. Reisner paid his respects to Sarah, expressed his condolences and bid everyone goodbye.

David sat opposite Carla. They did not exchange hugs, but nodded amiably.

"David, I thought you did a good job handling that fellow and getting things on track," said Aaron.

"Thank you. That's my job."

"So what happens now?" asked Les.

"Well," said David, "I'll have the right people in my office take care of the paperwork and get the ball rolling. Remember that we are dealing with a government bureaucracy in a Central American country whose utmost objective is to protect its own interests. Things will move slowly. Sarah will have to decide if she will waive her rights to challenge the reports prepared by the three parties."

"You mean she has to waive that right before seeing the reports?" asked Les."

"That's the way it works."

Sarah appeared at the door with Nancy by her side.

"Sarah, we can go over the paperwork details tomorrow or the next day. Right now, you should take it easy," said David.

Sarah continued into the room with Nancy walking at her side. She sat and looked at her friends.

"I can't tell you how much your being here means to me. I may be in shock, I don't know. Maybe we all are. It seems like a nightmare, but I know I'm awake and this is all real. All I want right now is to bring Martin home. Perhaps some of his remains should stay in El Salvador, and I would agree to that. But I want him here. This is his home. I don't want there to be two thousand miles between us. That may seem selfish, but that's what I want. I don't care how he died. Whether something was done to him or not doesn't change that. It won't bring him back. We never spoke about it, but we knew there were risks. And maybe sometime later, I'll want to know more. But right now, all I want is to bring him home."

When she was finished speaking she was looking right at David.

"I'll take care of it," said David.

"Thank you," said Sarah.

"There is one more thing," said David.

They all looked at him.

"The Salvadorans will not release the remains unless a family member or a representative with the Power of Attorney is there in person to sign the necessary papers. No electronic transmissions of any kind are permitted. This is a requirement we will not be able to negotiate. If we leave it up to the government or the MATES agency to represent Sarah, it will take weeks, probably months before the process is completed. And who knows if there is any certainty or accountability to be sure they don't screw up."

"Are you suggesting that Sarah go in person?" asked Regina.

"I don't think that's a good idea," said Nancy. "Sarah is in shock, to say nothing about how they treat women down there."

"My firm can hire someone to represent her," said David, "but that has a down side. If some bureaucrat starts asking questions of someone with no knowledge of Martin's family or his work, delays can occur. The people our firm hires are not rocket scientists; they are well paid, glorified messengers. They can't handle anything much beyond name, rank and serial number. I can't recommend that option in this case."

"You know" said Sarah hesitantly, "I've had two miscarriages. We so much wanted to have a child. What you don't know is that after the last one, we learned I could no longer have children. I don't know if it hurt me more knowing that or knowing Martin would never be a father. He never complained about it. Sometimes we talked about adoption, but we couldn't discuss it without ending up in tears. So we just went along and did nothing."

Everyone shifted uncomfortably, not sure if this was a confession, or an expulsion of the pain she carried that so often showed in her eyes. They had been much more comfortable listening to David talk about processes, procedures and bureaucrats. Nancy put her arm around Sarah.

"She cannot go to El Salvador," she said and all nodded or spoke in agreement.

"I'll go," said Anthony.

Everyone turned in his direction.

He went on, "It will take a few days before the paperwork is done. I can be brought up to speed on what I have to know and be prepared by then. I have a valid passport. And I have the time."

"But Anthony," said Bernadette, "you have your job starting up next week."

"You have a new job?" asked Les.

Bernadette answered, "Anthony has been rehired by his old company. Or at least it's ninety-nine percent done. They have made him a great offer to return, and he is supposed to start before the week is out."

Les started to offer congratulations, but stopped abruptly, realizing this was not a festive moment.

"I'm sure I can negotiate a delay," said Anthony. "Another week won't matter as long as they know I'll be back. Besides, there is that one percent or maybe two. I haven't even decided if this is the right thing yet. In any case, I have the time, or I can make the time. Everyone else here has more pressing obligations. We don't want a stranger to do it. I can do it. I want to do it."

His offer was followed by a brief silence. Finally Nancy spoke.

"Anthony, if you can do this, it's a wonderful solution. It's also very thoughtful and caring of you. We should all share in the burden. David is already helping with things on the legal end. Aaron and I would like to share the cost of your travel and whatever other expenses you incur."

"Thanks, but I don't need…"

"Anthony," Nancy went on, "this is not a negotiation. You're doing something we all want to be a part of. We're doing this for Sarah and Martin. You are undertaking a huge task here. Don't try to deny us our share."

"I can arrange the travel; planes, hotel, and whatever it takes," said Carla.

"We also will help with the expenses," said Les.

Regina added, "We'll arrange a memorial service for Martin based upon your return."

"We can share in the cost for that as well," said Carla.

"I'll call you tomorrow to let you know how soon we can brief you and how long we need to get everything ready," said David.

Sarah stood up and walked over to Anthony. He got up from the chair and she hugged him with tears running down her face. Then she went to each person and hugged them in turn. Martin would be coming home.

Chapter 20

When they arrived home, Bernadette went straight to the liquor cabinet and poured herself a glass of amaretto. She left the bottle on the wet bar, but did not offer Anthony a drink. He helped himself to one still very aware that she had been silent on the short ride home. He decided to wait for her to speak before bringing up what they had just been through. After a few minutes of sitting quietly, sipping her drink Bernadette looked at him.

"You should have discussed this with me first. It should have been *our* position that you would go. You should've considered me in all of this."

Anthony studied the amber color of the liquid in his glass.

"It just came out," he said. "It seemed right and it just came out. It's not the kind of thing you think about."

"Going to a foreign country to bring home the remains of a person killed in an explosion and delaying the start of a job that seems like a gift from God and there's nothing to think about, nothing to discuss with your wife?"

"Sometimes you have to act in the moment, or else the moment passes," he said.

"Is that what this is? A metaphysical response, a Buddhist response, a Philosophy 101 response? Anthony, this is not a simple thing you're doing. It has potentially important consequences. It's dangerous. A man was killed and we may never be sure of the circumstances. You're not going to be treated as an honored guest down there. And what if Trenholme doesn't agree to a delay?"

"He'll agree," said Anthony.

"What about me? What if something happens to you? What if they throw you in jail?"

Anthony smiled, "Hey come on. This isn't a Matt Damon movie. The only real danger is dealing with bureaucrats that may run up the number of days it takes so they can jerk me around a bit."

"You should still have given me a heads-up," she said.

"There was no time. You are looking at this the wrong way. This is for Martin and Sarah. This is not about us."

Bernadette paused. "This is for *you*," she said coldly.

Anthony stood up and walked to the bar. He poured himself a refill and turned back to face Bernadette. He circled the rim of his glass with his finger.

"Maybe it is," he said. "Maybe it's to save my soul."

"I thought you didn't believe in the soul," she said.

I don't," he said. "Not the way you do about collecting sins or scoring points and ending up in Disneyland in the Sky or the DMV below."

"Then what? What's all this about your soul?"

"I don't know. Maybe I just want to do the right thing. To be able to look at myself and be able to say I did the right thing. To be able to say that about something important. I can't explain it any better than that."

Just then the doorbell chimes rang.

Anthony opened the door and it was Carla. He invited her in.

"Hi guys," she said. Carla sensed that there was tension in the room.

"Look," she said upon entering, "I spoke briefly to David before he left. He said that one of the issues that may come up is that the officials down there may be looking for bribes at prices that may be a little out of our price range. I made a call to my boyfriend, who will cover whatever is necessary. He will set up an account for Anthony that he can access electronically. Anthony will be able to transfer money to a bank in El Salvador or any place else, if that becomes necessary. There's no need to share this information with the others. I'll tell you everything you need to know when I get the travel documents taken care of."

"That's very generous of him," said Anthony with a tone a touch more sarcastic than appreciative.

"I'm a great lay," she said with a smile.

Carla turned to Bernadette. "This is a good thing Anthony is doing. He stepped up when it had to be done. I'll be in touch."

When she left, Bernadette refilled her drink.

"Looks like your fan club is growing," she said.

Anthony decided not to say anymore. He went into the den and began searching the internet for information about El Salvador. Bernadette went to the bedroom to read. They spent the rest of the weekend apart in the same house. He, mostly in the den gathering information he thought he would need; she, reading and tending to chores around the house. They ate together, but hardly spoke.

On Monday morning, Anthony placed a call to Henry. He had not slept much the night before. His thoughts had bounced from one person to another. He remembered the night of "kebobs a la Martin" when Martin told him that he was welcome in his home at anytime. That same night he saw Sarah's sadness and her anger without understanding what he had done to upset her. He thought about Bernadette's anger because he had not considered her before volunteering to go to El Salvador. He thought about how to handle Trenholme. He had made his decision about going back to SkyTel. Perhaps it was influenced most by the visit from Carla.

Anthony concluded that doing good work was easier done if you had resources and influence. Saints were a thing of the past, Mother Teresa notwithstanding. To get anything done it took money and connections. Otherwise you could be feeding the hungry, clothing the poor and sheltering the homeless without your own pot to piss in. In the end, the hungry, poor and homeless would still keep coming. To make things better would require that all the SOBs who had money would share it, and those that had influence would use it. Philanthropic motives might be self serving, but a big donation did more to help than serving a bowl of soup. He would go back to SkyTel, take the job, advance his career and be generous and do good deeds along the way. Besides, he knew that if he were working a soup line, he would end up telling the recipients to stand up straight and get their resumes up to date. He could contribute more by accumulating wealth and influence Convinced of this, the thought of being chummy with Trenholme and Albright still gave him a chill.

Trenholme picked up the phone after Jeanne Marsh managed to squeeze ten minutes of hostility into thirty seconds.

"Hello, Anthony. Good to hear from you. I was just about to call you."

"Sure, that's what they all say," said Anthony smiling.

"Well, young man, I have good news. I was able to convince Edwin that your stock options should remain yours under the condition that the acquisition by NordSTAR is successful. I also modified the language of the agreement saying that your contribution had to be directly related to the acquisition, thereby eliminating any possibilities of a challenge. If they buy us, the stock options are yours and will be vested immediately. Can I assume that you accept the terms and will start as soon as you and your attorney can review the contract?"

"That's great to hear, Henry, but there is a problem."

"What is it?"

"Something has come up," said Anthony. "Something very serious that requires my going to El Salvador this week. I may have to be there for a few days, maybe as much as a week. In the worst case, ten days."

"Anthony, I assume that you are being entirely forthcoming and that you are not negotiating."

"Henry, I will accept the offer based on your description of it, and I'll commit to staying for the duration of the project, but I need time to take care of this matter."

Anthony paused, and then went on.

"Henry, the life of a close friend was taken while he was in El Salvador. I have to go to retrieve his remains. This is not a negotiation. I will use whatever time I have down there to bring myself up to date on SkyTel matters, and will hit the ground running when I get back. If we add the worst case of ten days to my time of departure, I will be at SkyTel in two weeks. Assuming that the contract you have prepared reflects what you have offered, you can tell the NordSTAR people that I'm on board, and that I'll give them my first report three weeks from today."

"It's not NordSTAR I'm worried about."

"I can't help you there," said Anthony.

"Anthony, I want to settle this as soon as possible. Please stay near your phone and I'll call you back in ten to fifteen minutes."

"I'll be here," said Anthony as he hung up.

He went to the bathroom and doused his face with cold

water. He took a cold bottle of a mango flavored iced tea out of the refrigerator, drank half of it and carried the remainder back to his desk. Once seated, he closed his eyes and tried a silent mediation concentrating on the sound of his own breathing. His mind insisted on racing through the past twenty four hours until the phone rang.

He picked up the receiver. "Anthony Bartolo," he said calmly, using his business voice.

"Anthony, this is Henry. I have explained your situation to Edwin who is here with me now and is on the line. He would like to speak with you, and he may ask you to repeat some things you have already shared with me."

Anthony was hoping to avoid this. His body became tense. The intensity of his dislike for Edwin Albright had never been greater.

"Anthony, this is Edwin. What's all this crap about a dead body in El Salvador?"

"Good morning, Edwin," said Anthony. "I'm sure Henry explained everything just as it is. I must go to El Salvador. I will agree to the terms Henry described. I'll use the time there to bring myself up to speed. I'll meet with NordSTAR in three weeks, and I'll do my best to get the deal done. This is not a big deal and won't affect the outcome of what I do for SkyTel."

"Listen to me Anthony," said Edwin. "I have gone way beyond my tolerance level to appease those Kraut bastards and to let you profit from my hard work. You be here on Wednesday and let someone else bring back the corpse. Those third world savages have so little respect for human life, you can't even be sure you're getting the right body. If your friend had to go there to get some strange pussy that's his problem. I have a company to worry about. You be here on Wednesday."

"I'm sorry, Edwin. I can't do that," said Anthony, squeezing the phone.

"In that case, here is what you can expect. This afternoon I will have our attorneys draw up a lawsuit charging you with breach of contract, and we'll sue your ass so badly you'll need medical insurance just to stitch it up."

"Don't threaten me, Edwin," said Anthony trying to keep his composure. "Besides, I haven't signed a contract.

"But you agreed to one. I heard it and Henry heard it."

"You know that will never hold up," said Anthony.

"It doesn't matter. All that matters is that our attorneys will keep you tied up fighting it for two years. Whatever money you have left, and then some, will go toward buying some attorney another yacht for defending you. And you won't find another job when a prospective employer finds out that you are being sued by your old one. You'll be toast. You be here on Wednesday!"

As Albright was about to hang up, Anthony said, "Thank you Edwin, for confirming that I made the right decision. You do what you have to do. I'll send you a post card from El Salvador."

Albright slammed the phone down. Henry spoke just as Anthony was about to hang up.

"Anthony, I will call you back in five minutes. Don't go anyplace."

"I don't think there's any point in calling back," said Anthony.

"Anthony, I have gone to bat for you in these matters. Not altruistically, that's true, but for the company and my own interests. I'll call again in five minutes. Please be there. You owe me that."

"I'll be here," said Anthony.

Anthony's body was as soaked as it might be after a workout or kayaking. He washed off his face again and was drying it when the phone rang. He put the towel around his neck and picked it up.

"Yes, Henry," he answered.

"Anthony, I have to apologize for Edwin's boorish behavior. I can certainly understand your disdain for him and the things he said, but the man has a fragile ego and he cannot withstand what you or I might consider reasonable arguments or points of view. He doesn't know how to accept or deal with being challenged or questioned about anything. He takes it all as a personal attack. Such is the way great minds sometimes work."

"Yeah, tolerating Krauts and savages is a real hardship."

"Anthony, you have to rise above this. I am not suggesting that Edwin is justified in his words or actions. I am just trying to help you see that they are his and his alone. They are what they are. I abhor them, but no one can change him. You have to see what is at stake here, what is at stake for you. Don't throw this opportunity away."

"Henry, I must go to El Salvador. Then I must prepare to be sued."

"Go to El Salvador. Take care of your friend. Do whatever is necessary for whatever time it takes. Don't worry about a lawsuit. There will be none regardless of your decision. I will take care of that. Just don't close your mind to coming back."

"You can do all that?" asked Anthony.

"I can."

"Then why didn't you head this off?"

"Edwin is less intransigent when he is exhausted. Right now he is vulnerable and knows deep down that he is a

162

pathetic human being. I can work with him now in ways that I could not before the phone call. I'll see him as soon as I hang up. In a few days, it will be as though nothing happened. The phone call will not have happened. Go, take your trip. Call me anytime while you are gone if you need any reassurance. When you come back, Edwin will welcome you back to the team."

"That sounds hard to believe," said Anthony.

"Edwin is hard to believe sometimes. Leave everything to me. Don't make a decision now. Just think about it. Keep an open mind and think about it. We'll talk when you get back, or if you need to call before then. Let me take care of it."

"No promises," said Anthony.

"Only that you will think about it."

"Agreed."

Chapter 21

After the phone call with Trenholme, Anthony decided to go to the local library rather than continue researching El Salvador on the Internet. He did this primarily to get out of the house, but also decided that it would be a good idea to get some books he could bring with him on the trip. He preferred reading and putting Post-it notes on key pages to reading computer screens. The Hempstead library disappointed him with a limited selection and in particular by not having a book written by Joan Didion called *Salvador* describing her experiences there at the start of the twelve year civil war. Reviews in the NY Times and LA Times had suggested that this was the book to read to understand the country, its culture, history, people and politics. Fortunately, it was still on the shelves of a local bookstore even though it had been published more than twenty five years ago. He also picked up a travel guide despite knowing that Carla would provide whatever information he needed.

On the way home, he stopped at the coffee shop. He changed his mind about getting the coffee to go and elected to stay and have a slice of lemon pound cake with his coffee as a poor substitute for lunch. He remembered how lovely Sarah had looked sitting across from him there when she told him about Martin's upcoming and unexpected trip to El Salvador.

He scanned the travel guide stopping to look up each time the door opened. He learned that El Salvador was the smallest of the Central American countries. It was dwarfed by its neighbors, Guatemala on the North and Honduras on the East. On its Pacific coast, the Gulf of Fonseca, which looked like a manageable kayak trip, separated it from Nicaragua. Although the travel guide listed plenty of places to stay and things to do, it placed repeated emphasis on the high crime rate and do's and don'ts for tourists. Anthony grinned to himself as he thought *Hey, you're talking to somebody who grew up in Brooklyn*. With that, he picked up his books and left for home.

Bernadette wasn't home when he arrived at the house. He checked out some El Salvador related websites suggested by the travel guide and studied some maps. Bernadette arrived home before he got to the Didion book. They shared a dinner with little more than perfunctory conversation. After dinner, he went to the den and picked up his copy of *Salvador*.

It was an easy read considering the subject matter. She referenced the 1980 assassination of Archbishop Romero at the San Salvador Divine Providence Cancer Hospital, the murders of Jesuit priests, their housekeeper and her daughter, and the rape and murder of four U.S. nuns. These events triggered the armed insurrection that turned into a civil war and captured the attention of the world.

Anthony noted her emphasis on the brutality of the ruling regime's death squads, and the support it received from the United States government out of its fear of Communism spreading in the region. He no longer considered the travel guide's warnings of crime to be anything like what he had known growing up in Brooklyn. In El Salvador beheadings and dismemberment had become the punishments of choice.

What impressed Anthony most was that Didion was genuinely terrified during her stay. Despite being treated as

165

a V.I.P by the U. S. Embassy, commonplace arrests, kidnappings, detentions, and the *disappearance* of citizens and visitors frightened her, as did the obliteration of any sense of civil rights. Meanwhile, the American population had been clueless about the atrocities taking place in this country which is closer to Hempstead, New York than Hempstead is to Denver, Colorado. El Salvador had been looked upon as a good source of coffee, not unlike the cup Anthony had enjoyed earlier in the day. Perhaps due to his preoccupation with career, marriage, houses, and GPS systems, Anthony was oblivious to the history of the catastrophic internal struggles of this tiny country

Bernadette was asleep by the time Anthony had finished the book. He wanted to talk to her about it, but knew it would be unfair to wake her. His ignorance of the modern history in this hemisphere was at odds with his self image. Anthony fancied himself as knowledgeable of world affairs going back to the start of World War II. His curiosity drove his study of history and particularly armed conflicts which had always fascinated him. He enjoyed getting into heated discussions and speaking knowledgeably of world events, but had dismissed the "Banana Republics" which had failed to attract his interest. In college, the region never came up. In bull sessions at work he and colleagues could always engage in an informed discussion of historical events, but Central America was completely off his radar, and apparently that of everyone he knew. The exception was Martin.

Martin must have had an in-depth understanding of this part of the world. He must have known why Salvadorans still needed health care assistance from the United States more than fifteen years after the hostilities ended. Before falling asleep, Anthony promised himself to learn as much about El Salvador as he possibly could; this strange country with a population less than that of New York City. It would help him understand what Martin knew and why he was drawn to the place, and maybe why he lost his life.

On Tuesday morning Anthony was awakened by the phone ringing long after Bernadette was gone. The answering machine began recording the call before he could pick it up. He listened as David proposed that he come to his office the next day to meet with him and his colleagues to prepare for his trip. David left all the details including a suggested start time of ten o'clock, and asked that Anthony confirm his availability by two o'clock that day. Anthony went through his morning routine, got cleaned up, made the bed and had some toast and coffee before returning David's call. He waited for the lunch hour hoping to avoid having to speak to David. A woman answered and explained that David was out to lunch. Anthony asked her to advise David that he would be there for the meeting the next morning which she amiably agreed to do. Then he went to the den and continued his research on El Salvador.

At 2:00 P.M., he received another phone call. This time it was Carla.

"Anthony," she said, "I have prepared all the preliminary travel documents you'll need for your trip. I talked with David earlier today and we concluded that Sunday would be the best day for you to depart. That will give you a full work week down there to access the people you'll have to get approval from in order to repatriate Martin's remains. Before I go ahead and book flights and a hotel, I want to be sure that Sunday is good for you."

"Yes. Sunday works," he said. "I could be ready as

early as Friday, but I guess there would be no point."

"Do you want to discuss this with Bernadette first?"

"No, that's okay. She is cool with it. We kind of figured anytime from Friday on."

"Okay, then," said Carla. How about if I bring all this stuff to your house on my way home? I can come by at about four o'clock. I'll explain everything about the arrangements, how changes can be made once you're there, and all the details you'll need to know."

"What date do you have for my return?" he asked.

"We have the following Saturday targeted as a return date, but we arranged the ticket so that it can be changed easily if there's a need to do so. I will explain how that's done when I see you."

"Okay," he said.

"Anthony?"

"Yes?"

"Is four o'clock a good time?"

"Oh, yeah, sure. I'll see you then. Thanks for doing all this, Carla."

"I'll see you at four."

Anthony was interrupted again at 3:00 P.M., this time by the door chimes. It was a FedEx delivery Anthony was not expecting. It was an envelope containing the documents from Henry Trenholme. He signed for the delivery and took them inside. He opened the packaged and saw a folder on which there was a note from Henry saying that everything is fine. The folder contained a contract, an amended Confidentiality Agreement and a bound report of the negotiation status between SkyTel and NordSTAR. He thought for a moment about bringing the contract to David's office tomorrow to have him review it. Despite being impressed with David's performance at Sarah's house, he thought better of it. *I won't give him the satisfaction,* he thought as he put everything back in the folder. He went to the computer to research El Salvador's history for another hour before Carla showed up.

Carla arrived shortly after 4:00 P.M. carrying a large, soft leather briefcase. Anthony invited her in, took her coat and offered her coffee, tea or a glass of wine. She asked for a glass of water instead. They went to the kitchen where he got the water, and they sat at the small table to go over the papers.

"Okay," she said. "Let's start with the travel documents. You will be flying out on United from JFK on Sunday at 8:20 A.M. A car will take you to JFK so you don't have to worry about leaving your car there. We'll also arrange to have you picked up when you return to New York. You'll arrive at El Salvador's International Airport which is about forty miles from San Salvador, the capital, at 12:30 P.M. local time which is an hour earlier than here. The flight is non-stop and less than five hours. Your ticket is business class because for reasons known only to us in the secret order of travel specialists, there is no first class service. If I were to explain why, I'd have to kill you."

She smiled seeing that the tired joke did not get a reaction from Anthony, and went on.

"You will be greeted at the airport by a guide, one Mr. Hernández. We have used him before. He is very good at what he does. He will be holding up a sign calling out Mr. Anthony. It's better not to publicly display any more information than necessary. He'll take you to your hotel in San Salvador. You'll be staying at the Sheraton which is a first class hotel on the main drag, very safe, very comfortable."

Anthony wondered out loud, "Is this the same Sheraton

where murders took place right in the lobby during the early years of the war?"

Carla looked at him.

"Anthony, I have no idea, but the war there was a long time ago. This is a safe hotel."

"Sure, sure," he said. "I just read about that incident, and I was curious."

"Anthony, are you sure you're ready for this?"

"No question," he said. "It's just that I've become fascinated by the history of the place and aware of how ignorant of it I've been."

"Then I should not have to advise you of the high crime rate, the need to stay in tourist friendly areas and the absolute necessity not to wander or travel anywhere at night on foot. You'll also understand why Mr. Hernandez will accompany you wherever you go, day and night and that he is armed."

"Isn't that going a bit overboard?" asked Anthony.

"No," Carla said. "It's not."

Anthony decided to take her at her word.

"Included in these papers," Carla went on, "are a voucher for the hotel for the first week and a separate voucher for or as much as two more weeks. That shouldn't be necessary, but it's better to plan for changes now rather than later. Mr. Hernández's fees and use of the car will be billed directly to my company. All you have to do is sign the voucher he presents to you.

"David will give you the names and locations of the government agencies and the personnel you'll have to meet. He'll also provide all the forms necessary for you to claim Martin's remains and take them out of the country. The MATES organization is working with the government to have the remains secured and packaged for transportation. They are to be checked as your personal belongings on your return flight. You cannot carry them on board. One of the forms David will give you is for the airline. With that form they will accept the sealed remains and deliver them to you upon your arrival in New York. Exactly how that is done will be explained in the instructions you get from David."

"You're very thorough," said Anthony.

"We're almost done," she said as she reached into her briefcase and pulled out a black vinyl bag with a drawstring that she placed on the table.

"This is a cell phone that is set up to place calls either locally while you are in El Salvador, or back to the U.S. from there. It is already programmed with the numbers of the San Salvador Sheraton, U.S. Embassy, and the local government office David will put you in contact with, and the private number of Mr. Hernández."

"Is Mr. Hernández also known as Matt Damon?"

"Anthony, this is serious business."

"I know, I'm sorry," he said, smiling.

Carla continued, "The phone is also programmed to call US numbers including my office, David's office, your home number, Bernadette's cell and Sarah's number in case you want to give her an update on your progress."

Anthony reddened, but said nothing right away.

"Can I ask you something?" he said after a pause.

"That's what I'm here for," said Carla.

"Did David?… Is part of why you and David?… Did David have his? … Is David after Berna-"

"Anthony, stop. If you have any questions about David and your wife you should ask one of them."

"You're right, I'm sorry. It's just that…"

Carla was quiet for a moment then spoke.

"David cheated on me about two years ago. It was brief. I confronted him, and he admitted it. We had counseling, and worked through it. I forgave him, or at least I thought I did. But the trust was broken and I couldn't accept that. We went on as usual, but our marriage was never the same. We both knew it. I started seeing someone, first out of anger, revenge perhaps, but eventually it became something else. My own definition is respectful love. Respect is something that's very important to me. Obviously my relationship with David changed. We both understood what was going on without talking about it. I would tolerate his flirting, and even his dalliances. He wouldn't question me."

Anthony looked into her eyes not wanting to ask the question, but wanting to hear the answer. Carla paused, and then spoke.

"As far as I know, David has never made any serious advances toward Bernadette. Now let's get back to business. I had mentioned access to funds should they be necessary to motivate the bureaucrats to expedite matters. This envelope contains instructions about how to retrieve the money. All you have to do is go to the Banco Cuscatlán. Their locations and everything you need to know is in this envelop along with a card that looks like an ATM card. You'll have to give the card to a bank officer if you want funds to be transferred. Do you have any questions?"

Anthony thought a minute.

"Yes, I do, but I need a cup of coffee first. It will take me five minutes. Can I get you anything?"

"I'll have a cup, black, please, and I'd like to use the bathroom."

"Sure, you know where it is. I'll make the coffee."

Anthony was seated at the kitchen table when Carla returned.

"The coffee smells good," she said. "So, let's get to your questions."

"Well, the plans and accommodations look great. I may come up with a question or two before I leave, and obviously you have been very thorough..."

"But?" she said.

"You haven't made any arrangements or provided instructions for me to get to the clinic where Martin was killed."

"Anthony, the place was burned to the ground. This wasn't Mount Sinai Hospital. This was something between a shack and a bungalow. There's nothing there to see or learn from. And it has nothing to do with collecting his remains."

"Yes, I know, but I want to see it. I want to see the people that knew him, the people in the area around the clinic."

"I don't think that's a good idea," said Carla. "You're a stranger to these people. If you ask questions, the likelihood of getting answers is low. Besides it's far from San Salvador which is fairly cosmopolitan. In the city, you may have to put up with government bureaucrats, but overall you'll be safe. You'll find good food and water. The people there are wonderfully hospitable despite having their civil war embedded in their psyches. And that probably holds true in the small towns and villages. It's just that they are less controlled. It's not easy to tell where you're safe and where you're not."

"Carla, this is very important to me. I want to see the place where Martin worked. Please help me do that."

"Anthony, this is not a good idea."

"Please, Carla. Set it up for me. I'll take full responsibility for my safety. I'll sign any waivers you need to protect you or your company."

"It's not my company I'm concerned about. Why do you have to this?"

"I don't know how to answer that exactly."

"Does Bernadette know this part of your plan?"

Anthony looked straight at her.

"Oh Jesus," she said. "David said you might be difficult."

"Like you said, the schmuck is a good lawyer," said Anthony.

"If I do this, I want an agreement from you that Mr. Hernández will be with you twenty-four/ seven," she said.

Anthony smiled, "How can I turn down having Matt Damon at my side? Thanks Carla," he said.

"I'll have to put some work into this, but I should have what you need in a day or two."

"I can't thank you enough," he said.

"You just better get there and back in one piece or I'll really kick your ass."

Anthony looked closely at Carla and realized that he had misjudged her. While he thought she was attractive, he had thought she was a bit of an exhibitionist, and used her looks and wiles to achieve success in business and relationships. He realized now that she was very professional, took her work seriously and put a lot of importance on her friendships and relationships.

Bernadette arrived home as Carla started putting her things away and Anthony collected the materials she brought. She was surprised to see Carla, but after she understood what had taken place, she invited her to stay for dinner. Carla graciously declined, gave her a hug and left.

"So," Bernadette said, "when are you leaving?"

"It looks like Sunday if all goes well with my meeting with David and his partners tomorrow."

"And when are you supposed to get back?"

"The following Saturday, assuming that all goes according to plan.

"Will you need a ride to the airport?"

"No, Carla has arranged for a car to pick me up."

"Great. That's just fucking great, Anthony," she said.

Chapter 22

On Tuesday morning, Anthony waited for Bernadette to leave before he prepared for his visit to David at his Manhattan office. He tried to keep Bernadette's open hostility out of his mind and hoped she would cool down before Sunday. He knew that a gesture on his part such as sending her flowers or buying a gift would just further piss her off. At the same time, he could not back down from his quest. Traveling into the city, his excitement about his unfolding adventure grew. His enthusiasm about going to El Salvador had been sensed by Bernadette and it angered her. She was excluded from it, annoyed by her friends' response to him, and concerned that her world was being shaken by forces she didn't fully understand. Anthony knew that any explanation he could provide about what motivated him would only feed her anger and fears. Ignoring her concerns was best for now.

When he arrived at the offices of David's firm, he could not help but be impressed. Located on the thirty sixth floor of a midtown Park Avenue building, the spacious reception center led directly to a glass enclosed conference room with a commanding view of downtown Manhattan extending to New York Harbor. The receptionist invited him into the room and asked if he would like something to drink, or a newspaper to read, or anything else while the attorneys were on their way. He helped himself to a bottle of water from an iced container atop the wet bar and thanked her. She turned and left as Anthony looked at the marble pedestals supporting the glass top of the conference table and the sculptures placed at strategic positions in the room. The message to prospective clients was clear: "We are world class." David was obviously doing very well. Apparently he had enough clout to get assistance from his colleagues in a pro bono venture in which the firm would not normally get involved *No wonder I hate the bastard*, he thought.

David entered a few minutes later followed by a colleague who introduced himself as Russell Collins. Russ, as he called himself, was the firm's chief counsel for operations in Central America and the Caribbean. The agricultural exports from these regions into the U.S. were substantial and the complex export/import regulations, banking operations and transportation requirements necessitated legal services provided by the firm. David allowed that Russ could even come up with genuine Cuban cigars from time to time.

"So, Anthony," Russ began, "David has given me a summary of the purpose of your trip to El Salvador. We have prepared a number of forms and letters for you to bring with you. Some will require your signature, which if you can provide before you leave, we can notarize and keep on file to save you the trouble of doing so. Each form or letter has a side memo that explains its purpose, who will likely ask for it, and what you can expect when it's presented. There are copies of each in English and Spanish. There's also a set of anticipated questions and answers that you should study before any meetings there. Nothing very complicated, but errors in form and procedure are a bureaucrat's dream especially when dealing with Americans. I understand that you have personal knowledge of the deceased and a means of contact with his spouse in the event that becomes necessary."

"Yes, that's correct," said Anthony.

"If you like we can go through the documents right now, take care of the signatures and be good to go."

They all agreed and a secretary who was a registered Notary Public was brought in. All the papers were completed in fifteen minutes.

"That was easy," said Anthony.

David spoke. "Carla tells me you want to visit the site of the clinic where Martin was killed."

"Yes, I do," said Anthony.

"Nothing remains of the clinic," said David.

"Yes, I know," said Anthony. As if to justify his intentions, Anthony offered, "Perhaps, I can set up a plaque or something as a remembrance of the clinic and Martin."

"It turns out that the MATES agency has that covered," said David.

"Well, I would like to go anyway. In addition to the business of acquiring Martin's remains, I intend to do so."

"Anthony," asked Russ, "How much do you know about El Salvador?"

"As much as I could learn over the weekend."

"Well," Russ continued in what Anthony interpreted as the most condescending tone he had ever heard, "It is a very complex place with a rather sordid history, and not without its dangers once you get away from the capital or major cities."

"Well," said Anthony in return, "I don't know about sordid, but it seems to me that El Salvador, especially because of its history is like a microcosm of the world. Everything people or rather governments can do to fuck up the world has been done there. It's like a laboratory experiment of how not to construct a society, or at least an experiment that demonstrates the consequences of oppressing a benign populace. Despite having this place to study, we have learned nothing. Fifteen years after a long and horrible civil war, there is still rampant poverty, an absence of civil rights and the brutalization of many innocents."

"That sounds a little preachy from someone who has discovered the place over the weekend," said Russ. "I have spent a considerable amount of time in El Salvador, Guatemala, Nicaragua, Honduras, Costa Rica and so on. Trust me, each of those countries has its own identity, and they're not easy for an outsider to understand."

"I'm sure that's true," said Anthony, "but, some things seem so simple that not understanding them boggles the mind."

"Well, there you go," said Russ. "They appear simple to you because they are too complex to understand without being a student of their cultures."

"Okay, let's see where I have it wrong," said Anthony. "The Spanish conquistadors came to El Salvador in the early 1500s. They found an indigenous people, the Pipils I believe they were called, most of whom are extinct today. Their economy was based on agriculture, but they cultivated knowledge of astronomy, mathematics and hieroglyphics. The conquistadors laid claim to the land and their superior armies subordinated the Pipils, took over their land and built plantations that exported crops to Europe at a great profit. The plantations and most of the land were ultimately acquired by a small group of Europeans called the Fourteen Families who used any means possible to suppress the natives who had become enslaved to work the land. Three Hundred years after the conquistadors arrived, El Salvador gained its independence from Spain, but strangely enough, a small segment of the population, all European descendants, retained all the wealth and continued to use the indigenous population as slaves.

"After slavery was eventually abolished, the descendants of the Pipils were landless and impoverished. From that point forward there were a series of rebellions starting in the 1800's that were brutally suppressed. Fast forward to 1980 and we have diverse groups of oppressed people uniting to rebel and ultimately start a civil war which lasts for twelve years. During this time our country, the home of the free and the brave, poured millions of dollars to support the regime in power despite death squads and atrocities that make Guantanamo look like a day care center. Our government was afraid that these people who didn't have enough to eat might expand the communist threat that was growing in Nicaragua.

"So now we have peace in El Salvador, the Pipils represent less than five percent of the population, the country's most famous product is homicide and its best known export to the U.S. is the Mara Salvatrucha, considered one of the most brutal gangs operating in Los Angeles competing toe to toe with the Columbian and Mexican drug cartels and into the trafficking of illegal immigrants. All of which is an unintended consequence of the conquistadors fucking with the farmers who were minding their own business.

"Today El Salvador has an average of ten murders a day making it one of the most violent countries in the world. After a previous government ran a post civil war society that didn't do enough to stop crime with its "Hard Hand" program, which was a euphemism for curtailing civil rights, the next administration introduced its "Super Hard Hand" program which I am sure will solve everything. And while all this is going on, the core of the Salvadoran people are by so many accounts the nicest, kindest and hardest working people despite being subjected to brutality from the government on one side and the gangs on the other. Now, just what part of this complex culture, don't I understand?"

Russell's face had turned a pale white while Anthony was running off at the mouth and his color had still not returned. He looked to David who appeared very matter of fact and not at all upset.

"And why are we helping him?" Russell asked David.

"I guess he was trying to make the point that he knows what he's getting into," said David, "and he still wants us to help him go to the site of the clinic. One of the papers in the packet he signed was a release saying that we had advised him against it and that he would do so only at his own peril. So before we hear any more about the tragic consequences of the Pipils, let's give him the information he needs, wish him well and get back to work. All of us will have the clear understanding that the firm's efforts are exclusively to assist Anthony in retrieving Martin's remains and today's history lesson never happened. Can you both agree to that?"

"Of course," said Russell, "and since your friend has such an in depth knowledge of the Salvadoran experience, I shall excuse myself."

"Yes," said Anthony, "and I apologize for the outburst. I realize that you're extending yourselves to help, and I am sorry if I appeared ungrateful."

"Apology accepted," said Russell. With that he left the conference room.

Anthony looked at David.

"I hope I didn't get you in any trouble," he said.

"You didn't," said David, "but I'll tell you what you did. You alienated a lifeline. If you get in trouble down there - and after listening to you this morning, I think that's a great likelihood - the guy who could do the most to get you out of trouble whether it be with the authorities or gangs is Russell. I think it's safe to say that you pissed him off."

"Maybe the difference between him and me is that I care," said Anthony.

"No, Anthony," said David. "The difference is that he's a grownup."

Taking Flight

Chapter 23

From Wednesday on, Anthony continued to learn more than he would ever need to know about El Salvador. Not even the unread contract from SkyTel could detract him from the study of his obsession. One note that caught his attention was that despite measures taken by the current regime to ban guns in public places, some estimated 300,000 illegal firearms were carried by the citizenry of El Salvador. Suddenly, knowing that Mr. Hernandez would be armed seemed more comforting than alarming. Anthony thought it was ironic, if not a little spooky, that he would be leaving on November 16, the anniversary of the killing of six Jesuit priests, their housekeeper and her daughter at the Jesuit University campus in El Salvador. It was thought, but never proven, that they were killed by a death squad believed to be operating with the consent, if not the direction of the government. Carla, meanwhile, had sent him the information he needed to find the destroyed MATES clinic outside Perquín, a town of less than 6,000 people that he would research further.

If Anthony could wrap up his mission in a week or so, he would be back in time to celebrate Thanksgiving with Bernadette and her family, a chore that united them in their need for patience and tolerance. Family gatherings at his in-laws were something she found more difficult to deal with than he did.

Bernadette had remained cool to Anthony despite his efforts to reach an accord before he left on Sunday. She went through the motions of being cordial while making it clear that she was pissed. She turned down suggestions that they go out to dinner during the week because she was tired after a day at work. She declined a similar invitation for Saturday night, because there would be several last minute preparations for what she referred to as "your adventure." When Saturday arrived, he insisted on talking about his trip and the strain it was putting on their relationship. She resisted at first, but finally gave in.

"You just don't get it, Anthony," she said. "Here you are going off on this adventure like the Lone Ranger or some damn action hero in order to find something meaningful in your life. And you made the decision to do this without even talking it over with me. Did you give any thought to how I might feel about it? Do you know what that means? It means that your life with me is not meaningful enough. That all the talks we've had about our goals, about starting a family next year, about how we would be different from our parents, about how we would grow old together, about how we would live the different stages of our lives, and about how we would always be best friends and partners was all bullshit! And to make matters worse, you have broadcasted that to my oldest and dearest friends.

"I have supported you through your job loss and the disappointments from your old business buddies and here you are going off into the sunset and leaving me alone. My family and friends must be thinking 'he can't be very happy at home if he is going to Central America to shave a few weeks off having the remains of a dead friend returned to the U.S.;' *my* friend's husband by the way. 'Why he's even risking his job in order to do it.' That's what has caused *me* to put a strain on our relationship."

"You are looking at this the wrong way," he began.

"The wrong way?" she interrupted. "What part is wrong? Is it the part about your search for something meaningful? Is it the part about you wanting to be a hero? Is it the part about you making this decision without discussing it with me first? Is it the part about how this overrides everything we've planned together? Is it the part about how I have supported you and would never have done something like this to you? Is it the part about how other people see this? Just what part am I looking at the wrong way?"

"Let's not leave it like this before I go away," he said.

"Why is that?" she asked. "Because something might happen to you down there? Because it is not the safest place to be? Because I might end up without you? Did it ever occur to you that these are reasons we should have talked about this first?"

"The danger part is grossly exaggerated," he said.

"Sure. That's why Carla assured me that you will have an armed bodyguard with you the whole time."

Anthony looked surprised.

"Oh, you don't think Carla and I talk? You don't think I ask about things like your safety? Have you completely blocked out who I am and what you mean to me?"

"Look, I am sorry for not discussing it first. You're right. I didn't consider you when I volunteered to go. I should have. I was just as shaken up as you and everybody else about Martin's death. I was on autopilot when we were at Sarah's. I just wasn't thinking clearly."

"If we had talked, and I asked you not to go, if I pleaded with you, would you have changed your mind?"

Anthony looked at her and paused before answering.

"I'm sorry. To be truthful, I still believe it's the right thing to do," he said.

"Well that's not good enough," Bernadette said.

"That's the best I can do," was all he could say.

Bernadette spent the rest of the day shopping and killing time away from the house while Anthony made up a list of what he would need for the trip. He packed everything except his shaver which he would use and pack in the morning. He put the important papers, travel documents, special cell phone and some books in the black shoulder bag he normally used for his laptop computer. He picked out the clothes he would wear on the flight; jeans, blue plaid shirt, his best walking shoes, light gray sweater and a gray tweed sport coat. He was ready to go, but his sense of adventure was replaced with a hollow feeling not unlike the one he had the day he lost his job.

Anthony did not sleep well Saturday night. At 5:30 A.M. he got out of bed not sure of how long he had actually slept. He was careful not to wake Bernadette. Perhaps he was afraid she would not get up to see him off. He tried to write a conciliatory note before he left, but all he could come up with was "I'll call you from the Sheraton. Love, Anthony."

The limo arrived at 6:15 A.M. Anthony opened the door before the driver could knock. He had slipped a Time magazine and a Phillip Roth paperback into the outer compartment of his shoulder bag for airplane reading. His other bag was a rolling overnight suitcase that he would carry on board. At this time on a Sunday morning, getting to JFK by 7:00 A.M. would be a piece of cake.

Anthony sat quietly in the back of the limo as they went from his home to the airport in the opposite direction of his route to work. This observation reminded him that he had still not read the contract Henry Trenholme had sent. He had considered reading it on the plane, but thought it would be better to do once he reached his destination. When the car arrived at the airport, the place was much busier than Anthony expected. He offered a tip to the driver who declined with a smile, telling him that it was all taken care of. The United flight was operated by an outfit called TACA that used the UAL terminal and personnel in New York.

The check-in in process went smoothly. Anthony was one of a dozen or so travelers in Business Class. His fellow passengers appeared to be a mix of Americans and Salvadorans. There were no women in this section of the plane. The Americans, probably businessmen, were dressed casually in jeans and khakis while the Salvadorans were dressed in their Sunday finest. To Anthony, all the Salvadorans appeared to have a slight build including the passengers who passed through on their way to Coach. Some had fine facial features; others had coarser features hinting at their indigenous heritage. Another observation Anthony made was that most of the Coach bound Salvadorans had bad haircuts.

Anthony's thoughts went back to his childhood when his father would take him to Alfredo's Barber Shop in their Brooklyn neighborhood. His father would be welcomed and serviced by Alfredo, the owner and barber of the first chair. His son Luigi was the barber of the second chair. Anthony was assigned to Luigi who had very bad breath and didn't know how to cut hair. When Luigi would stand alongside Anthony and make idle conversation, Anthony, trapped as he was, would look down and hold his breath for as long as he possibly could. In the end, Luigi's foul breath found its way into Anthony's nostrils after which Anthony would ask for a tissue so he could blow his nose.

The part of the haircut Anthony hated most was when

Luigi soaked the side of his face and ears with soapy shaving cream. After trimming Anthony's sideburns, Luigi would remove the residual soap with a towel always leaving some in and around Anthony's ears. When the haircut was over and Anthony politely thanked Luigi, he would immediately go the restroom to dry his ears and examine the pin-up calendars on the back of the restroom door. He usually had to wait another ten minutes or so for Alfredo to finish his father's haircut. Once, on the way home, he asked his father why he always had to get a haircut from Luigi. His father explained that that way they could get their haircuts at the same time. When Anthony protested saying he did not like Luigi's haircuts, his father replied by telling him that the man has to make a living. That was the last they spoke of Luigi's haircuts. For the longest time, Anthony imagined adulthood as freedom from Luigi's scissors, soap machine and horrible breath.

The flight served an American breakfast accompanied by Salvadoran coffee which was good not just in comparison to airline standards, but to Anthony's own. Anthony read his magazine and made a false start of the Roth novel before dozing off. He was awakened by the gentle hand and voice of the steward asking him to put up his seat tray in preparation for landing. The pilot set the plane down smoothly and taxied toward the terminal. As they approached it, Anthony saw a large outdoor sign that read "Welcome to Aeropuerto Internacional Comalpa." Anthony had arrived in El Salvador.

Upon deplaning, Anthony stopped at the first restroom he could find. After collecting his suitcase and completing passage through Passport Control, he walked a narrow corridor that led to the airport proper. He immediately saw a sign bearing the name 'Mr. Anthony.' Mr. Hernández gave a disarming smile as Anthony looked at him and nodded. Mr. Hernández had already broken the mold by being a big man even by the most western standards. He was tall, with broad shoulders, broad mustache wearing an impeccably tailored white suit and white fedora that sat upon an excellent haircut. Jim Croce's lyrics found their way into Anthony's mind: *Big, bad Leroy Brown, biggest, baddest man in town.* Anthony's respect for Carla continued to grow. Mr. Hernández reached for Anthony's rolling suitcase with one hand and offered to shake his hand with the other.

"Welcome to El Salvador, Mr. Anthony," with only a slight trace of accent that added charm to the way he spoke.

"Thank you for meeting me," replied Anthony. "It's good to be here."

"Come, I will take you to your hotel. After you are checked in, I will give you a brief tour of San Salvador. Then we will have dinner and you can rest until we go tomorrow to the Government Offices where you have an appointment at 9:00 A.M."

"It's really not necessary for you to spend your entire evening with me," said Anthony.

"Señor, the Señora Carla was very clear about what we have to do. With all respect, she is boss."

"Gracias, Mr. Hernández. I appreciate all that you are doing for me. Please call me Anthony."

"You are very welcome, Mr. Anthony. Now if you follow me, we will go to the hotel. The drive will take maybe a little less than one hour. You can relax until we get there."

The airport was as modern a fishbowl as any in the U.S. The tall windows were framed in white plaster on the inside and white stone on the outside. The concourse looked like any other with its mix of shops and food services. There was no shortage of police, or perhaps soldiers throughout the terminal. From the Customs exit to the rotunda and main concourse, guards with automatic weapons were present. Rather than conveying a sense of security, they gave the place an ominous ambiance.

Anthony's sense of excitement started to build again as they walked to the exit under the watchful eye of the ever present armed guards. He followed Mr. Hernández to a black old model Mercedes Benz with tinted windows all around. The shiny car was immaculate and the chrome trim appeared almost new. As Mr. Hernandez lifted Anthony's suitcase into the trunk, he bent forward slightly. Anthony could see a strip of leather under his suit coat that was surely part of a holster.

Mr. Hernández opened the rear door and gestured for Anthony to enter.

"I would prefer sitting up front, if you don't mind," Anthony said.

"As you wish, Señor," Mr. Hernández said with a trace of a smile.

As they drove on the highway leading to the city, Anthony was impressed by the modern road with two lanes in each direction separated by an island of trees and indigenous plants. Every few miles there were checkpoints with more armed guards. Their car was stopped only once. Mr. Hernández showed the guard some papers and was waved on. Along the way, there were huts with vendors selling coconuts, mangos and other varieties of fruits and vegetables at the side of the road. Closer to the city there were small buildings with corrugated roofing that could have been small factories, stores or houses. Since it was Sunday it was hard to tell if these places were built for commercial or residential purposes. In the city, there was instant congestion and air fouled by buses, taxis and a few trucks. Street vendors were present on every corner. Anthony commented to Mr. Hernández about the universal crowding of cities.

"Ah, this is good," he said. "Tomorrow when all the offices and businesses are open, the crowds will be much bigger."

Anthony noticed some buildings that were clearly ready to be demolished and others that looked new and modern.

Mr. Hernández commented, "We have earthquakes, Señor. Some are very bad. Sometimes the buildings are taken down very quickly, sometimes very slowly, or not at all."

Pointing to one in major disrepair, he said, "That building has been like that for six years."

A few turns later and they were on a tree lined boulevard. The street vendors were no longer visible. Instead, the street corners were occupied by guards similar to those at the airport. They pulled into the driveway of the Sheraton. Instead of going to the marked reception area, Mr. Hernández drove directly into the garage and parked on an upper level. They each grabbed a bag and took an elevator to the lobby. Upon entering the lobby, Anthony knew he was in a world class hotel. *If this is an emerging or developing country*, he thought, *they got this part right.*

Anthony was greeted warmly when he checked in. After a minimal number of forms and signatures, He and Mr. Hernández were escorted to his room by the bell boy. The room turned out to be an elegant suite with a luxuriously furnished living room, bedroom, a small separate dining area and a bathroom built for four.

"Very nice," he said aloud.

Mr. Hernández tipped the bell boy who turned on the air conditioner before he left.

"You can rest for a while," he said to Anthony. "My room is right next door. I will come to pick you up at Five O'clock. I will give you a call first. If you need anything before then, do not hesitate to call me."

Mr. Hernández left. Anthony thought about making some calls, but instead, he removed his jacket, shoes and sweater, laid down on the bed and fell right to sleep.

Taking Flight

Chapter 24

Anthony was startled awake by the unfamiliar ring of the phone. Two loud, high pitched bursts of sound interrupted a dream he was having wherein he, Edgar Albright, and Henry Trenholme were arguing about Anthony's stock options while Bernadette and David sat quietly in chairs along the wall. The dialogue was unintelligible and faded as soon as the sounds entered his consciousness. He found the phone on the nightstand to the right of the bed and picked up the receiver.

Still groggy, he answered with an uncertain, "Hello?"

"Mr. Anthony," said Mr. Hernández on the other end of the line, "I thought it was time to take a little tour of the city before we went to dinner."

"I'm sorry. I fell asleep. Can we skip the tour for now? I'd like to freshen up before dinner and make a few calls."

"Yes, of course."

"Thank you. I hope I didn't mess up your plans for the evening," Anthony said apologetically.

"Not at all, Señor. Perhaps I should meet with you in one hour."

"That would be perfect," said Anthony. "By the way, how shall I dress for dinner?"

"For tonight, we shall have dinner in the main dining room of the hotel. A jacket and tie are required."

"Thank you again, Mr. Hernández, I'll be ready in one hour.

"Mr. Anthony?"

"Yes?"

"These calls you will make. Will you use your cell phone?"

"Yes."

"Good, that is best for calls of a personal nature."

When he hung up, Anthony realized that Mr. Hernández was advising him that the hotel phone might be bugged.

Anthony showered and shaved, pleased that the hotel used the same house voltage as in the U.S. He was also pleased that the currency was U.S. Dollars so he wouldn't have to go through the currency exchange process. He put on a luxurious guest robe that was hanging on the bathroom door and then laid out the fresh shirt and pants he would wear to dinner. He hung up his remaining jackets, pants and shirts in the closet nook, but left everything else in the suitcase. There was a small safe on the floor of the nook. Following the instructions on its door, he programmed a four digit combination code to secure it for later use. Anthony took the cell phone and some notebooks out of his carry-on bag and sat on the bed. He called Bernadette first.

"You have reached the Bartolo residence. Please leave a message at the beep," replied the answering machine.

"Bernadette, it's me. Pick up if you're there, please."

After no reply, Anthony continued.

"Okay, I guess you're out. I just wanted you to know that I'm at the hotel in San Salvador. Everything about the trip went smoothly including being picked up by Mr. Hernández who seems like a very nice guy. I'm safe, comfortable and will be going to dinner shortly with Mr. Hernández. You know how to reach me if you need to. I'll call you tomorrow. Love ya. Bye."

He dialed another programmed number.

"Hello, Carla speaking."

"Hey, Carla, it's Anthony."

"Hi Anthony, how was your trip?"

"Well, I was just calling to let you know that everything went very smoothly. The ride to the airport and the flight were on time. Mr. Hernández, who seems like a really nice guy by the way, was there to meet me and took me to San Salvador straight away. I'm settled in the hotel which is more than was necessary, and we're headed for dinner in a few minutes. I just wanted to thank you again for the job you did in arranging all this."

"I'm glad it went well, but quite frankly I'll be a lot happier when you're out of there and back home."

"I'll be fine," he said.

"Good. Be well, and call me if you need anything."

"Right. Thanks again, Carla. Bye."

"Bye, Anthony."

He decided to make one more call.

He punched in the number and waited for two rings before the familiar voice answered.

"Hi Mom. It's Anthony."

"Well, it's certainly been a long time."

"Yeah, well I've been busy."

"So what's wrong?"

"Nothing's wrong. I'm just calling to say hello."

Anthony's mother had moved to Naples, Florida six months after his father had died from a heart attack that followed a massive stroke three days before.

"How's Florida?"

"Lots of Jews and Cubans."

Anthony smiled to himself. *Some things never change,* he thought. Anthony detested his mother's views of the world and her prejudices. He never forgave her stance against Rita. He also never forgave what she had done to his father eighteen years ago by having an affair. His father had been the strong, silent type who weakened after that, never confronting her, but never recovering from it. Anthony couldn't allow that maybe she had just found a compelling love that she couldn't deny. He mentally cast her as a whore as the old biddies in their neighborhood would have done.

"It's not as bad as Miami, but they're all over the place, she said."

"Well, Brooklyn was a melting pot. You should feel right at home," he said. "Besides, it was your choice to move there."

"I couldn't stand the cold anymore."

"Maybe you should have moved to Arizona."

"What am I, a cowboy?"

"I'm calling from El Salvador, Mom. The weather here isn't bad considering that it's November."

"El Salvador. Isn't that where they had the war after killing the Bishop? Why didn't you go to Aruba, or the Bahamas, Bermuda even?"

"Mom, it's business. I'm not on vacation."

"Must be some business. What are they doing now, putting computers in bananas?"

"Have you been well?" he asked.

"Except for the usual aches and pains, I'm fine. Am I going to see you for Thanksgiving? Is that why you're calling?"

"No. We'll be going to Bernadette's family's house."

"Well, how about Christmas?"

"Maybe. I'll have to see, but for now, don't count on it. Do you want to consider coming up?"

"In December? You know I hate the cold."

"Well, we'll talk about the holidays as they get closer."

"Anthony?"

"Yes?"

"Are you sure nothing's wrong?"

"I'm sure, Mom. I just wanted to say hello. I have to get going now. Take care of yourself and stay warm."

"Call me again soon."

"I will. Bye now."

"Bye, Anthony."

Anthony hung up realizing she had not once asked about Bernadette. *How did my father stand it?* he asked himself.

Anthony finished getting dressed and put the cell phone, notebooks, papers and other items from the carry-on in the safe. He wore what little jewelry he had, and carried his cash and one credit card in his wallet. He was wiping his dress loafers with the shoe cloth provided by the hotel when there was a knock at the door. He put the cloth down, grabbed his sport coat and opened the door to see Mr. Hernández waiting.

"It is a good practice, Mr. Anthony, to ask who it is before opening the door. From this point on, I will knock like this" he demonstrated three rapid knocks on the door followed by a pause and a fourth knock. "But it is still good to ask who it is," he said as he entered the room.

"Is there really a reason for concern?" Anthony asked feeling like he was being scolded.

Mr. Hernández scrutinized the room, picked up the hotel phone listened to the dial tone and put it back down.

"It is not a usual occurrence, Mr. Anthony, but kidnappings have occurred from time to time. It is always good to be cautious."

"Kidnappings in a hotel like this?" Anthony asked incredulously.

"Guests are seldom kidnapped from cheap hotels."

"Point taken," said Anthony.

They left the room and were heading toward the elevator when Mr. Hernández opened a door leading to a stairwell. Although they were on the fourth floor, Mr. Hernández said he preferred the stairs.

"They are less confining," he said, "and there are fewer surprises when you open the doors."

Anthony wasn't sure if Mr. Hernández was overstating the implied security risks, but decided not to question him again. At the lobby level they exited the stairwell and walked toward the elegant dining room. They were greeted by the Maitre D' who obviously knew Mr. Hernández. He took them directly to a corner booth distinguished by a placard designating it as reserved. Once seated, Mr. Hernández suggested they have some wine. Anthony agreed and immediately deferred to Mr. Hernández to make a selection. He spoke in Spanish to the Maitre D' who seemed very pleased. The Maitre D' summoned the sommelier and gave him instructions. When the sommelier turned away, the Maitre D' repeated his welcome to the guests and advised them that their waiter would be Raul, who would be attending to them momentarily.

Anthony wasn't sure if this was standard treatment at this restaurant, or if it was turned up a notch because he was with Mr. Hernández.

"This is a very nice restaurant," said Anthony. "They seem to know you well."

"I am here quite often with clients," said Mr. Hernández. "In San Salvador, people who do business together treat each other well to maintain the business."

"Well, I appreciate your bringing me here and having dinner with me."

Taking Flight

Mr. Hernández studied Anthony for a moment before speaking again.

"You are different from most of the clients that Señora Carla sends to me, as she said you would be."

"Oh, how so?" asked Anthony.

"First, let us prepare our order. This restaurant has fine meats and fish. There are a few Salvadoran specialties on the menu, but to be sure, those will be better in some small places where we will dine in the next few days. The clientele here are mostly from the U.S. and Europe, a few from Asia, so the local dishes are not the most popular, or the best."

"In that case, I could enjoy a good steak, medium rare with side dishes as you suggest."

"Very good. In my case, I shall have the lamb which is prepared very well here."

The sommelier arrived with the wine. He offered Anthony the cork, which he took, examined and sniffed before nodding. A sample of wine was delicately poured into Anthony's glass.

"I think you should do the honors, Mr. Hernández."

Mr. Hernández smiled in acknowledgement.

"Please. You shall do for me the honor," he said.

Anthony sipped the wine, letting it roll over his tongue and against his palate.

"Wonderful," he said, feeling a little self conscious, wondering if anyone had ever sent back a bottle.

The sommelier and Mr. Hernández seemed pleased and the wine glasses were filled. The two men toasted to their good health and good business. No sooner were they done when the waiter, Raul, introduced himself to Anthony and welcomed his guests. Mr. Hernández ordered their dinner in Spanish. Raul asked one or two questions, also in

Spanish. Mr. Hernández answered and Raul disappeared.

"So," Anthony said, "you were saying I am different than Carla's usual clients."

"Yes. Yes. Usually they are, let me see… They are what I think you would call uptight, tense, and somewhat nervous in their surroundings here. They seem to be expecting to be kidnapped, and you are thinking that is a silly idea. Perhaps, because they come here on matters related to business whereas your visit is more personal in nature."

His comments reminded Anthony of why he was here.

"My business here is personal. It is the result of the death of a friend," he said somberly.

"Yes. Señora Carla has told me fully of your purpose. I offer you my sincere condolences."

"Thank you," said Anthony. "Perhaps, we should talk about tomorrow."

"I would recommend that we enjoy our dinner first. A good meal is best when talk of business is put aside. After our meal, we shall have a coffee, perhaps a brandy and then we shall talk about tomorrow."

"Sounds good to me," said Anthony.

Dinner arrived shortly. They kept the conversation light. Anthony told Mr. Hernández that he had read books about the history and culture of El Salvador, and that he found them fascinating. He said that he was a little puzzled by what seemed like contradictions about the people here, and he hoped to learn more about them in the next few days. Mr. Hernández talked admiringly about the United States. After a pause he remarked that Anthony's country and people seemed to have contradictions of their own, and perhaps they could discuss them over the next few days as well.

Anthony agreed. "I'll look forward to it."

When dinner was finished, Anthony complemented Mr. Hernández on the excellence of the meal. They ordered brandy and coffee to wash it all down.

"Your mission here, Mr. Anthony, this is good. This is a noble thing to look after your friend," said Mr. Hernández.

"It's not so noble" replied Anthony, "as much as a sense of duty. Someone had to do this, and I was the most available person."

"Señora Carla said you would be modest about your mission, and that you would know as much about El Salvador as perhaps me by the time you left."

"I doubt that very much, but I admit that I have found the little I have learned of this country to be very interesting. However, let's not talk so much about me. How have you come to this profession? Have you ever been to the U.S.? Do you have a family here?"

Mr. Hernández smiled. "Many questions, just as the Señora said."

"I don't mean to be rude, but I would like to know more about you, especially if you're going to be helping me these next few days."

Anthony studied Mr. Hernández for the first time. He guessed he was about fifty. He noticed a vertical scar on his neck slightly angled from front to back as it disappeared under his shirt collar. Mr. Hernández looked at Anthony carefully and spoke in surprisingly candid terms.

"Most men my age," he began, "were on one side of the war or the other. I was with the rebels, who the U.S. government used to call the guerillas, or insurgents. Before the war, I went to the university. My parents were modest farmers, but I received a scholarship, only one of a few offered by the government that year. I studied civil engineering and was working for the government building bridges and buildings. Shortly after the war broke out, I joined the other side and began blowing up the bridges I helped build.

"I became a Colonel in the army. I had men who became very good at destroying things. To protect ourselves, we also became good at using weapons… and our hands. When the war was finally over, I could not go back to my profession. To sit with papers or to go to building sites was too confining. Besides, the government would never trust me completely with critical structures. I would always be under its careful study."

"Study?" asked Anthony.

"As I said, you were on one side or the other. Eventually, everyone wore themselves out and a peace agreement was reached, but does not mean that one side trusted the other. So I decided to use the skills I learned and become a private businessman helping wealthy visitors to El Salvador. It gives me the freedom to go and come as I please and the pay is very good, much better than for an engineer."

"I'm not a wealthy businessman," said Anthony.

"Perhaps, but you come as a friend of Señora Carla which is more important. She sends much business to me, usually lawyers. The U.S. it seems has many lawyers."

"Have you been to the U.S.?"

"Only once. To New York, but I am a Salvadoran. I am tied to the earth here. I may visit the U.S. again, but always, I will return. My family is here."

"Tell me about your family."

"Mr. Anthony, if you do not mind, I think it is time we talked about tomorrow."

As he said this, Mr. Hernández lifted the coffee pot that Raul had left and poured Anthony a cup. In doing so, his jacket parted slightly and Anthony could see a holster and weapon.

"That's the second time I could see you are wearing a gun. Wouldn't it be better to conceal it more?"

"Many people have guns here. It is better that they know I have one too. The question is whether I have two. That it something the other fellow does not know."

"Do you have another?" asked Anthony.

Mr. Hernández smiled again. "If I tell you, I have to kill you," he said, this time with a hearty laugh.

Anthony wasn't sure if he had learned that line from Carla or not, but Mr. Hernández surely enjoyed using it.

Once composed, Mr. Hernández signaled to Raul for another round of brandy. Raul complied and left the bottle. "It is time to discuss your schedule," said Mr. Hernández.

"Of course," said Anthony. "Thank you for telling me what you did."

"Very well then," Mr. Hernández started. "Tomorrow, we will meet with Mr. Calderón. He is the person, who on the papers you have is referred to as "The Director." I can help with any translation that may be necessary, but Calderón can speak English well when he chooses. He was on the other side, and does not trust me. He will not trust you very much either, but you must not take this personally. It is very important that you show him respect. You must refer to him as Mr. Director, or Sir. Never address or answer him without using a title. You must always speak softly to him as though he is your superior. Señora Carla says this may be difficult for you, but it is very important. If Calderón suspects that you are not showing respect, he will stop the meeting and postpone the discussion for several days at least."

"Sounds like we're in the old Soviet Union."

"Mr. Anthony, this is your mission. My advice is to help you be successful."

"I'm sorry. I shall follow your advice to the letter."

Mr. Hernández continued, "Señora Carla tells me that you have all the necessary papers to request and collect the remains of the deceased doctor and to transport them to the U.S. She emphasizes that you have been instructed to sign some papers only in Calderón's presence at the time he instructs you to sign them. As you go through the procedure, he will tell you what is to be done, and in what order. You must follow these steps exactly."

"I have the picture," said Anthony.

"Very good," said Mr. Hernández as he poured them each another brandy.

"May I ask one more question?" said Anthony.

"Yes, of course. As many as you like."

"You tell me the importance of calling Mr. Calderón by his title and treating him with respect. Yet, you call him "Calderón," or "Mr. Calderón.'" Why is that?"

"Because he is a traitor. Because he is a prick."

Now, it was Anthony's turn to smile. He was really getting to like this man. He raised his glass to propose a toast.

"To dealing with traitors and pricks."

Mr. Hernández acknowledged the toast, and then suggested that they turn in so that Mr. Anthony would be fully rested for the next day. They got up to leave before a check had arrived.

Anthony asked about the bill.

"It is trust, Señor. Raul will take care of putting it on my bill. Trust is everything among Salvadorans."

Taking Flight

As they exited the restaurant, Mr. Hernández bid farewell to Raul and the Maitre D'. They in turn bid farewell to Anthony. Mr. Hernández provided a survey of the lobby, pointing out the various shops that Anthony might find of interest. As they passed in front of the Concierge desk, Anthony nodded to the young man sitting there, who stood without saying anything. Mr. Hernández continued to the stairwell door.

"The exercise of the stairs will be good for our digestion," he said to Anthony.

"I could use that," replied Anthony, feeling good about the dinner, the brandy and the conversation with Mr. Hernández.

They climbed the four flights of stairs. Mr. Hernández casually peered through the small rectangular window in the door, seemingly out of habit, then opened it and stepped into the hallway. He escorted Anthony to his room, waited for Anthony to open the door with his key card and bid him goodnight.

"We shall have breakfast at 7:00 A.M. We will leave at 8:00 A.M. and hope that Calderón does not keep us waiting past 9:00 A.M. Have a good rest, Mr. Anthony, and welcome once again to El Salvador."

Anthony felt genuine warmth from Mr. Hernández as they shook hands. He thanked him again for the evening and shut the door. After removing his jacket and tie, Anthony opened the safe and took out the cell phone. He tried calling Bernadette again even though it was already 11:00 P.M. in Hempstead. Again the machine answered. Thinking she might be asleep, he did not leave a message. Anthony went back to the safe and removed the folder containing the papers David had prepared for him. While reviewing them, he found himself getting restless. He had already slept for a few hours earlier in the day. He was stimulated by the dinner conversation and his sense of adventure had returned. After staring at the same sheet of paper for ten minutes, Anthony put it down and decided to take a walk.

He pulled a sweater out of his bag, put the key card and his wallet in his pocket and left the room. He did not want to disturb Mr. Hernández. He applied his newly learned skill of using the stairway to descend to the lobby. Upon reaching it, he headed to the main entrance, passing the empty concierge desk on the way. He left the lobby through the revolving door and found the sidewalk and street well lighted and very quiet. He decided that once around the block would be enough. He turned left heading away from the main entrance of the hotel. He could hear his footsteps and feel the humidity that was not unlike that of Hempstead. As he reached the corner, he turned left again. There were ground floor shops whose entrances inside the hotel were closed for the night. The display windows were dimly lit, each with alarm system decals in the corners. An accordion style gate separated the display area from the shop interior. The sidewalk areas between the shop windows were much darker than the hotel's main entrance. When Anthony stopped to look at one of the displays, he thought he heard footsteps. He was already three quarters down the street, but was unsure of what was around the corner. He decided to go back to the main entrance. As he turned back, he was facing a tall skinny man in grey hooded sweatshirt.

"Americano?" said the man.

"Si," replied Anthony.

"Give me your dollars," the man said quickly as he pulled a gun from his belt.

"Okay, just take it easy," said Anthony as he reached for his wallet.

When the man saw Anthony reach for his rear pocket, he pointed the gun right at his face.

"Whoa," said Anthony. "This is my wallet. Money, money."

The man started waving his gun up and down.

"Down," he said. "Down."

Anthony instinctively kneeled down and put his hands up.

"I have dollars," he said quickly.

The man waived the gun up and down again.

Anthony showed him an open hand and said "Dollars" again as he slowly reached for his wallet. He lifted it carefully from his pocket showing the man that it was indeed a wallet.

The man responded by waving the gun up and down once more. As Anthony slowly placed the wallet on the ground, he noticed a movement from the other side of the street which was even darker than where he was. *Oh shit,* he thought, *there's more than one.* He could feel his heart racing. There was a pounding sensation in his ears.

"Watch, ring," the man said.

"Okay, pal. Just take it easy. You can have whatever you want," he said as he slipped off his watch and removed his wedding ring.

"Necklace," said the man, waving the gun again.

Anthony went blank for a second. "You mean a chain. I don't wear one. I don't have a necklace."

"Take off your shoes." Puzzled, Anthony put his hands behind him reaching for his loafers and took them off with as little body movement as he could manage. He put each shoe in front of him with the wallet, watch and ring.

The man stepped closer, raised the gun to Anthony's forehead and put his fingers inside Anthony's shirt collar. Satisfied that Anthony was not wearing a chain, he put his hand on Anthony's face and shoved him back so that Anthony was on his butt, his hands propping him up from behind and his feet in front of him. The man quickly moved to his knees to collect Anthony's belongings, leaning on the ground with his gun hand. He suddenly stopped moving and remained in a half kneeling position. Anthony raised his eyes to see Mr. Hernández holding a gun to the back of the robber's head.

"Pick up your belongings, Señor."

Anthony paused a minute before he realized that Mr. Hernández was talking to him. He scrambled to pick up his things.

"Am I glad to see you, Mr. Hernández," said Anthony.

Mr. Hernández gave him a foreboding look. He said something in Spanish to the man still kneeling on one knee. The man slowly gave up his gun. Mr. Hernández ordered the man to both knees, then removed the magazine from the handle of the gun, and emptied it of bullets. He removed the bullet from the chamber, returned the magazine to the handle and stuck the gun in the back of the man's belt. Then he picked the man up by his neck and shoved him with a Spanish epithet. The man took three or four off balance steps. Before running away, he turned and shouted something back to Mr. Hernández.

"How did you know to come?" asked Anthony.

"The concierge was to alert me if you left without me. Unfortunately, he was not at his desk when you passed, but Raul saw you leaving and called me. That was a very foolish thing to do, Mr. Anthony."

"I just wanted to take a walk. I thought the street

around the hotel would be safe," he explained feebly.

"Think of any street at night as you would think of taking a walk through Central Park at night."

"I'm sorry. I owe you my safety, perhaps my life."

"Instead, you can buy me a drink. The bar is still open and I think it will do us both good."

"That's a deal," said Anthony, truly grateful for not being further chastised for his error.

They were at the bar letting the warm flow of brandy calm them down. On the way in, Mr. Hernández had a chat with the concierge that was more than an embarrassment to the young man.

The events of the past few minutes were still going through Anthony's head.

"Why did you give him back his gun?" he asked.

Mr. Hernández looked at him somberly. "Most likely, he belongs to a gang. If he went back to them without his gun, he or they would have to retaliate. This way, he does not have to explain anything. If he remains silent, there is no retaliation and he does not lose face."

"What did he say when he left?"

"I will see you again, Hernández."

"Oh shit, I gave him your name!"

"Perhaps when he inquires about my name, it will encourage him to remain silent and forget this matter."

"Do you think that's likely?"

"We shall see."

"I am deeply and sincerely sorry for putting you in danger, Mr. Hernández. I won't do anything like that again."

"I was in the war for twelve years. This boy was perhaps not even born then. He is in more danger than me. We shall hope he will understand that. Now, we should turn in for the night and stay in our rooms until I call for you in the morning."

Anthony put out his hand which Mr. Hernández accepted, neither knowing that their lives would be linked forever.

Taking Flight

Chapter 25

Despite the several shots of brandy, Anthony was not ready to sleep after Mr. Hernández escorted him to his room. He showered again in an attempt to wind down, but the experience of the night took over his mind. He decided to prepare for his morning meeting. He opened the safe and removed the documents and instructions from David. He went over them as diligently as he would any business project. Going through the prepared questions and answers, Anthony was once again impressed by the thoroughness and professionalism demonstrated by David and his colleagues. By 4:00 A.M., he felt ready for every contingency. He put the papers he needed in the black bag. Anthony decided to stay awake rather than risk oversleeping again. He stretched after standing and elected to do some yoga exercises.

He began by slowly rotating his neck, reminding himself to breathe properly. He bent at the waist to stretch his back and leg muscles, then to the next position by dropping to his knees and extending his arms letting his hands and forehead rest on the floor. Next, he sat with his legs folded, back straight, his palms facing upward resting on his inner thighs and listened to his breathing trying to reach "Samadhi," the ultimate contemplative state free from any stimuli. For a moment he felt completely relaxed, but the events of the night once again penetrated his thoughts. Instead of concluding with "Namaste" or an "Om", he said "Fuck 'em all." He shaved again and finished getting dressed. He chose to wear his business suit and treat those he would encounter this morning as business adversaries that he would bend to his will. He was ready for war when Mr. Hernández called at 6:50 A.M. He picked up his black bag and waited for the special knock on the door.

The hotel dining room provided a buffet breakfast with a chef cooking eggs to order. Even though he had promised himself he would eat lightly this morning, Anthony found himself devouring eggs, bacon, biscuits and potatoes and washing them down with wonderful coffee. He followed this with a plate of tropical fruit to cool and cleanse the palate and cheer up his taste buds.

Mr. Hernández commented, "It looks like having a gun poked in your face is good for your appetite."

"I thought I wasn't hungry when we came in. I should also be tired, but I'm wide awake and very alert. I'm anxious to get started."

"Very well then, we shall leave now in case the traffic is heavy."

"How long will it take to get there?"

"Without traffic, only 15 minutes, but there is always traffic so expect it be 40 to 45 minutes."

"I'm ready," said Anthony.

They left the dining room and went out the exit leading to the garage. When they reached the car, Mr. Hernández circled and looked under the vehicle before unlocking it and inviting Anthony to enter.

The street outside the hotel had maintained its sense of calm, but when they turned onto a main boulevard, a new energy took over. The streets were crowded with cars, trucks and bicycles of all sizes and vintage. On every corner were street vendors selling everything from food to trinkets and a variety of services geared toward visitors to the city. The shops were not open yet, but a chaotic mix of restaurants, grocery markets, and clothing and appliance stores was preparing for the day's business. Then, as though to provide a familiar setting for Anthony, there appeared Pizza Hut, McDonalds, Burger King and the friendly visage of the Colonel at KFC. Buses belched, garbage trucks grinded, horns honked and vendors shouted. There seemed to be no shortage of pollution, noise, disorder or any other big city charms.

Mr. Hernández calmly made his way through the maze and after two turns they were on another boulevard occupied only by office buildings and what looked to be apartment buildings. Instead of street vendors, corner booths were occupied by the police or soldiers. Anthony could still not tell the difference. When they reached their destination, Mr. Hernández turned the car into a garage entrance that was monitored by an armed policeman/soldier instead of an attendant. Mr. Hernández showed him some papers, identification and cash.

"Did you pay him off?" asked Anthony as they entered the garage, "or was that a parking fee?"

"The police are not well paid. Recognition of their services is always appreciated and rewarded. Soldiers are a different story."

"How do you tell the difference between the police and the soldiers? They look the same to me."

"They have different weapons, Mr. Anthony. Soldiers always carry automatic rifles. Police carry only pistols. Soldiers always wear sunglasses, even at night. There is also a difference in the way they walk. The policeman looks tired or bored. The soldier looks like he is on a mission."

"You can notice a difference in the way they walk?"

asked Anthony.

"In a day or two, you will notice the difference. Let's hope it is a distant observation."

Anthony took his black bag and they exited the car. He followed Mr. Hernández to an awaiting elevator.

"No stairway, this time?" queried Anthony.

"A key card is required. The stairway is used only by people who work here or have special passes."

The elevator reached the second floor. Mr. Hernández motioned to exit.

"Remember, show respect, no matter how hard," he said to Anthony as they stepped into a waiting room.

The room was furnished with molded plastic chairs along two walls. Anthony saw a closed sliding glass window. On the window sill was a bell with a sign written in Spanish. Mr. Hernández rang the bell and gestured to Anthony to take his place at the window. They waited exactly seven minutes until 9:00 A.M. when a matronly woman slid the window open, and in Spanish asked Anthony the nature of his business. After a slight nod from Mr. Hernández, Anthony spoke.

"Buenos Días, I am Señor Anthony Bartolo. I have an appointment with the Director, Señor Calderón at this time, por favor," Anthony said, hoping she would accept his English bracketed by his limited Spanish as an attempt at being respectful.

He handed the woman the appointment papers, explanation of his business and forms requesting the permission he was seeking.

"Please have a seat, Señor. The Director will advise you when he is ready to see you."

"Will that be long?"

"The Director will advise you when he is ready. Please

be seated." With that the woman slid the window shut.

Anthony got the message, turned and took a seat. Mr. Hernández joined him.

"The question you asked will add ten minutes to your waiting time."

At 9:25 A.M., the window slid open again. The matron reappeared.

"The Director will see you now. May I have your bag, please?"

Anthony got up and looked to Mr. Hernández who nodded. Anthony handed the bag to the woman through the window. The woman buzzed the door to his right. Anthony instinctively rushed to open the door. When Mr. Hernández started to follow, the woman spoke again.

"No, Señor. Only Señor Bartolo," she said.

"He is my translator," said Anthony.

"That won't be necessary," said the woman

Mr. Hernández reluctantly took his seat while nodding again to Anthony.

Anthony entered the large office area that held about twenty desks each occupied by a man in a white shirt and black tie. A policeman in front of a work table was examining the contents of Anthony's bag. He removed a Leatherman multi-purpose tool that Anthony liked to have with him when he traveled. It was the only model with a variety of tools that excluded a knife blade. It was sometimes questioned when he went through airport security, but invariably was permitted. The policeman looked at Anthony waving his index finger from side to side before putting the Leatherman in a brown manila envelope. He returned the bag to Anthony. The woman appeared beside Anthony and instructed him to follow. She led him to an office door at the back of the room. Anthony could see a man seated at a desk through the venetian blinds on the window next to the door. He was on the telephone and ignored the woman's knock. When he hung up the phone, he shouted. The woman knocked again, opened the door and motioned Anthony toward the visitor chair.

Anthony walked to the desk and extended his hand.

"Señor Director, I am pleased to meet you."

Mr. Calderón gestured to the visitor chair. Anthony withdrew his hand and sat.

"You are Señor Bartolo? American?"

"Yes sir," replied Anthony.

Calderón was slightly built, balding and sported a thin mustache that he continually pressed with his index finger and thumb.

"That sounds more Spanish than American. You are sure you are not Salvadoran?" he said laughing.

"I'm sure, Mr. Director."

"Perhaps, Italiano? You are maybe related to the Sopranos?" he said laughing again. "We know all about the Sopranos from the DVD."

Oh, Jesus Christ, Anthony thought to himself. *Here we go again. At least he appears to be in a good mood.*

"Mr. Director, I am seeking your help in a matter of great personal importance."

"Yes. Yes. Yes. I understand. You wish to have the remains of the American doctor returned to the United States. There are certain regulations that must be satisfied in order for that to happen. We have heard from the representative of MATES, and he tells me that you have been advised of our regulations, and that you have brought all the necessary papers."

"Yes, I have, sir."

"That is good. This is a matter of quite some importance. If a foreigner dies on Salvadoran soil, we must be sure that everything surrounding those circumstances is proper. The permission to export the remains has certain special requirements."

Calderón extended his hand toward the woman who was standing to the left of Anthony. She handed Calderón the papers Anthony had given her. Anthony drew additional documents from the black bag and laid them out in order on Mr. Calderón's desk. He kept his notes on his lap.

"I understand some must be signed in your presence," said Anthony.

"That is correct. You appear to be very well prepared. Usually Americans think they do not have to meet Salvadoran regulations."

"It is my intention," said Anthony, "to fully satisfy the requirements of the Salvadoran Government so that I will be permitted to return to the United States with the remains of my friend."

"Ah, so you are a friend, not a lawyer, not a fellow doctor?"

"That's correct. I am a close personal friend of the doctor's family, and I represent them in this matter as explained in these papers."

"Why is there not another doctor from the MATES, or a lawyer representing them here? How have you been chosen to do this task?"

"Well, it is simply a matter of who could represent the family's best interests at this time."

"It is interesting to me that another doctor did not come. Is that because they did not agree with how the deceased doctor conducted his affairs?"

"I'm here to assist the deceased doctor's family, not the MATES organization or its lawyers, just the family, his wife."

"His wife?" said Calderón.

"Yes."

"Does the deceased doctor have any children?"

"No, sir," Anthony replied, "but may I ask what any of these questions has to do with my request?"

"Ah, Señor. Now you sound like an American. It is my job and my authority to ask questions. It is your job to answer them."

Anthony took a cleansing breath.

"Yes, of course. I only want to follow your government's regulations and complete my mission here."

"Your mission? You speak in the terms of a soldier. Are you a soldier, Señor?"

"I am just a businessman and close friend of the family."

"Did you know that the fellow that brought you here, Hernández, was a soldier?"

"I know nothing of that," said Anthony slightly exasperated.

"Señor Bartolo. You have come to my office with many documents that have obviously been prepared by people who have done business in El Salvador. In fact, you are very thoroughly prepared, but you are not a doctor in the same organization as the deceased, or a lawyer. With so much help at your disposal, you expect me to believe that you did not know that Hernández is a former soldier. I find that very hard to understand, Señor. Perhaps, you do not consider Salvadorans sophisticated enough to understand the workings of these things."

"Mr. Director, I assure you that the use of Mr.

Hernández's services was provided to me by the agency that made my travel arrangements. I have no knowledge of his background, nor do I consider it relevant to my business here."

"It is I, Señor, who shall determine whether or not his presence here is relevant."

"Yes, of course, Mr. Director. May we go through the papers?"

Mr. Calderón took a long pause. Then he smiled.

"Of course, we shall go through your papers."

Calderón began his examination of each document. Without saying a word, he would shove one at a time toward Anthony and point to the signature line. Each of Anthony's signatures was followed by a rubber stamp placed over it by the woman who dutifully stood by Calderón's desk.

Anthony believed Calderón had had his fun with him and was now getting on with the business at hand. He thought back to the guard at the unemployment office and how all bureaucrats must receive the same training in harassment techniques. Thirty minutes passed before Calderón asked another question.

"Señor, this document asks the final location of the deceased doctor's remains. The answer provided is the United States."

"That's correct," said Anthony.

"No, Señor. It is not. How and when will the family inter the remains of the deceased doctor?"

"The family has been making those decisions during my stay in El Salvador, I'm not sure of the final arrangements," said Anthony.

Mr. Calderón pushed on the desk and rolled his chair back.

"I am afraid that is unsatisfactory, Señor."

"I don't understand, Mr. Director. All the forms to complete this business are before you. Great care was taken to be sure that each regulation of your government would be satisfied. There's no mention anywhere that the disposition of the remains needed to be disclosed other than that they would be returned to the United States."

"Not all things are defined in forms, Señor Bartolo. It is of great importance to the government of El Salvador that the final resting place of the deceased doctor's remains be determined and fully disclosed. The Catholic Church sanctions cremation only when the remains are to be interred in consecrated ground. The Church is very clear in this requirement, and thus it is the requirement of the government that the Church be respected in this matter, and that you and the deceased doctor's family also respect its wishes."

"Mr. Director, with all due respect, sir, the deceased doctor wasn't even Catholic. He was just doing a humanitarian service for the people of El Salvador!" said Anthony as he tried to control his temper.

"That may be so, Señor. Perhaps if he had not chosen to put his clinic near the town of Perquín, which as you may have discovered with all your preparation was a town inhabited by rebels, and now that the war is over is still inhabited by people that fought against our government. Perhaps, if your good doctor had understood that the services and priorities he could have provided to government employees would have been acknowledged and appreciated in unfortunate circumstances such as these, I could find some way to help you. Perhaps, I would have been able to influence my superiors, but under the circumstances, I must have the specific final resting place of the deceased doctor's remains clearly defined and verified before they can be released for export."

"I tell you what," said Anthony, aware that he was losing ground quickly, "I can make a phone call right now and get you the information you need. It will take only a matter of minutes. I can have you speak directly to the parties if you wish. If you need the information in writing, I can have it emailed or faxed with a signature in a very short time. Hopefully, this business can be completed today."

"I am sorry, Señor, but that is impossible. I have many appointments today. In addition, the forms you have signed today must be completed again so that all documents are signed on the same day as the approval is given. If you have a spare set of unsigned copies, we may use them. Otherwise I suggest that you have a new set sent to you, or that you return to the United States to obtain them."

Anthony had to suppress the urge to grab and shake the hell out of Calderón. He took a deep breath realizing he had to play the long game. He remembered why he was here. It was his turn to be the grownup.

Anthony looked at Calderón and said, "Mr. Director, I appreciate the time you have given me this morning. I'm sorry that I did not consider the matter that has made our request impossible for you to approve today. I realize now that I was not sensitive to the requirements of the Church or your government in this last matter. Of course I will take every step to fill those requirements, and I request that you will reconsider our appeal at the earliest possible time."

Calderón looked at Anthony for what seemed like a long time before answering.

"Call my office on Monday, one week from today for the date of your next appointment. I will try to see you the following Thursday or Friday. I will give you the exact day and time when you call. That should give you more than enough time to get the documents you need."

Anthony worked hard not to gasp. He was sure his eating crow had earned a better response. *Think marathon, not sprint*, he told himself.

"I shall call on Monday. Thank you very much Mr. Director."

Anthony collected all the documents while Calderón watched. They both stood as he prepared to leave. The woman led him toward the door. He bowed slightly toward her and left going straight for the door that led to the waiting room. Mr. Hernández stood when he entered. Anthony nodded slightly as he continued toward the exit. He led the way to the elevator and the car which Mr. Hernández unlocked with a remote control.

When they were inside the car, Anthony looked at Mr. Hernández.

"It looks like I'm going to be here for a while."

On the way back, Anthony explained what had happened leaving out Calderón's references to Mr. Hernández.

"He is a prick," said Mr. Hernández.

"We just have to consider him our ten percent shit factor," said Anthony. "I will explain what that means at the bar if you will allow me to buy you a drink later, perhaps a few."

"Mr. Anthony, I will be happy to drink with you and have dinner with you so long as you do not afterward take any walks by yourself."

"That's a deal, but first I have to explain to my wife why I won't be home for Thanksgiving which will be just as dangerous."

As they continued toward the hotel, Anthony realized

that he had not retrieved his Leatherman from the policeman. *That makes it a perfect morning.*

Chapter 26

At the hotel, Anthony went straight to his room. He removed his jacket and tie before taking out the cell phone. He was glad to see the maid service had been completed. Anthony and Mr. Hernández had agreed to skip lunch so that Anthony could take a nap and make up for the sleep he missed during the night. He started to call Bernadette's cell, but thought better of it. He would call her at home tonight to let her know of the changes that would have to be made to his schedule. He thought about calling Carla, but did not want to risk her passing the new information on to Bernadette. He would call Carla and David after speaking with Bernadette later, or in the morning. They would have plenty of time to make the necessary adjustments. Anthony removed his shirt, shoes and trousers and hung up his suit. He set the clock radio for 4:00 P.M., laid on the bed and drifted into a deep sleep.

When the radio came on, a Spanish speaking man was talking very excitedly about something Anthony could not follow. He felt slightly disoriented, but was able to brush away the fog and recount the events of the day. He freshened up and called Mr. Hernández who agreed to meet Anthony at 6:00 P.M. for dinner. Anthony took the time to read the correspondence he had brought from Henry Trenholme.

It was all there; reinstatement of Anthony's employment at SkyTel, the continuation of his stock options, salary and bonus details, everything. Trenholme had gone out of his way to make the language straightforward and to the point. Anthony found nothing to dispute. He put the papers back in their folder and returned them to the safe. He freshened up and thought about the meeting with Calderón and how he should proceed. He was still considering his options when Mr. Hernández knocked on the door.

They decided to stop at the bar before heading to the hotel dining room. Anthony ordered scotch on the rocks. Mr. Hernández had a rum and coke. Anthony recounted most of the discussion with Calderón again and explained his father's theory of the ten percent shit factor to Mr. Hernández.

"Your father sounds like he was a wise man," said Mr. Hernández.

"He was a good man," said Anthony in response. "Perhaps, we should discuss what today's meeting with Calderón does to my schedule," he added.

"Very well, I am at your disposal," said Mr. Hernández.

"I hope so," said Anthony. "I won't be able to do what I came here to do without your help. I hope you'll continue to assist me."

"Your mission is a noble one. I will do everything I can to help. Tell me your new plan."

"It's a little fluid right now. If Calderón stays to his word, I will meet with him again next week. Thursday is Thanksgiving Day in the U.S. I'm sure you know it's a very important holiday. My wife will be upset that I'll not be with her. As I see it, however, there is no way around meeting Calderón on the day he proposes."

"That is correct," said Mr. Hernández. "Your wife does not share your enthusiasm for your mission?"

"It's a long story, but the short answer is 'No.'"

Mr. Hernández nodded and Anthony went on.

"The choice I have is to return home and come back for the meeting with Calderón or stay in El Salvador until the meeting. Staying would give me more time to meet the people my friend knew and served. If I make the trip home I would have less time in the village, but my wife might be pacified."

"I understand," said Mr. Hernández.

"I don't know how difficult it will be to find lodging near the village or in Perquín on short notice if I don't go back to New York."

"Let me know what you decide", said Mr. Hernández. "I am certain that we can work out arrangements. If necessary, we can use Señora Carla's help. These are not difficult problems to solve."

"I will call my wife after dinner and let you know what we decide." Anthony raised his glass to Mr. Hernández. "I appreciate your help and understanding."

Mr. Hernández raised his glass in return, "To the success of your mission, Mr. Anthony."

They touched glasses and finished their drinks. After another round, they ordered dinner in the main dining room where Raul was at their service.

It was 8:30 P.M. when Anthony returned to his room. His first order of business was to call Bernadette. He was pleasantly surprised when she picked up the phone on the first ring. He greeted her warmly and was leading up to the news of the day when she interrupted him.

"Anthony, something has happened."

"From the tone in her voice, he immediately thought about her parents.

"What is it?"

"It's Nancy. She's in the hospital." Bernadette paused,

still obviously shaken. "She attempted suicide."

"Jesus," was Anthony's first response.

"What happened? Why? Is she going to be okay?"

"She took pills. Aaron found her and called an ambulance. At the hospital, they pumped her stomach. They say she'll recover, but she has to have a psychiatric evaluation before she can be released."

"What brought this on? What about Aaron?"

"Nancy has some issues. Not with Aaron. She's ..."

"I know about Nancy," said Anthony.

"You do? How could you? Why didn't you ever mention that to me?"

"I found out accidentally. Then it just never came up."

"That's a pretty important thing to never bring up."

"Well, you never mentioned it to me either. And you've known about her a lot longer than I have."

"That's different."

Anthony decided to let that pass.

"Look," he said, "this is terrible news. I like Nancy and I like Aaron. We should support them in any way we can. Do you know of anything we can do for them?"

"As a matter of fact," said Bernadette," I am going to spend some time with them. Aaron has his practice to take care of, and besides, he's a wreck."

"What are you going to do?"

"Nancy is scheduled to come home on Wednesday. I am going to take some time off and stay with them for a week. I'll look after her, prepare some meals for them and just keep her company during the day. It's not a good time for her to be alone."

"Well, one of the reasons I was calling was to bring you up-to-date on what's happening here. It turns out that the local government big shot is not completely satisfied with the paperwork. He wants some changes made."

"Did David make a mistake?"

"No. David and his colleagues actually did an excellent job. This guy is just an angry civil servant using undefined technicalities to give us a hard time."

"Did you piss him off?"

Anthony decided not to answer. "The bottom line is that we need new paper work, and I can't get another meeting with him until next week on Thursday or Friday."

"You're going to meet with him on Thanksgiving?"

"It's not Thanksgiving here."

"This keeps getting better and better Anthony. This means I have to have Thanksgiving dinner with my parents without you. Just thinking of that gives me a headache."

"I'm really sorry about the change, but I had no control over it."

"You could have just stayed here."

"I was thinking of coming home for a few days. Then I'd return here next Monday and stay until the end of next week."

Bernadette was silent.

Anthony continued, "I can probably get a flight out tomorrow afternoon, Wednesday at the latest. I have to talk to Carla."

"You know what I think?" said Bernadette.

"What?"

"I think that since I am going to be at Nancy's for a week, you should just stay down there until you finish up," she said crisply.

"I can be home from Wednesday or Thursday until Monday. That will give us some time to talk about everything that has gone on. Maybe I can help with Nancy and Aaron."

"Anthony?"

"Yeah?"

"Just stay there until you're done."

Bernadette hung up.

With his jaw clenched, Anthony looked at the dead phone.

"God damn it, Bernadette," he said.

He sat on the bed and thought about their conversation. He was upset about Nancy. He speculated that something must have gone badly with her lover and felt sorry for her. At the same time, learning of this strengthened his resolve not to be defeated by his deteriorating relationship with Bernadette, or the meeting with Calderón. Both of these situations needed to be managed carefully. He decided to wait until morning to call Carla since flight changes for his return wouldn't have to be made immediately. He called Mr. Hernández and they agreed to get together and make some new plans.

When Anthony informed Mr. Hernández that he would be staying in El Salvador until Friday night of the following week, Mr. Hernández made a proposal.

"If you wish, we can stay in San Salvador. I can take you around the city and show you sights that most people like to visit. There are many famous churches and memorials. El Salvador memorializes the war as though its countrymen were fighting a foreign power instead of each other.

"That sounds interesting, but…"

"Or, if you like, we can visit Perquín which is very close to the village of the clinic. Perquín draws many visitors. It was a stronghold of the rebel forces during the civil war. Many foreigners go there to do research and see the war memorial so there are good accommodations. They

229

are almost all run by locals who display pride in their country while they remain sensitive to the cost of the war."

"I like the idea of going to Perquín sooner than later," said Anthony.

"I can also offer a change from the plan to stay at a hotel in Perquín. I have many friends there. If you like, I can arrange for us to stay at the home of a family, good friends I have known for most of my life. They have a home that is humble in comparison to this grand hotel, but it is comfortable and it will give you the opportunity to know some very good people who are true Salvadorans, unlike the prick, Calderón.

"Staying with your friends sounds terrific to me if it's not an imposition. Of course, I will pay for our accommodations," said Anthony.

"The accommodations are very reasonable," said Mr. Hernández, "and the hospitality is Salvadoran."

"I will be honored to be their guest."

"They will be honored to have you. I took the liberty of advising them of this possibility after our dinner this evening."

"Tell me about them."

"My friend Jorge lives with his wife, Consuelo. They have two children, a boy, nine years, and a girl, seven years. Jorge and his wife have a shop. They sell souvenirs of the war, coffee, tea and treats for the Europeans and North Americans that visit Perquín. He conducts local tours of the battle sites, cemetery and the war memorial. He also uses his pick-up truck to provide transportation to and from surrounding villages."

"You mean like a taxi?"

"Not exactly. He helps small farmers get their goods into town, takes villagers needing serious medical care to the hospital in Perquín, and does small things that make village life tolerable for those who wish or are forced by circumstance to remain there."

"He sounds like an American entrepreneur," said Anthony.

"The entrepreneur is not an American idea, Mr. Anthony. The word comes from the French."

"Of course," said Anthony feeling a little embarrassed.

They worked out a few more details before retiring for the evening. Anthony would call Carla and David in the morning to bring them up-to-date. He'd also call Henry Trenholme to let him know of his adjusted return date and that the terms of the new agreement with SkyTel met his requirements. He and Mr. Hernández would check out of the hotel, have lunch, and do a quick auto tour of San Salvador before setting out for Perquín.

231

Chapter 27

Following breakfast in the hotel dining room on Tuesday morning, Anthony returned to his room to make the phone calls. Because of the time difference in New York, he called Carla on her cell phone instead of at her office.

"Hello, Anthony," she answered, recognizing the origin of the call.

"Hi Carla, How are you?"

"Well, this is one of those times when shit happens."

"I heard about Nancy. It's terrible."

"I saw her last night. She looked like death warmed over. Thank God she'll be okay, at least physically. I wanted to shake the hell out of her and hug her at the same time. She is really one of the good people. Aaron is too. They're a bit of an odd couple, but somehow they make it work. They give each other what they need to survive in a world where they don't quite fit. At least they did until now. I just hope they can pull it together."

"Carla, if you know or learn of anything they need that I can provide, please let me know. I want to help."

"I'm sure that Bernadette staying with them will be a big help. We can all figure out what to do next, but the main thing is to let them know that we care about them."

"I'll help any way I can. In the meantime, Carla, we've had a glitch down here. To keep it short, I need a new set of papers from David and most unfortunately, I have to meet with the government officer again next week on either Thursday or Friday as he determines.

"On Thanksgiving?"

"That's the way it goes. My guess is that I'll haul out of here as soon after the end of business on the Friday after Thanksgiving. I was hoping you could change my ticket instead of me negotiating with the airline."

"I'll take care of it. Are you sure about finishing by Friday?"

"As sure as I can be."

"Have you thought about coming home and returning there next week?"

"Ah, Bernadette and I discussed that, but we agreed to this plan since she'll be staying with Aaron and Nancy."

"I'll take care of the tickets. What about the hotel?"

"Mr. Hernández and I are going to Perquín later today. We'll be staying at his friend's house until next Wednesday. On Wednesday, we'll come back to San Salvador. Then, I leave for home as we discussed."

"Sounds like you got more than you bargained for."

"Yeah, well, we knew it wasn't going to be simple."

"Anthony?"

"Yeah?"

"You may not realize or fully appreciate this, but staying at the house of a friend of Mr. Hernández is a big deal. He's never done this for my clientele. It's an honor. You must have really impressed him."

"I'm not so sure of that. He may think I'm the dumbest of the clients you've ever sent. I'll tell you more when I see you."

"It's an honor. Trust me," she said.

"I'm impressed by him. Now, I have to call David. I'll get back to you as things develop."

"Okay. As I make new travel arrangements, I'll have any papers or messages sent to you at the hotel. Just make sure they know when you'll return and that you wish them to hold any mail or messages."

"Got it. Thanks again, Carla."

"Take care of yourself, Anthony, and stay in touch."

Before calling David, Anthony made another call. After three rings, there was an answer.

"Hello."

"Hi Sarah, this is Anthony."

"Anthony! How are you? Where are you?"

"I'm in San Salvador, and I'm just fine. I'm calling to let you know that we had a minor snag with the bureaucrats here that requires some new paperwork in order for me to obtain Martin's remains."

"Oh, dear."

"David and I will work out the details shortly. But there is something important that you have to do."

"What is it?"

"The office down here wants to have a definitive location as the final resting place of Martin's ashes. There is an unwritten mandate from the church that such a place be what the church considers consecrated ground. In other words, a catholic cemetery."

"But, we're not catholic."

"I know. It's just a bureaucratic hoop to jump through to expedite matters. It means nothing."

"What do I have to do?"

"Okay, you may want to write this down. There is a cemetery way out on Long Island. I forget the name of the town, but all the cemeteries there are adjacent to one another including the big national cemetery used by the military. Anyway, there is a Holy Cross cemetery in that town. You need to call the cemetery and request that Martin's remains be interred there. That will create a record. Do what you have to do to initiate the process. You can always back out later."

"Suppose they ask me if Martin is catholic?"

"Sarah, you have to do what is necessary to satisfy this insane demand from a civil servant who just wants to screw with us. You won't be doing anything illegal or immoral as far as the cemetery is concerned because Martin's ashes will never get there. The church here can't care very much if it won't put its demand in writing. The government here won't ever know what happens once Martin's remains leave the country. To put it bluntly, it's all BS, but it perverts the goal of bringing Martin's remains home."

"I understand."

"I'm going to have David call you. When he does, you should tell him that you plan to have Martin's remains interred at Holy Cross cemetery."

"Will you or David get in any trouble over this?"

"The best thing you can do to cover David is to advise him that these are your wishes. Then, he'll only be carrying out his client's instructions. As for me, as long as the papers are completed correctly, I'm out of here without a problem."

"Are you sure you shouldn't just come home and let the MATES people handle this?"

"I'm sure. If we can satisfy this one detail, everything will be fine, and I'll be back in New York with Martin's remains a week from Friday."

"They're keeping you down there?"

"It's just a short time until we can get the papers right and have another meeting."

"Anthony, I didn't want this to become so much trouble for you. Aren't you supposed to start your job next week?"

"Sarah, please. Let me handle this. Everything will be fine. I want to finish this and bring Martin home. It's going to be okay. I just didn't want to go around you and leave David exposed from his firm's perspective. It'll be okay."

"Have you heard about Nancy?"

"Yes," said Anthony, remembering that Sarah knew about his encounter with Nancy at the marina. "It's awful. I feel for her and Aaron."

"You know, Bernadette and I saw her last night. She was all drugged up, mumbling through tears, her mind bouncing between guilt, loss and pain, but do you know what she asked us?"

"What?" said Anthony.

"She asked if you were okay in El Salvador and would you be back soon?"

Anthony had to take a few breaths before he could respond.

"Sarah, I'm fine and I'll be back soon. Can I tell David to call you to get your instructions to designate Martin's internment at Holy Cross cemetery?"

"Yes."

"Good, Sarah. You're doing the right thing."

"Anthony?"

"Yes?"

"Thank you and please be careful down there."

"Bye, Sarah."

Anthony washed his face with cold water before making the next call. After being put on hold for a short time, David came on the line.

"David, this is Anthony calling from San Salvador. I need something."

"Should I get Russell in here?"

"I don't think that'll be necessary," Anthony said.

Anthony went on to explain what Calderón wanted and that he, Anthony, had spoken to Sarah and she advised him that Martin's remains would be interred at Holy Cross cemetery.

"Now why would she do that?" asked David.

"Not sure. It may have something to do with Martin spending so much time down here in a Catholic country. I didn't want to ask. She's still very upset about Nancy."

"Are you jerking me around?"

"Why would I do that? Why don't you just call Sarah and ask for instructions regarding the final resting place of Martin's remains?"

"How quickly do you need the revised papers?"

"Sooner, rather than later. I meet with Calderón next week. If the papers get here by Monday we'll be all right."

"You're a piece of work, Anthony. How does Bernadette feel about your being down there an extra week?"

Anthony didn't like the idea of his bringing up Bernadette.

"She's okay with it. She'll be staying with Aaron and Nancy for a week or so."

"That's some story," said David. "The dyke gets dumped and Aaron gets her stomach pumped."

"Send the papers to my hotel with instructions that they be held until my return. If there are any questions, you can ask Carla. I'll be moving around a bit."

"Don't catch anything," said David.

Anthony hung up and went to wash his face again. Rather than talk to Henry Trenholme directly, he decided to send an email with the service provided by the hotel. *Better to make this a one way conversation*, he thought. He changed into jeans, sport shirt, sweater and a pair of loafers. Before he packed his clothes, he went down to the shop in the lobby and purchased a garment bag. He returned to his room and put his business clothes in the new bag that he planned to leave at the hotel until his return. He packed the clothes he would need for the next week into his travel bag and put the papers for recovering Martin's remains and those related to SkyTel in the smaller bag. They would be safer with him.

Anthony thought about his "lost" Leatherman tool and wished he had retrieved it. He called the front desk and advised them of his plans including his expected return one week from Wednesday. The hotel agreed to accommodate him, to hold his garment bag and to collect and hold any mail or messages that arrived for him until he returned. He called Mr. Hernández and confessed that he made a trip to the gift shop without him, but that he exercised extreme caution. They agreed to leave the hotel together as soon as Anthony dropped off his garment bag at the front desk and sent an email to Trenholme.

Taking Flight

Chapter 28

Anthony and Mr. Hernández completed their business at the hotel and went directly to the car. Mr. Hernández still wore a white suit but had replaced his shirt and tie with a crew neck sweater. He put his and Anthony's travel bags in the trunk of the car. Anthony kept the smaller black bag with him up front. Mr. Hernández told him they would move the luggage to the rear seat later so the trunk would be free for supplies they would pick up before going to Perquín.

They left the hotel and began a whirlwind tour of San Salvador. Anthony found the street grid in San Salvador similar to that of Manhattan with main arteries running North to South and East to West. He learned to look for street names on the curbs rather than search the sparse signage. Mr. Hernández said their tour would include an overview of the city, but they would avoid the east side of town, an area called Soyopango which was notorious for its gangs. Even the police, he said, did not patrol this area and entered in force only when a serious disturbance was reported.

They drove past the government building where the meeting with Calderón had taken place and on to Av Cuscatlán where they turned toward the city center. The congestion on the streets and sidewalks was far greater than what they had experienced the day before. It was as though the entire country was putting on an exhibition for Anthony Bartolo. Mr. Hernández slowed and pointed out the Bibliotheca Nacional on the right, an impressive building that would have looked comfortable in the center of Madrid. On the next street to the left was the Palacio Nacional, presently the seat of government. Across from it was the Plaza Barrios.

"Many demonstrations and protests took place in the Plaza during the bad times," explained Mr. Hernández. "While some groups occasionally protest here to voice their grievances, the plaza now is mostly a gathering place for tourist groups, pickpockets and street vendors."

Continuing on, they reached the Catedral Metropolitana.

"The tomb of Archbishop Oscar Romero is in the basement of the church. In 1993, the church was visited by Pope John Paul II. At that time, the tomb was on the main floor."

"Can we stop and go inside?" asked Anthony.

"Of course," said Mr. Hernández.

Mr. Hernández turned onto Calle Delgado and found a parking garage. From there they walked back to the Cathedral.

"Mr. Anthony, it would be wise to put your watch and ring in your front pants pocket. A good place for your wallet also."

Anthony understood and did as Mr. Hernández suggested.

"How do I look?" Anthony asked.

Mr. Hernández smiled and said, "Not so much like a tourist, but not so much a Salvadoran either."

"Well, that's a little progress," said Anthony.

As they approached the church, they saw a group of women standing near the steps listening to a man wearing a black suit.

"They are Evangelicals," said Mr. Hernández. "They

also admire the legacy of Archbishop Romero."

"Really?" said Anthony.

"He is a hero to all who preach to help the poor and those who believe that the meek shall inherit the earth."

"How do you know they're Evangelicals?"

"By their dress. In El Salvador, the Evangelicals are very conservative. More so than Catholics, Episcopalians and Lutherans. Notice that the women are all wearing scarves or kerchiefs. Also they wear only dresses and skirts, no pants."

"You would make one fantastic tour guide," said Anthony.

"Perhaps when I retire from this business," Mr. Hernández said, accepting the compliment.

Anthony looked up to take in the building. The blue and yellow checkered dome sported the bright colors seen on so many billboards and buildings in San Salvador. The front of the church had a stucco façade with a colorful campesino motif that Anthony later learned was painted by Fernando Llort, an internationally acclaimed Salvadoran artist who at times has been compared to Joan Miró and even Picasso. The bright colors were said to express the value of women, the community and the Salvadoran face of God.

"This building is a monument to the peasants of El Salvador. Romero to them was a saint, and the artist saw the peasants as the soul of the country," said Mr. Hernández.

"And to you, Mr. Hernández, was he a saint to you?"

Mr. Hernández gave Anthony a long look before answering.

"It is unusual many times for a powerful man to really understand the life of the poor; to study and know their daily lives, and to believe in them. To believe that they should have a better life is not a common thing for the rich and dominant. He did not start out that way, but he learned and wanted to change their lives. In the end, that cost him his life. So perhaps he was a saint.

"This Cathedral was rebuilt at the end of the war. The Church and the government were very smart to have such a monument for the people and their saint. It gives them a salve to nurse their wounds."

"Are you saying this building had a political inspiration?"

"Everything the church and the government do have as you say, a political inspiration."

"But I thought the church was on the side of the poor people and the government on the side of the powerful," said Anthony.

"The Archbishop now is Opus Dei, the most conservative of the church's thinkers. Romero would not have kept his job if he worked for them. The Evangelicals, who you will see more of in the rural areas are sincere in their assistance to the poor, but they believe that suffering in this world will be rewarded in the next. That does very little for the small farmer trying to feed his family."

They ascended the steps and went inside the church. Anthony was reminded of the first time his father took him to St. Patrick's Cathedral in Manhattan. As a boy, he was in awe of the church. The stained glass windows, side altars, racks of votive candles, the main altar and especially the Cardinals' hats hanging from the very high ceiling created lasting memories. He remembered the feeling of being overwhelmed as he and his father had walked quietly toward the front of the church. The only sounds had come from the clicking of their heels walking across the marble floor.

As Anthony walked around this cathedral, he came to a portrait of Archbishop Romero underneath which was a brass plaque describing his tomb below the building. Appearing almost as a supporting pillar to the portrait was a tall brass collection box inscribed with a dedication to the poor. A nearby stairway leading to the lower floor and the tomb had a chain across it with a sign reading "Closed" in three languages. He continued down the center aisle toward the main altar. He saw the Stations of the Cross colorfully portrayed in the windows on each side. When he reached the altar railing, he kneeled wanting once again to feel that sense of awe. He wanted to feel a presence greater than himself. He wanted to believe. He waited and finally stood, disappointed and angry at his own expectations. He turned toward the side exit and left the building aware of the bulk of Mr. Hernández behind him.

When they reached the car, he turned to Mr. Hernández.

"Can we go on to Perquín now?" he asked.

"As you wish, my friend, as soon we get our supplies."

Mr. Hernández drove to a quieter part of the city where they found what to Anthony looked like a country general store. They purchased three five gallon drums of gasoline, three similar size containers of water and two plastic table cloths. Mr. Hernández selected four chickens that had been alive that morning. The storekeeper unhooked them from an overhead rack and carefully wrapped them in brown paper before putting them in a paper sack. He added ten sugar coated pastry crusts that to Anthony looked like the shells of the Italian canolies he loved. Finally, they bought bottles of rum, whiskey and beer.

They moved the luggage to the rear floor and back seat

of the car. The chickens, pastries and alcohol were placed on a plastic cloth put on top of the suitcases. Another cloth was used as a cover for their cargo. They put the gasoline and water in the trunk using a rope to tie down the lid. Anthony admiringly noticed Mr. Hernández's skill at using seamen's knots.

As they drove off, Mr. Hernández explained, "The electric power in Perquín is not so reliable; much better than in the villages, but not as good as San Salvador. Jorge has a generator for which we have bought gasoline. Without it, his refrigerator would be useless to store food unless he can find ice when the power fails. Refrigerators and generators are not common in Perquín unless you are wealthy. Jorge is not very rich, but makes a good living and has these for his family. The water supply is also unreliable, especially in the villages where it is available only once a week. When you visit the village of the clinic, you shall take water with you as a gift to the village. Also, you shall use it to drink while in Perquín. Salvadorans can drink the local water without a problem, but Americans sometimes find our water disagreeable. The gasoline and water are the "rent" you will pay for lodging. The chickens are a gift to Jorge and his family in return for their hospitality. The sweet pastry is for the children. The whiskey and beer are for the adults. The entire cost is less than for one day at the hotel in San Salvador."

"Sounds like a bargain. Are you sure it's enough?"

"For a tourist, the price would be much higher, but you will be treated as family."

They drove forty miles in the direction of San Miguel on the Interamericana Highway. Mr. Hernández pointed out that Morazán, just north of the city proper, was a rebel stronghold during the civil war and the location of some of the most intense fighting.

"The war museum in Perquín, which I am sure you will see, has many reminders of the losses suffered here."

The country became more mountainous and remained so as they continued north connecting to Highway 7 toward Perquín, another twenty-five miles away in the direction of Honduras. Within ten miles of their destination there were signs for El Mozote and Perquín.

Mr. Hernández spoke quietly of El Mozote.

"This is a village that could help you understand El Salvador if you saw it," he said. "It is very small. There are no hotels. The only places to eat are small snack bars. El Mozote has many ghosts that still haunt this country."

"I'd like to see it," said Anthony.

"It is the village where I lived before the war," said Mr. Hernández.

They drove east a few miles off Highway 7 until they reached a signpost announcing their destination. They parked in an open area near the small church that was adorned with brightly colored murals. The pictures of families together with children playing nearby provided a sense of peace and harmony. They continued to walk and came upon a plaque that started just above the ground and was slightly higher than Mr. Hernández was tall. The inscription was in Spanish. Mr. Hernández removed his hat.

"These are the names of the people that were massacred here by the government troops at the start of the war. Almost eight hundred people in one day, many of them children," he said solemnly to Anthony.

Anthony took some deep breaths as he acknowledged the surroundings.

"These," Mr. Hernández said as he pointed to four lines on the plaque with his index finger, "are the names of my wife, my son and my two daughters who were killed on that day."

Anthony instinctively made the sign of the cross because he didn't know what else to do or say. They moved on to a nearby rose garden that adorned the mass grave of the children slaughtered that day. Despite the cool November weather, many flowers were in bloom.

"I was away at my job. When I learned what happened, I joined the rebel forces. No matter how many bridges I destroyed, or whatever else I did, it never changed for me what happened here that day."

Mr. Hernández broke a rose stem and laid the flower on the ground. The two men stood silently. Anthony waited until Mr. Hernández turned back toward the car and followed. As they reached the car, Anthony turned to face Mr. Hernández.

"Thank you for bringing me here."

Mr. Hernández unlocked the car and they continued their journey to Perquín in silence.

The mountainous terrain had trees on all sides. It reminded Anthony of the Adirondack Mountains in upstate New York where he had spent several summers. While much of the landscape they had seen this day was not all that impressive, he thought the area from El Mozote to Perquín would make a great Chamber of Commerce poster.

When they reached Perquín, they drove down Calle de Los Héroes. Mr. Hernández conducted a quick tour of the small city while they still had some daylight. He pointed out the Museo de la Revolución which was dedicated to the history of the civil war with displays of photos, posters, weapons and artifacts of war. More impressive to Anthony was a visible crater behind the building that still contained the remains of a helicopter that had carried an infamous army officer of the Atlacatl Battalion to his death. Mr. Hernández pointed out that the tour guides in the museum are former rebels who revel in telling the story of the downed helicopter. Anthony understood what Mr. Hernández had meant about ghosts. El Salvador had a history and culture that were centered in death. Not death caused by natural disaster, disease or famine, but by man, accompanied by horrific atrocities. That the long war left an indelible scar on the psyche of past and present generations was no longer a wonder. The wonder was how could this or any other country survive such a past?

"Now, I shall take you to see Jorge and his family," said Mr. Hernández.

"Is it customary to have a drink shortly after introductions," asked Anthony.

"Sometimes, yes," said Mr. Hernández.

"Well, I hope this is one of those times. I don't want to appear rude, but tonight, I could really use a drink."

"Then it is good we have brought some with us."

Chapter 29

Mr. Hernández left the busy thoroughfare and drove to a more residential area where houses were grouped closer together. From there, he continued further into a more rural area where houses occupied about a half acre of land some of which was used to contain gardens and house fowl and small animals. They came upon a pink, green and white single level stucco house that was smaller than Anthony's house in Hempstead, but larger than those crowded together in the center of Perquín. A carport adjacent to the left side of the house hovered protectively over a blue Ford pick-up. As they turned off the road, the long gravel driveway greeted them with a crunching sound that set off the distant barking of a dog. Anthony and Mr. Hernández got out of the car and climbed the three steps to an open porch that contained four mismatched chairs; a wooden rocker, two wickers with arms and a cane back that could have been a former member of a dining set. At the center of the porch, the front door opened and a tall, thin man with dark, thick wavy hair and a heavy mustache came out to greet the men. He was wearing a Rolling Stones T-shirt, jeans and a pair of flip flops.

"Hola," he said approaching Mr. Hernández.

"¿Que tal, Jorge?"

"Bien, gracias."

The two men shook hands and with their left hands each embraced the shoulder of his friend.

"Quisiera presentarte a Don Antonio," said Mr. Hernández.

Jorge extended his hand, "Bienvenida, welcome Don Antonio. I can speak English, but not so good as the Colonel."

"Mucho gusto," said Anthony. "That is close to the limit of my Spanish."

The three men laughed and agreed to speak English in honor of their guest.

Jorge called over his shoulder, "Consuelo."

A lovely woman opened the door. She was petite, with dark hair, fine features, large dark eyes and a welcoming smile. She was followed out the door by two children who ran past her to greet Mr. Hernández with a hug.

Jorge presented his wife to Anthony with pride.

"Don Antonio, to you I introduce my esposa, Consuelo. Consuelo, this is Don Antonio, a friend of the Colonel."

They each said "Mucho gusto" at the same time and laughed.

Anthony could see from the roundness of her belly that she was carrying a child, but wasn't sure if it was appropriate for him to say anything, so he remained silent.

Mr. Hernández unhooked himself from the boy and girl and took Consuelo's hands in his and while looking at her stomach said, "Es precioso, no?"

She smiled and called her children over to her and asked Jorge to introduce them to Anthony.

"These are my children, Juan, after the Colonel, and Maria."

Juan put out his hand immediately and said "Nice to make your acquaintance, sir."

Impressed, Anthony replied, "The pleasure is all mine, Juan," happy to finally know Mr. Hernández's given name.

Maria stood by her mother and did not return

Anthony's extended hand, burying her face in her mother's ribs.

"Maria, say hello to our guest," said Consuelo.

Maria turned her head toward Anthony and said, "Hello, Señor. Bienvenida."

"Hello, Maria. It's is very nice to meet you."

Maria buried her face in her mother's ribs again until Mr. Hernández announced that he had something for them. He retreated to the car and took out the brown bag containing the sweets. They reached for them and Juan immediately took a bite. His mother scolded him for not saying "thank you" first and told them they must wait until after dinner to enjoy their dessert. When Maria looked disappointed, Consuelo allowed her one bite to be even with Juan. Maria dutifully thanked Mr. Hernández before taking a bite substantially larger than the one taken by her brother.

"Come children, back into the house," said Consuelo.

"Can't I stay?" asked Juan.

"You can stay if you help carry the things from the car," said Jorge.

Juan agreed and Maria was happy to go back in the house with her mother holding the sugar coated pastry.

"We have plenty to take from the car," said Mr. Hernández.

Anthony stood still for a moment and said to Jorge, "You have a beautiful family."

"You have children, Don Antonio?"

"No, not at this time," Anthony replied, not mentioning that he and his wife had a set of priorities including careers, bank accounts, and other material goals that they hoped to fulfill before her biological clock started to stagger.

"Perhaps soon. I wish you good luck," said Jorge.

Taking Flight

"Thank you, I wish you good luck with your coming child."

"Gracias, Antonio."

Anthony was thankful that Jorge had dropped the title.

The men and Juan emptied the trunk and rear seat of the car. The gasoline was brought to the rear of the car port. The water was placed behind the house near a back door that led to the kitchen. Jorge carried the liquor and beer. Juan wrapped his arms around the sack with the chickens and brought them to his mother. Mr. Hernández and Anthony brought their luggage into the house. When they were done, Mr. Hernández and Anthony returned to the porch and sat on the wicker chairs. Mr. Hernández raised his left foot to his right knee to remove his shoe. As he did, his trouser leg was raised enough to reveal a leather holster that contained a small pistol, his second gun. Mr. Hernández shook the shoe until a small piece of gravel fell out and replaced it on his foot. While they were still alone, Anthony could not resist commenting.

"That's a pretty small weapon compared to the one you used the other night outside the hotel," he said. "Does it have any pop, or is it just for show?"

Mr. Hernández gave Anthony an impatient look.

"No gun is just for show. A second gun is used only in very bad circumstances. Are you familiar at all with guns?" said Mr. Hernández as he removed the gun from its holster.

"A little," said Anthony. I used to go to target practice with my father, but I would use a rented gun. I've never owned one."

"This," said Mr. Hernández "is a very fine weapon. It is a Walther PPS. The magazine carries eight 9mm hollow round bullets that provide much, much pop, as you say; as much as the Glock under my coat. The only sacrifice is distance for which the Glock is better."

"Aren't you afraid that thing will go off in its holster if you run, or trip or something? Does it have a good safety?" asked Anthony.

"This gun will not go off by itself if you drop it from Jorge's roof. The trigger safety is never on because of the circumstances in which the gun might be needed."

"Aren't you concerned about the children getting hold of it?"

"When it is not on my ankle, I press this release," he demonstrated for Anthony as the magazine separated from the handle, "and the gun cannot be fired."

He handed the disabled gun to Anthony

"Impressive," said Anthony, observing the compactness and rich detail of the weapon.

"Enough about guns," said Mr. Hernández. "We must join our host."

Anthony was pleased to see that he would have his own room. It was small with a single bed and a bureau on which rested a wash basin, a towel and an empty glass. At the foot of the bed was a gauze bundle that Anthony learned was a mosquito net. It wouldn't be necessary this time of year unless some rogue mosquitoes invaded the area. He put his clothes in the bureau drawers and a small closet. His toilet articles and shaver went on the bureau. He used the bathroom as he would at home or in the hotel. The next day he would learn the flushing practices and uses of the shower and sinks that were consistent with balancing an expensive and sometimes erratic water supply and sanitary requirements. He learned that the property also had an outhouse in the back for those days when water was limited or not available.

That first evening, Consuelo made a wonderful dinner

using two of the chickens brought by her guests. She complemented the chickens with local vegetables and rice. Later, Mr. Hernández would explain that the main meal of the day was usually served in the afternoon, but tonight's dinner was in honor of their guest. After dinner, the men went to the front porch with the rum and whiskey. Jorge brought out glasses, one of which contained an ice cube for Anthony. Anthony made a mental note to drink without the luxury of ice in the future.

Anthony and Mr. Hernández had whiskey and Jorge enjoyed the rum while lighting a cigarette after offering one to his guests. When they declined, Jorge explained that he smoked only one a day, after dinner.

"I could never do that," said Anthony. "I used to smoke, but once I quit, I knew that if I ever had one, I'd be back to a pack a day."

"Does it bother you that I smoke?"

"No. Please don't stop for me."

Anthony saw that the cigarettes were American made and asked Jorge if they were sold here.

"Oh, yes. Sometimes, my friends living in the states send them to me. If they are not stolen at the Post, they get here."

"You have friends in the U.S.?"

"Most Salvadorans have friends or relatives in the U.S. Also in Canada, Australia, Italy and France."

"How come?" asked Anthony.

"El Salvador is not a rich country. There are some people that are rich, of course. Others that are, how do you say, in the middle?"

"Middle class."

"Yes, yes. Many middle class families have relatives in Europe. Salvadorans who left the country at the start of the war. Others from this class went to the U.S., Canada and Australia. Also the poor campesinos, the farmers who left after the war and went to America and some to Canada to take jobs there. It is the only way they can make money. They send money home to help their families. Sometimes, even as laborers, they make more in one month there than they can make here in one year's time."

"I thought things were better now."

"You mean since the war?"

"Yes," said Anthony.

"For me, things are better, I have more money. I have a house. The Colonel taught me much about making money by selling to the wealthy. I opened a shop with souvenirs for the rich tourists, and I provide services for them. Usually they are professors from the U.S. or Europe who come here to study the war. They wish to see the photos, the graves, and the helicopter in the street. We have made many dollars telling the story of that helicopter. Each year, the battle to shoot it down gets longer, and the man inside becomes a bigger monster than the year before. The professors get excited about the purchase of a rock from the crater in which it sits. They lose sight of the misery and the suffering. The rock becomes a symbol of the war for these people. A war they see as in the past, but for many Salvadorans things are no better. "

"But your son is obviously being educated well. He speaks English perfectly. He showed me his books earlier. Surely he will be successful," said Anthony.

"Yes. We have a tutor for him in addition to his school. The school is expensive. The tutor is expensive. That is why we do not live in a bigger house," he said laughing. "My hope is that he will go to the University and perhaps become a doctor one day."

"That's a good goal, Jorge."

"Yes. But for many it cannot even be a dream."

"And your daughter?"

"She also goes to school and is very smart. The University today takes many women. At some point we shall decide between a dowry and the university. I think for her to be a lawyer will be good."

"And the young people in the villages? Do they go to the school that Juan and Maria attend?"

"The schools are not free. This is not the United States or Cuba. We must pay for the schools, books, even the pencils. Most of the villagers are struggling to eat, to stay warm, and to stay healthy."

"So they get no education at all?" asked Anthony.

"In the villages, life is different. Children get schooling from either a local who has been out in the world and returned, or one who visits from a city like Perquín. Payment is sometimes in dollars, sometimes in chickens, or eggs, or clothing."

"It sounds like the country schoolhouse approach used in the early days of the U.S.," said Anthony.

"Perhaps," said Jorge. "The children are taught by this person as arranged by the elders of the village. One or two may go on for more schooling in the town if the villagers agree to pay, but mostly when the boys reach thirteen or fourteen years, they are sent to the U.S. to join other Salvadorans and get jobs. They send money back and stay there as long as they can."

"But that would wipe out the future generations here."

"This is already happening. Young men, boys really, leave, some never to return. The ones that stay and help their families bother less and less to work in favor of waiting to receive money sent back. Then there are the gangs. Before the war, there were no gangs and everyone worked hard, but that only led to poverty and punishment from those who had everything."

"You make it sound hopeless," said Anthony.

"Ah, that is the curse of the Salvadoran," said Jorge. "We always have hope. We always think we can overcome. We see your country as a source of hope even though the U.S. was on the side of the government during the war."

"It's hard to understand that."

"Do you know, Antonio, that your country's war in Iraq had soldiers from El Salvador on its side?"

"I'm embarrassed to say I didn't know that."

"We have little at stake in that war. We haven't enough money to feed our poor, but we have an army alongside your rich and powerful country. Our soldiers go willingly because Salvadorans love the U.S. as a source of hope and as a good friend."

Anthony shook his head.

Juan and Maria came out to say good night. They had finished their homework, had their pastry for which they thanked Mr. Hernández profusely as they showered him with hugs and giggles. Juan came up to Anthony and extended his hand and said "Good night, sir."

Anthony shook his hand and touched his shoulder as he had seen Mr. Hernández and his father do earlier. The boy smiled and went inside. Maria came up to him and stood there shyly. Anthony uncertain of what to do extended his hand. The young girl put out her hand.

"Good night, Señor," she said and then turned and ran back into the house.

Jorge followed the children inside to participate in their nightly ritual.

Anthony looked at Mr. Hernández. "Once again, I

want to say that I am honored that you brought me here."

"I think we shall have another whiskey" said Mr. Hernández.

He smiled when Anthony answered by saying, "I'll have mine with no ice."

When Jorge returned, they talked about the children the way all adults talk admiringly about children. It was clear they were done for the night regarding any talk about the war, politics or poverty. They flirted with some mundane subjects until they hit upon soccer or "*futbol*" which is very popular in El Salvador.

Anthony told them the sport was becoming more popular in the US, particularly in New York.

"When the great Pelé played there, he won the hearts of the most hardened New Yorkers with his feats of wonder, once described in the New York Post as *Feet of Wonder*."

They each had a soccer story to tell, all of which were enhanced by the whiskey and rum.

As they were getting ready to call it a night, Jorge asked Anthony how he would like to spend the next day. He invited Anthony to join a small tour group of Canadians that were here to see the historic sites.

Anthony paused then carefully qualified what he was about to ask with exclamations of appreciation for the offer and the hospitality received today.

"If it's all right," he said looking first at Jorge, then Mr. Hernández, "I would like to go to the village tomorrow."

"Of course," said Mr. Hernández.

"I understand completely," said Jorge.

Anthony wasn't sure if he had offended them.

Mr. Hernández seemed to understand what he was

thinking.

"A lot has happened since you have arrived. Now it is important for you to see the place where your friend gave his life," he said.

"Thank you for understanding," he said, looking at both men.

"We shall have breakfast together in the morning so the children can see you before you go. Consuelo will make sure that you eat enough to get you through the day," said Jorge.

"I think I've already eaten enough for tomorrow," said Anthony. "I can't tell you how much I enjoyed being with you and your family tonight."

They went inside the house. When Anthony reached his room, he took the cell phone out of his bag, looked at it for a long while and then put it back and went to bed. As he drifted off to sleep, he heard the voices of the other men having a long discussion in a language he could not follow.

Taking Flight

Chapter 30

Thursday morning was announced by roosters near and far just after dawn. Anthony awoke feeling well rested and excited about the prospects of the day. He was ready to get started when it occurred to him that the others in the house might still be asleep. When he heard voices from the kitchen, he decided that it wouldn't be intrusive to get up and going. He dressed, brushed his teeth and joined Consuelo and Maria in the kitchen. They had a school notebook on the table in front of them. Consuelo looked up and smiled.

"Good morning," she said, "I hope you slept well."

"Very well, thank you."

"We are working on Maria's English lesson. She is having trouble with her words. I am not so good to explain them."

"May I try?" asked Anthony.

"Of course, if it would not be trouble for you,"

Anthony sat at the table next to Maria and looked at the vocabulary exercises in the notebook. The first word was 'library'.

"Library is bibliotheca. Say 'lye brair ree'," he said slowly, pronouncing it phonetically.

"Lye brair ree" she repeated back.

"Bueno," he said, excusing himself while he went to his room to retrieve his Spanish/American phrase book that he had long abandoned.

When he returned they went to the next word.

"Glass?" said Maria.

"Glass is vaso ... for bebida."

"Glass, vaso?"

"Si, bueno," said Anthony.

As they continued through the list of ten words, each getting a little more challenging, Consuelo started making breakfast. When they completed the list, Mr. Hernández and Jorge were standing at the entrance to the kitchen looking on admiringly.

Maria looked up and smiled at them. Anthony felt a little embarrassed by his audience.

Jorge said, "You are a good teacher, Antonio."

"I think she has a good ear for language," said Anthony.

Maria cleared the table as Consuelo finished preparing breakfast. Just as the food was ready, Juan came out. Dressed, but looking half asleep, he was greeted with family applause for finally joining them. He took an exaggerated bow, which added cheers to the applause.

They shared a sumptuous breakfast of eggs, beans and rice.

Anthony protested, "If I eat like this every day, I'll become too fat."

"This is in case you have no lunch today in the village," said Consuelo.

They ate and drank coffee while the conversation went on about food, the children's school, plans Jorge and Consuelo had for the house, what they planned for the arrival of the new baby and the expected weather for the day.

"And for dinner tonight," added Jorge, "Consuelo makes the best papusas you will ever taste. They will be lighter than last night's dinner, so they will not make you fat."

They laughed as Anthony patted his belly.

"It is time for school," announced Jorge. "We will walk. We do not need the bus or the truck on such a nice day. Children, say goodbye to our guests."

The boy and girl each hugged Mr. Hernández. Juan came over to Anthony and shook his hand. Maria put her arms around Anthony's neck and gave him a tight hug.

"Gracias, Señor Antonio, Buenas días."

"Buenas días, María," said Anthony.

Consuelo cleaned up after declining Anthony's offer to help. Anthony and Mr. Hernández moved out to the porch as they watched Jorge leave with the children.

"I think we should talk about the day and your friend," said Mr. Hernández.

"Okay," said Anthony, expecting to hear a schedule or an agenda for the day.

"Your friend, the doctor, was a good man. He helped the villagers who needed his care. The people respected him, and they saw that he was different from the other doctors who came here and did good works. The other doctors stayed distant from the people. They kept to themselves. They worked very hard, but did not join in any of the festivities of the villagers. They had their lodging in Perquín. Your friend would talk to the people. He became very interested in their art, their music, their customs and celebrations."

"How do you know all this?" asked Anthony.

"Jorge knew your friend. Not too well, but Jorge knows many villagers who have spoken about him. Sometimes, Jorge would transport the doctor to or from the village, or pick up supplies for him."

Anthony's guard went up. The feeling of camaraderie that enveloped him since last night was replaced by a wariness of Jorge's intentions.

"So, why didn't Jorge mention any of this? Why are you telling me now?"

"Jorge and I talked for a long time last night after you went to bed. He was not sure of what or how much he should say to you."

"Which means he doesn't trust me?"

"It means he does not know you. You are from a different place. He sees foreigners all the time. He knows they do not think like Salvadorans. He was concerned about what you will do while you are here. As he sees it, you come here for reasons that are not entirely clear. Then you will leave here, and what you do will remain."

"Why are you telling me this?"

"I have told him that you are an honorable man, and that you are not here to cause harm. That you will respect and understand what you will learn."

"I'm not sure I understand," said Anthony.

"Your friend, the doctor was a special man. Not just for the care he provided to these people, but because he cared about them. They in turn came to care about him."

"So what is wrong with my knowing this? How could my knowing this cause any harm?"

"There is more," said Mr. Hernández.

"What?" asked Anthony.

"For now," said Mr. Hernández, "Jorge and I agreed that it would be best if you had your experience in the village. Meet the people you want to meet. I will introduce you to the elders in the village. You will be free to present yourself, ask questions, and see the clinic. If at the end of this, the villagers agree, Jorge will tell you the rest."

Anthony was having a hard time shaking the feeling that Jorge did not trust him and was faking his warm hospitality.

"So was all this a big welcoming act?"

"No, no, my friend," said Mr. Hernández, "but if I may say so, you are acting American again, very impatient. You want things to happen quickly that must take a little time."

"Do you trust me?"

"Yes, I do, and for that reason, Jorge is treating you as a guest in his home. But for him to discuss your doctor friend requires that the villagers know you better and trust you."

"Why do you not share these concerns?"

"Perhaps because you did not run away when I came upon the thief that was threatening you. Perhaps because I can see that your concern in coming here is sincere. Perhaps because you did not choose to tell me that Calderón said bad things about me. Perhaps because when you have lived for twelve years as I did in the war, you learn quickly who you can trust and who you cannot."

"How do you know what Calderón said to me about you?" asked Anthony, completely surprised.

"The woman who was your escort is an old friend."

Anthony shook his head in wonder. "So, what happens now?"

"I will take you to the village and give you an introduction to the elders. You will also be free to wander so long as I know where you are. When you are done, we will return here. You can decide each day what the next shall be."

"I'm not so sure that I should stay here."

"Don't mistake Jorge's respect for the villagers as a disrespect of you. He truly likes you, as his family does. If they were at all uncomfortable with you, they would ask us to leave."

"As you suggest, let's play this one day at a time," said Anthony.

"Soon you will have 'confianza,'" said Mr. Hernández.

"What's that?"

"The trust and confidence of those in the village. When they get to know you as I do."

The two men prepared themselves for the twelve mile journey to the center of the village. They put two containers of water in the trunk of Mr. Hernández's car. It would be an introductory gift from Anthony to the elders. On the drive to the village over an uneven dirt and gravel road, Mr. Hernández explained to Anthony that he would get to meet the important members of the village. Some would greet him more favorably than others. The younger men would be the least trustful."

"Why is that?" asked Anthony.

"They will be somewhat envious of you, simply because you are an American. Also, the single women will want to size you up. You would be considered a prize for them."

"Come on," said Anthony. "I'm married and only here for a short time. These people are religious, and you just told me that I haven't earned their trust yet. Where is the prize in that?"

"You are American. You are rich to them. You would not be the first American to take a Salvadoran mistress."

"Wouldn't such a person be cast out from her village?"

Mr. Hernández laughed. "The church would tell her she is sinful, but to the unmarried women, you would be a prize. Other women would be jealous of her. The church is important to the villagers for births, baptism, weddings and funerals. For money and luxury, Americans are much more valuable. That is why the men would not like you so much, unless it was their sister that you took as a mistress."

"That's not why I'm here," said Anthony as the car rocked from side to side.

Suddenly, Mr. Hernández pulled over to the side driving the car over sage and rocks. A cloud of dust slowly revealed an oncoming bus that took up most of the road. They waited off to the side until it passed.

"How do you decide who yields?" asked Anthony.

"The bus is much bigger," said Mr. Hernández.

They reached the village after driving another mile that was turbulent enough to make Anthony feel lightheaded and unsteady. When the car stopped, he asked Mr. Hernández if he could take a minute to collect himself.

"Wait here," said Mr. Hernández as he got out of the car.

Anthony watched Mr. Hernández walk toward a large circular fountain with a stone perimeter that stood about two feet above ground. It was the centerpiece of the village around which was an outer circle of small buildings. Those on the left consisted of a few shops and a Western Union satellite office that Anthony later learned was used to receive wire transfers from the expatriates sending money home. The buildings on Anthony's right were a cantina, a storefront with the sign "Escuela", and a clinic bearing a red cross. Straight ahead was a small church. There were five men standing in front of the fountain who welcomed Mr. Hernández. Several other villagers watched from a distance. An older woman wrapped in a black shawl stood alone looking at the men from the front of the church.

After the greetings were over, Mr. Hernández walked back to the car. He opened the door and asked Anthony if he was ready to meet the village elders. Anthony nodded. They each retrieved and carried a container of water.

Anthony walked behind Mr. Hernández as they made their way toward the men. When they reached them, he realized that two of the "elders" were no older than he. The three other men were in the age range of Anthony's parents. After they placed the water containers in the bone dry fountain, introductions were made by Mr. Hernández. It was clear that the younger men had a better command of English than the older.

Anthony explained to them that the doctor who was killed at the clinic was a personal friend, and that he came to El Salvador to retrieve his friend's remains. He hoped to bring them back to the United States so that his family could honor his passing. Mr. Hernández interjected that the government had possession of the remains, but they would be turned over to Anthony the following week.

"So why do you come here, to our village?" asked one of the older men.

"I would like to see where my friend worked. I would like to speak with the people he served and ask them what they liked about him so that I may tell his family."

Mr. Hernández interjected something in Spanish that Anthony took as an interpretation for the older men.

"What are you expecting to learn?" asked one of the younger men. "He was a doctor. He helped people who had bad teeth or a damaged mouth. People liked him. Now he is dead. What more is there to know?"

"My friend first came here out of a sense of duty because he was a doctor and wanted to offer his help to people who might not otherwise receive it. After coming here a few times, this place became very important to him. He collected art and music from El Salvador because he was moved by the people and the struggles they endured."

Once again, Mr. Hernández intervened in Spanish.

Anthony continued, "He knew the history of this country and shared the pain of its people and their hopes for better times. It is my hope to understand that a little better so that I and his family and friends will not feel like he died in vain. He loved this place and I wish to bring an understanding of that love to those who loved him."

The second younger man spoke, his voice rising, "Many, many Salvadorans have died including some from this village. Many are left without mothers, fathers, brothers, sisters and children. No one from America cares about them, but one doctor dies and you are here, and the government works to send him home. Our village stops everything to listen to you."

Mr. Hernández started to say something, but Anthony put his hand on his arm.

"I understand that the losses we have experienced are not the same," said Anthony.

"I think you understand nothing, Señor," the young man continued. "Tell me, if a Salvadoran went to America and he was killed there, would the Americans stop to explain to one of us, what he did, why he liked America, why he was such a nice man, a good man?"

One of the elders raised his hand and said something to the young man who then turned away.

The elder spoke, "We shall show you where the clinic is, what is left of it. But for now, let us go to the cantina where we will have a drink and you can tell us more about yourself, and we shall speak about your friend."

Anthony looked at Mr. Hernández who nodded. The last thing Anthony wanted to do was to sit and drink, but he realized that he was still being sized up. If he were to stand a chance of achieving "confianza," he would have to go along.

They walked to the cantina and all seven men took seats around a table while the proprietor brought out bottles of beer. The younger man who had challenged Anthony sat sideways looking away from the others at the table. Anthony knew that he would have to win him over if he was to gain the confidence and cooperation of the others. As Anthony looked back toward the fountain, women had gathered to fill water bottles from the containers they had brought. The old woman who had been standing in front of the church was now at the fountain. She ignored the water, but continued to watch the men.

Chapter 31

"So, Señor," one of the elders who had been quiet until now asked Anthony, "Tell us who you are. Where are you from in America? What is your family like? What is your profession? What do you think of our country?"

"Gentlemen," Anthony began, "if you will forgive me I will speak in English because my Spanish is so poor. With your permission, I will rely on Mr. Hernández to help me communicate if there is something I do not say clearly."

The elder nodded indicating that Anthony should go ahead.

"My name is Anthony, Antonio, if you prefer. I am from the town of Hempstead outside of New York City, in an area called Long Island where I have a home with my wife, Bernadette. We have no children yet, but hopefully that will change in the future. I am a businessman in the field of communications technology. Um… the business of telephones and computers."

The men looked at Anthony, their faces seemingly indifferent.

"I think it would help me," continued Anthony, "if you would tell me your names before I go on."

The men looked at each other considering the proposal. The elder turned back to Anthony.

"I am Hector," he said and put out his hand.

The man alongside him said, "Ignacio" and also shook hands with Anthony.

Anthony looked to the next man who responded by saying "Donato" who nodded instead of offering a handshake.

The next in line, one of the younger men, said, "Ernesto" while he twirled a toothpick in his mouth.

The last was the young man who gave Anthony a hard time while they were at the fountain. He clearly had an excellent command of the English language and was not afraid to use it. He looked at Anthony without saying anything. Anthony just looked back at him and waited.

"My name is Eduardo, Ed if you like," he said.

"Thank you," said Anthony. "I have only been in El Salvador since Sunday. So what I know of your country is what I have read in books. As we know, books cannot tell the whole story of a place. I want to see what I can for myself by spending a few days here, and as I said earlier, I would like to see where my friend worked and meet some of the people who knew him and impressed him so much."

"And what have you learned since your arrival?" asked Ignacio.

"That the people who work in the government offices here are not that different from those in America," Anthony said hoping he would get a smile or favorable response.

Eduardo shot back, "Do those people ever come to your house with guns, Señor?" He got up and walked toward the fountain.

Anthony realized that his attempt at humor had failed.

"Eduardo has a, how do you say, a piece of wood on his shoulder," said Ignacio.

"A chip," corrected Ernesto. "A chip on his shoulder."

The men all nodded in agreement.

Hector stood and said, "Perhaps we have met enough for today. Tomorrow, we can bring to you some of the people the good doctor has helped. They will tell you of him. If you like, we can also have our school teacher meet with you. She had helped explain the needs of these people to the doctor."

Anthony realized they were done for the day. Maybe they needed to discuss him amongst themselves. He was disappointed by the abrupt ending of the meeting, but thought it had ended on a positive note with a promise of more to come.

"I would like that very much," Anthony said in response to the offer.

Mr. Hernández came to his side and said something to the others in Spanish. They nodded.

"Come. Mr. Anthony," he said. "I will take you to the clinic."

"Oh, great," said Anthony, his spirits picking up. They would get more out of the day.

The two men turned to walk back to the car when Anthony saw Eduardo talking to the old woman by the fountain. The woman was looking over Eduardo's shoulder at Anthony and Mr. Hernández.

"What's going on with Eduardo and the woman?" he asked Mr. Hernández.

"I think the answer to that will come tomorrow. Try to be patient."

They reached the car and drove slowly away from the center of the village until they reached a dirt road that had been hardened by the regular passage of vehicles. In less than a quarter mile, a blackened cinderblock shell of a one story building appeared. The roof was completely gone. Empty spaces that were once a doorway and two windows stared menacingly at the visitors. To Anthony the building seemed a miniature replica of the burned out apartment buildings that populated the slums of the south Bronx. The ground crunched under their feet as they walked on a pathway of dirt, debris, rock and ground glass. Anthony recalled how a McDonald's restaurant in California had been razed and replaced by a park-like monument within two days of a tragic shooting by a crazed gunman. The clinic, or what was left of it, was just another damaged building in El Salvador, one of many. No monuments would be built here.

Mr. Hernández waited outside as Anthony walked through what was once an entrance. The inside of the building had a dividing wall that separated two rooms that when combined would fit in his living room at home. Despite the warm afternoon air, there was a chill inside the cinder block walls. The wooden floor had cracked boards and was missing a large section along one wall. There were large rusted cans, broken bottles, charred beams and remnants of wrecked furniture all about. Anthony stepped over the obstacles carefully testing each place he put his foot before resting his weight on it. There were burned out cabinets along the wall. If they once had doors, they had been taken off. As he made his way into the second room, there was a table resting sideways with two legs half buried under more wreckage. File cabinets without drawers lined the walls. What once contained charts, notes and files that recorded the health of the community this building served, that Martin served, was now a collection of charred metal serving no one.

Anthony approached the bare pedestal for a machine or perhaps a mechanically operated patient chair. He bent to touch it and determined it was stable. He sat and studied the mess covering the floor looking for something familiar or recognizable. When his eyes dropped to his dust covered shoes, he put his head in his hands.

"What the hell am I doing here?" he asked himself in a

low voice. "Is this what happens when somebody does something useful? Does he end up as a piece of unrecognizable garbage? Does the place where you give your life turn into a shit hole? Do the people that had been helped here even care? Couldn't they have at least cleaned the place up?"

He stood slowly and looked through a space that once held a framed window. He could see Mr. Hernández standing outside and realized that he had been overheard. The big man's head was bowed, and he was holding his hat in his hand. In the other direction, he saw another figure in the distance. He squinted until he was sure he recognized Eduardo. The young man turned and walked away not attempting to hide. Anthony reached into the debris around his feet and picked up a handful of pebbles, dirt and charred remains of something wood and put them in his pocket.

"Fuck these people and their goddamn games," he said.

He made his way back to the building entrance and walked up to Mr. Hernández.

"I'd like to leave now and I'd like to get a room at the hotel in Perquín," he said.

They drove away stopping at Jorge's house where at Anthony's request Mr. Hernández went to collect both their belongings while Anthony waited in the car. Anthony looked straight ahead and turned toward the house only when he heard Mr. Hernández bidding his friends goodbye. When he did, he saw Maria wave silently in his direction. Anthony waved back and then faced forward before anyone else came out.

Chapter 32

The men drove back to the central section of Perquín. They passed the museum they had driven by the day before and continued until they came to the Hotel Perquín Lenca. It had the appearance of a refined mountain lodge designed for those who wanted a rustic setting with all the creature comforts of a first class hotel. It had been built by a former American relief worker that adopted El Salvador as his new home, and free market capitalism as his new way of life.

Anthony and Mr. Hernández left the car, registered in the elegant lobby and took separate, adjacent cabins that had modern bathrooms, fireplaces and a sitting area separated from the sleeping quarters. They agreed to meet back in the lobby in thirty minutes. The secret knocks on the door were no longer deemed necessary. Being aware of his surroundings was now instinctive to Anthony. Mr. Hernández viewed Perquín differently than he did San Salvador. If he didn't know all fifty-five hundred residents, they most certainly knew him. As his client, Anthony was perfectly safe.

Anthony put his clothing and personal belongings away. He emptied his pocket of the dirt, pebbles and charred wood he had picked up from the clinic floor and put them in a plastic cup on the bathroom sink. He replaced the plastic wrap over it and put the cup in his suitcase. He grabbed the black bag and started to remove the SkyTel folder, but put it back. He took out the cell phone and called Bernadette, first at their home number and then to her cell phone, reaching voice mail in both instances. He left a brief message at each to let her know that he had called. He sat on the Indian weave sofa and tried to unravel the myriad thoughts going through his head.

Bernadette obviously did not want to take his calls. Jorge had disappointed him. Why wouldn't she at least answer? Anthony had taken an instant liking to Jorge and had expressed his appreciation for what seemed like his host's mutual regard and respect. He felt well received by Jorge's family. To learn that Jorge was withholding information was upsetting. If Bernadette was still angry, why couldn't she just say so and eliminate any question of her well being? That smug Eduardo saying in reference to Martin: "He helped people... People liked him... Now he is dead... What more is there to know?" Did they write him off that easily? The clinic left as a burned out shell seemed disrespectful. Would that be Martin's legacy? Did he not deserve more? If there was anything wrong with Bernadette, one of her friends would contact him, certainly Carla would. His last conversation with Jack Mullen fought its way to the top of Anthony's thoughts. *Jack was laying it on the line telling Anthony that his fellow employees were not unhappy to see him go. That Anthony did not distinguish between being forthright and being disrespectful to his colleagues. Why wouldn't Bernadette pick up the damn phone? Was he being unfair to Jorge and the villagers?*

"No," he said out loud. "They should have acknowledged that I was a friend of their friend."

Anthony looked at his watch and realized that he was running late for his meeting with Mr. Hernández.

The huge fireplace in the lobby of the main lodge was roaring. There were groups of Germans and French talking loudly in their native tongues in a setting that looked like

Indiana Jones was expected to walk through the door. Anthony spotted Mr. Hernández near the front door and asked if they could go to a quieter place for a drink. Mr. Hernández nodded, pushed open the door and suggested they walk to the La Cocina de Ma'Anita just two blocks away.

When they arrived, the small bar was already full of patrons so they took a table in the dining room for more privacy. They agreed to drink rum over ice and Mr. Hernández ordered a bottle. They sat in silence until the waiter brought glasses, imported rum and a small glass decanter of ice cubes. They added ice to their glasses and Mr. Hernández poured rum for both. He raised his glass to Anthony.

"To a better day tomorrow," he said.

"I hope I didn't insult or offend you today," said Anthony.

"I understand that you are a good man on a noble mission," said Mr. Hernández.

"Do you think I screwed up today?"

"The villagers will see you tomorrow not knowing your feelings. I will talk to Jorge. He was surprised by your leaving, but he will understand."

"But, is he offended?"

"Mr. Anthony, you left the hospitality of his home and family. This was a surprise to him. He does not understand your anger."

"Sometimes, I don't understand it myself. Often, when I think over something I've done, I start thinking about what I should've done instead. I constantly struggle trying to figure out what is right."

"Why do you do this struggle?" asked Mr. Hernández.

"I'm not sure. To find the truth I guess."

"The truth is not always the same to everyone, Mr. Anthony."

"I understand that, but still..."

"Still?"

"A person has to believe in what is right and act on that belief."

"Do you think you can find the truth in anger?"

"That sounds like a question to which there is no answer."

"Then we should have more rum," said Mr. Hernández as he poured each of them another drink.

Anthony let the rum glide down his throat and enjoyed its warmth.

"Rum may become my new best friend," he said.

Mr. Hernández smiled back.

"I really didn't want to offend Jorge," said Anthony. "He has been good to me, but when I learned that he did not reveal everything he knew, I was disappointed. I got angry. Why wouldn't he trust me? I have no agenda except to understand the experience my friend had at this place. I mean no harm to anyone."

"Perhaps, you know that better than he. He may just need some time to know you better, or perhaps, you do not know yourself all the reasons why you are here."

"What does that mean?" asked Anthony.

"Mr. Anthony, as I listen to everything you have told me about why you are here, what your friend meant to you, what you are trying to do for his family, I believe you. One hundred percent ... but there is something else."

"I'm not following you."

Anthony hadn't realized they had finished another glass of rum until Mr. Hernández poured again. He reached over and took another ice cube from the decanter with his fingers and plopped it into his glass.

"May I speak freely?" said Mr. Hernández."

"Of course. I have nothing but respect and admiration for you, and you saved my life. Fire away," said Anthony as the rum made its way to all the little nerve endings that had not been fortified by any food since morning.

"When you met with Calderón, he did not give you what you came for. He made you change your whole plan. You did not like that, and you did not like him, but yet you did not get angry."

"I was conducting business," said Anthony.

"Yes, and then Jorge and his family offer you their home and hospitality, but he does not tell you everything you wish to hear even though you are still new to them. So you get angry. You have no patience. You want everything to happen quickly."

"He didn't trust me and that made it personal," said Anthony defensively.

"And when the people of the village agreed to meet with you, and asked a few questions and invited you back the next day, you were angry with them."

"I felt they were playing with me."

"And when you saw the ruins of the clinic, you were angry again."

"I believe they should have done something to clean the place up."

"Then why would you not go to them and ask them to help you do that."

"I guess if I offered money it could get done," Anthony said with a mocking tone.

"That is more anger, Mr. Anthony."

"What's your point?" said Anthony testily.

Mr. Hernández paused for a moment and looked at

Anthony straight in the eye.

"I'm sorry for the attitude," said Anthony. "It just sounds like you're accusing me of doing or saying things I shouldn't have. I do that to myself all the time. I don't want to lose your friendship."

"My point, my friend, is that if these things of which we have spoken make you angry, there is something inside of you that is causing the anger, not Jorge or the elders."

Anthony could not think of anything to say. He started to raise the glass to his lips when Mr. Hernández raised his own and tapped Anthony's before draining the rum. Anthony took the opportunity to pour for both of them, this time not bothering with the ice. They drank this round without speaking. Anthony poured another, this time raising his glass to Mr. Hernández before sipping.

"I guess I screwed up," said Anthony. "My life has been a bit of a mess lately. There have been problems with my work and my wife. My friend was killed, another friend tried to take her own life, a couple separated although I wouldn't say they were both my friends."

"Did you not get angry before these things happened?"

Anthony and the rum laughed, "I couldn't say that."

Mr. Hernández laughed in return.

"It seems to me," said Mr. Hernández, "that you get angry when things do not go as you would like. That is not unusual, but you get very angry when you think that someone does not trust you or believe you."

"Wouldn't that bother you?" asked Anthony.

"I trust very few people therefore I am seldom disappointed."

"I don't trust many people either. I trust myself most of all. I am disappointed in myself when I fail to do what is right."

"And when you fail others, does that disappoint you? Make you angry?"

An image of Rita made its way into Anthony's consciousness.

"I think we should order some food," he said. "I'm getting looped."

Mr. Hernández recommended the grilled steak with roasted vegetables and Salvadoran tortillas which he described as different from those found in Mexican restaurants in the U.S. Anthony agreed to the selection.

"Would you like wine or beer with your meal?" asked Mr. Hernández.

"I think I should just stick with the rum or have some bottled water," said Anthony, slurring slightly.

"Wise choice," said Mr. Hernández.

"So what do you think I should do?" asked Anthony.

"I think we should enjoy a nice dinner. It will be good to get something in your stomach besides the rum," said Mr. Hernández.

"That not what I meant," said Anthony.

Mr. Hernández was quiet for a moment before he spoke. "I think tomorrow we should go back to the village and meet with elders. You should listen to what they have to say and answer their questions. Then ask them any questions you may have. If you wish to speak to them about clearing the clinic site, you should do so. Give them a chance to disappoint you. You have nothing to lose."

"And will you tell me what the others may know that I don't."

"I think it is best that you hear certain things from people in the village who knew your friend better than I or Jorge."

"How will I know if they are telling me everything?"

"It is important that you listen."

"But..."

"And try not to get angry."

The food arrived and as was their custom in their short acquaintance, they savored the meal and the rum and discontinued talk of the day's business.

Before they called it a night, Anthony made a request.

"Tomorrow, I will meet with the elders and listen as you suggested," he said. "I will do my best to remain calm, but before we do that I would like to make some purchases with your help."

"What is it you wish to buy?

"I want to buy some overalls, work shoes, work gloves, a hat, shovel and a wheelbarrow."

Mr. Hernández looked at Anthony before speaking, but did not comment or question Anthony's request.

"There is a General Store in town that has such things. We can pick them up in the morning."

"Thank you," said Anthony. "Now I think I'd better get to my room before the rum decides to punish me."

Chapter 33

Anthony woke up earlier than usual feeling tired and with a foul taste in his mouth. After taking a long shower, he shaved and brushed his teeth and felt a little better. He did some stretching exercises and made coffee with the amenities provided in the room. Knowing he wasn't scheduled to meet with Mr. Hernández for another hour or so, he thought about the day before. As the meeting with the elders, his experience at the clinic and his conversation with Mr. Hernández ran through his mind, he felt very isolated. His thoughts drifted to Bernadette, Sarah, Carla and Nancy, but brought no comfort. He knew he should follow up with Trenholme about the job contract, but wasn't motivated to make the call. He was still upset by Jorge's holding back whatever it was he knew about Martin. Instead of concluding that he should reconcile his actions to what was expected by the others, he decided to keep his own counsel. He would take one issue at a time. He would fulfill his obligation to meet with the elders, but his personal objective for today was the clinic. He wanted to be outside, to do something physical. Everything else could be addressed later. He knew what he needed to do today.

He met Mr. Hernández at the appointed hour and they had a hearty breakfast and more coffee. They did not speak other than Mr. Hernández affirming that they would stop at the general store before meeting the elders. He offered no more advice or insights into Anthony's behavior.

As they got up to leave, Anthony said, "I want you to

know that I appreciate everything you've done for me."

"Whatever I have done, I have done because I believe you are a good man with a good purpose," Mr. Hernández replied.

It took about fifteen minutes to reach the general store which turned out to be larger than Anthony had expected. In addition to a full complement of work clothes and tools for the farm and garden, it had merchandise ranging from camping gear and casual clothing to basic foods and souvenirs. Anthony selected a pair of bib overalls that he could wear over his street clothes if necessary, a denim shirt, and one pair of heavy socks, work boots and a western style straw hat. In the tools section, he picked out a long handle shovel, a broom and dust pan and a heavy duty wheelbarrow. Before he completed his purchase he remembered to get work gloves, deciding to get some extras in case they got muddy or torn. The store accepted his credit card and Mr. Hernández helped him load everything into the car. Mr. Hernández excused himself and went back into the store. He came out with a large bag and a six pack of water bottles.

"I cannot imagine you using those tools without a good supply of water," he said.

"Thank you," said Anthony. "Forgetting water could've been a serious mistake."

The two men and their cargo headed for the village.

"If you don't mind and if you think it will be safe, I would like to leave all this stuff at the clinic before we meet with the elders," said Anthony.

"It will be safe," said Mr. Hernández confidently.

They drove as close to the clinic as the road would allow, emptied the car of the gear and clothing, and then drove the short distance back to the village center. The

elders were already there seated outside the cantina drinking coffee. They sat in the same order as the day before except that in Eduardo's place was a woman. Anthony guessed she was in her forties. She wore a long sleeve white blouse with a pointed collar, a multi-colored long skirt and blue kerchief. As he got closer, Anthony could see she was wearing rimless eyeglasses and no makeup. Her only jewelry was a plastic bracelet on each wrist, one red and one yellow. They matched the colors in her skirt.

The men invited Anthony and Mr. Hernández to sit and ordered coffee for them without asking. After greetings were exchanged, the woman was introduced to Anthony as Señora Cabrera, the village school teacher who came from Perquín four days a week.

"Very nice to meet you," said Anthony.

"It is my pleasure, Señor," she said.

Señora Cabrera went on to provide her background information to Anthony. It became obvious that she was well educated. Her work was her personal effort to promote education for the children of the village. She had traveled to Europe and the United States as a younger woman, and occasionally served as a resource to foreigners doing research on El Salvador's civil war. She had lost her husband in the war. She asked Anthony questions about his professional background and appeared able to keep up with Anthony's references to communication technologies. Then she switched to a more personal line of questioning.

"You have no children at this time?"

"No," said Anthony, thinking that she already knew this.

"May I ask why?"

Anthony felt the blood rushing to his face thinking this

was none of her business, and had nothing to do with why he was here.

"My wife and I made a decision to wait until our careers were established, and we were in a secure financial position before starting a family," he said.

"And are you in such a position now?"

Exercising as much self control as he could, he said, "Yes."

Anthony began to feel as though he were being questioned by an attorney with an agenda. He recalled advice he had once received to answer questions in such a setting with as few words and information as possible.

"And do you expect to begin a family soon?" the woman asked.

"The matter is under consideration," he said trying to be evasive by not saying too much.

"Do you have a desire for a large family or small?"

"Well, that's all relative, but one has to consider the cost of education and providing opportunities for one's children."

Then he added, "Do you have children of your own?" He risked alienating her by going on the offensive, but he had enough of this line of questioning.

"Your friend, the doctor, he had no family?" she asked, ignoring his question.

"He had a wife, but they had no children. I am representing her in the matter of returning his remains to the United States."

"Were the doctor and his wife also waiting to be in a secure financial situation?"

"Señora, you must know that the doctor was financially secure. You may not know that his wife had suffered two miscarriages and is now unable to bear children."

"I see," she said when Anthony interrupted.

"Señora Cabrera, I am sincerely trying to answer your questions, but I must confess I do not see their relevance. I understood the purpose of your meeting with me was to help me understand how the services provided by my friend helped the people of this village, and how those people felt about him. Your questions are not helping me."

Anthony rose and said to the elders, "Gentlemen, I thank you for the time you have given me this morning."

He turned to Señora Cabrera. "Señora," he said, "I appreciate the opportunity to speak with you. Perhaps we shall have another talk at a later time."

Again he spoke to elders, "With much respect, I would like to stop our conversation now so that I may go to the clinic where I have some work to do before the day gets very hot. If you will excuse me, I will attend to that now. I will be at your disposal should you wish to talk further. Buenos Días."

The elders rose, but none offered to shake hands. Anthony gave a slight nod with his head, turned and walked away. As he did, he spotted the old woman watching them from in front of the fountain. Anthony looked directly at her and she stared right back.

Anthony started the walk toward the clinic aware that Mr. Hernández was not coming along. *He's probably explaining my rude behavior to the Supreme Court of this shithole of a village*, he thought.

When Anthony reached the clinic it was approaching 10:00 A.M. He was ready to work up a good sweat. He brought the work clothes inside the charred ruins of the building. He took off his outer clothes and replaced them with the denim shirt, overalls, socks and work shoes. He donned his new hat and put on a pair of work gloves. He positioned the wheelbarrow outside an opening in the cinder block structure and carried the water, shovel, broom and dust pan into the building. He put his street clothes over the water bottles to protect them from the sun. After surveying the mess from the inside, he stepped out and checked his surroundings. A ragged grove of trees was about fifty yards from where he stood. He walked to it and found that it was quite dense, but had open patches that were covered with a mix of fauna and debris. He designated the largest open space as his dump site and walked back to the building.

Anthony opened one of the water bottles and took a swig. His plan was to start in the second room and remove the biggest movable objects first. Starting with the overturned table, he pulled on its legs and dragged it to the opening. Once there, he wished he had purchased a hand truck, but had to settle for balancing the table on the wheelbarrow and maneuvering it to the dump site. He had to stop twice to prevent it from falling off, but managed to get the table to the clearing. He made his way back and went straight for the file cabinets. They were even more awkward to get onto the wheelbarrow and harder to balance, but one by one he got them to dump site. He thought his next objective should be the pedestal he had sat on the day before, but it was much too heavy for him to move, never mind lift onto the wheelbarrow. *This will serve as a chair to rest my weary bones, and be the last to go*, he thought as his spirits improved with the work. "Fuck 'em all," he said. "Fuck 'em all."

Anthony walked backed to the first room and methodically picked up and carried bottles, cans and light debris to the wheelbarrow and carted it all to the dump.

After an hour or so, he was impressed by how much the dump site contained but dismayed by how little the clinic seemed to be cleared. He went back to second room and started hauling the charred furniture remnants. After three such hauls, he felt the twinge in his back that he recognized from his chair lifting exercise at Martin's house and his venture of underwater kayaking. An aching back and the arrival of the sweat he'd sought prompted him to take a break. He grabbed the water bottle and took a seat on the pedestal. He removed his hat and raised the bottle over his head letting water spill onto his hair and face. Even though he was hurting a little, his spirits were better than they had been in the last two days. He took another drink and the water spilled over his lips, chin and down the outside of his throat. After taking some deep breaths he rotated his back from side to side. Standing, he raised his arms and stretched upward, then leaned to each side. When he straightened he took another gulp of water and rested the bottle on the pedestal. He put his hat back on and looked through what was once a doorway where he saw a man watching him from a distance. Rather than check him out, Anthony went back to work.

Despite the stretching, the break caused his back to stiffen so he went back to picking up the smaller litter. After filling and transporting the wheelbarrow, he went back and repeated the process. The ache in his back was uncomfortable, but tolerable. Following two more trips to the dump site, he found company when he returned to the building.

"Buenos Días, Antonio," said Eduardo.

"Buenos Días, Eduardo," he said.

Anthony said nothing more and went back to filling the wheelbarrow with cans, bottles and scrap. Without a word,

Eduardo began picking up the waste around his feet and added it to the wheelbarrow. Anthony pointed to the extra work gloves resting on the floor.

"You may want to use those," he said as he left with the wheelbarrow.

When he returned Eduardo was wearing the gloves and had collected pieces of broken furniture that lay on the ground just outside the building. Anthony brought the wheelbarrow to a rest and watched as Eduardo filled it.

"Take a break," he said to Anthony. "I'll get this one." He left following the trail Anthony had taken. When Eduardo returned, Anthony handed him a fresh bottle of water.

Without conversation the men continued their labor for two more hours. There was still plenty of debris lying around, but the big stuff except for the pedestal was gone.

"That's enough for today," said Anthony. "I need a beer."

"That is the best thing you have said since you arrived at our village," said Eduardo.

Anthony went inside and changed back into his street clothes. The two men walked to the cantina. On the way, they saw a few people in the square Anthony didn't recognize. He saw Mr. Hernández standing by the school building talking to the old woman who had been keeping a close eye on Anthony.

"Who is that old hag?" Anthony asked Eduardo.

Eduardo smiled, "She lives in the village. I know her very well. She is interested in you. She is interested in all strangers."

"Can I buy you a beer?" asked Anthony.

Eduardo was still smiling and looked to be preparing a smart answer, but just said, "*Sí*."

After Anthony and Eduardo finished two beers, Mr. Hernández came over to the cantina.

Anthony said, "I'd invite you to join us for a beer, but I'm getting ready to crash and would appreciate a ride back to the hotel."

"No problem. After you have some rest, I am sure we can find more beer," said Mr. Hernández.

Without acknowledging Eduardo's help other than to shake his hand, Anthony and Mr. Hernández departed. On the drive back, the road seemed bumpier than in the morning. Anthony braced himself with his hands against the passenger door and the dash board trying to keep his back straight and his body from bouncing.

"So, who is the old woman you were talking to?" asked Anthony.

Mr. Hernández smiled, "I thought you would know that," he said. "She is Eduardo's mother."

Chapter 34

When they returned to the hotel, Anthony stopped in the restaurant kitchen and asked for a bag of ice. When he reached his room, he wrapped the bag in a towel and applied it to his back. He maneuvered his body on the sofa until he found a position that was comfortable and provided some relief. His mind was trying to unravel the spoken and unspoken words of the day when he drifted off into the peaceful sleep that often rewards physical labor.

The phone startled Anthony. He jumped up from the sofa, turned and picked it up.

"Anthony Bartolo," he answered instinctively knowing that he did something wrong, but wasn't quite sure what it was.

"Mr. Anthony, I don't know if you were planning on having dinner tonight, or if you want to rest in private," said Mr. Hernández at the other end of the line.

Anthony brushed the sleep away from his eyes.

"Sure, dinner sounds good, what time is it?"

"Seven o'clock."

"I was asleep Mr. Hernández, and I need to freshen up. Can we meet in twenty minutes?"

"Of course. I shall be in the lobby."

"Can we eat at the same place as last night?"

"Certainly. Take your time and I shall wait for you by the fireplace."

"Thank you. I'll be there shortly."

Anthony was fully awake now. He picked up the towel and discarded the plastic bag containing ice water before taking a quick shower. He dressed casually in jeans and a sweater which would be fine for tonight.

It was closer to a half hour before he joined Mr. Hernández in the lobby.

"So how do you feel after your day of hard work?" asked Mr. Hernández.

"Actually, I feel pretty good. My back is a little tight, but it's okay. I had a great nap."

The evening air felt invigorating as they walked to La Cocina. Once inside they went straight to the dining area which was buzzing, ordered a bottle of rum and dinner.

"It didn't go well with Señora Cabrera this morning. I tried to be cool, but I felt as though I was getting the third degree. I thought I would be the one asking questions and getting information."

"She was just doing as she was asked," replied Mr. Hernández.

"By whom?" asked Anthony.

"The elders of the village."

"I don't get what's going on with Eduardo and his mother. He was giving me a hard time yesterday, and she's creeping me out. I thought she was putting some ancient curse on me the way she stared and followed me around. Today, he gives me a hand without a word of explanation, and she's talking to you. Can you please explain what's going on?"

"She wishes to speak with you in the morning. She will speak about whatever is on her mind. She asked if you would meet with her in the church at eight o'clock."

"In the church?"

"That is her wish."

"Do you think I should go?"

"If you wish to hear what is on her mind, you should

go."

"In other words, you want me to hear it from her."

"There are some things you should hear for yourself. Since her English is poor, I can assist, but I think it is important for you to see and hear her as she speaks."

"Is Eduardo going to be with her?"

"Perhaps. I am not sure."

"You realize of course, that this is driving me nuts."

"For that we have some rum. Enjoy your dinner and give some thought to what you have experienced here."

"That's all I've been thinking about."

"Tomorrow, many of your questions shall be answered. The elders think well of you, Mr. Anthony."

"I'm surprised to hear that."

"I am not," said Mr. Hernández as he refilled their glasses with rum.

The walk back from the restaurant cleared his head. The puzzle of the old woman was still on his mind. He didn't make any phone calls or even think about calling anyone. He did some stretching exercises hoping to heal his back before going to bed. Despite having had an earlier nap, Anthony fell asleep right away.

On Saturday morning, Anthony awoke feeling refreshed and met Mr. Hernández for breakfast as planned. He dressed in the same street clothes as the day before, not wanting to overdress for his meeting with Eduardo's mother. He planned to work at the clinic again when they were done talking. He would change into his work clothes when he got to the clinic.

Before leaving for the church, Mr. Hernández said they should discuss their schedule.

"Señora Carla called me this morning. No one has heard from you, and she was not sure if you still planned to return to San Salvador on Wednesday."

"I haven't called her in a couple of days, but I've left messages for my wife," said Anthony."

"I advised her that you will probably return to San Salvador as planned, but that we are waiting to hear from Calderón before we know for sure."

"That's about as much as I could've said," said Anthony.

"She sounded worried, Antonio."

Anthony sat back with the realization that this was the first time Mr. Hernández addressed him in this manner. The look on Mr. Hernández's face was of concern.

"Everything is fine," he said, "I've been trying to figure out what's going on with the villagers. I have some decisions to make about my career and future, and I have to do some fence mending with my wife. I can do these things best if I take them one at a time. Today is the day for Eduardo's mother and the work at the clinic. Tonight I will call Señora Carla."

Mr. Hernández looked at him.

"And I'll call my wife again," Anthony added.

"Let us go to meet Eduardo's mother," said Mr. Hernández.

They arrived at the village shortly after 8:00 A.M. The cantina was opening up, but none of the elders was present. The two men walked to the church. Mr. Hernández held the door open and followed Anthony inside. The inside was more pleasant than Anthony expected. There were two stands of votive candles on each side of the entrance. Wooden pews separated by a center aisle ran from the back of the church to the plain altar in front. Behind it was the decorative main altar that had not been used since Vatican II other than to house the tabernacle containing the savior of man, the very meaning of El Salvador. Above it was a colorful crucifix bearing a Jesus that had the high cheekbones and dark hair found among the indigenous peoples and mixed races of this country. Anthony did not find it amusing as he had had the blond, blue eyed Jesus looking down on the multitudes of Hempstead, Long Island.

Sitting alone in one of the pews was Eduardo's mother praying, her lips moving rapidly with fingers sliding over a string of beads.

As she saw Anthony and Mr. Hernández, she rose and called out,

"Eduardo."

Eduardo stepped out from behind the wall that separated the main altar from the sacristy and came forward to stand at the side of his mother.

"I have arranged with the priest to use a room in the back where we can talk privately," he said. He extended his arm in the direction in which they should walk. Anthony and Mr. Hernández followed as Eduardo led them to the meeting room.

The room was sparsely furnished with a gray metal table and four gray folding chairs. The walls were bare except for a small crucifix on one wall. Eduardo and his mother took seats on one side of the table. Mr. Hernández and Anthony sat facing them with their backs to the door. There was an awkward moment of silence before Eduardo spoke.

"Don Antonio, may I present my mother. She wishes to speak with you. She can understand English better than she can speak so she will speak in Spanish and I will translate for her. In case I have trouble finding the right words, I'm sure Mr. Hernández can help us."

Anthony knew that Eduardo would not need any assistance, but he wanted to show respect for Mr. Hernández. Anthony felt that he was the only one in the room who had no idea of what was going on. He took a deep breath and slowly and audibly exhaled. Then he nodded in consent to Eduardo. The old woman began to speak. Anthony was surprised at the strength of her voice and clarity of her speech. They were completely the opposite of what he expected from this haggard old woman. After the first few sentences, Eduardo repeated what she said in English.

"I am the mother of Ynez Órnelas. My daughter worked for the doctor and was killed with him. I am also abuela, grandmother to Ynez's child. I now care for this child who is without mother or father. You see the father of this child was the doctor, your friend. This is known by all in the village. The child's name is Martina. She is soon to be two years old."

Anthony's back straightened as the words and their meaning filtered through all of his suspicions. The woman seemed to sense what he was feeling and paused so he could absorb this news. Anthony said nothing so she continued and Eduardo dutifully translated.

"My Ynez and your friend worked together since the time of his arrival here. Whether they were in love or were just lonely, I do not know. When the child was conceived, Ynez was very happy. Your friend agreed to support Ynez and the child which he had done faithfully. He established a fund to provide for them. There was also an insurance policy in case anything happened to him. When the child was born, they both loved the child and grew closer to each other, but it was clear that the doctor also loved his wife in the United States and would never leave her. An old woman like me can understand how it is possible for a man to love two women in different ways, but not everyone in the village was sympathetic to him. Eduardo, for one, has always believed that the doctor should have married Ynez."

Anthony looked at Eduardo who, when he finished speaking for his mother, looked down at the table then slowly raised his head and looked at Anthony.

Speaking for himself, Eduardo added, "I cared for my sister a great deal. I wanted what was best for her. I did not like the idea of the American doctor having her as his mistress."

Eduardo's mother scolded him. The words were not clear to Anthony, but the meaning was. She did not like her daughter referred to in this way.

Anthony was reeling. Martin, who Anthony had put on a pedestal, especially since his death, was not a saint after all. His image of a truly noble person who provided humanitarian services to people in need with selfless dedication was severely tarnished. Martin had been leading a double life. *Was Martin's continuing work with MATES motivated by his desire for his mistress or the child she had given him? A child that Sarah couldn't.* Anthony put his head in his hands and tried to process what he was hearing.

The woman continued, "I can see that you are troubled by what you have learned. My son was also troubled when Ynez was first with child. But as he came to know your friend better, and he saw how happy Ynez was, he saw your friend differently. Eduardo realized that his sister was a woman, not a foolish girl. Your friend did not run back to the United States, never to return."

Anthony was still having a hard time digesting this and questioned Martin's motivation and his ability to live a lie.

"When you first came here," the woman continued, "I

suspected that you knew about the child and would try to take her from us. It is clear to me now that this is not your reason for being here. My son has told me that he thinks you are a good man even though he has known you for such a short time. Mr. Hernández, who I have known all my life, also tells me that you are a good person with no such purpose. Jorge and Consuelo say much the same thing."

The mention of Jorge's name startled Anthony. Without recalling all of his thoughts and feelings about Jorge, he intuitively realized why Jorge was reluctant to reveal any of this, and once again felt he had misjudged the person and situation.

He looked at Mr. Hernández, "I must apologize to Jorge."

"There will be time for that, Antonio," said Mr. Hernández.

Anthony looked at Señora Órnelas not sure if the meeting was over when she spoke again, and Eduardo translated.

"Since I have learned that your intentions are not what I first suspected, I have given this matter much thought. My fear had been that you would take our beautiful Martina from us, and I was determined to prevent that. My purpose was to protect the child. Now I have reached a different conclusion which is why I asked to meet with you this morning."

Anthony looked into the eyes of the woman and saw a different person than the old hag that was following him around the village square. The lines in her face were drawn by hard times. Living through twelve years of war and the recent loss of her daughter had taken their toll. Her eyes though weary showed more warmth than he had seen before.

"I am an old woman," she said. "My health is not good. I cannot provide the care for this child as her mother would. My son, Eduardo is a good boy, but he is not prepared to give this child a proper home, although this was our first intention. The child has no other family, another price of the war. So I have concluded that perhaps the child, Martina, belongs with you. Perhaps, she belongs with the childless wife of the doctor. I do not know her or your wife, but the elders, Eduardo and I have "confianza" that you will do what is best for the child. Whether Martina should return with you to the United States or not is a decision we entrust to you. If you decide this is not in the interests of the child, she will stay here and this village will be sure that she is always safe and cared for. It is a question of where and with whom she can have the best life. We Salvadorans have spent too much time killing one another. Each side distrusts the other even though the fighting has stopped. There are no assurances that war will not happen again. These men always think of war as the solution to our problems. I am afraid they will forget that the peace was decided because everyone was tired of the war which cost so many lives and solved nothing. I must think, we must all think of what is good for this child. I leave that question in your hands."

Anthony's head was spinning. He worked hard to not overreact.

"Señora Órnelas," he began deliberately, "I am overwhelmed by what you have told me. I'm honored by your trust, and I hope that I may continue to deserve it. Since we are talking about the life of a child here, I must speak to the others you have mentioned and search my own heart before I respond to your proposal. At this time, I ask that you give me some time to do so before I reply."

"Of course, Señor," she said. Eduardo then translated "May I suggest that you join us at Mass tomorrow morning at which time you may see our beautiful Martina? That may be helpful in your considerations. It is at 9:00 A.M."

Anthony was about to tell her he no longer attended Mass, but realized that that was irrelevant and it would be a deal breaker to decline.

"I will be honored to join you," he said.

Señora Órnelas stood and the men followed suit. She put out her hand and said without help from Eduardo, "Until tomorrow."

The men shook hands, Eduardo and his mother left the room. Anthony sat back down thinking about what to say or do next. Mr. Hernández put a hand on his shoulder.

"What just happened?" said Anthony.

"The world has changed for you," said Mr. Hernández.

"What am I supposed to do now? What do these people expect of me?"

"You only have to ask what you expect of yourself, Antonio."

Anthony just shook his head. "This is very fucked up," he said.

Mr. Hernández smiled and said, "My friend, I think we should go to the clinic again. Hard work seems to clear your head and going there will help you."

"You know that sounds like a great idea," said Anthony, "I think I can lift that pedestal and carry it to the dump site by myself right now, but I should go back to the hotel and make some calls. The clinic will still be there tomorrow."

"Then I shall take you back to the hotel," said Mr. Hernández.

"Would you mind staying with me so I can talk to you about all this?'

"Not at all. Do you wish to talk with rum or without?"

"Definitely without," said Anthony. "I need a clear head to sort all this out before I get on the phone."

Chapter 35

Anthony and Mr. Hernández returned to the lodge at about 10:00 A.M. The two men sat on a sofa facing the fireplace in the nearly empty lobby. They helped themselves to coffee from a nearby serving table and sat quietly for a moment before either spoke. Finally, Anthony cleared his throat and began saying out loud what had been running through his mind for the past hour.

"I'm not certain that my thoughts are very well organized yet, but if I may, I'd like to share them with you. If you have comments or see things differently, I will appreciate hearing what you have to say. Please don't be concerned about disagreeing with me or offending me. If you think I'm being a jerk, just say so. In doing so, you would be a true friend."

"With permission such as that, I will do what I can," said Mr. Hernández.

"I want to do the right thing here, but Señora Órnelas' proposal borders on the bizarre," said Anthony. "First of all, we are talking about taking a child out of the country and the village where she was born. Taking her from the only remaining family she has and bringing her to the United States which is about as different from her village as can be. I don't even know if it's possible to get her out of the country. Look at the grief we're going through just to collect Martin's remains!"

Mr. Hernández interrupted, "Antonio, this matter will be easier for you to deal with if you do not confuse logistical issues with the more important ones. If you decide to accept the Señora's proposal, the matters of passports, papers, permission to leave the country and so on, can be handled, and handled very quickly. They are not a matter for your concern."

"I don't understand," said Anthony.

Remember this country has been at war with itself for many years. The fighting stopped after twelve years, but the opposing camps remain. A person leaving this country with "proper papers" never seen by government authorities would not be a new thing. We have many Salvadoran expatriates living around the world. Some are educated, others are not; some are artists and engineers. Others are laborers, and some had been imprisoned. Some have returned and departed several times often with new identities. These are things that have been learned in El Salvador in order to survive. These matters should not be a concern for you. Passports, birth certificates, citizenship papers, new identification papers are possible. Trust me on this, Antonio."

"I've learned to trust anything you say. I'll try to concentrate on the human issues."

"Bueno," said Mr. Hernández.

"All right, let's assume that I present the proposal to Martin's wife. The first thing that will go through her mind is that her husband, whom she loved and whose work here she supported without question, had a mistress and a child whom she knew nothing about. She will feel deceived and betrayed. She would have to be able to forgive him which may take some time, *if* she can do it at all. On top of this, we are asking that she take his child as hers as a constant reminder of his infidelity. That's an awful lot to ask. Hell, I don't even know how *I* feel about all this."

Mr. Hernández shook his head slowly. "I will speak

bluntly to this matter. It some ways, my thoughts may be Salvadoran and therefore different than yours. In other ways, they may be what they are because I have lost my family in a war. I was a soldier in that war. I have seen many barbaric acts on both sides, Salvadorans against Salvadorans. A man cannot live through this without it affecting how he sees the world."

"Please go on," said Anthony.

"When the war was over, we signed a piece of paper and the fighting stopped. Those that were dead were gone. We are supposed to pray for their souls and forgive their murderers. This, everyone says, is the right thing to do. In time, the wounds heal, but they leave scars. As new generations come, the war becomes a collection of stories from the past, a visit to a museum, a day of mourning for the fallen and perhaps a new monument to praise. I know in my heart there are people I cannot forgive and events I cannot forget, but I must not act on them. And so I live my life with my memories as best I can in the present."

Anthony looked a little puzzled wondering how this was relevant to the decisions he had to make.

Mr. Hernández continued, "So here you have your friend. What does he do? He comes to this village to help the people here. While doing so he meets a woman. Perhaps he is lonely, perhaps he falls in love, or perhaps he is just attracted as a man is naturally attracted to a woman. And she is attracted to him perhaps for similar or different reasons. We shall never know. And they have an innocent child who now has a questionable future in this country. Her grandmother is not well and knows it, and so she has made a proposal she believes is in the interest of the child. She may be wiser than us."

Anthony shifted in his seat still not hearing anything he

didn't already know. Mr. Hernández, sensing that Anthony was getting restless, went on.

"My point is this. Can what your friend did be compared to the things men do to each other in the name of causes, flags, and governments? Is what he did so unforgivable? Is this the same betrayal as when one surrenders his own family and friends to murderers? Is this the same as when land is taken away from people who are then enslaved for generations? Is what he did so unforgivable that his child should suffer for his sins? How can we be asked to forgive armies that have slaughtered their brothers and not forgive your friend who came here to do good, met a woman and had a child?"

Anthony sat quietly putting his open hands against each side of his face, his fingertips meeting at the bridge of his nose.

"These are good questions," he said, "but I'm not sure they're fair, especially in the case of Martin's wife. To compare an act of atrocity to one of infidelity tends to trivialize being unfaithful. Trust is important in a relationship. Integrity is important in a relationship. Being unfaithful violates that trust and integrity."

"And is forgiveness not possible?"

"It can be hard, harder for some people than others."

"And when it comes to the child?"

"That makes it more complicated. It bends my mind. When I hear of married people who hate each other, but are unwilling to consider divorce because of their children, I know their children often suffer more. I hear of couples getting a divorce who use their children as pawns in a war of spouse against spouse. These are issues that cannot be resolved with a remedy that fits all."

"But we are not talking about divorce, Antonio. We are

talking about the fate of this child."

"We are also talking about the fate of the people who have to make these decisions. It would be unfair to judge them on the belief that there is one solution that is absolute and correct. Martin's wife would have to make such a decision. I could not fault or judge her based on what she decides."

"So you would forgive and accept whatever she decides to do?"

"Yes. I would."

"Can you not also forgive and accept what your friend has done?"

"I don't know. Besides, it's not the same for me as for his wife."

The hotel steward came by to advise the men that the serving table would be removed as the lodge prepared to open the restaurant for lunch. This was their last opportunity to have more coffee. They decided to take a break. Before they rose, Anthony spoke again to Mr. Hernández.

"I appreciate your counsel very much. I'm still struggling with these issues, but there is one decision I have made."

"And what is that?"

"I had been considering not saying anything of this to Martin's wife to spare her the knowledge of her husband's double life here. I had thought this might spare her from unnecessary pain. I've decided however, that she should know the truth and what is being proposed so she can decide for herself. Withholding that information would not be respecting her right to know, as painful as that may be."

The two men got up shook hands and agreed to meet later for dinner. For now, Anthony would take care of his phone calls and Mr. Hernández had business of his own.

Before leaving, Mr. Hernández added, "There was another option in the proposal from Señora Órnelas."

"That's a little too Salvadoran for me to think about right now. The first order of business must be with Martin's wife."

"I will see you at dinner, Antonio."

Chapter 36

When Anthony returned to his room, he freshened up and tried to meditate on the purpose of his calls, but couldn't get into it. He was anxious to get started. Since it was Saturday, he was hoping that everyone would be at home. At the last minute he changed his mind and decided to call Bernadette first instead of last. She picked up on the first ring.

"Hello"

"Hi, it's me."

"What's up?" Bernadette said curtly.

Anthony could sense that she was still pissed.

"Well, I just wanted to check in and see how you were. I've left some messages for you, but haven't heard back."

"I'm fine."

After a pause, Anthony answered her first question.

"Well, I'm in this small town of Perquín. It has a lot of history and is a few miles from where Martin had his clinic. I've seen the remains of the building and met a number of people who knew him. Everything down here has a way of becoming delayed, but I'm more or less on schedule and expect to be on a return flight next Friday or Saturday."

After another streak of silence, he continued.

"So are you going to your folks on Thanksgiving?"

"I already told you I wouldn't do that. I am going to see them on Wednesday. Everybody leaves work early the day before the long weekend, so I'm going to do that and drive out to have dinner with them and come home."

"What are you going to do on Thanksgiving Day?"

"Oh, probably just stay home, or maybe drive out to the beach. Maybe drop in on Nancy. I don't know yet."

"How is Nancy?"

"She's doing okay. She's getting counseling."

"And how are you?"

"I'm fine, but I was just on my way out the door when you called."

"Bernadette, I'm sorry I've had to stay down here so long, but the more I learn the more I believe it was the right thing to do."

"I'm happy for you."

"I'm sorry you're still upset."

After more silence, Anthony added, "I have to call Sarah now. Some new things have come up that need her attention. I'll explain later or when I come home."

"Well, don't let me keep you. I have to do some shopping. Bye."

After she hung up, Anthony looked at the phone and said out loud, "You're milking this for all its worth. I hope you're enjoying it."

Anthony walked around the room twice before calling Sarah. When she answered, he still wasn't sure where to begin.

"Hi Sarah, how are you?" he said minimizing the amount of cheer in his greeting.

"Anthony, it's so good to hear from you. Carla called me and said no one had heard from you for a few days. She was as close as she gets to being rattled. She said you weren't at the hotel in San Salvador and that you weren't returning her calls."

"Carla knew I was leaving the hotel. I've come to a small town near Martin's clinic and have been surprisingly short on time. Sometimes at night my ambition to make calls or check for messages dissolves, but I'm fine," he said, again tuning down the happy tone.

'So how is it going?" she asked.

"Sarah, I've learned some things and there's a lot we have to talk about. Is this a good time or do you have some place you have to be?"

"There's nothing special going on. I can talk. Are there more problems with the paperwork?"

"No, Sarah. The paperwork will take care of itself. David's working on it and it should be in my hands on Monday or Tuesday. If there are any more problems, I won't know until I meet with the government officials next week, but I think everything is under control."

"So what else do we need to talk about?"

Anthony paused for a minute.

"Sarah, this is a serious matter," he said. "I'm not sure if you can handle it right now with the loss of Martin still so new, but there are some things you have to know. And the last thing I want is for you to be hurt again."

"Anthony, just say it," she said with an impatient and nervous tremor in her voice.

Anthony cleared his throat.

"Martin has a child here, a girl not quite two years old."

Anthony paused to give her time to absorb what he had said. Finally, Sarah responded.

"Go on," she said, exercising as much control as she could.

"The girl's mother was also killed in the explosion and fire at the clinic. The child is now in the care of her grandmother who is not well."

"Are you sure it's Martin's child?"

"Yes. I'm sure."

"Have you seen her?"

"My first chance to do that will be tomorrow morning."

"Then how can you be sure? Could it be that someone is trying to take advantage of a situation?"

"Sarah there is no situation. Martin made provisions for the financial support of the girl. Whether you do anything or not, the child is provided for financially."

"What do you mean if I do anything?"

"There is a potentially life changing aspect to this."

"Anthony, give me a second. Let me just steady myself for a minute."

"Do you want me to call you back in a little while?"

There was a short pause on the line.

"No," Sarah answered. "Don't go away. I just want to catch my breath, get some water and sit at my desk. Please don't hang up."

"I won't Sarah. We'll take this one step at a time."

While he was waiting, Anthony tried to prepare his words carefully.

"I'm back," she said, her voice stronger than before.

"Okay, Sarah. I'm going to tell you things and you will be asked to make a decision. You don't have to make it today, and you can talk this over with whomever you feel can help you. There is no right or wrong with what you decide. If you wish, this conversation will remain between the two of us. As of now, no one back home knows anything about what I'm going to tell you."

"It involves the girl?"

"Yes."

"Tell me."

"As I said, the grandmother raising the girl is not well. Her only interest is the child's welfare. The girl also has one uncle here who is a good man, but not very prepared to raise a child. The grandmother is also concerned about the girl's prospects living in their village without either parent. The country and this village are still recovering from years of war. Basic needs such as water and electricity are randomly available. Opportunities for education are marginal."

Anthony paused again realizing that he was building a case.

"This is the way it is for many children and people down here, but they manage very well by helping and caring for each other," he said.

"You said I would have to make a decision."

"Sarah, the grandmother has proposed that the child be brought to the United States and be raised by you, if you so wish."

He could hear Sarah fighting for air and stifling a sob. He waited again giving her the time she needed to keep herself together. Sarah must have put the phone down because he could hear only undecipherable, muted sounds. Minutes passed.

"Anthony this is hard," she said when she was able to speak again.

"I know Sarah. I thought about sparing you from this, but that was not a decision for me to make. As I said before, there is no right or wrong here, no judgment, and you don't have to decide now."

"If she were to come here, how soon would that be?"

"I can't say for sure, but it's possible she could return with me."

"Is it possible for me to come there and see her, meet her, get to know her a little?"

"It's possible, but I have the sense that doing so would

inadvertently create an official process that would be drawn out and of questionable outcome. Everything would just get infinitely more complicated."

"What do you think I should do Anthony?"

"I think you should search your heart, be honest with yourself and make the best decision you can."

"Would you think less of me if I said no?"

"No, Sarah, I promise."

"Would you think less of me if I said yes and accepted a child my husband had with another woman? Doesn't that seem a little desperate?"

"Of course not, Sarah. I swore to myself that I wouldn't try to influence your thinking in any way, but I do have an opinion about this."

"Please tell me."

"I don't think you should care about what I or anyone else thinks, or how some might consider the child's origins. I came here to retrieve Martin's remains so they could be brought home. They were to comfort you and give you a sense of being reunited with Martin, whom you loved and who loved you."

"And who had a child with another woman," she said with a soft sob.

"Yes, he did, Sarah. That's part of this, but the child is innocent and is a person who Martin has left behind. A living legacy that will always have Martin inside of her. We have services and build memorials for those we lose. Can this be compared to nurturing a life left behind by the person we lost?"

"So you think I should take her?"

"I'm just saying that you should search your heart and not consider all the crap that people invent to sustain misery. Whatever you decide will be okay, but make your decisions based on what your heart tells you to do."

"Suppose I get angry at what Martin has done and take it out the child?"

"You wouldn't, Sarah. We both know that."

Anthony could hear Sarah inhale deeply.

He continued, "Sarah, do you remember the night at your house when I helped with the chairs?"

"The night you called me a princess and I bit your head off?" she said with a combination of a sob and a broken laugh.

"Yeah, that's the one. Well that night, at that moment, I thought you were the most beautiful creature in the world. I wanted to take you in my arms and make you mine."

"I remember the moment and there was a spark, and the attraction was mutual."

"That's right Sarah. That happens sometimes. People are complicated. Neither of us intended anything, but for reasons we may not fully understand, there was an attraction."

"Yes, but we didn't act on it."

"That's true, but how close were we? What if the circumstances were different?"

"You mean what if we were thousands of miles away in a godforsaken place where water and electricity were a luxury?"

"You've got the idea."

"Are you sorry we didn't act on it?" Before he could answer she added, "I'm sorry, I'm sorry. I sound like I'm fishing."

After a moment he answered, "I'm not sorry, but you've had a special place in my heart since that night. So does Martin. I would not exchange that for anything."

"Thank you Anthony."

314

"Look, I think we've talked enough for one night," he said. "There's a lot to think about. Why don't you sleep on it? Tomorrow, you can decide if you want to talk to someone, get advice or whatever you need. I'll call you in the evening, and you can tell me how you want to proceed. Whatever you say will work for me."

"You said you'll see her tomorrow. Will you tell me about her, no matter what?"

"If that's what you want," he said.

"I feel like I should make a decision now, but I know I'll make it more confidently tomorrow. My insides are a wreck. I'll appreciate the time to just internalize all this."

"I think that's the right thing to do."

"Anthony?"

"Yes?"

"You had no idea what you were getting into when you agreed to go to El Salvador for me, did you?"

"That's for sure, but you've no idea how enlightening an experience it's been for me. I still haven't processed everything that has happened, but the world is looking different to me now."

"Different good or different bad?"

"Just different. I think it will be different good."

"Anthony?"

"Yes."

"Have you talked to Bernadette?"

"I talked with her before I called you, but I didn't discuss any of this."

"Is everything OK?"

"We're a little strained right now, but we'll be all right."

"I'll talk to you tomorrow. Goodnight, Anthony."

"Goodnight."

Anthony put down the phone, realizing that he was soaking wet. He had perspired as much as when clearing the clinic the day before. He decided to freshen up before calling Carla. After a shower and an hour nap, he placed his third call of the day.

"Hi Carla."

"Where the hell have you been, Anthony?"

"I love you too, sweetheart."

"Don't piss me off. You haven't checked in since you left the hotel. You haven't told me where you are. You don't check your cell phone. You don't check with me."

"I've missed you too," he said laughing. "Besides, I told you we were going to Perquín."

"Anthony, you've been down there for a week now. Haven't you realized that you're not strolling through Disneyland? That can be a dangerous place especially out in the boonies where you are probably walking around in a Yankees cap shouting 'Mug me! Mug me! Try and mug me! I'm Big Bad Anthony from New York!'"

"Actually, I'm wearing a Mets cap. It's definitely a National League kind of place. They don't like the designated hitter rule."

"It's a good thing I have Mr. Hernández watching out for you."

"He's become my new best friend."

"So I changed your ticket to have you come home a week from today, since Friday was questionable. You'll receive everything you need at the hotel in San Salvador. Do you expect them to jerk you around anymore, or is next Saturday good?"

"It should be okay. I'll know more when I meet with the government officials, but as far as I can see, Saturday looks good. If anything has to be changed, you'll be the first to know."

"I want to hear from you every other day until Thursday. Then you call again on Friday and Saturday before you leave."

"Isn't that a little excessive?"

"You know if I give Mr. Hernández a bonus, he'll kick your ass for me."

"Carla?"

"Yes?"

"You've been great. I really appreciate what you've done."

"Yeah, yeah. Just be careful down there. And Anthony?"

"Yes?"

"Make sure you give Bernadette a call."

"I already did. First call today."

"Watch out for yourself, Anthony. Give me a call on Monday."

Chapter 37

Anthony spent the rest of the afternoon walking around Perquín. He walked through the War Museum, but he may as well have been at a supermarket. He couldn't stop thinking about his earlier telephone conversations.

Having skipped lunch, he and Mr. Hernández had an early supper at the lodge. They drank beer, but stayed away from the rum. Anthony told his friend about the conversation he had with Sarah, and that while he would talk to her again the next day, he was not certain she would make a decision quickly.

When Anthony asked Mr. Hernández what he had done with the afternoon, Mr. Hernández just shrugged and said he saw a few friends and had taken care of some business. They agreed to retire early and to meet for breakfast before going to the Sunday Mass at the village church.

The following morning, Anthony awoke to the sound of the cell phone. His first thought was that he had overslept, but when he saw that it was only 6:00 A.M., he got nervous. *Nothing good happens with early morning phone calls*, he thought.

"Hello," he answered.

"Anthony, it's Sarah."

"Hi Sarah. Is anything wrong?"

"No. I'm an absolute wreck, but other than that everything's okay." She continued speaking very rapidly.

"I'm sorry to call you so early Anthony but you said you were going to see the girl this morning, and I wasn't sure when you would be leaving, and I didn't want to miss you, and I wasn't sure if you were an hour earlier or later than here, and I have been up all night thinking, and I wanted to reach you before you met the girl…"

"Sarah, Sarah, calm down. I'm here. It's 6:00 A.M. I haven't gone anywhere yet. I don't have to be at breakfast for another two hours. Just settle down and tell me why you called. No, wait. Let me go to the bathroom first and I'll call you right back."

"No."

"Sarah, I really have to do this."

"I meant no, I'll stay on the line."

"I'll be right back."

Anthony went to the bathroom, washed his face and soaked his head in an attempt to wake up. He returned to the bed and picked up the phone.

"Okay, Sarah, I'm here."

"Anthony, I want to do it," she said, excitement still in her voice. "I haven't slept all night thinking about everything we talked about, and I want to do it. I would like the child to come and live with me. I would like to raise the girl as her mother, if she will have me. I don't want her to suffer the loss of her family there, but if she wants to come, I want to have her. I will visit her grandmother and she can come here whenever she wants, but I don't want this opportunity to pass."

"You sound pretty certain," he said.

"Anthony, I'm scared to death. I've thought about everything we discussed and more. I've cried. I've laughed. I've cried and laughed at the same time. I'm absolutely certain this is what I want to do. I am overwhelmed thinking about everything I have to do. I'm not certain I can get everything done in time, but I don't care. I know this is right. I know it, I know it. I know it."

"Sarah?"

"Yes?"

Anthony paused, "I was going to ask you a bunch of questions that no longer seem necessary. I'm very proud of you."

"I'm really scared."

"You would be crazy if you weren't"

"Will you tell her about me when you see her?"

"I don't know how much I'll be able to say to her, but I'll tell the grandmother today unless you want more time to make a final decision."

"I don't need any more time. I don't need any advice. I don't need to see her first. I'll give her and her family as much time as they need. I'll do whatever I have to do as long as she and the family want her to be with me."

"Let me get to work on it. I'll call you later this evening with more information. Sarah, I think you're doing a wonderful thing."

"Thank you Anthony, I love you for doing this."

"Likewise kiddo."

When Anthony arrived at breakfast, Mr. Hernández was already seated sipping a cup of coffee. Anthony sat and Mr. Hernández poured him a cup.

"You must have slept well, Antonio. You have a smile on your face."

Anthony related the phone call he had received from Sarah to Mr. Hernández who listened intently.

When Anthony had finished, Mr. Hernández raised his cup of coffee to make a toast. "Congratulations," he said.

Anthony looked puzzled. "Why are you congratulating me?"

"Today, you are Salvadoran. That means from now on,

you will see things differently than you have seen them before."

"Well, I 'm not sure about that, but I appreciate the thought."

Mr. Hernández raised his coffee cup again,

"To achieving "confianza" Antonio. You have done very well here."

Anthony raised his coffee cup in acknowledgement and suddenly felt very proud.

"Thank you, Mr. Hernández."

"I think it is time for you to call me Juan."

"Thank you, but I'm not ready for that yet. To me you are Mr. Hernández, a man of great strength, wisdom and integrity."

"I am humbled that you think so, Antonio."

After breakfast the two men left the lodge to attend Sunday Mass and to meet Martina Órnelas. They arrived at the village church a few minutes before the Mass began. As they entered the church, Donato, one of the elders, greeted them and escorted them to the second pew behind the group of elders. The Mass began and there was no sign of Señora Órnelas, Eduardo or Martina. Anthony went through the rituals of the Mass as he had so many times as a boy. He began to worry if something had gone wrong or changed. *My God*, he thought, *what will it do to Sarah if something has changed?*

As the priest began the offertory of the Mass, Donato passed a straw collection basket with a green felt lining from pew to pew. Anthony dropped a five dollar bill in it and passed the basket to his right. He grew increasingly anxious and continued to search for the Señora and the girl. The priest came to the front altar facing his parishioners and waited for the offering to be brought forward.

Everyone turned to face the center aisle and then Anthony understood.

Entering the aisle from the rear was Señora Órnelas in a beautiful dark green silk dress that reached the floor. Her grayish white hair was covered by a silk scarf. Her face still bore the lines of age and hardship, but today she was transformed into a regal persona. Eduardo was with her in a dark blue suit, white shirt and light blue tie. His hair was slicked back, his face clean shaven. He carried the straw basket containing the offertory collection.

Between Eduardo and his mother walked a young child who held on to Eduardo's forearm with one hand and Señora Órnelas' hand with the other. Martina wore the kind of white dress usually reserved for young girls when they receive their First Communion. She giggled and her eyes widened as she saw the faces of people she recognized. Anthony's eyes took her in, and he could see Martin in her face. The trio brought the basket to the altar and placed it on the step before it. They turned and came to the pew occupied by Anthony and Mr. Hernández. The men moved in to make room. Señora Órnelas stood next to Anthony.

As the Mass went on, Anthony went through the motions of the ceremony while stealing glances at the child. She sat, then stood on the seat first facing the altar, then turning to face the row of people behind her while pulling on the hem of her dress. Before serving the Eucharist, the priest blessed the crowd and offered a sign of peace to which the parishioners responded by offering a sign of peace to the priest and their neighbors. While many of the congregation shook hands and said "May peace be with you," Señora Órnelas turned and embraced Anthony warmly. He reciprocated awkwardly. At the serving of communion, Anthony followed the Señora to the priest who offered the Host to Anthony's cupped hands while reciting "Body of Christ." Anthony responded "Amen" and put the wafer in his mouth thinking this would be a likely time for a lightning bolt, but he returned to the pew unscathed. The wafer melted in his mouth with familiarity despite the many years since his last communion.

Upon exiting the pew at the end of the Mass, Martina ended up between Anthony and Señora Órnelas. The parishioners smiled approvingly as they made their way to door. When they reached the entrance to the church, a few people were talking to the priest, but most of the crowd had dispersed. While the priest was occupied, Señora Órnelas formally introduced Martina to Anthony. The girl looked at him shyly, not letting go of the woman's hand.

"I am very pleased to meet you," said Anthony bending and extending his hand. The child just looked at him. Señora Órnelas guided the girl's hand to Anthony's and he shook it gently. After he looked closely at the girl, he commented aloud, "She certainly is Martin's child."

"And my daughter's," said Señora Órnelas.

"Of course," said Anthony. "May we talk?"

"Yes, but first, come," she said.

She took Anthony by the arm, and walked up to the priest with Anthony in tow. The child stayed with Eduardo.

"Padre Onofrio, this is Antonio."

The priest extended his hand, "Ah, the American. Very pleased to meet you, my son."

Instead of saying he wasn't his son, Anthony answered, "Pleased to meet you, Padre."

"You must come to the blessing today," said the priest.

Anthony looked puzzled, but the Señora pulled him away before the conversation could continue. "Let us go where I can sit," she said, and led him to the rear pew.

323

Anthony followed, as did Eduardo and Martina. Mr. Hernández waited outside.

The old woman sat and beckoned for Anthony to sit beside her.

"You have something to say?" she said in Spanish and waited for Eduardo to translate.

"Yes," Anthony began, trying to chose his words carefully, grateful for the translation pauses that Eduardo would provide.

"I have discussed your proposal with the wife of my friend. She is honored that you would consider her for such a responsibility. She has agreed to accept and will honor whatever considerations you may have. She also wants you to know that she will willingly bring the child back to El Salvador for visits and accept you in her home so that you and Eduardo may visit the child whenever you wish to do so."

The woman nodded. "I am too old and too ill to travel, but it warms my heart to know that I will be able to see the child again during whatever time I have left. Eduardo too, should see the child perhaps in the U.S. She is an angel and all I have left of my daughter."

Eduardo got up to shake Anthony's hand.

"This is a good thing, you have done, Antonio, but it is also very hard for us, especially for my mother."

"I understand," said Anthony. "It is you who have done a good thing. You, the Señora and the wife of my friend, who is a good woman who will love the child as well as give her a good home. She will be sure Martina knows of her mother and all her family."

Señora Órnelas wiped a tear from her eye, and then stood.

"Now, it is time to go to the blessing," she said.

Taking Flight

Anthony still did not understand, but he rose and followed her, Eduardo and Martina out the door. Outside the church, the square was empty except for Mr. Hernández. The woman turned to Anthony and put a hand on his cheek, but said nothing. Anthony looked at her in the bright daylight thinking that the deep lines in her face could tell many stories.

"Please do not be worried for the child," he said.

"Thank you for what you have given to her and to the woman who will care for her."

The woman hugged him briefly, and then appearing taller than she had seemed before said, "Let us go."

Mr. Hernández brought his car around so the woman would not have to walk far. He drove them to the clinic and parked a short distance from the building. It was surrounded by what must have been the entire village. Everyone seemed in a solemn mood. Anthony helped Señora Órnelas from the car. Eduardo lifted and held Martina in his arms. Anthony walked forward with Mr. Hernández at his side. All the elders were present as was the priest. He caught sight of Jorge, Consuelo, and their children. As he walked toward them, Jorge stepped forward. They shook hands and Jorge clutched Anthony's arm.

"I owe you an apology, Jorge. I didn't understand why you didn't tell me of things you knew until I learned about Martina. I was a jerk, and I'm very sorry."

"You do not need to apologize, my friend. I would have done the same thing."

"I don't think so, but thank you for saying so."

"You are welcome in my home at anytime."

"Well, I'm not sure how things will work out exactly, but I think I'll be having some company soon, in addition

325

to Mr. Hernández."

"Bueno, Antonio. This is good news. Consuelo, please come here."

Consuelo and the children joined the men. Jorge told them of Anthony's news. Consuelo hugged Anthony.

"You must come to our house," she said.

"Thank you, I will," said Anthony.

Their son walked up to Anthony and said, "Nice to see you again, Señor."

Anthony shook his hand, and replied in kind.

"Nice to see you, Juan."

Maria walked up to Anthony, a little more reserved than at their last meeting.

"I am happy that you and my family are friends again, Señor."

Anthony hugged her and said, "We were never not friends, Maria. I was just a little *estúpido.*"

They were still laughing when they heard the priest call for the crowd's attention. As the villagers gathered around the priest, Jorge explained to Anthony that it was the custom of the village to leave ruins such as battle sites and places where helicopters were downed, as they were, as a reminder of the events. The village reacted the same way when the clinic was destroyed. He also explained that the clinic was the property of the organization that built it, but MATES no longer seemed interested in the structure.

"And so we learned from you, what we should do in this case," Jorge said as they walked closer to the shell of the building. They stopped a few feet away so that Anthony could see four wooden crosses, each with the name of a victim carved on the horizontal cross bar that was about two feet above the earth. Anthony could also see that the building had been entirely cleared out and cleaned up. The only remaining item in the building was the pedestal Anthony could not remove two days earlier. He looked at Jorge, who nodded, pointing to the entrance. Anthony went in and could see that on the pedestal was a wooden plaque on which the words "In memory of our friends from America" were carved. Anthony worked to keep his emotions in check. Jorge led Anthony back outside.

The priest then began a blessing of the site spoken in Spanish. Anthony could make out the words for 'doctor, friend, and death'. At the end of the blessing, Señora Órnelas was handed a rose by Father Onofrio. She took Martina's hand and together they placed it in front of one of the crosses. They were followed by two others; Donato, who was the father of Juanita Herrera, the clerk killed at the clinic. He in turn was followed by the surviving mother of Jesus Moreira, the orderly and handyman. The priest then handed a rose to Anthony who brought it to the cross bearing Martin's name. Anthony dropped to his knees and placed the rose at the foot of the cross. His body shuddered, but he fought back the sob that was fighting to be released. He placed his hand on the top of the cross and patted it like he would pat a friend on the shoulder. Then he stood and returned to stand alongside Jorge. The priest then completed the ceremony with a final blessing making the sign of the cross and a loud "Amen" to which everyone responded "Amen."

Chapter 38

When the ceremony at the clinic was concluded, everyone returned to the village square. As in any community with a heartbeat, such an emotionally draining event is followed by a celebration. Food, drink and music were the ingredients that brought relief to the pain of suffering and loss. Today would be no exception. The perimeter of the fountain was filled with tables on which were trays of foods prepared for a festival dedicated to saints, heroes, ancestors and fallen friends. The cantina made sure that rum, wine and beer were in ample supply. A multi-generational group of men and boys with a variety of horns and string instruments played music that was alternately joyous and sad. Two women shared vocals of local songs that brought tears to some. After a modest amount of food and beer, Mr. Hernández gathered Anthony, Jorge, Eduardo and all but one of the elders aside and suggested that they meet in the room at the rear of the church.

While the festivities went on outside, the men worked on a strategy to send Martina to the United States. Anthony listened at length while different suggestions were made in Spanish. Sensing his discomfort, Mr. Hernández explained in English.

"Antonio, it is the opinion of the men that to apply for a legal passport and other papers necessary to allow the child to leave the country would take a long time and be subject to many obstacles. There is also the possibility that such permission would be denied since neither of the child's parents is living and the grandmother cannot travel because of her health."

"What about Eduardo?" asked Anthony. "Couldn't her uncle escort her to the U.S. with all the legal points covered?"

The men looked at the floor. Mr. Hernández explained.

"Eduardo has had some problems with the police and the government authorities. It is unlikely that he would be successful trying to leave the country legally. If the girl were with him, the possibility of her leaving the country would be over."

Eduardo looked sheepishly at Anthony and shrugged his shoulders.

Mr. Hernández continued. "It is proposed that the girl have papers identifying her as the daughter of Jorge and Consuelo. You will be escorting her to Miami so that she may visit with Consuelo's sister who really happens to live in that city as a legal immigrant. You will have letters from Jorge and Consuelo giving your permission as her escort."

"How can she be properly identified as their daughter?"

"Mr. Hernández pointed to one of the elders. "Hector here can draw up a passport, birth certificate and other papers making her their daughter."

"What about on the other side, incoming at the U.S.?"

"You will go through customs on the U.S. citizen side with a child properly documented and with notarized letters of consent signed by Jorge and Consuelo granting permission to take her from El Salvador to the United States. It will be less difficult there than on this side."

"What is the risk here?"

"There may be an official here who has not yet been corrupted who will challenge your authority to take the child with you."

"What happens in that case?"

"You will go to prison for twenty years," said Mr. Hernández with a straight face.

Anthony looked at him nervously and the men burst out laughing.

"In that case," said Mr. Hernández, "we will be sure a higher official who has been corrupted will intervene on your behalf."

"You're sure this can work?"

"As we discussed yesterday, Antonio, it has many times before."

"My father used to tell me to never mess with the Feds or MasterCard."

"I am sure he was wise, but in El Salvador even MasterCard has to deal with corrupt officials."

"So you're suggesting that we do this when I leave on Saturday?"

All the men looked at him. Mr. Hernández nodded. Ignacio, who had been quiet until now, spoke.

"Don Antonio, there is always a risk that something will go wrong. If that happens, we will fix any new problem separately. As long as the papers are in order, the chances of a problem are very small."

"Is Calderón involved at all in this process?" asked Anthony.

"No. He only has to do with making life difficult for the poor and those who will not offer bribes."

"So when I see him about Martin's remains, he won't know about any of this?"

"We don't think so, but we can never be sure."

"You know, if I'm bringing Martin's daughter with me, I'm not sure I even need his ashes. I will have his living legacy. Maybe we should just drop that and avoid Calderón altogether."

Mr. Hernández spoke, "It would not be wise to change anything you have scheduled with Calderon. It would only raise suspicion that something is going on. He is a prick, but he is not stupid. If he denies your request for your friend's remains, it would not be unreasonable for you to leave the country, but if you did not keep the appointment, he would wonder why, after all your time here."

"You're sure about the papers?" asked Anthony.

All the men nodded.

"And they can be ready by Friday?"

Hector spoke up, "I will make a passport and papers that the late J. Edgar Hoover could not challenge. I promise you."

After a long pause, Anthony said, "Okay. Just keep me out of jail."

"We will work out more details tomorrow. Now it is time for rum," said Mr. Hernández.

When the men left to go outside, the festival was in full swing. Anthony drank some rum and ran the plan through his mind. He had just agreed to commit a serious crime in a foreign country. It was indeed time for more rum.

Chapter 39

Anthony was woken by the phone again on Monday morning. Once it again it was Sarah.

"Hi Sarah," he mumbled.

"Anthony, you were going to call me last night, When you didn't I was afraid something bad had happened. Please tell me you're all right and that what we talked about is still okay."

"Sarah," he said, "I can't talk much right now, but I'm fine. Everything we talked about is all okay. I'll be able to give you more details later, but trust me, everything is great. There was a lot of celebrating last night, and I'm afraid I over did it. That's why I didn't call. Frankly I have a very bad headache right now, and I need to get myself together before I can say much more. I'm really sorry for not calling, but I promise to call you later. Everything is fine except my aching head."

"Okay. I trust you, and I'm sorry about your headache. Bye."

It was 7:00 A.M. and Anthony felt terrible. A foggy memory of the night before slowly revealed itself. Eduardo was going to take Señora Órnelas and Martina home until Martina would go with him to the home of Jorge and Consuelo. Anthony had learned that Señora Órnelas was very sick, much more so than he had known. Draping her body in silk did not stop or slow down what was ravaging her from the inside. There was something else that had bothered him about the events of last night; something that he couldn't remember that had left him uneasy.

Taking Flight

"Oh, I'll never do that again," he proclaimed out loud as he began the torturous process of returning to the land of the living. He found some chewable Maalox Tablets in his bag and immediately put four in his mouth. When he went in the bathroom, he found a note on the mirror from Mr. Hernández asking him to call when he was up and around. Apparently he wanted to give Anthony as much time as he needed. Anthony had an almost military routine that called for shaving before a shower. Today that would change. He would not only shower first, but would stay under the stream of water until his insides stabilized and his headache became tolerable.

An hour and a half after waking to Sarah's call, Anthony was dressed and although still shaky, ready to go back into the world. It was 8:30 A.M. when he called Mr. Hernández on his cell to learn that he was in the Lodge restaurant with coffee waiting. Mr. Hernández smiled sympathetically as Anthony joined him. Anthony's eyes said everything. Mr. Hernández poured him a cup of coffee and put a couple of pills on the table. Anthony, who wouldn't normally put anything into his body that he hadn't personally researched, took the pills without a word and washed them down with coffee.

He picked at his breakfast while Mr. Hernández read the newspaper. To his surprise, he felt considerably better in about half an hour. He looked at Mr. Hernández who put the paper down.

"Did I do anything to embarrass myself last night?"

Mr. Hernández smiled, "For a man looking forward to twenty years in a Salvadoran prison, I would say you did quite well. You did nothing dishonorable. You were sometimes comical and incoherent. I didn't know you could sing."

"I can't," said Anthony.

Anthony drank more coffee and the night before became clear.

"Señora Órnelas is dying isn't she?"

"She has had the cancer for some time. She is not yet sixty years."

"She must have been something before she was ill."

"She was. She was a soldier during the war. A man had to work hard to keep up with her."

"I bet," said Anthony. "So you think the plan for Martina leaving with me on Saturday is good, that it will work?"

"I would not suggest it if I thought otherwise."

"I believe that. May I ask you something about your friends?"

"Of course."

Last night, when we had the meeting, all the elders from the first day were there except one of the younger men. I think his name was Ernesto."

Mr. Hernández looked carefully at Anthony. "He was not asked to be there for purposes of your safety."

"Whoa, what does that mean?"

"Not everyone trusts Ernesto. We thought it would be best to not include him in our discussion."

"You mean he's …. like a spy or something?"

"Or something. A few things have occurred that have put his trust in question. Until that matter is resolved, he will not be included in things that could put anyone in danger."

"And what if he is a spy or something?"

Mr. Hernández could read the question in Anthony's mind. "We are soldiers, not barbarians. If he is doing things that could be harmful to the people of the village, he will be cast out."

"And that's it?"

Mr. Hernández did not back away from the question. "If he were to betray someone in the village and cause serious harm, there would be justice."

"Would he get whacked?"

"This is not like the movies, Antonio. Justice will be according to the harm he has caused. No more, no less."

Anthony knew it was time to stop this line of questioning.

"I'm feeling a lot better now. Thank you for the pills."

"We must meet with Jorge tonight to go over many details of your departure on Saturday."

"The girl is sweet isn't she?" As soon as he asked the question, Anthony remembered that Mr. Hernández had lost his children in the war. He couldn't pull it back, but wished he'd kept his mouth shut.

After a slight pause, Mr. Hernández said, "Yes. She is a beautiful child."

Anthony switched subjects. "I promised Sarah that I would call her back when my head cleared. I also have some other calls to make. Do you mind if I take care of them now?"

"That would be good. Keep in mind that your flight plans may change a little. Nothing major. Just don't have Señora Sarah expect to meet you as currently planned until we talk to Señora Carla tomorrow."

Anthony was a little puzzled, but at this point he knew that the best thing to do was to trust Mr. Hernández who saved his life once, and would not risk it now.

"Okay," said Anthony. Shall we meet, in say, two hours?"

"That is good. I have some business with Hector. You

will be fine here. If you need for anything, you know how to reach me."

Anthony got up to leave. As he stood looking at Mr. Hernández, he said, "Now this is an American term, and it means only good things," he said. "You are coolest fucking dude I have ever known. Meeting you has been the most unforgettable experience of my life. It has been a privilege to get to know you."

For the first time since Anthony had known him, Mr. Hernández was caught off guard, but he quickly collected his himself.

"Thank you very much, Antonio."

"Thank you, Juan."

Chapter 40

Anthony returned to his room with two things on his mind. He picked up the cell phone and called Sarah. When she answered she said she was at work and would call him back in a few minutes. He got comfortable on the sofa and waited for her call. His mind drifted to the conversation with Mr. Hernández about Ernesto. *Why would someone betray his closest friends? What could be his motivation? Money? A job? The only other classical motivator was a woman and that didn't seem to fit here. What or who could he betray? Politically and emotionally these people may be at odds with the authorities, but the war was long over. The village didn't have anything illegal going on like a drug trade or weapons smuggling. Hector had joked that the reason the government ignored their practice of forging documents was because stopping it would cut off a source of income to corrupt officials and the illegal documents were used to export and import their own people who brought money from foreign jobs into the country.* His thoughts were interrupted by the phone.

"Hi Anthony, it's me, Sarah. Are you feeling better?"

"Yes, much," said Anthony. "I'm sorry about this morning and not calling you last night, but the whole experience was kind of mind blowing. I'll save the details for another time."

"I understand. I was just worried. This is so important."

"I know, but I want you know everything is okay." For reasons, he didn't fully understand himself, Anthony decided to speak cautiously. "As I was saying earlier, everything is going along just fine. I'll be bringing the package home with me on Saturday. You should check with Carla in case of any last minute schedule changes."

Sarah was silent on the other end.

Anthony continued. "I'm looking forward to coming home. This is a beautiful place in some respects, but kind of primitive in others. I'm glad my business is winding down. I hope the bureaucrats here settle up and ship me out."

"Anthony?"

"Yes?"

"Is everything…

He interrupted her. "Everything is fine. I'll see you Saturday."

"Okay, but one more thing."

"Sure."

"Make sure you call home soon, okay."

Anthony looked at the phone for a second. "Sure. I'll do that. Bye, Sarah."

"Bye."

Anthony concluded that he had been spooked by the Ernesto business and tried to shake it off. He took lemonade from the courtesy bar and brought out his business papers before making the next call.

After two rings, Jeanne Marsh's voice said, "Mr. Trenholme's office."

After being in El Salvador for over a week, getting seriously mugged and agreeing to participate in a major felony, he still didn't like Jeanne Marsh, but he lost interest in playing mind games with her.

"Jeanne, this is Anthony Bartolo. I'd like to speak with Henry, please."

Anthony heard the recorded music come on without a word. That was Jeanne's way of saying she didn't like him either.

Trenholme came on the line. "Anthony, finally," he said. "I was hoping that poor mail, phone, fax and email systems were the cause of not hearing from you."

"Henry, I don't want to jerk you around so I'll come right to the point. It's not going to work. I'm not coming back to SkyTel."

"I take it you are not posturing or negotiating."

"That's correct. You put everything I asked for in the contract, but I can't do it."

"May I ask why?"

"I don't know if I understand it myself yet, certainly not well enough to explain to someone else."

"Have you ruled out just delaying your decision until you figure it all out?"

"Yes, I have, Henry. I haven't decided what I'm going to do next, only what I'm not going to do."

"I guess Edgar drove you over the edge."

"Actually, Edgar is only a part of it, a very small part. It has more to do with figuring out how I want to live my life, not the kind of job I want. Speaking of Edgar, I can tell him directly if you prefer. We have had our differences Henry, but you did live up to your end of our bargain, so I'll bear the wrath of Edgar's fury if that will take the heat off you."

"No, that's not necessary, Anthony. Besides, I get a certain satisfaction from telling Edgar he can't get everything he wants."

"Good luck, Henry."

"Good luck to you, Anthony."

Anthony took one more walk around the room before

picking up the phone again. He waited only one ring after dialing Bernadette's work number.

"Bernadette speaking," she answered.

"Bernadette, it's Anthony."

"I'm kind of busy right now, can you call me later at home?"

"This is important and I thought you should know right away."

"What is it?"

"I've turned down the SkyTel job offer. I've decided it's not what I want to do."

"Oh! Another life changing decision that we don't talk about first."

"I was afraid if we talked about it, I might change my mind."

"Good job, good salary, stock options you lusted after. Possible career with NordSTAR later. What a terrible circumstance."

"I'm trying to figure out my life."

"What're you going to change next? Me? How will I find out? In the mail?"

"I'll be home on Saturday. I'll explain more then."

"The only explanation that is important to me is why we can't talk these things over *FIRST*? Goodbye, Anthony, I have to keep *my* job."

Taking Flight

Chapter 41

After making the calls, Anthony re-packaged and packed the SkyTel papers with a sense of relief mixed with uncertainty about the future. He had no idea of what he would do professionally. He decided not to second guess himself and figure this out when he returned home. Bernadette's response to his news was totally justified, he concluded. Anthony thought he could do a better job of mending that fence in person than from here. Although Bernadette wasn't receptive to much of what he had to say lately, she would think differently, he thought, once he described his experiences here. She would get it. She would understand.

For now, there was plenty to do. Anthony called the hotel in San Salvador and learned that a package sent from David's firm had been received. He was also told that he had a message from the office of Director Calderón regarding their meeting. Anthony didn't want to guess what was going on with Calderón so he placed a call to his office and found out that their meeting was scheduled for 9:00 A.M. on Thursday morning. When he reached Calderón, Anthony was surprised and unsettled by the pleasant and almost friendly tone of the man. Calderón spoke to him personally, and seemed very pleased that he was able to accommodate Anthony's revised schedule. Anthony thanked him and assured him that the corrected application for the retrieval and return of Martin's remains would satisfy the requirements of the Salvadoran government.

Anthony considered different approaches to the next

few days. When he and Mr. Hernández met again in the lobby he presented his ideas.

"This evening I will spend some time with Martina so she can get to know me a little better before we travel. After she goes to bed, we can meet with Jorge, Hector and whoever else is needed to work out the specifics of getting her out of the country. Then I think we should return here so I can study the departure plan. If I'm going to risk becoming an international fugitive, I'd like to practice every lie I may have to tell so each will sound believable. It would also help if you could teach me a few Salvadoran expressions that a parent would say to a child to comfort her, instruct her, and suggest eating, and so on."

"You will be very well prepared Antonio, I assure you."

"I will also need to know what questions I should expect to be asked and what the appropriate answers should be. In your experience at this sort of thing, you must have many suggestions."

"We will begin tonight," said Mr. Hernández.

"Finally, I don't trust Calderón. He spoke to me today like we were old friends. I'd like for us to go to San Salvador tomorrow night and have all day Wednesday to prepare for any changes he may throw at me before Thursday's meeting. If I have to contact anyone in New York, I'll have time to do so."

"Antonio, you are thinking like a soldier."

"I'm thinking like somebody who doesn't believe in the tooth fairy."

Mr. Hernández reassured Anthony, "We shall prepare well. I shall be at your side until you and the child are boarding the airplane."

"Thank you, Juan."

Taking Flight

A short while later, Anthony and Mr. Hernández returned to the village. They went to the little house where Señora Órnelas, Eduardo and Martina lived. The old woman was dressed in a simple native dress. She struggled to rise when the men entered, but they implored her to stay seated. Eduardo came into the room with Martina holding his hand. The toddler was dressed in jeans and a child's T-shirt bearing pictures of Sesame Street characters. Eduardo reintroduced the girl to Anthony and Mr. Hernández. They tried their best to look friendly and less like intimidating, oversized people. Anthony sat on the floor and asked her simple questions in English the girl could not understand. She turned to her abuela for guidance. Señora Órnelas reassured the girl by saying something in Spanish and then asked her to show a picture of her "madre" to Anthony. Martina went to a small table next to the chair where her grandmother sat. She picked up a small plastic frame containing a picture of her deceased mother and brought it to Anthony. For the benefit of all in the room, he told the girl that her mother was "hermosa" and suggested that she bring the picture with her. Eduardo advised him that another was already packed with her things.

When it came time to leave, Eduardo brought out a suitcase and a shopping bag of belongings and supplies that Martina would need. Mr. Hernández bid the Señora farewell for now, and Eduardo kissed her on the cheek before carrying the bags out to the car. From her chair, Señora Órnelas hugged the girl as tears filled the lines in her face. She removed a small crucifix on a gold chain from her neck and put it over the child's head.

"Vaya con Dios," she said, and then struggled to stand dismissing Anthony's motion to stay seated. She hugged Anthony and held him very tightly as she repeated, "Vaya con Dios."

Anthony helped her to sit again. He took Martina by the hand and walked to the door.

"Vaya con Dios, Señora."

The three men and the girl, along with her belongings, climbed into Mr. Hernández's car. They left the village and went to Perquín. When they arrived at the home of Jorge and Consuelo, the family came out to greet them. Consuelo took the girl inside beckoning Anthony to follow.

"She needs a diaper change," said Consuelo.

"Uh, oh. That may be a little over my head," Anthony replied.

"Come, I will show you."

Anthony was surprised to see her reach into the bag Eduardo brought for her and take out Pampers.

"I thought they were a luxury for the modern world," he said.

""In El Salvador, Pampers and cell phones are everywhere," said Consuelo.

She showed Anthony how the diaper was to be changed, the child to be cleaned and then suggested that he do it. He balked at first, but then managed the task with only a little assistance from Consuelo.

"You will make a good father some day," she said.

"If I can manage this, I can rule the world," Anthony replied very proudly.

He returned to the porch where the men were having a beer. Jorge got one for Anthony and then offered a toast to Anthony's first successful diaper change.

"More importantly," said Anthony, "the child survived!"

The family gathered for dinner and Anthony again sensed the wonder that he experienced his first night here.

This gathering seemed a million miles away from the stress and constant striving of his life in Hempstead. Here, the reward that came with having so little outweighed the price for having so much.

After the main meal, Consuelo served a wonderful dessert made of sweet custard. The evening ritual began with the woman and children leaving the men to their business. Soon after the children retired for the night, Jorge brought up the need to discuss the plan for Martina. He made a phone call that brought a pick-up truck driven by Donato with Hector seated beside him to the front of the house. The rest of elders climbed out of the back and joined the men on the porch. All were present except Ernesto.

With a brief introduction from Mr. Hernández, Anthony repeated his plan to go to San Salvador the next night, and his concern about Calderón. Hector described the passport and birth certificate he was making for Martina. Notarized letters from Jorge and Consuelo were prepared and would be signed giving Anthony permission to take her to visit her aunt in Miami.

"We will arrange for Consuelo's sister to meet you at the Miami airport in case there is a need for her to be there. Once you clear customs there you can continue with Martina to New York on a flight that leaves four hours later," said Hector.

"You know," said Anthony, "there's a lot of sensitivity to smuggling children into the U.S. Many television programs have been presented on the subject."

The men looked at each other and agreed to give that some thought if Anthony felt it would increase the risk.

"I think it's important," said Anthony.

The men nodded in acknowledgement.

Anthony proceeded to ask a bunch of "what if?"

questions. Each was answered deliberately. It was clear that his concerns were possibilities they had anticipated or experienced before. Anthony was impressed with their responses and satisfied they would consider his input to the plan. They all shook hands. Since the elders would be taking care of the travel documents, Anthony's only unfinished business was to contact Carla about changing the flights to include a stopover in Miami. He would do that in the morning.

Jorge brought out beer for everyone. In a more relaxed moment, Anthony noticed Mr. Hernández engaged in a conversation with Ignacio during which Mr. Hernández looked very solemn while Ignacio became increasingly agitated. Something was not right. Anthony was uncertain if it had something to do with the plan or not. He felt satisfied that he had participated in the latest version of his departure strategy. He would think it through again tomorrow and make sure the Salvadorans had the American perspective of visitors and returnees to the country. There were five more days before Anthony departed. For tonight, the "clarification" of Martina's birth certificate, parentage, travel documents and agreement to return via Miami was enough.

The elders drank beer with their hosts, told a few stories and wished each other well. Before departing, Hector reminded Anthony that all the documents would be delivered to Jorge on Friday. They would meet again then. They elders piled back into the pickup and left for the night. A short while later, Anthony and Mr. Hernández said good night to Jorge and Consuelo. Anthony looked in on each of the three children before he and Mr. Hernández returned to the Lodge.

On the drive back, Anthony brought up his observation

of Mr. Hernández and Ignacio talking and asked if there was anything wrong.

"It is more of the problem with Ernesto," said Mr. Hernández. "It seems that he is being recruited by one of the gangs in San Salvador. It is not a problem that should give you any concern."

Anthony was uneasy with his response, but decided not to push. At the lodge, they called it a night and agreed to meet for breakfast at 8:00 A.M.

Chapter 42

After a restless night, Anthony was up early Tuesday morning. He packed his bags and belongings before breakfast. On his way to the dining room, he pushed the entrance door with one of the bags he was carrying and felt a strain in his lower back. He twisted his body as he walked trying to stretch it out, but a nagging pain persisted. He was seated at a table before Mr. Hernández showed up promptly at 8:00 A.M. After they ordered, Anthony made a suggestion.

"I don't have a stroller or small carriage for transporting Martina. I thought perhaps we could pick one up before we leave on Saturday. It will help in case my back acts up, which it did again this morning." he said.

"That should not be a problem," said Mr. Hernández. "If you like, we can stop where we bought your supplies and bring it to Jorge's house so it will be ready when we leave."

"Good. Let's do that," said Anthony. "For now, I'd like to call Carla and have her prepare tickets for Martina and me to travel to New York via Miami."

"Very well, I will have the people here prepare our bill."

After breakfast, Anthony returned to his room and called Carla. He wasn't sure how much Sarah had shared with her, but Carla took down all the information about the flight changes and the ticket for Martina without question. She repeated everything back to Anthony and advised him that the tickets would be at his hotel in San Salvador by

Noon the next day. She reminded Anthony that her friend's original offer of money was still on the table, if needed.

"I don't think I'll need it," replied Anthony. "And quite frankly, I hope it stays that way, or else I'm in trouble."

"Be very careful Anthony."

"I will Carla. Thanks again. Let Sarah know the travel plan, okay?"

"I will. Travel safe."

On the spur of the moment, Anthony decided to make another call.

"Hi Mom, how are you doing?"

"Wow, two calls in one week. This is an honor. What's wrong?"

"Nothing's wrong, but I've had a change in my travel plans. It turns out that I'm going through Miami on my way to New York with a four hour layover. I thought if you could handle the drive, we could meet at the airport for coffee or lunch, or something."

He prepared himself to hear how difficult the drive from Naples to Miami would be, or how horrendous the airport traffic was.

"What time does your flight arrive?"

"It's scheduled to be there at 11:30 A.M."

"Where shall we meet? They don't let you go to the gate without a ticket anymore."

"How about the United Air Lines counter in the main terminal?"

"Good. I'll be the one wearing a red carnation."

"See you Saturday, Mom," Anthony said shaking his head.

"Anthony?"

"Yeah?"

"You're sure nothing's wrong?"

"Everything is fine. I'll see you at the United counter Saturday morning."

"Bye, son."

Anthony checked the room one more time before taking his bags to the lobby. Mr. Hernández was at the front desk. Anthony settled the bill and they left the building with a sense of purpose. Their first stop was at the general store in Perquín. When the proprietor explained to Anthony that the only children's strollers he had were a few rentals he kept on hand for tourists, Mr. Hernández intervened and the proprietor picked out the best one and sold it to Anthony. They packed it in the trunk of the car and headed for Jorge's house. When they arrived, Anthony was surprised to see Jorge at home.

"This is an important day," he said. "I wanted to be here to see you and the Colonel. The shop can wait."

"I appreciate that," said Anthony.

Consuelo joined them bringing Martina with her.

"I thought it would be good for me to be with Martina again so she'll be okay with me when we leave on Saturday," said Anthony. "We also bought her a stroller."

"Good," said Consuelo, but first, she needs another diaper change and you need the practice."

Anthony rolled his eyes and followed Consuelo into the house. He performed the task thinking it wasn't really as challenging as brain surgery as long as you held your breath. With Martina in a fresh pamper and clothes, he introduced her to the stroller and made a game out of her first ride. The child giggled as he wheeled her back and forth and made some wheely turns. When the ride was over, he lifted her out of the stroller and gave her a gentle squeeze that she returned.

Taking Flight

With the exception of trying to interpret the body language during some private words between Mr. Hernández and Jorge, Anthony relaxed most of the day enjoying the simple and tranquil surroundings. Later they enjoyed an outdoor lunch and talked about pleasant memories and future plans. In the late afternoon, Jorge went to collect the children from school. Juan and Maria were happy to see Mr. Hernández and Anthony.

"The baby cried during the night," said Juan. "She woke me up."

"Baby's do that sometimes," said Maria. "Don't be such a baby yourself."

"You see my friend," said Jorge to Anthony, "when you have children, you must get a striped shirt like the referee at the *futbol* games so that you can keep order. When they get out of hand, you give them a yellow card for a warning. When they behave badly, you give them a red card and they must go to their room."

Consuelo added, "He talks like he is in charge, but he lets the children get away with everything. I am the one to hand out the yellow and red cards," she said as they all laughed.

"Do you see how less shy Martina is with me now?" Anthony asked proudly.

"She likes you. You are doing very well with her," said Consuelo.

Anthony wished the time here could go on, but knew it was time to leave for San Salvador. He put Martina down for a nap before they left and commented that he was getting the knack of caring for the child.

"You should not wait too long before you have one of your own," commented Jorge. "A man needs family."

"I feel like you are part of my family," said Anthony.

They all bid each other goodbye, comforted by the fact that they would be together again soon completely unaware that once again their lives would change forever.

Taking Flight

Chapter 43

Driving back to San Salvador on Tuesday evening, Anthony recognized the road signs, landmarks and the towns they had passed on their route to Perquín. Even as the sky turned dark, the terrain had a familiar feel. Neither he nor Mr. Hernández said much during the first half of the trip. They stopped briefly in San Miguel so Anthony could stretch out his back and walk around a bit. Once back on the Interamericana Highway, Anthony recited his instructions to get him and Martina through airport security in San Salvador and Customs in Miami. He spoke the Spanish phrases he learned to use when interacting with Martina. The exercises reminded him of games his parents would play with him on road trips.

It was dark when they reached San Salvador, but the traffic was still congested as they slowly made their way through the city. Anthony could make out and identify the major buildings they toured only ten days ago. When they finally reached the hotel, Mr. Hernández pulled into the garage and parked. Because of the hour and their having skipped lunch, they agreed to have dinner in the hotel before checking in.

"We can get the bags later," said Mr. Hernández making sure that nothing was exposed in the cabin of the car.

"I'm all for that," said Anthony.

They entered the hotel lobby from the garage and headed straight for the dining room. They were greeted by the Maitre D' as old friends and taken to a quiet table. Raul,

353

whom Anthony remembered from their first night soon appeared and extended a warm welcome to both men. He made some suggestions and they each selected a "Kansas City" steak. They ordered beer instead of wine and agreed to skip the rum tonight.

Anthony enjoyed the familiarity of the place. He did not feel as much an outsider as he had the first time he dined here. Mr. Hernández had become a friend and not just a contractor hired by Carla's agency. The Colonel was the bonding agent between San Salvador, Perquín and the village where Martin had served and died. He was the link to Jorge and Consuelo, Señora Órnelas, Eduardo and Martina. He was the connection to the elders in the village and the spirit behind the blessing of the clinic and the memorial to its victims. He was now one of the most important people in Anthony's life.

When dinner was over, they agreed to save the final preparation for Anthony's meeting with Calderón until the next day. Raul bid them a warm good night and they went to the lobby to register. As Anthony was filling out the guest card, he inquired about messages and mail. The clerk brought him the packet that had arrived from David's law firm and a large envelope from Carla's agency. Assuming that they were complete and correct, he tucked them under his arm to review in the morning. The clerk advised Mr. Hernández of a message that came in earlier in the evening. After glancing at it for a moment, he asked Anthony to wait at the desk.

"With your back not doing well, I shall get the bags from the car and join you shortly."

Anthony was surprised that Mr. Hernández was willing leave him alone. He assumed that he was no longer regarded as a rookie and could take care of himself, at least in the lobby of a world class hotel.

"I'm sure I can manage. Let me help," said Anthony.

"I insist, Antonio, to avoid the anger of Señora Carla."

"I tell you what," said Anthony, "I will grab one of these luggage carts and meet you at the garage entrance."

"The cart will be fine, but wait here for me."

Anthony felt that he was being treated like the naïve tourist after all, but decided not to argue. Mr. Hernández disappeared through the doorway leading to the garage.

Anthony walked to the end of the registration desk where he found and selected a luggage cart. To pass the time he opened the mail packet. Without removing the papers he could see the law firm letterhead and plastic markers indicating where signatures were required. He closed the packet and opened the envelope from Carla. He made out a list of instructions and electronic tickets bearing bar codes. Satisfied, he left everything intact. *Tomorrow*, he said to himself. His eyes wandered around the lobby taking in the potted plants, guest chairs and tables displaying magazines and newspapers.

Not wanting to upset his friend, but growing impatient and becoming uneasy, he left the cart and walked toward the garage door. After looking at it for a long thirty seconds, he turned the knob and pushed. No sooner did he open the door when he heard the popping sounds; three of them followed by footsteps.

"Juan," he called out.

"Juan, are you out there?"

"Juan, I'm coming to the car."

Anthony went into the garage half walking, half running toward the car. He turned at the end of a row of parked cars in order to reach their space. As he did, his head jerked up, his spine arched backward as he stared in disbelief. Mr. Hernández's twisted body was lying behind the car, the trunk lid open, the keys visible in its lock. One suitcase was on the ground. Three bloody pools were spreading over the back of his white linen jacket. His right arm was bent under him in the direction of his shoulder holster. His left knee was bent, his right leg extended.

"Oh no, oh no," cried Anthony as he bent over his friend. He dropped the packet and put a hand under Mr. Hernández's head and another on his shoulder.

"Jesus fucking Christ, don't let this happen!" he shouted.

"Juan, Juan, can you hear me?"

Anthony heard a soft groan as he tried to roll him so he could see his face.

"Okay, okay, you're alive. I'm going to help you. It's going to be all right. Please don't fucking die on me."

Anthony tried to cradle him putting a hand on his back where he could feel the sticky liquid spreading. Mr. Hernández was moving his lips trying to say something. Anthony put his ear close to his face.

Mr. Hernández half moaned and half whispered, "Ernesto."

Anthony stiffened and looked at Mr. Hernández again and said, "I'll get help. Just hang on, I'll get help." Anthony started to rise when he heard a familiar voice.

"Now, give me your dollars, Americano."

Anthony looked over his shoulder and could make out a skinny figure coming from the shadows. The mugger from last week had returned. Anthony turned back toward Mr. Hernández and gently surrendered him to the floor of the garage. He took a deep breath desperately trying to keep himself together.

"Don't shoot," he said. "You can have my money. You

can have his money too."

As he lifted his hands away from Mr. Hernández, his right hand slowly made its way to the wounded man's left ankle. Still with his back to the robber, and looking over his shoulder, he spoke again while taking the small pistol from its ankle holster.

"Just don't shoot. Please don't shoot," said Anthony. "I have plenty of dollars. *Mucho dinero!*"

Anthony shifted his feet as he turned half way to his left, the pistol concealed in his right hand. The robber was waving his gun toward the garage ceiling indicating that he either wanted Anthony to raise his hands or stand up. Anthony stood slowly, his profile facing the skinny man wearing the same gray hooded sweatshirt. The arm of the man was extended toward Anthony holding the same gun that Mr. Hernández had returned to him.

I can do this, I can do this, Anthony thought to himself.

"Mucho dollars," said Anthony again as he stood erect and swiftly turned with his right arm fully extended. He pulled the trigger twice before his arm jumped so far off the mark a third shot missed the robber whose eyes reflected the terror his mind was just beginning to absorb. Anthony straightened his arm again and continued squeezing the trigger until all he heard were repeated clicks. The robber lay motionless less than six feet away, his gun still in his hand.

"You bastard," Anthony screamed at the young dead man. "He let you go! You fucking bastard!"

Seconds passed before Anthony turned back to Mr. Hernández. He dismissed the idea of getting help from the hotel.

"I'm going to get you to the hospital," he said. "Hang

on, please hang on."

Anthony took the keys from the trunk lid, threw the bag and his packet into the trunk, closed it and moved quickly to open the car's rear door. He threw the pistol on the front seat. He ran back to the limp body of Mr. Hernández, put his hands under the big man's arms and dragged him to the door. Gathering as much strength as he could, he lifted his friend feeling a searing pain in his back. He got Mr. Hernández's head as high as the window and pushed so that his body fell forward, face down on the rear seat.

"You've got to get to a hospital. There's no 911 here. We can't wait," Anthony said to the motionless body.

He grabbed Mr. Hernández around the waist. Anthony put one leg on the floor sill of the car and pushed as hard as he could. After two attempts, Mr. Hernández lay curled on the rear seat of the car. Anthony got behind the wheel and started the engine, talking to Mr. Hernández as he sped out of the garage.

"You're going to be okay. I'll get you to the hospital. I remember where it is. Just hang on. You're going to be okay."

Anthony headed up the street in the direction from which they came. The traffic had quieted down. He drove until he saw the sign for the city hospital. He turned left and continued on until he could see the building.

"Don't worry. I'll get you there. I promise I'll get you there."

He drove faster than he should until the hospital was in sight.

"You see? Do you see it? There it is. You'll be okay. It's right here. Just hang on a little longer."

Anthony pulled into a driveway and headed to what

looked like the emergency entrance.

"We're here. We're here," he shouted almost joyfully. "I'll get help."

He parked in front of sliding glass doors and jumped out of the car only to find that they were locked. He pounded and pounded on his reflection.

"Open the fucking door! Open the fucking door!"

Finally a man in scrubs appeared looking uncertain of what was going on. Anthony pointed to the car.

"Help him. Help him. The man has been shot," he screamed through the door.

Slowly, the man on the other side touched a key pad and tapped the code that opened the door.

Anthony ran pointing to the car and opened the rear door.

"He's been shot, please help him. Hurry! Please fuckin' hurry."

The man in scrubs moved quickly to the rear seat and climbed into the car.

Anthony watched pumping his fist up and down. Other hospital personnel came to the door. Anthony pointed to the rear seat and waved for them to come.

The man in scrubs backed out of the car and took a step away. He looked at Anthony and shook his head.

"Get him some blood," said Anthony. "He's lost a lot of blood. Get him some blood and you can revive him," he pleaded.

The man shook his head again.

"He is dead, *Señor*. There is nothing that can be done."

"Don't you know who he is?" said Anthony. "He is Colonel Hernández. Colonel Juan Hernández. You can't just let him die!"

"I'm sorry, Señor. There is nothing we can do."

The finality of it was beginning to reach Anthony. He moved to where the man was standing and stood until he moved aside. Anthony put his foot on the rear floorboard of the car. He leaned in and put his hands on the shoulder of Mr. Hernández.

"I'm sorry, Juan," he sobbed. "I'm sorry I didn't get you here in time. I'm sorry you met this guy because I was stupid. I'm sorry I let him hear your name that night. I'm sorry I let you get my bags for me. I'm sorry I let you die. I'm so fucking sorry."

And then it all came out. The agony of Martin's death, his almost fatal mugging, his introduction to Martina, his faulting Martin for living a lie, the ceremony honoring the victims at the clinic, his alienation of Bernadette, his anger toward his mother for betraying his father, and his own betrayal of Rita. He sobbed over the lifeless body of his friend. His body shook violently as he tried to find some relief in the tears and sobs that consumed him. When the sounds and the movement and flow of tears finally subsided, he moved back out of the car. He turned and saw at least ten hospital personnel standing there looking at him with sad and worried expressions.

The man in scrubs came up to him.

"I'm very sorry Señor, for the loss of your friend. With your permission, we would like to take him inside."

Anthony looked at them with a confused expression.

"What good is that going to do?"

He closed the rear door of the car and turned to face them.

"I'm taking him with me," he said.

"Señor, there are procedures we must follow when a dead person reaches the hospital. Please let us do our job."

"I'm really tired of procedures and regulations and

processes and fucking people that think paperwork is more important that saving lives or returning the dead to where they belong."

"Please Señor, this is a terrible thing that has happened, but we must take care of the deceased."

"I'm taking him out of here. As far as you are concerned, this never happened. No reports, no papers, no authorities are necessary. You can do what you want, but I'm taking him with me, no matter what."

The man took one step forward. Anthony looked at him, unyielding.

"No matter what."

Anthony moved around to the driver's side of the car, got in and started the car. He put it in reverse and backed out slowly so that those in the way could move to safety. Once he was facing the street, he pressed the accelerator and sped off.

Anthony kept an eye on the rear view mirror as he retraced the route that brought them to San Salvador. Because of the hour, he decided to gas up before leaving the city. He drove to the general store where they had purchased food, water and ice before their first trip to Perquín. He parked in the back away from a few other vehicles. Once inside, he purchased two blankets, a hooded sweatshirt and a box of bullets for the pistol. With the clerk's acknowledgement, he put the sweatshirt on in the store pulling the hood over his head before paying the bill, adding on enough to fill the car with gas. Once outside, He put both blankets over the body of Mr. Hernández. Anthony pulled the car up to the gas pumps in front and filled the tank. He was thankful that there were no police cars in sight as he and Mr. Hernández left for his final trip to Perquín.

Chapter 44

Anthony made sure not to speed or do anything on the road that might attract attention. Driving late at night was enough to be noticed by police. It occurred to him that if he were in New York now, he would have patrol cars, state troopers and SWAT teams for company. He turned North at San Miguel and headed to Highway 7 that would take him toward El Mozote and then Perquín. There were no lights in his rear view mirror or on the road ahead. After driving for almost three hours, he tried to relax his body and wished he had a cup of coffee. He thought about turning on the radio but concluded that everything would be broadcasted in undecipherable Spanish. Besides, the quiet of the car helped him stay alert and awake. It wasn't until he saw the road sign for El Mozote that he turned to look at the back seat barely making out the dark blankets. It occurred to him for the first time that he had killed a man tonight. Justifiable, he thought, but he killed a man nevertheless. He couldn't let go of the thought until he admitted to himself that he may have pulled the trigger whether the robber was armed or not. He killed in response to seeing his friend lying helplessly on the ground, shot in the back. He fired to avenge Mr. Hernández, not in fear for his life.

As he passed the turnoff to El Mozote, Anthony recalled their visit to the cemetery and memorial there. *How do you survive such losses?* So many Salvadorans must carry the scars of loved ones lost and perhaps the guilt of surviving. The perpetrators of personal horrors were not foreign powers, but brothers in blood and culture. Oh what Shakespeare could have done with the history of this tiny country.

Anthony slowed the car as he approached the city limits of Perquín. At 3:00 A.M., not even the roosters were awake. He drove slowly until he approached Jorge's house. He could hear distant dogs barking as the car rolled over the gravel. He sat for a minute before leaving the car. When he opened the car door, he heard the front door of the house open although no lights were on. Jorge was standing on the porch wearing only a pair of shorts and wielding a rifle. As Anthony exited the car, Jorge lowered the weapon and walked slowly toward him. The two men met near the steps leading up to the porch. Anthony just stood looking at Jorge, grief masking his face, his arms extended at a downward angle, palms up. His mouth opened, but he couldn't speak. He pointed to the car.

Jorge did not need words to understand what he was about to see. He walked slowly to the car. After looking inside, he opened the rear door and leaned in. He pulled back the blankets and bowed his head saying nothing. He turned and walked back to Anthony who was still facing the porch.

"I couldn't leave him there," said Anthony.

"Come inside," said Jorge.

As they climbed the porch steps, a light went on in the house and Consuelo appeared at the door. Jorge whispered something in Spanish and she gasped, instinctively looking inside to where the children were. She held the door open as Jorge guided Anthony into the house. Jorge brought Anthony to the kitchen and told him to sit while Consuelo went about closing the children's bedroom doors. She came back to the kitchen and made some coffee and brought out some rum. She busied herself getting glasses, cups and saucers and bringing them to the table. She turned away from the men and grasped the edge of the sink, her head bowed. She wiped tears from her eyes and poured coffee for the three of them while Jorge poured a shot of rum into each glass. He gently pushed one of the glasses toward Anthony who had been staring at the table top. Anthony picked up the glass but did not drink.

"You did the right thing by bringing him here," said Jorge.

Anthony explained what happened in the garage and at the hospital while Jorge and Consuelo listened quietly.

"It was my fault," he said. "I let him go to the car in the garage by himself. If I were there it would have turned out differently."

"Antonio, the Colonel was a soldier familiar with danger. This was not your fault."

"I thought about what happened on the drive back. How could the robber have known we would be at the hotel in San Salvador last night? I didn't understand at the time, but Juan whispered a name."

"Ernesto," said Jorge.

"You knew?" said Anthony.

"We learned that Ernesto was being recruited into a gang from Mara Salvatrucha. The same gang as that of the thief you killed tonight. The village life was not enough for Ernesto. We left a message for Juan at the hotel warning him that Ernesto's initiation was to tell the gang when he would return to San Salvador. Juan must have dropped his guard just for a moment. That is how men die. In a short second, you make a small mistake and you are dead. It was not your fault. A mistake was made."

"It was because he didn't want me to lift my luggage,"

Anthony said in an exasperated tone.

"No. He didn't want to expose you to danger. That was his job. That was his way. He must have checked the garage and not seen the robber before going to the car. That was the mistake."

"He was not a man who made mistakes, especially when he was warned that something was going on."

"When men plot to kill other men, they have the advantage, always," said Jorge.

"I want Ernesto," said Anthony. "He used me to get to the Colonel. I have to settle that."

"Ernesto must already be gone from the village. Justice will be done at the right time. For now, we must take care of the Colonel, and you must get some rest. We still have the child to think about."

"I can't sleep."

'Drink your rum and lie down for a while. I have some calls to make and I will drive to village shortly. When I come back, I will wake you if you are asleep. There is much to be done."

"Can you forgive me?"

"There is nothing to forgive, Antonio. It is part of living in El Salvador."

Anthony stood and the men embraced. Consuelo came over and took Anthony in her arms.

"Jorge is right. This all comes from the war."

"Get some rest now," said Jorge. "I will come for you soon."

Consuelo led Anthony to the room where he had stayed during his first visit. He lay on the bed and Consuelo removed his shoes. She went to turn off the light.

"I'm sorry," said Anthony. "I'm so sorry."

"Rest," she said as she turned off the light.

Chapter 45

Anthony woke up at 7:00 A.M. on Wednesday morning. It took him a minute to realize where he was. He heard voices coming from another part of the house. He sat up in bed and saw Maria and Juan looking at him from the doorway.

He rubbed the sleep from his eyes and said, "Hi kids."

They came in and hugged him silently. He put his arms around them. They knew. No one here was shielded from tragedy. Innocence left the young very early in El Salvador.

"I love you guys," he said with a squeeze. Fighting back tears, he disengaged himself and told them that they had better get ready for school. They turned and left without speaking.

Anthony went to the small bathroom and freshened up before joining the voices coming from the living room and the kitchen. The elders and Jorge were there. Some of their wives were working with Consuelo in the kitchen. They stopped talking when Anthony entered the room.

Anthony looked at each of the men, one by one. Then he spoke to the group.

"I'm sorry for the mistakes I made that led to the Colonel's death," he said. "I share your grief."

The men nodded

"Join us," said Ignacio. "We are planning the day for Colonel Hernández. Salvadorans know how to honor a soldier and put him to rest."

Anthony sat on a foot stool as he listened to the men who spoke alternately in Spanish and English so that he could follow along. He contributed nothing, but gained an understanding of how important a figure Mr. Hernández had been to these men. When the plans were completed, Anthony spoke.

"I want Ernesto. It is my duty and my way to honor the Colonel."

Hector replied. "I don't think the Colonel would agree that this is your duty. We all want Ernesto. His betrayal of the Colonel has hurt us deeply. Ernesto has turned his back on the village and his family. He must just now understand what he has done. Let him live with that feeling for now. His time will come."

Unsatisfied with the answer, Anthony said nothing in response. Since the crowd could not fit in the kitchen, the men moved out to the porch where the women brought out a large breakfast of eggs, bacon, biscuits and bread. Anthony guessed that they had arrived early in the morning and were ready for a meal that would sustain them through a difficult day. He was surprised at his own hunger, ate heartily and drank lots of coffee. The men talked of some of the accomplishments that Mr. Hernández achieved during the war. They shared stories about his skills as an engineer and his cunning as a soldier. He noticed that when an unresolved question about the plan for the day came up, they deferred to Jorge.

Jorge then got up to announce that he would be taking the children to school which would be limited to a half day today. The men stood when he did and wished him well until they would meet later in the day. Anthony thought in their goodbyes to Jorge he heard one of the elders refer to him as "Colonel."

Jorge left with Juan and Maria. The elders departed with their wives soon after. Anthony asked Consuelo if he could take a shower and she got him some extra towels. Anthony got his bag from Mr. Hernández's car approaching it slowly and opening the rear door to see that his friend's body and the blankets were gone. He took his bag and mail packet from the trunk. Consuelo was cleaning the mess left from the breakfast on the porch.

As he was going to his room, Consuelo said, "Today, you should wear the best clothes you have with you."

Anthony nodded and went in the house. As he went through his ritual of shaving and showering, he came to the realization that there was no time for personal grieving. He had a job to do participating in a solemn ritual that the people of the village and Perquín considered sacred. The assassination of Archbishop Romero had rocked the entire country and sparked a revolution. The death of Juan Hernández was no less a loss to this community. Anthony would carry himself with the dignity his friend deserved. When he was done dressing, some of the elder's wives had returned to help Consuelo prepare what appeared to be a silk shawl, perhaps for one of them to wear. To keep himself busy he looked over the papers sent by David's office and the travel documents sent from Carla. After studying them carefully, he returned them to their original packaging.

Shortly before Noon, Jorge returned with the children who were instructed to dress in the clothes Consuelo had set out for them. Jorge changed into a suit and tie. Consuelo came out in a beautiful bright and colorful floor length silk dress. The children joined her. Juan was wearing a white shirt, red tie and blue pants. Maria was wearing a white blouse and plaid skirt. Both wore black leather shoes. The elder's wives praised their appearance. They all gathered in a circle before getting ready to leave. Maria led them in a

Taking Flight

Spanish prayer at the end of which Jorge said "Amen" which the others repeated. Before Jorge and the children got into his pickup truck, he asked Anthony to drive the women to the village in Mr. Hernández's car. Anthony followed his instructions.

When they reached the village the perimeter of the fountain was covered with flowers. A hearse was at the entrance to the church containing its driver, the priest and a coffin. The women left the car and joined their husbands in a small school bus. One of them was holding and caring for Martina. Replacing them in Mr. Hernández's car were Eduardo and Señora Cabrera who greeted Anthony with a warm hug. Anthony followed Jorge's truck to the main highway.

As they proceeded to El Mozote the highway was lined with people on both sides of the road. Men, women, children, the young and old were there, some holding flowers others waving tiny flags. It appeared as though the entire population of the village, Perquín and surely other places were there to honor the Colonel. How this could happen so quickly in a remote area such as this was something Anthony could not comprehend. Then he remembered someone saying to him, 'This is El Salvador.'

When they reached the memorial cemetery at El Mozote, cars and trucks overflowed on to the road. As the hearse approached a prepared gravesite, Jorge's truck and Mr. Hernández's car came to a stop. The crowd closed in an orderly and respectful manner. The driver opened the tailgate of the hearse as the priest got out from the passenger side. At the driver's signal, the elders stepped forward to their assigned places. Jorge beckoned to Anthony to join them. The coffin was gently drawn from the hearse. Consuelo stepped forward and placed over it the shawl the women had prepared that morning. The men lifted the coffin onto their shoulders and followed the priest to the gravesite. They placed the coffin on wooden beams that sat across the grave. Canvas straps lay across the beams.

The priest gave a blessing and led the crowd in several prayers. Each of the elders gave a short talk in Spanish honoring their fallen hero. Anthony glanced around the crowd and was jolted when he saw the woman from Calderón's office among the mourners. Seeing her reinforced the thought to Anthony, *this is for them, not for me*. Before Jorge spoke, he asked Anthony to say a few words. He had been told to expect this, but had not yet settled on anything. He stepped forward.

"I came to El Salvador to retrieve the remains of a friend so that his family could honor him in death. Here I met another man who became my friend who we mourn and honor today. I will never forget him."

He stepped back not sure if he said enough or too much.

Jorge stepped forward and began a eulogy that described how much the Colonel had meant to him as a young man, as a soldier, as a man who married and had his own family whose son bears the Colonel's name.

He ended by saying, "Today we bring him here to rest near his own family who he has already joined. He deserves that rest and the joy of being with his wife and children again after doing so much for all of us." He bowed his head and the mourners acted in kind. The Priest gave the final blessing as Consuelo removed the shawl. Four of the elders took hold of the straps while the beams were taken away. Slowly they released the straps hand over hand as the coffin was lowered into the ground. Starting with

Taking Flight

Señora Cabrera, the mourners approached the grave and dropped a flower to the coffin, made the sign of the cross and moved on. Colonel Juan Hernández was at rest.

Chapter 46

By the time Anthony was back at Jorge's house on Wednesday evening, he was drained emotionally and physically. The experience of the funeral was exhausting. In addition to the acceptance of his enormous personal loss, he recognized how the Salvadoran community, in which Mr. Hernández was a giant, had responded by honoring him in such a dignified way. Dealing with death was a way of life. The community seemed to be saying that no matter how great the loss, they would not be defeated. No matter how great the tragedy, they could survive. The spirits of the dead would live on and inspire those who went forward. The war may have long ended, but the struggles went on and these people would not surrender their fight for the survival of present and future generations. Their hopes and dreams would remain alive.

Earlier, Jorge had suggested that Anthony have dinner with his family and Martina whom they would bring home with them. Afterward he and the elders would discuss the next steps to be taken. After freshening up at the house, Anthony turned down a suggestion to rest before dinner. He gathered up Martina, brought her outside and placed her in the stroller. Juan and Maria joined him. With a child on each side, Anthony pushed the stroller in a large circle while Jorge watched from the porch.

"Do you like living in America," asked Juan

"Yes, I do," said Anthony, "but I have never thought about it as living in America. Just living at home."

"Isn't it big and noisy?"

"I suppose it is, but there are many places in America that are small and where people live quietly."

"We see pictures of big cities and movie stars. Once we saw a New Year's Eve celebration on a TV. I have never seen so many people," said Maria.

"It's quite a celebration," said Anthony. "I'm sure you celebrate it here as well."

"Yes, we have fireworks and always special food and music and dancing, but we always remember the dead which makes people sad."

"Part of celebrating a new year is remembering those we have lost. It is a sad time for many people in America as well."

"Do you like *futbol?*" asked Juan

"Yes, we call it soccer. It's not as popular in America as it is here, but many people have come to like it. What we call football is a different sport and much more popular, but soccer, as we call it, has become better known and is now played by many children."

"What is your wife like?" asked Maria.

"Well, she is very pretty and very nice."

"My mother is very pretty and very nice too."

"Yes, she is."

"And you are handsome like my daddy."

"Well, thank you, Maria. You and Juan shall grow up to be very pretty and handsome as well. And Martina will too."

"Is it important to be handsome and pretty in America?"

"That's a good question, Maria. I guess it is since people work so hard at it."

"Do you work hard at it?"

Anthony squirmed a little. "I suppose I do. I try to

wear nice clothes and comb my hair so that I will look my best, but you know it's much more important to be nice and an honest person."

"Do you work hard at that too?" asked Maria.

"Not as hard as I should," said Anthony with a laugh. "And how about you, what do you want to be when you grow up?"

Juan interrupted, "I want to be a *futbol* player and build bridges."

"Oh," said Anthony, "you may have to choose one or the other."

"Why? Everybody plays *futbol*. I can learn to build bridges."

"I want to travel all over the world," said Maria.

"I hope you can," said Anthony. "If you come to America, I hope you will come to see me."

"And your wife?"

"Of course."

"Can I come too?" asked Juan.

"You bet. In fact if you don't come, I'll be very disappointed."

"The men in the village have started to call my daddy 'Colonel,'" said Maria.

"I'm sure that it is an honor for your daddy. He is a man very much respected by the others."

"I hope that doesn't mean he will be the next to die," said Maria.

Anthony sucked in his breath.

"I think your daddy will live for a very long time," he said wondering if that was a good thing to say to children who have seen so much.

They walked quietly for a while, when Juan broke the silence.

Taking Flight

"Whew! What a stink!"

"I think Martina is ready for a change," said Anthony.

Anthony took care of cleaning and changing Martina, talking to her all the while to keep them both less anxious during the process. Consuelo came to collect her so he could wash before dinner. The evening meal began with a prayer during which they all held hands and prayed for the well being of Colonel Hernández's soul as he joined his family in heaven. Consuelo's eyes were moist as she got up to serve the meal. The conversation was light and included talk of people they had not seen for a long time before today and the children's school schedule of the next day. Juan and Maria were instructed to say goodbye to Anthony before going to bed since they probably would not see him until he returned from San Salvador.

"Am I going back to the city tonight?" asked Anthony.

"We will discuss our plans later," said Jorge.

With a little help from Consuelo, Anthony put Martina to bed. He returned to the kitchen and hugged Juan and Maria promising to see them again very soon, and reminded them that they had an invitation to visit him in America.

He left them and walked to the front porch. Jorge was just completing a call.

"Donato and Hector will be here shortly," he said to Anthony.

"Will we talk about Ernesto?"

"Antonio, it is best that for the remainder of the day we do not include any mention of Ernesto. Doing so will interfere with this day of devotion to the Colonel. There is time for Ernesto. It will come soon, I promise you, but it is not something for discussion today."

Anthony started to ask another question, but stifled it.

"Okay," he said.

Jorge brought out four bottles of beer as the truck with Donato and Hector rolled up. The men shook hands and sat waiting for Jorge to speak.

"Colonel Hernández is dead. There is nothing more that we can do about that except to honor him and finish his mission. Antonio came here to retrieve the remains of the doctor, and the Colonel agreed to help him. We have asked Antonio to bring Martina to the United States adding to his responsibilities, which he has agreed to do. These are the elements of the present mission. Does anyone wish to disagree?"

Anthony raised his hand to add dealing with Ernesto, but caught a cautionary look from Jorge and stopped. Donato and Hector remained silent.

"Very well, then. We must proceed in light of the new things that have happened. The death of the Colonel will now surely be known by all in San Salvador including Calderón. He must also know of the robber killed in the garage at the hotel where Antonio and the Colonel stayed when in San Salvador. His history with the Colonel will raise his interest. Whether he can connect the assassin to the Colonel or to Antonio is uncertain. Certainly there is no proof of any connection, but his curiosity will drive him to ask questions and listen to rumors. And there are always rumors."

Anthony raised his hand, waiting for Jorge to give him permission to speak. Jorge nodded.

"Isn't he likely to learn what happened?" asked Anthony. "Isn't he likely to contact the police? He knows the Colonel was my escort and that I'm scheduled to see him tomorrow. He can find out that we had dinner at the hotel last night. While I didn't see anyone in the garage, I did stop to get supplies and gasoline before coming back to Perquín. I also stopped at the hospital."

"He may suspect, but to have proof of a crime, especially one committed by an American, is necessary before he can make an arrest, even in El Salvador."

"I can beg off going to the meeting. I can claim to be ill and get a delayed meeting date," said Anthony. "I can leave the country on Saturday as planned, although I may not ever be able to return."

"While Calderón may not be able to act on any suspicions he may have, he can create some difficulties regarding your eligibility to leave the country. He is very much a part of the government bureaucracy that deals in these matters. If he suspected that you would try to leave and wished to block your departure, he could probably do so. It is my belief that he would become more suspicious if you did not attend the meeting as scheduled."

"So what do we do?"

"My proposal is that you go to the meeting as planned. Carry out everything as though nothing has happened."

"But, how do I explain my being at the hotel last night? We registered after having dinner in the hotel dining room. If everyone knows about everything as you suggest, he will know I was at the funeral. I spoke in honor of the Colonel."

"I have taken some steps," said Jorge, "to relieve this situation."

"What steps?" asked Anthony.

"There is no record of your registration at the hotel last night. That has been taken care of. Officially, you were never there, you or the Colonel."

"But we were in the dining room. We talked to the Maitre D' and the waiter Raul."

Donato smiled. Hector spoke.

"The Maitre D' and Raul are in the village as we speak. They were at the service for the Colonel this afternoon. They have taken care of the desk clerk, and he has taken care of the records of your registration. As far as the hotel is concerned...," he shook his head.

Jorge spoke again, "It will be easy for Calderón to believe that the Colonel was in Perquín when he died. You also were in Perquín, at my house, as my guest. Calderón has little interest in seeking justice for a gang member. He will be pleased that the Colonel is gone. He may even seek pleasure in obstructing your mission, but solving a crime against a thief is not something he will be concerned about."

"What about the police?" asked Anthony.

Hector interjected, "They will be happy to have one less gang member to deal with."

"You seem pretty certain about this."

"There is nothing certain, Antonio," said Jorge, "Information is often for sale. It spreads very quickly, but to move away from the original plan will create more suspicion and danger.

Anthony could not contain the question any longer. "What about Ernesto?"

Jorge just looked at Anthony. Finally he said, "Dealing with Ernesto at this moment will increase the level of danger to the mission." He finished the statement with an air of finality on the subject.

"How does all of the uncertainty affect the plan for taking Martina with me on Saturday?"

"That plan has changed," said Jorge. "The possibility that Calderón will obstruct or delay your departure makes your escorting her out of the country a greater risk. As you yourself pointed out, there are other considerations that challenge the wisdom of that plan."

"Are you saying that she won't leave with me?" Anthony asked incredulously.

"Yes."

Hector smiled. "She will leave as scheduled, Antonio, but not with you."

"What are you saying?"

"For now, let us leave it at that. You must trust us, Antonio. Your departure from San Salvador by yourself is the safest way. Martina will be handled separately. She will be brought to you at the airport in Miami shortly before the plane departs for New York, assuming of course that you get to Miami. The responsibility you have is insuring that she is taken care of once in the United States, and that she has the possibilities to live a better life."

"So who takes her to Miami?"

"Let's leave that for now."

"Are you saying you don't trust me with the rest of the plan?"

"Not at all, Antonio. You will know everything before it happens. It is not a matter of trust as much as a matter of safety for the others."

Once again, Anthony took Jorge's withholding of information personally. He felt that he had earned his trust. Jorge sensed this.

"Antonio, this is not a matter of personal trust. We are trusting you with the fate of a child's life. It is a question of tactics. This is how the Colonel would have planned it. I swear to you this is in the best interests of the girl and you."

Anthony swallowed.

"Okay," he said. "Now what?"

"You will return to San Salvador tonight with the

Maitre D' and Raul. You will register at the hotel and stay in your room. In the morning, you will take a taxi to Calderón's office and complete your business there. If things go well, you will return here with your friend's remains."

"How do I get back here?"

"You return to the hotel after the meeting. You will learn soon enough if Calderón plans to obstruct your departure. Stay in your room until you are ready to check out. I will pick you up at the hotel at 2:00 P.M. and bring you back."

"And if things go wrong?"

"If they cannot be fixed between the time you leave Calderón and the time I pick you up, we go to a new plan."

"And if…?"

"Antonio, please. One step at a time."

"When am I supposed to leave for San Salvador?"

"The men are waiting for you at the cantina. As soon as you are ready. Donato and Hector will take you there."

"And the new papers and travel documents?"

"They will be ready when you arrive back tomorrow," said Hector.

"Anthony shook his head and asked, "How did the war last so long?"

"Because the other side had many more guns," smiled Donato.

"There is one more thing, Antonio," said Jorge.

"Yes?"

"The gun you used. You must leave the gun here."

Anthony had not even thought about the gun, but he instinctively did not want to give it up. Whether it was a protective instinct, a personal connection to Mr. Hernández, or a reminder of what he had done, he wasn't sure. He looked at Jorge who held his hand out waiting.

Anthony closed his eyes and drew a deep breath, letting it out very slowly. "Yes. You're right. I'll get it from my bag."

Anthony retrieved the gun and turned it over to Jorge. Jorge put it on the chair beside him and embraced Anthony. "You have done very well my friend. This mission will be successful because of you."

"What caused the bad feelings between Calderón and Mr. Hernández besides their being on opposite sides during the war?" asked Anthony.

"After time passes, one does not always remember the cause, just the feeling," replied Jorge.

Anthony nodded. Donato and Hector helped Anthony with his bags and drove him to the cantina. They brought him to the two men waiting inside and wished him good luck.

Chapter 47

At the cantina, Anthony sat with the Maitre D' and Raul. They had a much more somber demeanor than the one they wore at the hotel. The men took Anthony through a brief list of instructions for the evening. At the hotel, he would register again, ask for a wake-up call, a bell captain to assist with his bags and arrange for a taxi to pick him up in the morning.

The drive back to San Salvador was quiet. When they finally reached the hotel, they did not drive into the garage. About a half block from the main entrance of the hotel, Raul got out of the car and crossed to opposite side of the street. The Maitre D' drove half way up again and let Anthony get out and collect his bags. Anthony walked the remaining distance while the Maitre D' followed along in the car slightly behind him. Anthony reached the hotel entrance, turned and saw Raul catch up with the car and get in. Anthony waited for the car to drive off before entering the lobby. He understood they had taken nothing for granted.

Anthony was settled in his room after going through the entrance and registration plan exactly as scripted. He resisted a temptation to go to the hotel bar for a nightcap, and an even stronger urge to go down to the garage. He knew sleep would not come easy tonight so he did what Anthony always did. He organized. He got all his papers in order, packed everything he would need for the next day's business, laid out his clothes, recharged his cell phone, and made check lists for his meeting with Calderón and the calls to follow. He played out several mental scenarios that might be useful in the morning's drama. His mind was still in Calderón's office when he fell asleep.

Anthony was awake for twenty minutes before the wake-up call interrupted his thoughts. A public appearance in the dining room would be wise, so he went downstairs in the manner taught to him by Mr. Hernández, nodded to the desk clerk in the lobby and went into the dining room and partook in the breakfast buffet. Before heading back to his room, he retrieved his bag containing his business clothes from the Concierge. He returned to his room, dressed for the day and took the black bag containing all his important papers, travel documents and a few personal belongings he did not trust to leave in the room or with the Concierge. The luggage he left behind contained only clothes and toiletries that he would never miss if lost, or worry about if searched. He questioned whether or not he was being slightly paranoid, but then reminded himself that two men had just been killed in this building. He had pulled the trigger in one case. He was in a foreign country and Mr. Hernández wasn't there to open doors anymore.

The taxi arranged by the desk clerk took him through the crowded and busy streets of San Salvador. The scene was familiar as the cab followed the route he had taken with Mr. Hernández, but had an entirely different feel. Curious observation and amusement were replaced by careful surveillance. He searched for anything that could endanger him, a pedestrian walking toward the cab, a car driving along side, or anything out of the ordinary. He arrived at Calderón's office on time and shortly thereafter was received by the matron he had met during his first visit and had seen at Mr. Hernández's funeral. She greeted him with no sign of recognition, using the same cold efficient manner as was expected in her role.

Upon entering the office area, Anthony spotted the same policeman that had confiscated his Leatherman. Anthony put his bag in front of the man and decided to test the waters.

"I'd like to pick up the item you collected from me on my last visit."

The policeman looked incredulous.

"You may do so by checking with Lost and Found at Police Headquarters."

"And where would that be?"

The policeman looked Anthony in the eye.

"I will leave a map for you," he said as he shoved Anthony's bags back toward him.

Well, I wasn't arrested, thought Anthony.

The matron continued escorting Anthony to Calderón's office, knocked when they arrived and entered when Calderón announced permission.

"Ah, Señor Bartolo, please be seated," he said as Anthony entered the office.

"Mr. Director, thank you for seeing me. I am pleased to present to you what I believe to be all the required papers including new ones that address the final disposition of the deceased's remains at a Catholic cemetery in Long Island, NY. Confirmation of such arrangements has been made by the officials at the cemetery and approved by the appropriate administrators overseeing such matters."

Calderón took the packet that Anthony offered and began leafing through its contents. He looked to his right and gestured with his hand to a polished wooden box sitting on a flat work table.

"There are your friend's remains, Señor. If these papers are in order, they shall be yours to take to the United

States."

"I appreciate the efforts you and your government have made on my behalf."

Calderón nodded and continued to scan the papers.

"I understand that you have come alone today," said Calderón without looking up.

"Yes, I did," said Anthony, offering nothing more.

"And where is your escort, Mr. Hernández today?"

"Mr. Hernández's whereabouts are no longer my concern, Mr. Director. He had been my guide in San Salvador, helped me to reach Perquín and the village that was the site of the MATES clinic where my friend was killed. My present stay at a hotel here in the capital and my return to the airport does not require a guide after having been in El Salvador these many days."

"He's dead, you know."

Anthony stiffened and was aware that Calderón noticed.

"Yes, I know," he said.

"Is that not of concern to you?"

"Of course, it is unfortunate and sad when anyone dies, but I hardly knew him."

"But, did you not speak at his burial? That is not something done by a person who hardly knows the deceased."

Anthony shifted in his seat. He took a deep breath and rolled the dice.

"Mr. Director, may I speak frankly?"

"Of course, Señor"

"I was asked by the agency that hired Mr. Hernández on my behalf to say a few words at his burial because they knew the man was an important person here. Their request for me to say something on their behalf was a business decision, not a personal or even a sincere one. That's the way businesses operate, especially businesses in New York. The man drove me around, had a few meals with me and got me to wherever I was supposed to be and was handsomely paid for his services."

Calderón looked at Anthony without speaking as if trying to determine Anthony's veracity.

"So you were not sincere and have no personal interest in this man, but performed such services as a business decision?"

Anthony looked him straight in the eye. His jaw tensed. He felt he was betraying a friend for practical realities as he did Rita, years ago. He wanted to reach across the desk and grab Calderón by the neck and squeeze the living shit out of him.

"Yes," said Anthony.

"And how is it that such a person comes from New York to retrieve the remains of a dear departed friend in order to lessen the grief of his widow? This sounds like a completely different person to me."

"That's different," said Anthony.

"And how is that different, Señor?"

Anthony sucked in as much air as he could and let it out slowly. He knew he was not going to win this game.

"With all due respect, Mr. Director, I came here to fulfill a duty, an obligation that I don't have to explain to you. What is required of me is to present you with documents that satisfy the Salvadoran government, the United States Government and the Catholic Church so that I can repatriate the remains of a man who gave his life helping the people of this country. I came here with the hope of expediting a process that the MATES agency said would be an extended one if they followed their own protocol. I have been here long enough, and now I'm ready to return home with or without that box of ashes."

"And where were you when Mr. Hernández was killed, Señor?"

"I was out getting laid by one of your beautiful Señoritas when the news spread through Perquín. If you like, I can give you her address. She was really hot!"

"That is enough, Señor. I am now late for my next appointment. I shall review your documents. If they are in proper order, you may pick up this box on Monday. If there is one signature out of place, one paper missing, the entire process will have to be repeated."

"Fine," said Anthony as he stood and turned toward the door. He considered a parting shot, but thought he had better get out while he could. He was startled upon opening the door to find he was face to face with the matron, her face as unrevealing as ever.

The woman hurried to keep up with Anthony as he headed toward the exit. Her hand reached the door knob before his, so he stopped in his tracks as she leaned in front of him to open the door.

Looking down at the floor as the door opened, she whispered, "*Vaya con Dios.*"

With a bag in each hand, Anthony bolted out of the building knowing he had fucked up the mission, denied his fraternity with Mr. Hernández, and still wanted to strangle Calderón. He tried for ten minutes to hail a cab until he realized that he was supposed to wait in line at a taxi queue like everyone else.

Back at the hotel, he went straight to his room and called the front desk to say he would be checking out at 2:00 P.M. He then went to the service bar and pulled out a bottle of club soda and chug-a-lugged until he could no longer stand the burn of the gas bubbles in his throat. While filling the bathroom sink, he yanked off his jacket and tie, opened his collar and stuck his face in the cold water until he had to come up for air. He peeled off the remainder of his clothes and sat on the bed in his shorts. It occurred to him that today was Thanksgiving Day.

Anthony dressed in preparation for the trip back to Perquín. He realized that Calderón never intended to let him walk out of that office with Martin's ashes, and that having them in site was just part of his game. Calderón's contempt for Mr. Hernández had been transferred to Anthony. A dozen years of war can fuck everybody up. Anthony reached into the bag containing his cell phone.

He considered calling Sarah to break the news that he would not be bringing home Martin's remains, but thought that was a message better delivered in person. If he got out of this country with Martina, that would more than offset the delay or loss of Martin's ashes. There was no point in calling Carla. Everything she could do had already been done. She had no control over what would happen between now and Saturday morning. It was time to call and mend some fences at home. If Bernadette stuck to her plan she would be home instead of at her parents' place, or maybe with Nancy and Aaron. He pressed the speed dial number while reminding himself that Bernadette had tolerated a lot of shit from him in the past two weeks.

The phone was ringing as she walked back from the bathroom. A short while ago she had been embarrassed by the loudness of her moans and the ferocity of her orgasm. Now, she walked naked and completely unselfconscious. She lay down in the bed and pulled the sheet over her body. He rolled over on his side propping himself up on his elbow facing her. His hand moved under the sheet and stroked her belly in a circular pattern.

"Happy Thanksgiving," he said.

She could barely make out Anthony's voice on the answering machine.

"Everything Anthony said about you was true," she said. "He was right about you all along."

"Bernadette, it's just the way it is," he said. "Every time I saw you, spoke to you, listened to you, all I could think about was this moment."

David had called her every day since Anthony had left. At first it was to keep her up to date on the business issues and legal arrangements of Anthony's trip. Then he would call just to check up and see how she was doing. She wasn't so naïve not to realize he was pursuing her, but she was flattered and knew she could control the situation. After the first week of Anthony's absence, he suggested they meet for coffee or a drink. After all he would say, "We have both been abandoned by our spouses, what was the harm?" She was smart enough to say "no" without suggesting "never." She enjoyed the attention. He proposed a workday lunch midway between their places of business in Manhattan. She responded with "it was not a good idea" but declined to say why. On Tuesday, he made his final thrust. He suggested they have Thanksgiving Dinner together. "Nobody likes to have dinner alone on Thanksgiving Day." She asked where he would propose they have this dinner because she was certainly not going to prepare it, go to his place, or eat anywhere where they were likely to be seen. She called it another "bad idea."

With this opening, he had offered that he would choose a very public place where he could guarantee her a turkey dinner with all the fixings and provide a second guarantee that none of her neighbors, friends, family, distant relatives, work associates or anyone in her past life or connected to her in any way would show up. She laughed when she asked what state this place was in. He said that it was less than an hour away from her house, but that its location was a secret to members of the Bar, and to reveal it would cost him his good standing and his ability to practice law in the Great State of New York. He waited while she paused.

She told him she would do it providing they used their own cars. "That's the deal, so you'll have to tell me where it is. He agreed to tell her where it was, but not the name which would technically not violate his oath. He added that she might figure it out when she arrived at the general location, but he would be looking out for her just in case. They agreed to an early dinner at 1:00 P.M.

At the appointed hour, she burst out laughing as she entered the parking lot of the most infamous greasy spoon diner on Long Island. A crude banner mounted on the low roof of the building waved in the November wind boasting a Thanksgiving Special Dinner, only $14.95*, 11:00 A.M. to 10:00 P.M. The reason no one she knew would eat here was simple; terrible food and lousy service.

He was at her car door as she parked. She greeted him with a "You sure know how to treat a girl." When he handed her a rose, she stopped laughing, but kept smiling as she gave him her cheek which he politely pecked. They entered the diner and after being told there was a fifteen minute wait for a table, decided to take two counter seats that had just been vacated. The food and ambiance was bad enough to be funny. Like two conspirators they each chose a hot turkey sandwich because it looked like the safest bet on the menu. When the meal came, the gravy scared them off so after two bites they had pecan pie and coffee, going so far as to let the waitress add whipped cream to the pie.

This had been much more fun than the day before when Bernadette had put on a brave face for her parents while explaining Anthony's exploits and concealing her own frustrations. She listened to the pending doom foreseen by her Mother. When dinner was over, David looked at her, but said nothing. She looked down at the counter and saw the rose in her lap. She looked at him while squeezing the back of his arm to assert her authority.

"Okay," she had said, "this is the deal. You follow me home. I will park in my driveway and open the garage door for you. You park in my space next to Anthony's car. You wait for me there. You can come in for one drink, and then you're gone."

He continued looking at her, stood and let her lead the way out. When they arrived at the house, Bernadette parked in the driveway behind Anthony's car. She opened the garage door remotely and let herself in through the front door. When she heard David pull in the garage, she opened the kitchen door leading to the garage. As he entered the house, she took off her coat, turned and walked to the wet bar. She was opening a cabinet door when he reached her and turned her around. "We don't need that," he said.

He reached over to turn on the bedroom lamp. She closed her eyes as he put his hand on her shoulder and turned her toward him as the phone started ringing again.

Taking Flight

Chapter 48

Anthony put down the phone after leaving a second message including all of his return flight information. He was sure Bernadette had decided to spend the holiday with her folks after all. He thought it better to leave a message than speak to her there. He could try again later.

Getting everything ready for his departure, he realized he would probably never return to this hotel or this city. He double checked everything before going down to settle the bill being ever so conscious of his surroundings. He thought about sticking his head in the dining room to see if Raul was there, but knew that would not be wise. After putting his receipts away he headed toward the main entrance. He remained just inside the double glass doors until he saw Jorge pull up in the truck. It was a bright afternoon outside, surely not one that would be spoiled by a gang member, policeman, a self important bureaucrat or a villager so anxious for a more exciting life that he would throw his own away.

He put two bags in the back of the truck and brought the smaller black one with him into the cab. Once seated, he shook Jorge's hand.

"I didn't get the ashes," he said.

"I know," said Jorge.

"You must use smoke and mirrors," said Anthony.

Jorge smiled, "Everything in time, Antonio, everything in time. Try and relax for now. Your mission in El Salvador is almost over. Tonight, you will rest. Tomorrow will be a day of final preparation for your departure, and on Saturday you will be home.

"I've made arrangements to meet my mother at the airport in Miami," said Anthony. "She lives in Florida now and it's been some time since we last met."

"How long is some time, if I may ask, Antonio?"

"Over a year. Since my father passed."

"That *is* a long time, no? Especially since she was widowed."

"Well, I have a feeling she's not alone, and she is not exactly my favorite person."

"I did not mean to pry."

"That's okay," Anthony said, "it's a little complicated."

Anthony leaned back against the head rest and closed his eyes. It wasn't until the gravel was crunching beneath the tires that he realized he had slept most of the way back. Donato and Hector were sitting on the front porch having a beer. The men greeted each other. Donato shrugged his shoulders when Anthony told him of his failure to secure Martin's remains.

"Bureaucrats have so little power, really," he said. "We shouldn't deny them the pleasure of creating difficulty for others. It is all they have."

"You're very philosophical today," said Anthony.

"The beer is very good," said Donato, laughing.

Jorge joined them after a brief discussion with Hector, handing Anthony a beer.

"Hector tells me that all the documents for tomorrow are done, and he wishes he could enter them in a contest for their beauty and authenticity," said Jorge.

Anthony raised his bottle in a toast, "To the art of expert forgery," he said.

"To the forgery of expert art," said Hector, to which

they all smiled and drank their beer.

"We shall review everything tomorrow, Antonio. For now, go, freshen up, and see if the children are done with their homework and if Martina is awake. Then join us for more beer."

Anthony took the cue and went in the house.

The smell from the kitchen was wonderful. On his way to the bathroom, he said a brief hello to Consuelo who was obviously busy. After cleaning up, he stopped in Juan's room where he and Maria were talking. They sat up straight as soon as he came in and gave each other conspiratorial looks.

'Hi guys," Anthony said. "What's going on?"

"Hello, Señor" they said in unison.

"I have to get Martina," said Maria.

Through the window, Anthony could hear sounds of more people arriving; voices of women as well as men. He started to leave when Juan asked if he could help him with a math problem.

"Sure, where's your book?"

"I have to get it," said Juan, his face reddening as he reached for his school bag. He went through the motions of getting the book out and turning pages when Consuelo called out,

"Juan, it is time."

Juan took Anthony's hand and led him to the front door. When they arrived at the porch, Anthony could see a line formed consisting of Jorge, Consuelo, Maria, Martina, Eduardo, Señora Órnelas, and Donato and Hector with their wives. Behind them stood a woman Anthony did not recognize at first. Then as she stepped forward, he saw it was the matron from Calderón's office carrying a small clay container. She handed it to Anthony.

"The box in his office was nicer," she said, "but the contents are more important to you, I'm sure."

Anthony was stunned as he took the container realizing what it was.

"His family will be very pleased, Señora, as I am. I can't thank you enough."

"Vaya con Dios, Señor."

Juan pulled on Anthony's hand and led him down the steps. The line of people opened before him and Anthony understood the conspiracy being shared by the boy and his sister. On a picnic table before him sat a festive Thanksgiving dinner. In the center of the table was a large roasted chicken with a miniature American flag stuck in its breast. Donato led them as they began to sing, "God Bless America" in Anthony's honor which they believed to be an American tradition. After a not too mangled attempt at the song, they each in turn wished Anthony "Happy Thanksgiving" shaking his hand or giving him a hug as he silently cursed the tears streaming down his face. To his relief, as he struggled to finds words, Juan yelled, "Time to eat, time to eat!"

For the remainder of the evening, Anthony remained rather quiet. He took in each of the people around the table trying to paint a portrait in his mind that would never fade. The goodbyes that night were heartfelt. The rum that followed the dinner provided warmth with no stupor. Anthony made no more phone calls that night, nor did he plan the next day's agenda before going to bed, nor did he dream of what had happened or what might come.

Chapter 49

On Friday morning, Anthony woke up to the normal noise of the household as the children prepared to go to school. He dressed quickly not wanting to miss them before they left. The family was having breakfast together when he joined them.

"*Buenos días,*" shouted Juan and Maria in unison.

"We thought we would let you sleep in this morning," said Jorge. "Tomorrow is a big day for you."

"I'm glad I got to see the children before they left for school," said Anthony as he gave Maria a gentle kiss on the top of her head and messed up Juan's hair. He gave Martina a kiss on her cheek. She mouthed a kiss back, but missed Anthony's face.

"I'm going to miss this," he said.

"Come, sit and have some breakfast," said Consuelo as she got up and went to the stove.

Anthony sat as she brought him a plate of eggs and potatoes. He poured himself some coffee and sat silently looking at the family around him.

Jorge broke the silence.

"After breakfast, I will take the children to school. I would like you to come with us and go on with me to my shop. I have something to show you."

"Sure," said Anthony. I don't have much to do today except pack and get my papers and tickets in order."

When they were ready to leave, Anthony gave Martina a big hug. This time she was able to plant a kiss on Anthony's cheek.

"You're a cutie," he said.

"She likes you, Antonio," said Consuelo.

"Come, children, it is time," said Jorge.

They waved to Consuelo and Martina as they piled into the truck and left for the school house. After dropping the children at school, Jorge looked at Anthony as they headed to the town and Jorge's shop.

"You have a look of sadness, Antonio."

"Jorge, I'm still trying to absorb everything I've experienced in El Salvador. In two weeks, more has happened to me than in two years of my other life."

"What is your other life?"

"The one I normally live, where I go to work, or worry about not going to work, have a wife, a house and friends. The place where everything is based on how my career is going, what my peers in my profession think of me, how my friends or my wife's friends judge me, and when and if my wife and I should start a family.

"Not long ago, I got very upset because a security guard at a state government office gave me a hard time. I was nearly devastated when people I had worked with turned away when I needed their help. They were people I thought had a high opinion of me. I was attracted to another woman, not because I was unhappy in my marriage, but because I wanted to be attractive to someone when my world seemed to be collapsing. How juvenile is that?

"When my friend was killed in El Salvador, I spontaneously volunteered to retrieve his remains. I don't know if it was an unconscious, noble reaction, or if I wanted to be a hero and impress people, or if I wanted to impress his widow, who was the woman I was attracted to. The next thing I knew, I was here and my wife was very upset with me.

"You know, she accused me of wanting my own little adventure down here, and for the most part, she was right. I enjoyed being the cavalry coming to the rescue. I enjoyed the encounter with Calderón and dueling with him. I enjoyed taking on the elders and clearing out the clinic. It *was* an adventure for me. It took on more meaning than the career I had thought so much of. And then everything changed."

"You are referring to the Colonel?" asked Jorge.

"Yes. I know I didn't cause his death directly, but I did some very stupid things. Unnecessary things that started a chain of events that didn't have to end the way they did."

"We all feel the loss of his presence, Antonio, but I do not think he would see his fate the same as you do."

"Maybe, but that's the point. Even in death, he would have remained as he always was, accepting faults without casting blame and forgiving the mistakes of others. I don't think I would've been as generous. I would have assigned blame for the mistakes I made and for what Ernesto did. My thoughts and actions would have been focused on blame and punishment."

"And this would help you deal with what happened?" asked Jorge.

"No. It would leave me as empty as I was after blaming the people that affected my job. Assigning blame and seeking revenge provides no satisfaction, no relief."

"I agree with you. There is a difference, as I said before, between revenge and justice. The first does not help anything. Justice is our way of saying what is or is not acceptable. The ache does not go away, but justice allows us to move on. We don't forget, but we remember, as in this case, not how the person died, but how he lived."

"Are you sure Ernesto will receive justice?"

"It was taken care of early this morning."

Anthony was stunned. "How?"

"You will see, but for now we have some work to do."

Perquín was quiet this early in the morning. Jorge parked the truck in front of his shop. When the men got out, Anthony noticed that Jorge was carrying the clay container holding Martin's ashes.

"We must prepare this for your trip," said Jorge.

Once in the shop, Jorge took out two small ceramic jars with colorful Salvadoran art on their lids. He turned them upside down to show Anthony labels that described the contents as "authenticated bomb crater rubble from the war zone in Perquín, El Salvador."

"One of our most popular items," said Jorge with a smile. He opened the clay container and poured its contents into the jars.

"This should get through U.S. Customs without a problem. If they have any concerns at all, they will be to determine that the jars have no drugs. If they bother to test the contents, do not object. I will add a few other artifacts of the war so that you will appear to be bringing home souvenirs, a very common thing for visitors to Perquín."

Anthony watched as Jorge sealed the jars with reusable tape, then selected a rebel arm band and a cross bearing the names of the slain Jesuit priests, wrapped them in soft white paper and put them all in a bag branded with the name of Jorge's shop. Some of Martin's ashes were left over in the clay container.

"Can we bring these to the clinic?" asked Anthony.

Jorge looked up at Anthony.

"Of course," he said, appreciating Anthony's request.

With the packaging of Martin's remains completed, Anthony picked out a few things on his own. They headed to the village and drove to within walking distance of the clinic. Anthony had carried the clay container in his lap, looking down at it during the bumpy ride. Jorge stayed behind as Anthony walked past the crosses bearing the names of the victims of the explosion. He walked into the shell of the building trying to think of something to say and settled for "Rest in Peace" as he poured some of the ashes on the ground. With less than a handful left, he returned to the crosses and put ashes in front of each, rubbing them into the earth. With the final few, he spread a thin trail connecting the crosses dedicated to Martin and Ynez Órnelas.

"Be together with love" he said.

Anthony carried the empty container back to the truck. As he got in he said to Jorge, "I would like to keep this as my own memento of all that's happened."

Jorge nodded. "Is there anything or anyone else you wish to see or do before we leave the village?" he asked.

"No. No, thank you," said Anthony.

Jorge started the truck and turned it around. Instead of heading back to Perquín, he turned in the direction of El Mozote. Anthony thought, he might be taking to him to the grave site and started to object, when Jorge raised his hand.

"There is one more thing for you to see, Antonio."

They drove another three miles along the main road that was now very familiar to Anthony. Approaching a grove of trees on their right, Jorge slowed the truck. Anthony wasn't sure why. Then he saw it as the truck came to a stop. Ernesto was hanging by the neck from the tree closest to the road. A yellow banner was draped around his body.

"So everyone will know he betrayed his village, his family and friends," said Jorge.

Anthony stared from the truck. After a minute, Jorge put the vehicle in gear when Anthony raised his hand. Jorge turned off the ignition thinking Anthony wanted to get out. Anthony just sat looking quietly. He realized that he was not repulsed by the sight as he would have been before his experiences here.

"A little more than a year ago, when my father died, I realized that I had experienced very few losses in my life. Usually, they were relatives or family friends who were very old and had lived a full life, the exception being my father. In just a matter of weeks, four people have died, two of whom I felt close to, one who betrayed the people I have come to know dearly, and one ... and one I killed.

"When my father died, my mother asked me to help with the funeral arrangements. We have what we call a viewing, where people can come and pay their respects. The next day there is a Mass at the Church followed by a graveside service where final prayers are said and those attending leave a flower with the deceased's casket. All similar to what we did Wednesday. Anyway, I didn't know a thing about how to prepare for any of this. Like most people, I called the local mortuary and spoke to a person who arranges everything for you. They ask questions so that a notice can be placed in the newspaper. They guide you through the selection of a casket, floral arrangements, prayer cards, and a guest book and arrange for a priest to lead a Rosary at the conclusion of the viewing. They arrange for cars to take the family from the funeral home to the church to the cemetery and back. In other words, there are specialists to take care of everything for you. Everyone is glad to have them because no one really knows how to do these things except the people in the business. You are so far removed from the process, you may as well be ordering furniture, or planning a vacation.

"Here everyone is personally involved in the process. People know how to handle death. Each person seems to have a role. When a death occurs, everyone goes into action in a way that seems like they've done it many times before. Death has its celebration just like a birth, a baptism or a wedding."

"And does this disturb you?" asked Jorge.

Anthony thought for a minute.

"No," he said, "you celebrate life and death with the same importance. I can't imagine anyone here saying, 'I'm sorry I can't be there to pay my respects because I'm taking a trip or have important business elsewhere.'"

"Is that what people do in your other life?"

"Sure, we even have appropriate measures to take in the event of our absence. We send flowers, baskets of food and Hallmark cards."

"Perhaps that is just the way things are in a modern society where everyone is so busy," said Jorge.

"Perhaps. I'm just trying to understand it all. A few weeks ago, I purchased a navigation system for biking and hiking. I was lusting after an antique bicycle. Today I am looking at a man hanging from a tree with the added knowledge that a few days ago, I took another man's life. I feel no remorse, no sense of satisfaction or victory over an adversary. I don't feel anything, but my life has changed."

"That is the often the way one feels when fighting in a war," said Jorge.

"What keeps you going? How can you continue? How do you not die inside?"

"Each of us dies inside a little, some more so than others. After a while, you become numb. You think of what caused the war; you think about a better life for your children, but in the end you think mostly about survival and when it will be over."

"There's got to be a better way," said Anthony.

"I hope so, but we are not the first, and we will not be the last to use war or killing to solve problems."

"I'm sorry for bending your ear. I'm probably not making much sense. It's just that my other life seems to have very little meaning to me right now."

"I understand completely," said Jorge. You have been through a lot."

"Let's go back, now" said Anthony. "I could go for a beer."

The house was quiet when they arrived. The children were at school, and Consuelo was tending to the vegetable garden behind the house. The men sat on the porch drinking cold beer.

"It is time to discuss your departure tomorrow," said Jorge.

"I'm ready," said Anthony.

"Earlier our plan was to have you take Martina with you. The obstacles were getting her a passport, forged letters from her "parents" giving you permission to escort the child, and so on. Things became too complicated. Calderón has transferred his anger from the Colonel to you. You shot the assassin in the hotel garage, which makes you more vulnerable each day that goes by. You are taking your friend's ashes as illegal contraband without the permission of the local authorities, and as you pointed out, U.S. customs may not look kindly on an American re-entering the country with a foreign born child. So the plan must be very simple, look very ordinary and most of all should keep you and Martina apart until you have reached Miami."

"Shucks, I had been kind of looking forward to charges

of murder, kidnapping, illegal flight and entry into the U.S. I bet I won't even qualify for frequent flyer miles."

"Antonio, it is good that you keep a wise guy attitude to a point, but the possibilities of what you describe are very real, especially while you are still in this country. There are people in prisons here that have been waiting for a trial for seven or eight years, foreigners included."

"I'm sorry. I understand how serious this is," said Anthony.

"Your flight leaves at 8:00 A.M. tomorrow morning. Because of the time difference you will land at Miami International at 11:30 A.M. You will have to clear Customs. Be sure to declare your souvenirs even though the dollar limit does not require you to do so. You will be an American returning home from the failed mission you had originally undertaken. If asked why you are stopping in Miami, you have a perfectly acceptable answer because your mother lives in Florida. There is no reason to lie, or have any false documents. The issue of your friend's remains should not be a matter of concern."

"What about Martina?"

"She will be on board the next flight to Miami once we are sure you have departed."

"She's not traveling alone, is she?"

"No," said Jorge, looking down for a moment.

"So?"

"Consuelo will be taking Martina."

"Whoa, how can you take that risk? My getting caught at something is one thing, but Consuelo? I don't like that."

"I don't like it either, but everyone agrees it is the safest plan. She will be met by her sister."

"I still don't like it."

"Consuelo has perfect documentation. Martina is now

documented as her niece, her sister's child and an American citizen by birth, with an American passport. Consuelo's sister is a blood relative who is a legal resident of Miami. There is nothing to question."

"How long does she stay?"

"Assuming everything goes as planned, Consuelo will return the next day," said Jorge.

"Meaning?"

"Your flight to New York leaves at 3:00 P.M. Consuelo will meet you at the boarding gate with Martina shortly before. You will board that flight with Martina. There are no Customs inspectors to pass from Miami on. You will have documents giving you permission to escort Martina to New York where she will be met by "relatives." We will have some Salvadoran friends at JFK just in case, but they should not be necessary just as the documents for escorting Martina should not be necessary."

"You really think it'll go that easily?" asked Anthony.

"There should be no problem with Consuelo and Martina."

"Meaning that the only potential problem is with me."

"If there is such a problem, it will be on Salvadoran soil. You might not make it out of the country, in which case Consuelo and Martina will not go to Miami."

"There is one other problem in Miami," said Anthony.

"What is that?" Jorge said with a look of concern coming over his face.

"You haven't met my mother," said Anthony.

Both men were laughing heartily when Consuelo joined them on the porch. She looked at them quizzically.

Jorge, still laughing said, "He would make a very bad soldier."

Consuelo walked back into the house shaking her head.

Taking Flight

Chapter 50

Anthony spent the rest of Friday checking and rechecking tickets and travel documents, packing what he would need in each bag and running his departure plan through his head. He and Consuelo reviewed their plan for meeting in Miami and even developed some worst case scenarios in the event that the authorities became suspicious or if Martina got sick or did not respond well to flying. Consuelo showed him the bag she was preparing for Martina. Anthony spent time with Martina playing little games, using Spanish phrases to communicate with her and walking around the yard with her. He helped her eat her lunch, changed her clothes and carried her in his arms as she was getting ready for an afternoon nap.

As he lay her down in her bed, he asked, "Are you ready for this?" He wasn't sure if the question was directed at her.

When Juan and Maria came home from school, Anthony listened as Jorge and Consuelo explained to them that their mother would leave on Saturday and return on Sunday night, and that Martina would be leaving and not returning.

"She will be staying with her new family in America," she said.

"She's lucky," said Juan.

"Will Señor Antonio be looking after her?" asked Maria.

"I will be nearby, and always ready to help, but she will be well taken care of and loved very much by her new family," said Anthony. Now when you visit the United States, you will not only be able to visit me, but Martina also."

"Mama, why are you taking Martina instead of Señor Antonio?" asked Maria.

"It is best because she is so young," said Consuelo.

"Why can we not all go together?" asked Juan.

"Because I have work to do here," said Jorge, "and I need you to take care of me."

"You promise to be home on Sunday, Mama?" asked Maria.

"I promise. And you must make sure you do all your chores and take care of your father."

"I promise," said Maria.

"Si, me too," said Juan.

The dinner hour was filled with small talk. Jorge told Anthony that Donato would drive Consuelo and Martina to the airport after Jorge left with Anthony. Donato's wife would stay with the children. Little else was said about the next day. The children stayed up later than usual because there was no school on Saturday and Anthony would be gone when they woke up. Bedtime finally came. Anthony held each child for a long time.

He said to both, "I shall look forward to the next time we meet. In the meantime, I have something to help you remember me."

He reached into his pocket and removed two miniature wooden crosses depicting the crucifixion in colorful Salvadoran abstract art, each with its own leather loop. He placed one over each of their heads. He had picked them up at Jorge's shop earlier in the day after receiving Jorge's permission to give them to Juan and Maria.

"Thank you, Señor, but we will not forget you," said

Juan.

"I will wear it every day," said Maria.

Consuelo thanked Anthony for his presents to her children, and then prompted them to go to bed. Anthony and Jorge moved to the porch.

"I feel that I should say something meaningful about what you and Consuelo have done for me," said Anthony, "but no words can describe what I feel for your family."

"There are times when no words are necessary, Antonio. You have a special place in our hearts."

The two men sat in silence for another hour before calling it a night.

Anthony wasn't sure if he had dozed off, but he was up at 2:00 A.M. feeling as though he had been awake the whole time. His adrenaline was pumping as he got out of bed and washed and dressed as quietly as he could. Jorge and Consuelo were already in the kitchen. Consuelo offered Anthony a cup of coffee and bowl of cereal which he accepted appreciatively. They did not linger and after a quick breakfast. Anthony turned to Consuelo.

"I'll see you and Martina in Miami. Travel safely and thank you for everything."

"Vaya con Dios, Antonio."

Anthony and Jorge packed Anthony's bags into the truck. Anthony took one last look at the house before climbing in the cab.

"Colonel, I'm ready," he said to Jorge. "Let's do it."

Jorge smiled, "Si, let's do it."

The sun was up by the time they reached the airport. They parked the truck and Jorge got out with Anthony to help him with his bags.

"I think we should part here," said Anthony. "I'm not being paranoid, but I think if I were leaving as I would under normal circumstances, I would go on my own from here. You probably want to wait for Consuelo, but I think we should separate now."

"That is good thinking. Perhaps, you would make a good soldier after all," said Jorge.

The two men shook hands with reserve in case they were being watched.

Anthony walked to a kiosk from where the airport tram took him to the United Airlines terminal. As he entered the terminal, he felt a bit more secure in the facility of an American owned company. He knew that had no bearing on his safety, but it felt good.

Following the plan, he checked two bags to Miami, and would go through Customs there and not in New York when Martina would be with him. He kept the smaller bag containing his papers and "souvenirs" to carry on. After collecting his boarding pass, he stopped at a newsstand and picked up a copy of USA Today. At the security entrance, he put his bag on the conveyor belt, emptied his pockets into a small bowl and put the bowl and his shoes into a plastic container that carried them through the X-Ray scanner. He was waved through the metal detector and passed without incident. He calmly walked to the end of the conveyor belt and waited for his bag, shoes and bowl of pocket contents. He noticed the operator scanning and rescanning his bag until an agent brought it out and asked him to open it on a nearby table. Anthony casually put his shoes back on, refilled his pockets and joined the agent at the table. His calm was starting to wither.

"Do you have any sharp objects or liquids that are not in sealed plastic bags inside, Señor?"

"No," said Anthony.

"Please open the bag."

Anthony pulled one of the tags of the dual zipper and opened the bag. The agent pulled the sides apart and leafed through folders and papers without removing them. He took out the ceramic bowls, souvenir arm band and the cross from Jorge's shop.

"Open the jars, please," the agent said.

Anthony took one and turned it upside down and showed the agent the "authenticity" label.

"Open the jar, please."

Anthony tried to conceal his increasing anxiety as he peeled off the reusable tape and removed the lid.

"Open the other jar, please," said the agent.

Anthony did so trying to look a little bored and annoyed with the request.

The agent looked into both jars and called for his supervisor to join them. Anthony started to perspire. He looked at his watch while waiting long minutes for the supervising agent to arrive and examine the jars. He placed his index finger on the ashes inside, rubbed his finger and thumb together and brought them under his nose.

"You are a collector, Señor?"

"Just a few souvenirs."

The agent looked at Anthony as though he had just discovered Adolph Hitler. Slowly and deliberately, he closed each jar, applying a label indicating they had been inspected.

"Have a nice trip," he said without a smile.

"Thank you," said Anthony returning the jars to his bag. He zipped it up and moved on without looking at the agents again.

Anthony continued on toward the gate where he found a seat near the unmanned kiosk. He put down the newspaper he was reading as an airline representative announced his flight and that boarding would begin in about ten minutes. Anthony would be boarding with second group. With his line of sight no longer blocked by the paper, he saw two men sitting opposite him dressed in dark suits with white shirts and dark ties. They appeared to be looking his way. He brought the newspaper up to cover his face uncertain of their occupation and interests.

When the time came to board, he made his way to the boarding line as casually as he could. He scanned a full circle before he spotted the suits standing further back. *Perhaps they were waiting to board with a later group, perhaps not preparing to board at all, perhaps they were agents of Calderón, perhaps the police, perhaps friends of Jorge...* Anthony slowly made his way to the agent who welcomed him and collected his boarding pass. He walked down the Jetway quickly, but came to an abrupt stop as the passengers in front of him stalled before entering the flight cabin. Once inside, a flight attendant greeted him absently. He inched his way toward his row. An elderly man was already in the window seat. Anthony nodded as he stowed his bag under the seat in front of him, sat and opened the newspaper holding it low enough to watch the remainder of boarding passengers. Fifteen minutes passed before the cabin door was closed. The suits never boarded. He put the paper down and rubbed his face. His armpits were soaked. He breathed a sigh of relief knowing he couldn't do this for a living.

The flight to Miami went without incident. He filled out a landing card that declared his souvenirs with a collective value of less than $100.00. As the descent to Miami International was announced, he became aware that his hands were made into fists and that his back had that familiar tightness. He sat upright during the final approach

412

and was jolted by the bump that accompanied the landing as the wheels touched down. He reached for his bag as the plane taxied to the gate. A familiar feeling from the experiences of many flights invaded his consciousness. He stood and held his bag in front of him following his fellow travelers out the door. The deplaning passengers automatically went to the international arrivals baggage claim area. After a short wait, he retrieved his checked bags and proceeded to the Customs station. When his turn came, he handed the agent his landing card and was waved through with a "Welcome to the United States." He stepped through the Customs exit and felt the relief that is often shared by international travelers when returning home.

Chapter 51

As Anthony made his way toward the restroom, he found he was observing the people around him with more than idle curiosity. At one point, he mistakenly thought he saw the two suits that had sat across from him before he boarded the plane. Even though he was on U.S. soil and had cleared customs, he still felt the need to exercise caution and look for any potential threat. He kept his bags close by at all times and pressed his foot against the larger bag while he washed his face. None of the restroom occupants challenged him or looked particularly suspicious. Back on the terminal floor, he checked the signs and headed toward the escalator that led to the United Airlines ticket counters. Anthony was a few minutes early, but his mother was already there dressed in a cream colored pants suit. He noticed that she had added some color to her hair that had lightened it and removed the gray. He walked up to her, put his bags down and gave her a perfunctory hug.

"Hey Mom, it's good to see you."

She hugged him and then took a step back.

"You look awful," she said, more concerned than scolding.

"I've been up since very early this morning," he said.

"The way you look can't be from missing one night's sleep. Your face is drawn. You look like you've aged since I last saw you."

"And you look younger. I'm happy to see you too," he said, shaking his head.

"Go ahead, laugh," she said, "but don't tell me this is

because you missed some sleep or were out partying for a night."

"I passed a food court on the way here. How about a cup of coffee or a bite to eat? I've got plenty of time before my next flight," he said.

"If you have enough time, there are places outside the airport."

"I think I should stay in case there are any flight announcements," he said firmly.

"This place is full of Cubans," she said.

Some things never change, he thought to himself.

"Cubans make some great dishes and their music is wonderful," he said.

"They're responsible for ninety percent of the crime in Miami."

"Yeah, in the good old days, the Mob had a corner on the market."

"Don't get smart with me," she said as he steered her toward the food court.

Anthony noticed a man in a light tan suit and straw fedora observing them as they left the United area. Approaching the food court, Anthony suggested they go to an enclosed restaurant where they could have table service and some privacy. His mother agreed. Once inside, a hostess greeted them and took them past a small bar to a booth in the back. Soon after, a waitress arrived. Anthony chose to have a chicken sandwich and coffee while she ordered a cup of Earl Grey tea. When the waitress left with their order, Anthony noticed the tan suit and straw fedora waiting outside. He concluded that the man had nothing to do with El Salvador, but all to do with his mother.

"So, how do you like living in Florida?"

"You know how I hate the cold."

"So that means you like it here?"

"There are so many transplanted New Yorkers here, you wouldn't believe it," she said.

"So that means that you like it here?" he asked again.

"It's better than Brooklyn," she said, "but Miami is not Manhattan."

"Full of Cubans, instead of Puerto Ricans?" he said adding a hostile edge.

"Did you invite me here to give me a hard time?"

"No, I wanted to see how you're doing."

Anthony paused, and then continued.

"And, I wanted to settle some things between us that are not so nice."

"Here? At the airport? While you're between flights? That's how you choose to settle things?"

She paused for a moment.

"All right, what's there to settle?"

They went silent as the waitress arrived with tea, coffee and Anthony's sandwich. Anthony leaned back against the booth. He could see the man in the tan suit occupying a bar stool.

"Anthony, you're going to make me sorry I came. I had the idea that maybe, just maybe, you wanted to see your mother to check on her life as a widow, as somebody trying to make a new life by herself in a new place."

"By yourself?" he asked looking in the direction of the bar.

"So what are you now, a detective?"

Anthony took a long look at his mother, then took a bite of his sandwich and chewed slowly before he spoke again.

"Look, I'm sorry, I don't want to argue with you, but there are some things about Dad that have always bothered me. I wanted to talk to you about them to clear the air, so we can move on and at least be comfortable with one another."

His mother looked at him again.

"You know you really do look awful," she said. "You were always a handsome boy and a good looking young man. Not pretty boy handsome, but you always had a good look about you with a spark in your face. You were attractive to people. That spark is gone. You look more road weary than tired."

"Can we talk about my father?" he said.

"Sure. To you he was always a hero. He couldn't do anything wrong. He played ball with you. He cried when you graduated college. He made magic in his garden. And those talks! You two could talk for hours about things you couldn't do anything about. Things that had happened and couldn't be changed or the way things should be instead of the way they were. And when you finished talking, nothing changed, but the two of you would act as though you had made everything better. You know, part of your father's charm was that he lived in a dream world, not the world everybody else lived in."

"You broke his heart," said Anthony with no more emotion than when he ordered his sandwich.

His mother looked stunned for a minute. This was not what she wanted to hear, not something she could argue.

"You think you know everything. You always have. I was entitled to have a life," she said.

"Why couldn't that life be with him?"

"It was. I never left him. I stayed with him until the day he died."

"But, you broke his heart. By the time he died, he was already long dead."

"You know, Anthony," she said, visibly upset, her eyes moist, "you think he and you were such great thinkers. That you had everything figured out and that you were such good souls while the rest of us were mere mortals. Well, let me tell you something. You sit here in judgment of me with the same look on your face that your father would have had. Like what I did wasn't good enough. It didn't meet your ideals."

Her voice was raised now. Anthony noticed the tan suit rising from the bar stool.

"Well, I've got news for you Anthony. I've had more than my share. Do you know what it's like for a mother to compete for her son's affection only to see him idolize his father while growing more and more distant from her?"

"You made choices."

"You're damn right I did. I wasn't ready to dry up and die. And I'll tell you something else, Anthony, and you listen good. You have your father up on this pedestal, and I know that'll never change. But you also think you and he were alike, and that's where you're wrong! You are much more like me in every way. In *every* way. Your drive, the way you are with people, the way you do things to suit yourself. It's true that your father was a kind and gentle man who was off in his own world, but you my son are very much in this world, and you get that from me. So before you tell me what a horrible person I am, you'd better look in a mirror!"

Anthony sat back in the booth. The tan suit was standing now, making no effort to conceal himself. Anthony and his mother sat quietly not looking at each other.

"I'd better go now," she said. "It's a long ride back to Naples, and you have a plane to catch."

"You're right," he said.

"What?"

"You're right," he repeated. "I guess I am more like you. It made sense as soon as you said it. I don't know if I'm happy about that, but it rings true. In fact if I wasn't I probably wouldn't have survived the last two weeks."

She looked straight at him. "Why, what happened?"

"It's too long a story," he said.

"Give me the short version."

Anthony breathed deeply before he spoke.

"I killed a man."

"Jesus!" she said.

For the first time ever, he saw a look of terror on his mother's face.

After absorbing what he had just told her, she whispered, "Are you in trouble?"

"Only if you turn me in," he said.

"Don't joke," she said.

"I'm okay. One could even argue that it was justifiable from a legal point of view."

"But?"

"In my heart I know I did it out of a thirst for revenge, and I may have done it even if my life wasn't threatened."

"But your life was in danger?"

"Yes."

"See, that would be your father questioning what you would have done if the circumstances were different. But they weren't different. You did what you had to do. And that you get from me. So maybe I did something good for you after all."

"I have to live with the knowledge that I killed a man. Wouldn't that bother you?"

"Maybe," she said, "but I would add the knowledge

that if I hadn't done so, I might be dead. Then I wouldn't have the opportunity to moralize and philosophize on the good and evil aspects of it. Personally, I'd rather have the chance to think about it. In the end I'd make the choice you did and move on."

"That sounds cold."

"Cold? Maybe, but things happen. You can't undo them. You move on."

"Not everyone can do that."

"That's true, but you're not one of them."

They were both calm now. The tan suit was seated again.

"I'm glad I had a chance to see you," he said.

"Me too, Anthony. Maybe next time we should bring helmets."

Anthony smiled, and then nodded in the direction of the bar.

"Are you going to introduce me?"

"Maybe we should save that for another day."

Anthony noticed that her face had softened. Her eyes were still moist.

"Yeah, that sounds right. The poor guy probably couldn't take both of us right now."

"Anthony?"

"Yes?"

"Thank you for seeing me and for telling me what you did. You know if you were in any trouble…"

"Yeah, I know"

They slid out of the booth and almost simultaneously said, "Have a safe trip home," as they hugged.

Anthony watched as she turned and walked toward the bar. The tan suit was standing and his mother slid her hand under his arm as they walked into the terminal.

Taking Flight

Anthony sat back down. When the waitress brought the check, he asked if she could bring him a shot of rum, to which she happily agreed. When she did, he looked at the glass for a minute then lifted it a few inches off the table and said in a low voice,

"To my father, the Colonel and Martin: Rest in Peace. For those of us who have survived so far, God help us."

He raised the glass to his lips and he savored the moment as the rum warmed his throat. He placed a tip on the table and paid the tab at the cashier's station. He asked the woman if they had breath mints. The cashier directed him to the newsstand a few shops away. This day still had a long way to go.

Chapter 52

Anthony had some time after his mother left to think over their conversation. He found himself admiring her toughness. He concluded that she needed it to survive in a world that she saw as challenging and merciless. After El Salvador, he had to concede that her perception had some merit. Anthony could draw the same conclusions after his job related experiences in New York. Still, he could not entirely forgive her transgressions because of the hurt she caused his father.

Funny, he thought, how easy it was for him to forgive Martin for leading a double life and betraying Sarah. He saw his own passing attraction to Sarah as less than a betrayal of Bernadette. He had no trouble being sympathetic to Nancy, married and carrying on an affair with another woman. He admitted that he had accepted, but had never quite forgiven himself for his betrayal of Rita such a long time ago. He was glad he and his mother were able to reach a place where they could at least be truthful with one another even though he withheld complete forgiveness as a matter of respect to his father. That's something a shrink could spend years figuring out. It boggled his mind. Perhaps forgiveness in a relationship is dispensed inversely to the closeness or importance of the person to be forgiven. That was as far as he could take the thought as he made his way back to the United ticket counter before embarking on the last leg of his journey home.

He checked his large bags and held onto the smaller

one containing Martin's ashes. He hoped it wouldn't be problematic when going through security. After getting his and Martina's boarding passes, he waited and looked for Consuelo. He thought of his mother and laughed as he took note of the number of Latinos in the terminal. He wondered if they were Cubans or members of the El Salvador security forces ready to whisk him and Martina back to their country. At about an hour prior to their scheduled departure time, Consuelo appeared with Martina and another woman.

Anthony scooped Martina out of the stroller and into his arms and gave her a loud kiss on the cheek, but was greeted with a frown as the child pushed him away.

"She is tired," said Consuelo. "It has been a long day for her."

As Martina twisted in his arms, he gently put her back in the stroller.

"Antonio," she said, "this is my sister, Rosaria."

"Rose," said her sister as she extended her hand displaying multiple gold bracelets on her wrist.

"Very pleased to meet you," said Anthony, as he shook her hand.

"It is my pleasure, Antonio. Consuelo has told me a great deal about you. I did not think a man who would do such good deeds would also be so handsome," she said, letting her hand linger in his.

Anthony withdrew his hand and turned back to Consuelo.

"They'll probably start boarding in half an hour, so we should get going soon. Does Martina need anything?"

"I just gave her a complete change of clothes. She had something to eat and drink on the plane. The best thing that can happen is that she will drink some juice on the plane and get some sleep. Everything you will need is her bag."

"Okay, then, why don't you walk me to the gates."

"I think maybe it will be better if we say goodbye now, Antonio. We will stay at the airport until your flight leaves." She handed Anthony a small bag for Martina.

Anthony thought about it and agreed on the odd chance that something should go wrong.

"Okay," he said. He gave Consuelo a big hug. "Thank you for everything you have given me. I'll always remember you, Jorge, Juan and Maria. I hope you come to the U.S. again in the future, since it is unlikely I'll be back to El Salvador."

"We shall never forget you," said Consuelo. "I wish you a good life, and I know you will be sure Martina has a good life."

"She will," said Anthony confidently.

"Vaya con Dios"

"Vaya con Dios, Consuelo."

He released her and looked at her sister. "Nice to have met you," he said.

Rose nodded and smiled flirtatiously as he lifted the strap of his bag to his shoulder and grasped the handles of the stroller. Consuelo put her hands on the sides of Martina's face and spoke to her in Spanish. Anthony understood the farewell and instructions to Martina to listen to Señor Antonio.

Anthony double checked their boarding passes and Martina's passport in case he needed it. He smiled at Consuelo and gently pushed the stroller in the direction of the gates. As he reached the entrance checkpoint, he showed the Security Agent their passes, his driver's license and held Martina's passport in his hand. To his relief, the agent checked both passes, his ID and waived them on. Once inside the queue, he tucked the documents away and steered their way to the baggage screener and metal detector. He placed his bag and the stroller on the conveyor and was asked to remove his shoes. Anthony was instructed to let Martina stand aside the metal detector as he went through it. Once cleared, he reached around to pick her up. Anthony put her down and held her hand as the agent scanned her body with a wand. Satisfied, the agent let them pass.

Anthony retrieved the stroller and placed Martina in it while standing in his socks. He picked up and carried his shoes and bag while pushing the stroller toward a row of unoccupied chairs. He put on his shoes looking all about him with the feeling of just having completed a grand larceny. His adrenaline was flowing as he stood and pushed the stroller toward the gate. A promenade of shops offered candies, souvenirs, clothing and jewelry. He wondered if anyone ever bought clothes here. He stopped at a near vacant kiosk and purchased two bottles of water and juice and shoved them in his and Martina's bags. As he approached the gate, passengers traveling with children were invited to board first. His first thought was not to do this to avoid drawing attention, then decided that not going forward would be more noticeable. He approached the airline representative at the Jetway entrance with their boarding passes in his hand.

As she took them, the agent said, "Oh, she is just darling."

Anthony smiled and that was it. He and Martina made their way down the Jetway into the near empty plane followed by a family with three children. He found their assigned seats, stored the stroller overhead and stuffed their bags under the seats. He put Martina in the window seat, strapped her in and sat beside her.

"Hey kiddo, are you okay?" said Anthony, temporarily forgetting all his Spanish phrases. He poured some juice into the non-spill cup that Consuelo had packed. To his relief, the girl smiled and took the juice.

Anthony's heart was still pounding after the uneventful boarding. He was finally on his way home.

The flight was, as Anthony would later describe it, "very dull, just the way I like it." The flight attendants were especially attentive as they remarked on the beauty of Anthony's "daughter." He offered no correction to avoid an explanation that might prompt questions he would rather not answer. As the plane roared down the runway and became airborne, he was finally convinced that he would not be removed from the plane, turned over to El Salvador Security Forces and taken back to spend the rest of his life in a windowless prison after Martina was sold on the black market. As relief settled in, he was sorry that he had not purchased a magazine.

Once they were above the clouds, his heart rate normalized, and he turned to Martina.

"Sweetie, I don't know how to explain any of this to you in Spanish or if you'd be able to understand it anyway, but there are some things I would like to tell you.

"When we get to New York, I will introduce you to a woman named Sarah. She's a very nice lady who will take care of you and will grow to love you more each day. You will become more and more important to each other, and over time both your wounds will be healed and be replaced by an enduring love.

"You'll meet other children, learn how to play games, go to school and blossom into a beautiful young woman. And of course, you'll eat lots of ice cream and pizza. El Salvador may have great coffee and wonderful papusas, but the best pizza in the world is right where we're going. When you have a New York pizza followed by a scoop of Ben and Jerry's, you will think you have ascended into heaven."

Martina looked at Anthony and smiled at the soft tone of his voice. As he continued speaking about the adventure waiting for her in New York, she nodded off and fell into a deep sleep. Anthony positioned her so that she lay against a pillow that rested on his arm. He could feel her warmth through the thin cushion. He thought back to the night that he and Bernadette made love without any protection and took the risk of her becoming pregnant. He wasn't clear about the time period needed to take the over the counter tests, but he was sure that if anything happened, Bernadette would've let him know. The idea of having children intrigued Anthony, especially now as he looked at Martina's angelic visage. He and Bernadette talked in terms of "someday," but always in an abstract sense. His thoughts drifted back to their night of lovemaking and he found himself missing her.

During the flight he overheard some passengers talk about traveling to the Big Apple to do some Christmas shopping and seeing a show. Until then, Anthony had been oblivious to the sense of it being a holiday season. He remembered not being able to talk with Bernadette on Thanksgiving Day. He wasn't sure if she would be at the airport or not when he arrived. It was true that he would have a driver waiting for him, but he secretly hoped she would show up anyway. He was confident that she would be more forgiving once they were together again.

When the flight touched down, Anthony stayed seated until the other passengers disembarked. When he and Martina left the plane with the stroller and bags in tow, he got them situated and went with her to a restroom. He had never appreciated children's changing tables in men's restrooms until now. He took a new diaper out of the tote that Consuelo had provided and changed Martina. He overlooked a wash cloth that Consuelo had also provided and used paper towels to wash and dry the girl's face and hands. He combed her hair with his own comb and made her as presentable as he could.

"You look very cool, Señorita" he said as Martina smiled back at him. "Let's go do New York."

They made their way through the arrivals terminal, down the escalators and through the long corridors leading to the baggage claim area. At first he couldn't remember his flight number or the baggage carousel that had been announced. Upon seeing the familiar faces of some fellow passengers, he made his way in their direction and waited at the carousel they selected. A few were complaining and joking about the screwed up system that required such a long wait and the conspiratorial motives for the seemingly intentional delays of the passengers' belongings.

"My six year old kid could have designed a better way," said one man.

I'm home, Anthony thought. "Welcome to the Big Apple, Martina."

As he was waiting, he heard voices calling his name. He recognized Carla's first.

"Anthony, over here."

He turned and saw Carla, a man he didn't recognize, and Sarah. They were behind the passengers crowded around the carousel. Anthony decided the bags could wait. He worked his way toward the outer perimeter of the crowd until he reached them. Sarah was tearing up as she saw Martina. She knelt down in front of the stroller and began to quietly cry while she took Martina's hand in hers and introduced herself to the child in Spanish. Martina was surprisingly receptive to the attention. Anthony let them have their moment. He turned to Carla.

"Hey sweetheart, it's good to see you. It's been quite a trip," he said as he gave her a big hug.

"I can't believe what happened to Mr. Hernández, and I'm so glad you're back."

Carla turned toward the man beside her.

"Jeffrey, this is Anthony whom you've heard so much about."

Jeffrey offered his hand which Anthony shook.

"Thank you for your generous offer of support." said Anthony.

"I was glad to do it. From the little Carla has told me, it sounds like you had quite an adventure," said Jeffrey.

Anthony nodded. He didn't want to trivialize his experience by sharing it with this stranger.

He turned again to Carla and looked beyond her in both directions.

"Bernadette didn't come," said Carla. "I offered her a ride, but she said she'd rather see you at home."

"Probably has something special waiting for you," offered Jeffrey with a big smile.

"Yeah," replied Anthony without a smile. "Thanks again, Jeffrey. Knowing there were funds available was a comfort even though they weren't used."

Anthony turned to Sarah and knelt beside her.

"She's a very lovable kid and a real beauty. Despite being cared for by a changing cast of characters, her disposition is good and I'm sure she'll adapt. Give her and yourself a chance."

"I will. I can't thank you enough Anthony. I never

expected anything like this."

"None of us did. It'll be a good thing. Just make sure you get a good lawyer right away to insure she can stay with you legally. They have ways of working these things out."

"I know. I've spoken to a very good attorney who specializes in out of country adoptions. He's assured me that everything can be taken care of, especially with Martin being the birth father and the cooperation of the surviving relatives."

"They're wonderful people, Sarah. You can't imagine." Realizing he may have indirectly referred to Martin's mistress, he changed the subject.

"It's good that you have a lawyer already. I assume David recommended him."

"No," said Sarah, "not David." Her face looked strange, like she wanted to say more, but couldn't or wouldn't.

"Listen," Carla interrupted. "We have a driver and a limo that we'll share until we get to Hempstead. We can drop off Sarah and the girl, and then you before he takes Jeffrey and me home. If everybody is okay with that, we can go as soon as you get your luggage."

They all looked at each other and shrugged.

"It's okay with me as long as Sarah is comfortable with that," said Anthony to Carla.

"I have a nanny at home to help me get started," said Sarah. "She even speaks Spanish. We have set up a temporary room for Martina until we can do it right. Anthony, you can see her tonight or whenever you want."

"Sounds like we have a plan," said Anthony. "Let's do as Carla suggested. Besides, I want to see Bernadette."

"To get your something special," smiled Jeffrey.

"Yeah, right," said Anthony wondering how Carla picked her men.

He reached for his carry-on bag and took out the package containing Martin's ashes.

"I can give these to you now or bring them over tomorrow," said Anthony.

"Why don't you bring them tomorrow so I can focus on Martina tonight?"

"No problem, I'll give you a call in the morning."

Carla said, "Anthony, do you think your bags are up?"

Anthony turned and looked through the thinning crowd around the carousel.

"I can see them from here," he said, as he walked to the rotating silver leaves that carried his bags and all the stories they could tell.

He picked them up, joined his friends and said, "Let's go."

Chapter 53

As the four adults and child moved to the sidewalk outside the baggage claim area, Anthony balked. When Carla completed her call to the chauffeur waiting in the designated limo area, Anthony stepped forward.

"Hey guys, I have a change in plans. You go ahead with the limo. I'm going to call Bernadette and have her come to pick me up."

"Anthony, that's silly," said Sarah. "The traffic going in the direction of the city will be much heavier than going to Hempstead. We'll have you home before she could get here."

"Yeah, but we have a favorite restaurant in Valley Stream, not far from here. I'd like to take Bernadette there before going home."

"Are you sure?" asked Sarah.

"Sarah, let Anthony do what he wants," said Carla impatiently. "Go ahead, Anthony, we'll catch up tomorrow."

The limo pulled up and the driver got out and opened the curbside door for his passengers.

"It'll just be the four of us, with the first stop in Hempstead," Carla said to the driver.

She turned to Anthony.

"I think having dinner out with Bernadette is a good idea," she said. "I'd like to talk to you about what you've been through once you're settled. It's a great relief to have you home again."

"Thanks, Carla. We'll talk."

Jeffrey extended his hand. "Welcome home again, fella," he said. "I hope to see you again soon."

"Thanks, Jeffrey."

Anthony turned to Sarah and kneeled down to be eye level with Martina at her side.

"You will stay with Sarah now. She is my friend, the one I talked to you about when we were on the plane. She will take good care of you. I'll see you tomorrow, so be a good girl and get some rest."

"Abuela?"

"No sweetie, your grandmother can't be here now. So Sarah will take care of you until you can see your abuela again. Now give me a big hug until tomorrow. I love you very much and Sarah also loves you. "

Martina looked confused, but hugged Anthony and gave no protest to staying with Sarah. Anthony looked up at Sarah.

"I know she doesn't understand a word of what I'm saying, or what it means for her to be here, but she seems to be going along," said Anthony.

"She must trust you," replied Sarah.

Sarah kneeled down beside Anthony and spoke to Martina.

"Sweetie, you will come home with me tonight, and I'll take care of you. I am so happy that you're here. I'll do everything I can to keep you safe and make you happy."

"I'll make sure she's comfortable tonight," she said to Anthony as they stood. "Then we'll take one day at a time. I'm a little scared. She's probably a little scared, but I'm so grateful she's here. I know we can make it work."

"Me too," said Anthony. "Have a good night and I'll see you tomorrow."

"Good night, Anthony," said Sarah as she gave him a

hug. Her eyes were tearing up when she stepped back. She turned and took Martina's hand.

"Come on sweetie, let's get in the car," said Sarah.

Jeffrey followed Sarah and Martina into the limo. The driver put the stroller in the trunk. Carla took a last look at Anthony.

"Are you going to be okay?" she said.

Anthony looked at her appreciatively and said, "I'm fine. By the way, I still have your phone. Can I keep it for tonight?"

"No problem," said Carla, "get it back to me whenever you can."

She stood another few seconds looking at Anthony. Saying no more, she turned and entered the limo as the driver held her hand. He closed the door, went around to other side, got in and in a matter of seconds the limo pulled away while Anthony looked on. He felt truly alone for the first time in quite a while.

Despite the cold air, Anthony stayed outside while he searched for the Carla's cell phone.

He pressed the speed dial number and waited.

"Hola!" the voice answered.

"Jorge, it's Anthony."

"Antonio, how are you?"

"I'm good. I'm sure you know that my meeting with Consuelo went well. Martina and I arrived in New York a short while ago, safe and sound. She's already off to her new home. Everything went perfectly. I'd like you to pass that on to Señora Órnelas and Eduardo."

"Of course. Everything went perfectly because it was such a perfect plan," said Jorge, laughing.

"Yeah, that's why I nearly wet my pants when any Latino came within fifty feet of me. I was wondering if you would've come to visit me in prison."

"Certainly," said Jorge, "that was also part of the plan. I would even bring you some of Consuelo's favorite dishes."

"Consuelo will return home tomorrow, right?"

"Yes, yes. The children already miss her and she can only take a short time with her sister."

"I met her sister. She was certainly very different than Consuelo."

"I am very fortunate that her sister lives in Miami," said Jorge."

Anthony did not reply.

"Antonio?"

"Yes, I'm here."

"What is it my friend?"

Anthony paused.

"My head is a little screwed up right now. I'm not sure what's going on. I was so focused on getting out of El Salvador, meeting my mother again, and getting Martina to New York, that I haven't had a chance to think about what it would be like to be home. The last two weeks seem like a lifetime and being here now seems so strange. I can't explain what it's like. My friends were here to meet me. They all looked and sounded so different to me."

"Antonio, perhaps it is you that is different."

"I'm not sure I'm ready to deal with that," said Anthony.

"Give yourself some time, my friend."

Anthony rubbed the sides of his forehead with his free hand.

"You're right," said Anthony. "I can coast for a few days. Everything will normalize by then. I just wanted to let you know that we made it, and Martina is in good hands."

"Martina was in good hands when you received her in Miami, Antonio. I appreciate you letting me know of your safe arrival. Thank you."

"You're welcome, Jorge, and thanks again for all you have done for me."

"Be well, my friend."

"You too, amigo," said Anthony.

After another pause, Jorge spoke again.

"Antonio, call me from time to time, or whenever you would like to talk."

"Thanks." said Anthony. "Adiós."

"Adiós, Antonio."

Anthony pressed the End Call button and rubbed his eyes. He put the phone back in his bag and walked toward the car rental kiosks.

At the Hertz counter, Anthony used the SkyTel Number One Gold Membership Card and asked for a midsized car. He specified that the car was for personal use and was to be billed to his personal credit card. In a few minutes he was in the Hertz shuttle on his way to the rental car lot outside the airport. He found the car waiting and ready to go. He put his bags in the trunk, took the cell phone with him, and as was his habit, tested the lights, directional signals, windshield wipers and brakes before leaving the parking area. He started the car, but before pulling out, he picked up the phone and placed another call.

"Hello."

"Hey, Bernadette, it's me."

"Hi, where are you," she said in an almost friendly tone.

"I'm at JFK. There's been a slight change of plans. I sent the others home. I'm going to get home on my own."

"Do you want me to pick you up?"

"No thanks, I've rented a car. Listen, there are a couple of things I have to do before coming home. They won't take long, but will be a lot easier if I do them now rather than wait for tomorrow or Monday. I shouldn't be late."

She answered after a slight pause.

"Okay," she said.

Anthony was relieved that Bernadette hadn't put up a fuss about his not coming straight home. This may have been a possible benefit or side effect of their already strained relationship. He put the phone down, guided the car out of its assigned space and pulled up to the exit gate. Once the car was cleared by the attendant, he drove out of the Hertz lot and headed for the Southern State Parkway. Driving eastbound, he passed the familiar Hempstead exit and kept on going. He turned off at the exit leading to the marina. As he pulled in to the parking area, he remembered his encounter with Nancy and realized that he had not asked Carla or Sarah how she was doing. A few lamppost lights gave a yellowish caste to the ground. Only two cars were in the lot. He guessed that the occupants were teenagers watching the "submarine races." The coffee shop was the only place open and he decided to take advantage of it. Anthony got out of the car, pulled his collar up to block the sea breeze and walked to the shop. Once inside, he could see they were getting ready to close up. Anthony considered getting a snack, but settled for a cup of coffee that was no longer fresh.

Outside, Anthony sipped the coffee and compared it unfavorably to the Salvadoran blends he had come to like. He walked to the edge of the marina where he could hear the water lapping against the poles supporting the deck. Oval pools of light from the lampposts were reflected in the water. The chill in the night air drove Anthony back to the car. It provided a warm and windless cocoon. He looked toward the ocean he could not see or hear and was denied its soothing rhythms. He put the coffee cup in a holder and made sure the door was locked. Anthony leaned back and closed his eyes. He inhaled deeply, slowly letting the breath escape his lungs through his mouth. He shifted his body so his feet could rest on the car floor without touching the pedals. Resting his hands on his knees, palms up, he again drew in as much air as he could before exhaling slowly. He tried to release the anxieties of the long day by reliving each encounter and dismissing it with an exhaled breath. His meditation wasn't working.

He took a sip of the coffee which was starting to cool. He put his head back again and a picture of the Schwinn Black Phantom came into his mind. *What a beautiful bike. It played to the buyer's fantasies with its graceful lines, bright chrome and glossy paint. It was probably a lot better to look at than ride, but that wasn't the point.*

His mind drifted to El Salvador and images of young Juan and Maria quickly morphed into Mr. Hernández slumped on the ground behind his car. His fingertips could feel the sticky blood that had stained the Colonel's suit coat. Anthony opened his eyes, rubbed his clean fingers on his trousers and came back to the present. He tried to think about a career strategy, but it was of so little interest to him now, he couldn't hold the thought. He spoke out loud.

"What I need to do is to take a few days to decompress. Then with a clear head, I can think about what I'll do next."

I better think about how to reconcile with Bernadette. Is that what I want? Did we really screw it up? Are we reconcilable? Has everything been my fault? What does she want? Did we learn that our relationship can't handle the crap that life deals out? Is what we do based on the approval of others? Is there anything deeper than that? How would we handle loss? How much are we ready to give to each other? These thoughts denied him the calm this long day had earned. El Salvador was a million miles away. The marina, *his* marina and the ocean offered no sanctuary.

Chapter 54

With no one else to call and no place left to go, Anthony started home. He recognized the familiar streets once he left the Southern State Parkway and tried in vain to organize his thoughts as he prepared to see Bernadette. Checking his watch, he was surprised to see it was just short of 11:00 P.M., but remembered it was set to Salvadoran time and was an hour later in Hempstead.

He parked in the driveway of his house half expecting to hear the crunch of gravel beneath the tires. He carried his bags to the front door and knocked, not remembering if his keys were packed away, or if he had left them home. He was hoping Bernadette would be awake, but wished that he could wait until morning for them to talk. Bernadette opened the door. She was wearing her robe over a night dress. Anthony had often commented on how "fetching she looked in her bathrobe." Bernadette had always laughed when he'd say that, answering "no one looks fetching in a bathrobe."

"Hi," he said as he stood on the front steps.

"Hi," she said stepping back and opening the door fully.

Anthony picked up his bags and dropped them in the foyer. He looked at Bernadette and wasn't sure if he should take her in his arms, or say, "We have to talk." Instead he said nothing and just looked at her until she spoke.

"Can I get you something? You looked tired."

"No thanks, I'm okay."

"Are you cold? You don't even have a jacket or

sweater."

"A little. Do you have any coffee made?"

"I can make some. Do you want to change or anything?"

"That's not a bad idea. Maybe I can do that and freshen up while you make the coffee."

"Okay, do you want something to eat?"

"No thanks."

"Your mother called. First time we've spoken in quite a while."

"My mother? What did she want?"

"She called to tell me she met you in Miami and that you looked like death warmed over. She didn't want me to be shocked when I saw you, and suggested I get you in for a checkup. She didn't bother to ask how I was."

"She tends to exaggerate," said Anthony.

"Not by much this time," said Bernadette.

"I'll change and be back in a minute."

Anthony went into their bedroom and looked around at the familiar bed, wall coverings, furniture and furnishings. He felt like a visitor as he sat on the bed and removed his shoes and socks and undressed. From a drawer in his dresser he pulled out a pair of old sweat pants, put them on and walked into the bathroom. He washed his hands and face trying to remove the long days travel from his skin. After soaking his hair, he wet a wash cloth and rubbed his neck, underarms and chest. He reached for a towel and enjoyed the luxury of the thick, absorbent cotton. He brushed his hair back, considered and then dismissed the idea of shaving. In his dresser he found a Tee shirt that he pulled over his head. His robe was hanging on the back of the bathroom door. It was freshly laundered and felt good around his body.

Anthony returned to the living room where Bernadette had poured coffee for him, and prepared a plate of fruit, cheese and crackers that were placed on the coffee table in front of the sofa. She was sitting in the opposing chair. Anthony sat on the sofa and thanked her.

"This looks great," he said.

"Your mother was right, you know," said Bernadette.

"A few good nights of sleep and some exercise and I'll be fine," he said.

Anthony devoured the food on the plate.

"Do want more?" asked Bernadette.

"No thanks. That was perfect," said Anthony. He sipped the coffee.

"I didn't expect you to look so drawn."

"What did you expect?"

"That you'd look like you do when you return from a business trip. Tired, but nothing like this. Do you want to talk about it?"

"Sure," said Anthony, "but it's late so maybe I should give you an overview and we can talk more tomorrow when we have all day."

"Okay, I'll think I'll pour a glass of amaretto. Can I get you one?"

"We don't have any rum, do we?"

"I don't think so, but I'll look."

"An amaretto will be fine."

Bernadette brought two snifters of amaretto from the wet bar, handed one to Anthony and took her seat in the chair opposite him.

"Thanks."

"So, you were going to give me an overview."

"Yeah. I don't know how much you've heard from Carla or Sarah, but the objective of my trip changed shortly after I got there. I don't remember if we talked about some of this because I didn't get through to you so many times. I'm not sure of what I actually have told you or just planned to tell you."

Bernadette closed the front of her robe and sipped the amaretto.

Anthony went on, "Anyway, the objective changed. While I was getting the runaround regarding Martin's ashes from some high powered clerk, I went out to the clinic where Martin was killed. It's just outside of a small village near the town of Perquín. The big news is that I discovered that Martin had a child by a woman from that village. The woman was killed in the same explosion that killed him. Conversations I had with the child's grandmother and Sarah led to me bringing her back to the U.S. Sarah was at the airport tonight to meet the girl and bring her home with her. There are some legal issues that have to be worked out, but with the girl on U.S. soil, Martin as her biological father and the consent of the surviving family, lawyers should be able to work out a way for Sarah to adopt or somehow get custody of the girl. That's it in a nutshell."

"So, Martin had a thing going on down there," said Bernadette."

"That's one way of looking at it."

"Is there another way?"

"Maybe that's a discussion for another time."

"How much did Sarah have to pay the girl's family?"

"That's an interesting thing. They weren't interested in money. They wanted what was best for the girl, which they thought was to be raised in the U.S."

"Who is they?" asked Bernadette.

"The girl has an uncle. The woman's brother."

"So they shipped the girl off, just like that?"

"Not just like that. It was a heart wrenching decision, but they thought it was in the best interests of the girl, especially since her grandmother is very ill."

"And you've lost weight, your face is drawn, and you have rings under your eyes. All this was caused by discussions between the girl's family, you and Sarah?"

"I'm not sure where you're going with that question, but the answer goes nowhere."

"Carla told me your bodyguard was killed."

"Yes, but that's another story."

"Sounds like it did turn into a Matt Damon movie," she said referring back to an earlier argument they had about his trip.

Anthony answered with silence.

"I'm going to have another amaretto, do you want one?" said Bernadette.

"Sure, why not?"

"So, is that it?" asked Bernadette as she handed him his glass.

"Well, there's actually a lot more. Mostly about the people I met and what I learned about myself, but those are things I thought we could discuss tomorrow."

"Any juicy stuff? Are the women down there hot? Martin apparently thought so. Did you meet any? Were you tempted? Did you get laid? Did you wish you had?"

Anthony wondered if she had been drinking before he arrived.

"I think I've covered enough for tonight. I'm ready to turn in."

"Are you expecting to get laid now? You know, like when you return from a business trip and get welcome home sex."

"I think I could just use a good night's sleep," said

Anthony as he stood up.

"Sounds like your needs must have been taken care of."

"Bernadette, I don't know what's going on. I know you've been pissed at me from the day I said I would take this trip, but this stuff about fooling around is coming from left field. So just drop it and we can talk more in the morning."

"I fucked David," she said. "In our bed. On Thanksgiving Day. While you were leaving me a message."

Anthony dropped down on the sofa. He put his hands together, clasped his fingers and brought them to his mouth, his elbows resting on his knees. His teeth were clenched on his index finger. He said nothing. He couldn't speak.

Bernadette looked as shocked as he did. She held her hands out, but there was no retrieving the words she had just spoken. If she had continued, she would have added "It was great." Now she wanted to say she was sorry. Neither expression would have widened or healed the wound just inflicted.

She put her glass down and walked quietly toward the bedroom. Anthony sat immobile for a long time, after which he got up and poured himself another amaretto. After the last of it warmed his throat, he lay his head back on the sofa and closed his eyes.

Chapter 55

Anthony awoke at 8:00 A.M. to the smells of cooking bacon, freshly made coffee, and a great need to relieve himself. He went to the bathroom, washed his hands and face, ran his wet hands through his hair, and returned to the living room. He picked a blanket up from the floor that he didn't have when he had finally had fallen asleep. He folded the blanket, put it on the sofa and walked into the kitchen. Bernadette was working over the stove.

"There's some fresh coffee and breakfast will be ready in a minute, if you want some."

Anthony grabbed a mug and poured a fresh cup of coffee. He looked at Bernadette who was lifting bacon strips from the griddle onto a serving plate.

"Eggs sunny side is all I can do with this thing without having them run all over," she said.

"After that bombshell last night, you're asking me if I want sunny side eggs?"

"We have a lot to talk about, so we may as well start with a decent breakfast."

He shook his head and took a seat at the kitchen table.

Bernadette brought Anthony a platter of bacon and eggs with wedges of apple, and another plate of toasted wheat bread.

She brought over a plate for herself and sat. Making Sunday breakfast had long been Anthony's ritual, but today was her day as the breakfast chef.

They ate in silence, not even attempting small talk, or proposing how they might spend the day. When their breakfast was consumed officially establishing an air of civility, Bernadette spoke first.

"I'm very sorry that I dropped that on you last night, but it's true. It did happen. I could give you a long explanation, or excuses, but none would matter or change what I did. I don't know yet if I'm even sorry for what I did because I was so angry at you. I felt lonely and abandoned. What is clear is that I did it, and that can't be changed."

She started to say more, but Anthony raised his free hand while he lowered the coffee mug to the table.

"Look, I can't discuss this right now, but I have a lot I wanted to say before hearing it. I think I should just go ahead and say what's been on my mind."

"Okay, I'm listening," said Bernadette.

"I'm not even sure where to begin, but I think I should start at the end instead of the beginning. The events of the past two weeks have changed much of the way I think and how I see the world. I'm afraid that if I try to describe them, I might trivialize their importance."

"Start wherever you like," said Bernadette sincerely.

"To begin at the end, I don't want to live the way we live anymore. Not in terms of my job, this house, our belongings, who we spend time with, and what we do with our time. Everything we do, everything we spend any time on separates us from what's important. Everywhere, there are people struggling for an existence; everywhere there are people abusing other people; everywhere people are trying to find hope for their children. The struggles, the abuses and searches go on and on with only a few good outcomes. And we live a life where our jobs occupy our minds and bodies ten or more hours a day. We eat food as fuel, watch TV to escape during the week and find ways to entertain ourselves on most weekends."

"You make it sound so shallow," said Bernadette.

"It is shallow!" said Anthony, his voice rising. "We close off the rest of the world. We can never have enough money, a big enough house or car, or enough ways to entertain ourselves."

"Anthony, we work hard, take a little time to have fun, and try to be good people and good members of the community. We give to charities, vote to protect civil liberties, personal freedoms and protect the environment. Maybe someday we'll bring children into the world who will continue to do good things. What's so bad about that?"

"Bernadette, we glaze over those things. The lion's share of our time and efforts go into creating personal wealth and acquiring Stuff."

"You're the one who acquires Stuff."

"You're right. I've collected a lot of toys, but you know what, we haven't reached one hundredth of where this road goes. People have multiple houses, cars, vacations and travels that make ours look like a pauper's night out."

"But they're not us. Why should we be responsible for them?"

"I'm not suggesting we should be. I just want to get off that road."

"Jesus, Anthony, you sound like someone from the hippy generation."

Anthony was surprised to hear her invoke Jesus' name.

"Bernadette, let me back up a minute. I don't want to go off on an anti-materialism jag. I really think that much of it is good and a hell of a lot better as a religion than what you get from most churches. What I really want to say is that I saw people who had very little in comparison to what we have, or can have. But they also had so much more. When they love, they love deeply; when they mourn, their hearts break; when they're joyful, it's abundant and contagious, when they suffer, they suffer together, when they pray, they pray for others. They live life to the fullest. Entertainment to them is sitting with a friend having a beer or glass of rum. Joy is someone getting married or having a baby."

"Or, in Martin's case, skipping the first part," said Bernadette."

Anthony got up from the table.

"I was afraid I'd sound like an idealistic preacher and not convey what I saw and felt and learned in a way that would be meaningful," said Anthony.

"I'm sorry for my dig at Martin. That was a cheap shot. But, Anthony you read up on all these religions. You read history and philosophy and you have a mind full of idealistic notions. You're always searching for something other than what we have. It's not easy keeping up with you."

"It's not easy for me either."

"Do you have anything specific that you want to do? All I hear is what you don't like about the way we live now," said Bernadette.

"I've given up my job. I don't want to find another one that's anything like it. I want to move away from here, far away, maybe out west."

"You mean California?"

"No, I was thinking more about New Mexico, Arizona. Someplace with small towns and a low profile."

"And what would you do?"

"I don't know yet."

"How would you live?"

"I don't know that either."

"When would you start this?"

"Soon. Now."

"And what about me?"

"You can come if you want."

"Don't you care about last night? Doesn't what I did bother you?"

"Yes. I care a lot and it bothers me a lot."

"What if it comes to bother you more than you can tolerate?"

"I don't know."

"That's not very reassuring. What if I won't go?"

"I'll go alone."

"Jesus Christ," she said, and got up and left the room.

Chapter 56

Anthony cleared the table and washed the dishes by hand, foregoing the dishwasher and left them on the counter rack to dry. He marched off to the bathroom to shave and shower away yesterday's grime and some of last night's hurt. Once freshened up and dressed, he went to the foyer to pick up his bags. He separated clothes that would be washed at home from those that would go to the dry cleaners. He found the plastic cup of debris from the clinic that had escaped questions from the Salvadoran police and U.S. Customs. He brought them out to the backyard and scattered them on the earth around the shrubs. Returning to the house, he put his personal items away and transferred the papers from the smaller bag to his desk. He carried the containers of Martin's ashes out to his car and placed them on the floor behind the driver's seat. As he straightened up he noticed a white object under a windshield wiper. He cursed to himself when he recognized David's business card, which he tore up and let fall to the floor. David not only didn't care that Anthony knew, he was bragging about it.

In the den, he put away the papers he needed to keep in a file cabinet. Those for Sarah, he put in a folder and shredded the others. He prepared a couple of lists. One was for Sarah and the other for Bernadette. He added notes and put Sarah's in the folder and Bernadette's in the desk drawer. Anthony made arrangements for the rental car to be picked up and returned to the airport. He found his wallet on the living room end table and his car keys in the cookie jar. He called out Bernadette's name, but got no response. He left a note saying that he would be back soon and left the house.

In ten minutes he was in Sarah's driveway. When he knocked, Sarah opened the door. Martina and the nanny were standing behind her. Sarah welcomed him with a big smile and a hug.

"I'm sorry I didn't call first, but I figured you'd be up by now," said Anthony.

"That's fine. We've been up for hours. Come on in."

He stepped into the foyer and stooped to give Martina a hug.

"Hi sweetheart, are they treating you okay? Are these strange people being nice to you? If not, you let me know, and I'll kick their butts."

"It's not good to say violent things to a child," said the nanny.

Anthony laughed, "This girl could tell you some things about violence you wouldn't want to know."

Anthony introduced himself to the nanny and turned back to Sarah.

"I have what I originally went to El Salvador for and some papers for you along with a list of contacts."

"Estelle, can you please take Martina into the kitchen," said Sarah to the nanny.

"Of course, Señora. Come along Martina," said the Nanny extending a hand to the girl.

Anthony waited until they went off hand in hand, Martina looking like she had lived here for all of her short life. Sarah stayed at the door holding it open despite the cold air, while Anthony retrieved the containers and the folder.

"What do you want to take care of first?" he asked.

"Let's bring them downstairs for now," she said, pointing to the containers.

Anthony followed Sarah to the room from where he had carried some bridge chairs a lifetime ago. He put the containers on a utility table that was set up against one wall and turned to Sarah.

"There they are," he said.

Sarah moved to touch the containers and put a hand on each one.

"Does one of these have to be delivered to the church we talked about?"

"Not unless you want to. That was just necessary BS to get them out of El Salvador. Funny part is they ended up being smuggled out with the help of several very good people."

Sarah turned to Anthony and put on hand on his cheek.

"Poor Anthony, you've been through so much."

"Shucks, Ma'am, wasn't nothin'," he said with an exaggerated drawl.

Sarah looked at him sympathetically.

"You know about Bernadette and David?" he asked.

She nodded. "David told Carla, and then warned her against using it in her divorce settlement. The settlement had already been worked out so Carla figured he just wanted to crow. Carla told me, and I confronted Bernadette."

"So, it's public knowledge."

Sarah didn't reply.

Anthony cleared his throat and changed the subject.

"There are some people you'll probably want to thank for getting Martin's ashes out of the country. I have all their contact information and the roles they played in the folder I left upstairs. Just always refer to the ashes as "the gift"

453

without identifying them further."

"I understand," said Sarah.

"The folder also contains the names of Martina's relatives, just two actually, her grandmother, Señora Órnelas and her uncle, Eduardo. The most important contacts are Jorge and Consuelo. They are wonderful people who will help you in any way they can, should there be a need.

"The folder also contains Martina's passport naming her as the daughter of Jorge and Consuelo, which we had to do to get her out of the country. Anyway, it's all explained very carefully in the papers that are in the folder. You can give them to your attorney as long as they're privileged. The passport is fake. Be sure he knows that."

"Can you come with me next week to meet with the attorney?"

"I won't be here, Sarah."

"You won't be here next week, or you won't be here for a while?"

"For a while, maybe a long while. But, you have my cell number and I will check in with you regularly to hear how Martina is doing. You'll probably get calls and email from El Salvador about her as well. Jorge is very internet savvy. You can send pictures; maybe even do some on-line video visits."

"You don't know how long you'll be gone?"

"No."

"Can you tell me where you're going?"

"I'm not sure yet, but I'll let you know when I get there."

"Anthony, I'm worried."

"Don't be. There's nothing to be worried about."

"Is Bernadette going with you?"

"I don't know that either, but I don't think so."

Sarah, put her hands to her lips. "That bastard."

"Look, David is a dirt bag, and I have no love for him, but this is not about him. I'll probably still be saying this when I'm sixty, but I'm trying to find myself. I'm not quite sure where I want to go, or how I want to live, but I have to look and I can't find it here. That's something I learned before I knew about David."

"Still, I hate the creep."

"Forget about him. Besides, I can hate him enough for the both of us," he said smiling.

"Oh Anthony, your life has been turned upside down because you tried to help me."

"No, no it hasn't. My life may just be beginning. I've been searching for a book of knowledge to tell me how to live and what to believe in. From this experience in El Salvador I've learned that there is no book. And God knows, I've read enough of them. I just have to go out and find what it is I'm supposed to do with my life. I can't find that out here or working as I have been. I have to start fresh and see what happens. The answers are inside me. They need to work their way out. I have to let them come out. El Salvador was a great start, but there's a long way for me to go."

"Will I ever see you again?"

"Sure you will. Not right away, but you will. I have to see Martina too. I'll keep connected, I promise."

Sarah put her arms around Anthony's neck.

"You've done a wonderful thing for me Anthony, and you were a good friend to Martin, the best. Please be safe and take care of yourself and know that you'll always have friends here."

"I will. I will. Can you do one favor for me?"

"Of course."

"Explain as much of this to Carla as you can and return the cell phone I left upstairs. I'll call her myself in a few days, but I can't handle her right now. She was my lifeline. She's been absolutely great, but right now I need a little space. I'm sure she'll understand."

"Anything else?"

"Yeah, how is Nancy?"

"She's good, getting better. I think she'll be all right. Aaron too."

"Tell her that I think she's cool too, okay. She'll know what I mean."

"Okay."

"Let me give you the folder and the phone and I'll leave you guys alone."

When Anthony returned to the house, Bernadette wasn't home. He went to his desk and opened the drawer containing his financial records, notes and his list for Bernadette. Anthony went about doing some laundry and packing. He packed clothes for two seasons centered on jeans, shorts, polos, three checked shirts, two sweaters, a sweatshirt, walking shoes and a pair of sneakers. He was able to pack everything he needed but two jackets into his larger bag. After putting aside the things he would wear or need the next morning, he put the bag in the trunk of his car along with a windbreaker and heavy jacket. No suits, ties, sport coats, dress trousers or dress shoes would come along for the ride.

Bernadette came home at about 5:00 P.M.

"Hi," she said, offering no explanation of her whereabouts.

"Hi, I'm glad you're home. I want to go over a few things."

"Sure," she said, "just let me change," as she took off her coat and turned away.

She put her coat in the hall closet and went to the bedroom. She returned shortly wearing sweats and sneakers. She sat and pointed her finger at him.

"You're on," she said.

"I'm planning to leave tomorrow. I'm driving west until I get to wherever I end up. You can come with me, or you can join me in a few days, or a week if you need time to deal with your job and family."

"You're serious about this aren't you?" she said.

"You bet. We can put the house in the care of a management company that can rent it, sell it or just take care of it for a while. Everything else is doable over the internet, and with a little help from our friends."

"You have to know it will never work, at least for you and me. I like my life here. I like my house. I like my job. I don't want to wander all over the country trying to save the world."

Anthony sucked in his breath and let it out slowly. This was the response he expected, that he intuitively agreed with, but it still saddened him.

"I wouldn't quite characterize it that way, but I can see that giving up what you have and your friends wouldn't be easy."

"Speaking of my friends, since none of them will speak to me, I met with David earlier. He advised me to get whatever we agree to in writing."

Anthony smiled. He quietly congratulated himself for not losing his temper.

"Do you still trust him after he practically announced

to the world that he nailed you?"

"Look, David is very simple to understand. He may be a dirt bag as you like to call him, but you know what to expect from him. Once you get past that, he's not so bad. *You* however, are very hard to understand. It's very hard to know what to expect from you. I thought we were building a good life here and you want to throw it all away."

"You threw something away as well."

"You had a hand in bringing that about. David happened to be there."

"All right, we're not here to talk about David. I have a proposition. It's very simple. You don't need anything in writing, but if you want I'll draft and sign an agreement. But tell that dirt bag if he comes near this house before I leave I'll shove his expensive briefcase up his ass."

Bernadette sat up straight and said nothing.

"Before I leave tomorrow, I'm going to the bank. I'll withdraw $10,000 from our account. There will be more than twice that much left. Then there are long term CDs and our investment portfolio. All of our assets can be directed with either of our signatures. They're all yours. Our financial guy can help you deal with all that. I will take the ten grand, my car, which is paid for, and my personal belongings. The rest is yours. The house is more than half paid for. Our mortgage is something you handle with your income. I'll have my cell phone with me. If you have any questions about any of this, you can always reach me. That's a better deal than any lawyer could get."

"Why are you doing this?"

"Because I need some money to keep me going until I get to where I'm supposed to be. I'm not as idealistic or impractical as you think."

"I don't mean that. Why are you throwing your life

away?"

"I'm trying to save my life, or at least find one I can feel good about."

"I can make you feel good. You know I can."

"Do you want what I said in writing?"

"No. Take as much as you need. If you need more later, take that too."

"Our budget and a record of all our financial holdings are on the computer. There is a paper back-up in a folder along with our insurance policies in my desk. Everything else is in the file cabinet. It's organized pretty well and it's easy to navigate. Everything is current. There are a few advanced payments I'm making that I'll mail in the morning.

"Thank you," said Bernadette.

"You're welcome."

"I can't believe this. Three weeks ago, our life was good and now I don't even recognize it."

"I'm sorry it turned out this way. I know I'm not easy to live with. I have trouble with that myself, but for me doing this is almost a matter of life and death. I know that sounds overly dramatic, but I believe it to my core."

"Fuck you, Anthony."

They remained civil for the rest of the night. They slept in the same bed. When she put her hand on his thigh he turned away knowing full well that he wouldn't be able to resist her for long. When the morning came, he stayed in bed until she left for work. Soon after, he went through his morning routine. He got dressed and decided to have a quick breakfast at the bakery on Sunrise before going to the bank. It turned out that the bank teller was unfamiliar with Anthony and of the multiple accounts he and Bernadette shared. He had to wait while she got the manager's assistance and approval for the large withdrawal.

Anthony returned home, and prepared notes for Bernadette explaining the different operating modes of their house security system, something he had forgot to include yesterday. He checked and double checked everything he had to do and had to have before he left. When there was nothing left to question, he went to the garage, opened the automated door and started the car. Not sure if Bernadette had ran it at all while he was away, he let the car run for a few minutes. Before backing out, Anthony reached down to the center console and disconnected the GPS system. He took the unit, its holder and power cord and placed them on the work bench. Returning to the car, Anthony backed out of the garage and put the car in Drive, turned on the radio and with the sun behind him headed west.

The End

Made in the USA
Charleston, SC
05 April 2013